The Ladies of the Stream

– GEOF WILLIS –

An environmentally friendly book printed and bound in England by
www.printondemand-worldwide.com

This book is made entirely of chain-of-custody materials

www.fast-print.net/store.php

The Ladies of the Stream
Copyright © Geof Willis 2013

01285 711381
07772465137
geofthepen@hotmail.co.uk

All rights reserved

No part of this book may be reproduced in any form by photocopying or any electronic or mechanical means, including information storage or retrieval systems, without permission in writing from both the copyright owner and the publisher of the book.

All characters are fictional.
Any similarity to any actual person is purely coincidental.

The right of Geof Willis to be identified as the author of this work has been asserted by him in accordance with the Copyright, Designs and Patents Act 1988 and any subsequent amendments thereto.

A catalogue record for this book is available from the British Library

ISBN 978-178035-565-8

First published 2013 by
FASTPRINT PUBLISHING
Peterborough, England.

To Paula,
my ever enduring wife and nurse.

Under the influence of Faith Havrincourt, five women plan the demise of a pair of despicable heirs on two large English country estates.

Knowing the chances of winning a court case against the men are remote in 19th century England Faith meticulously plans their deaths so as to make it appear a tragedy.

To win over friends and relatives she performs several sexual antics and subsequently holds them to personal ransom in order that they keep their silence.

The social crimes of the pair are finally revealed on 'the field of honour'.

Set in Gloucestershire the novel depicts many beautiful Cotswold villages and towns that the Coln River passes through on its way to its confluence with the 'Thames'.

The river itself is popular with fly fishermen who practice their craft of catching summer trout and the beautiful winter graylings, also known as The Ladies of the Stream.

Contents

1.	Coln Head	6
2.	The Preface	14
3.	Sennington Barn	24
4.	The Inquisition	31
5.	The Bull Hotel	44
6.	Uncle Charles and Aunt Maria	54
7.	Faith, Hope and Charity	56
8.	The Invitation List	64
9.	Charity	66
10.	The Summer Ball	68
11.	Azamgargh	80
12.	The Ladies' Liaison	83
13.	A Private Confession	85
14.	Writer's Block	87
15.	The Stranger	89
16.	Maidenhead	92
17.	The Castle Tavern, Holborn	102
18.	The Theatre Royal	105
19.	The Report	114
20.	The Backlash	117
21.	Infidelity Exposed	123
22.	The Set Up	127
23.	Marcel Desailley	129
24.	Ludlow Infirmary	132

25.	The Private Detective	135
26.	Faith and Gerard	143
27.	A Painful Journey	145
28.	Brockhampton Visited	147
29.	Lionel's Revelations	152
30.	Stefan's Nightmare	155
31.	Neil Portlock, The Truth	157
32.	The Return of Edgar Collison	166
33.	Liverpool	172
34.	Eugene	175
35.	Chedworth	179
36.	Edgar and Georgina	181
37.	Willie Greyffos	186
38.	Lionel and Stefan	190
39.	The Abduction	196
40.	The Search Begins	203
41.	Christmas Day, 1866	208
42.	Greyffos in Bibury	214
43.	The Brigadier's Offer	218
44.	The Ladies of the Stream	224
45.	Maria's Letter	229
46.	The Mill at Withington	233
47.	Neil Starbury	246
48.	Starbury v. Greyffos	250
49.	The Brigadier with Faith	257
50.	Stefan Confronts Faith	260
51.	Greyffos' Message	271
52.	The Collusion	276
53.	The Final Indictment	280
54.	Starbury's Ultimatum	286
55.	The Common Ground	292
56.	The Duel	294
57.	The Brigadier Reminisces	310
58.	The Wedding	320

Chapter 1
Coln Head

A horsewoman, elegant in appearance, eyed a well-worn grey mare up and down from her own mount. The mare was tethered to the aged oak gatepost of St Andrew's church at Sevenhampton. This was the second time she had passed the patient animal within the hour, but not a soul had come to claim her.

She dismounted and tied Eugene, her magnificent steed, alongside the disinterested beast, and walked through the arched entrance, wondering how many bodies, dead or alive, had passed over its ancient threshold in centuries gone by.

It was finally springtime, and after a particularly long, hard winter the daffodils and primroses were now out in abundance, succeeding the hardier crocuses and snowdrops. Their varied yellow heads danced joyously in the southwesterly breeze. Young buds on the deciduous trees were also beginning to break through, exposing their verdant green fronds as several barn swallows darted around in search of flying insects after an arduous journey from southern Africa.

To the lady's left beside the churchyard's ivy-strewn northern wall, an old man tended the fresh grave of his dear wife. Tears rolled down his wizened cheeks, but were soon dried by a tattered sleeve as he recalled memories of their long life together.

"Excuse me, Mr Holby. Do you know whose horse that is near to the gate? It has been idle there for some while now."

Oblivious to her approach, her enquiry startled the grieving widower, who jumped and placed a hand on his chest.

"My God!" he said. "Please don't do that!" He then shot a glance towards the church, and with his other hand over his mouth apologised profusely to the sky for his blasphemous remark.

The lady smiled at him apologetically before repeating her question.

With good manners he removed his flat cap and looked over the lady's shoulder to where the horse languished in the lane.

"There's a chap gone down to yon' stream, Mrs Cavner. I reck'n 'e'll be a'ter them ther' trout. It's the zeazon for 'em now. I en't ever ze'n the likes of 'im afore. I en't ever zet eyes on 'im in me life."

She looked towards the pathway that led down around to the back of the church. "How long has he been here?" she asked.

The old man pulled out his fob watch, which told him that it was at least an hour or more, but he shrugged his shoulders, as he didn't really know.

"Thank you anyway." She turned to go.

"Judging by 'iz attire, 'e en't no poor perz'n, Mrs Cavner. Nope, 'e en't a poor person," he repeated.

The lady politely thanked Mr Holby and offered her condolences about his wife's sudden and unexpected death before returning to Eugene.

The stranger had tantalised her mind. She wondered what he was doing loitering on her uncle's land? She considered whether to go and tell the gamekeeper and let him deal with the intruder. Instead, she took her horse by the reins and guided him around the church and out onto the water meadow beyond. There, she mounted the animal and they trundled down to the streamside, where the water ran slowly and appeared cold and clear, as the snow had long since melted and there had been little rain.

Most of the stream was lined with ash and willow, dotted intermittently with spiteful blackthorn bushes, brambles and clumps of nettles.

At first she could see no one, and the pair ambled slowly upstream as close to the river's edge as possible, occasionally disturbing an occasional woodpigeon or rabbit.

Soon she found the trespasser. He was a handsome man with dark tousled hair, a vague moustache and muscular features. He had removed his boots, and his riding breeches had been rolled beyond his knees, exposing his powerful calf and thigh muscles. He was paddling in the water and checking the undersides of both banks for any elusive fish.

Mr Holby had been right; his clothes did suggest that he was not a poor person by any means. Then why did he need to be catching trout, by hand indeed, on private land?

Soon his escapades would be ended, and he would not be able to go any further because the narrow stream disappeared beneath the lane at Brockhampton village.

Time was to be called on his boyish activities

"Excuse me! Do you realise whose land you are on?" she asked but there was no response. She tried again. "Excuse me. This is my uncle's land!" she shouted at him with her educated accent.

Struggling, he ignored her, but he then suddenly stood bolt upright with a beautiful brown trout in hand.

"How do you fancy him for supper?" he asked, smiling. He viewed his inquisitor up and down. She was an extremely fine looking lady with golden brown hair that had been rolled and pinned at the back. She was expensively dressed, wearing an amethyst-coloured tailored jacket braided and buttoned in gold, a long, black suede skirt and a white chemisette. Her jaunty, feathered riding hat and gloves matched her jacket.

Her penetrating blue eyes bore down upon him as he looked her over.

"The answer to your original question, ma'am, is that this is God's land." With his free hand he gestured towards their beautiful surroundings.

"My uncle will not be pleased having a trespasser here, so I suggest you leave immediately, but not before putting that back where you found it," she commented, eyeing the squirming fish choking in his grip.

He turned and threw the trout back into the pool, and for a second or two it lay stunned and drifted briefly with the current as it sieved water through it's gills before soon recovering and darting away.

He looked back at his alluring suppressor and smiled. "There. Does that make you feel better?" he asked as he climbed the bank before stroking her mount's face.

"A beautiful animal, ma'am; there are not many of these found over here in England. He's a *Morgan*, I believe: an American breed. They are very versatile horses," he said with eyebrows raised impressively.

She was taken aback slightly as he appeared to have a keen knowledge of the equine world, but she nevertheless considered his encroachment illegal. "Please! Can you leave my uncle's land?"

He had a deep suspicion that she didn't seem quite so forthright when she asked him a second time. She almost pleaded with him, he thought. "If you insist, ma'am. I was leaving soon anyway." He took out his pocket watch and glanced at the time. The itinerant poacher began to walk back downstream towards the church, carefully avoiding nettles and thistles.

"Excuse me! To leave this field it is quicker to walk that way," she nodded towards an iron swing gate and pathway leading up into Brockhampton village.

"But my boots and horse are this way," he replied over his shoulder, ignoring her advice and continuing in the opposite direction.

She didn't see the wry smile on his face as he went to collect his footwear. She followed, maintaining a distance of a few yards between them, determined to see him off the land.

He soon found his riding boots, and sat upon the damp grass to pull them on. Now suitably attired, he stood, and with two trout hanging from a forked hazel twig, he placed a hand gently on her knee as he held up the catch. "Supper?" he asked with a smile.

She swung her horse around, disgusted at his manners. "Who do you think you are?" she demanded to know, quite annoyed.

"Ma'am, I know who I am but equally, who are you? A mere woman, I understand." He waited for a reply as she regained control of the horse. "I don't have to tell you who I am! You are trespassing!" she scolded the handsome stranger.

"In which case, ma'am, I do not have to tell you who I am because you might also be a trespasser."

She had become irate with him but he was of the opinion that it was not normally in her nature to be so.

She said nothing and he turned to leave once more without looking back. She followed him to the narrow footpath that led around the bottom of the churchyard and into the lane outside.

On hearing her horse come to a stop, and knowing that she would have to dismount, blocking her path, he turned and offered his hand. "Ma'am, please allow me to help you."

Pursing her lips she had little choice. He acted as the perfect gentleman, taking her hand and helping her to the ground.

They fleetingly stood face to face, and his eyes looked deeply into hers.

Her heart fluttered in that trance-like moment, and she could not stop thinking about the figure of the man before her as he led her animal back through the lower graveyard to the church gate, where he loosely tied it next to his own ageing mare.

"What brought you here in the first place?" she asked, now standing on neutral territory.

He looked around, contemplating the old stone cottages and ancient church, and then once more he stared into her eyes. "Nobody has ever written about the Coln Valley and its quaint villages that have sprung up over the centuries. I think it's about time someone did, and so I came to find the source of this pretty little river, and by catching some fish I can deduce the health of its waters. I believe that somewhere near here is the source of the River Coln."

"Oh! And when do you plan to write your book?" she asked disbelievingly with her thoughts in disarray. Could this man standing before her, who pursues childish pastimes yet has a knowledge of horses whilst possessing one of the oldest and scruffiest mares along the Coln Valley, possibly be an author? Surely he is too young to be an eccentric.

"I will begin in the next two or three days, and will return here with pencil and paper in hand, and take in some stories and anecdotes from the local people. Firstly, I need to find the source of the river and then, over the coming months, I will work and write my way back downstream to Lechlade, where the Coln has its confluence with the great River Thames. It will take about a year, in which time all four seasons will also be fully ensconced within the narration."

As he now seemed very natural and confident she asked a question that had been on her mind. "Where are you from?"

He hesitated but then smiled before replying. "Bibury." It was all he said.

For a short while the attractive horsewoman was quiet, but suddenly she conceded. "Come. I will take you to see where the Coln rises from the ground." For some reason she unexpectedly seemed to believe what he had told her and, out of the blue, had developed some interest in his literary project.

Both mounted and set off side by side along the bridleway that passed the rear of Brockhampton Park and its splendid manor house.

She led him into a field north of the great house, to an area of marshy ground where several springs appeared through the open slopes.

Here he athletically jumped from his horse and stamped on the grassy earth below. The fresh spring waters bubbled up from under his feet in several places out of the Cotswold hillside and soon conjoined, beginning a downward southeasterly journey.

He studied the views around him until becoming quite satisfied that they were indeed at Coln Head. He patted her knee again and thanked her, and this time she didn't shy away as her horse stood resolutely still.

"Now that you have seen what you came here for, can you leave my uncle's land please?" she asked him politely but somewhat reluctantly.

"Certainly." He again took out his watch and having time in hand mused over what he should do next.

"Can I assume that there is an alehouse here in the village? He asked. "Whilst I'm here I may as well begin putting some ideas together in my head, and who better to ask than some local old men or indeed the landlord whilst I down a beer or two to loosen my mind?"

"Yes. There is the Cavner Arms in Brockhampton village; it is the only one. You will find the inn behind a little track, at the end of which is its sign. You cannot miss it. Aim for the tall chimney stack, which is part of the brewery attached to the same building."

"Would you like to accompany me?" he asked, hoping she wouldn't refuse. "I would appreciate some companionship from someone who resides here."

"I am afraid that it would not be a good idea for me – or any woman, for that matter – to be seen with a complete stranger in an alehouse. Besides, I do not live here and my limited local knowledge would be of little use to you." Deep down she regretted having to say what she did but it was the wisest thing to do. "I'll ride with you to the manor house but from then you'll have to go on alone."

As they sauntered back down the lane he asked her where she was from but she did not answer, instead they stopped at the rear entrance of Brockhampton Park.

"I'm afraid that I will be riding with you no further because here is where I am staying," she told him, showing little enthusiasm to return to the manor just yet.

He studied the house and then looked her up and down with a smile. "It seems that I am going to have plenty to write about. If you don't live here then where do you come from?" he asked her for the second time.

She was hesitant to tell him but eventually answered. "Shropshire. A place you've probably never heard of. It's called Cavner Arms."

He tried to put two and two together. She was from Cavner Arms in Shropshire and the local pub here in Brockhampton had the same name. "That is where Stokesay Castle is, am I right?" he suddenly asked.

She stared at him with a deadpan expression. Sat beside her was a handsome man with an apparently good education who was seemingly very knowledgeable.

"Yes, you are quite right. When will you be back? Soon?" she asked him.

He pondered over the days of the week. "Friday. I'll be back on Friday. First thing in the morning at the church, weather permitting," he turned to leave but then added in a strange accent, "Oh, by the way. Should anyone ask, my name is Stefan Desailley."

Her heartbeat quickened as she watched him ride away; something that had not happened for many years when meeting someone for the first time.

She wondered why he said 'should anyone ask'. Of course, she herself would have to ask about Stefan Desailley?

Seated comfortably at the bar in the Cavner Arms Stefan inquired only about Brockhampton Park and its current occupants. The landlord gave him as much information as he dared.

"The owners of the park are Sir Charles Corbett-Cavner and his wife, Maria Georgina. Their family have owned it for decades. Much of the land around here belongs to them, and they tenant out some of the farms and most of the smallholdings as well as the cottages in both villages. This pub and the malt house are also a part of the estate. Sevenhampton and Brockhampton are both part of the same parish," he added.

"And what of Stokesay Castle?"

"That belongs to the Cavner family as well. Sir Charles' brother, Frederick, owns it. The village near Stokesay Castle is named after their coat of arms and has the same name as this alehouse. It is all very complicated but the village in Shropshire also has an inn of the same name as this one, which was built for the local workforce by one of the past heirs. It is all a part of a massive aristocratic estate based in two counties: Shropshire and Gloucestershire."

Stefan thought for a moment. "When I was out and about this morning I was confronted by a most elegant woman astride a magnificent black horse. I saw her going back to the manor house. Who might she be?" It was a burning question that Stefan desperately wanted answered.

"She is Sir Charles' brother's daughter-in-law, Georgina Buchanan Corbett-Cavner. Sir Charles' wife is her godmother, and she is named after her. Both women are related somehow. She comes here on holiday two or three times a year, always alone though."

"Why do you stress the word *alone*?" Stefan asked.

"Everyone thinks she has a bad marriage but no one locally really knows. It is purely supposition. There are two children, a boy and a girl, and the boy will one day inherit the entire estate. She always comes on her own, never with her husband or children." The landlord said no more and seemed rather relieved when another customer walked into the old establishment.

Stefan mused over the information he had found out. He sat swilling the remnants of his beer around and around in his pot, staring across the bar deep in thought. A scruffy dog sniffed at his boots but Stefan took very little notice. The beautiful figure of Georgina Cavner was firmly implanted in his mind.

Georgina found Edward, her cousin, in the garden contemplating how improvements might be made that coming summer.

"Friday morning. Can you please come with me, Edward?" she implored.

Edward, the calm and collected son of Sir Charles Corbett-Cavner, quietly asked his excited cousin why.

"A gentleman wishes to write a book about the Coln Valley and I thought that while he does his research here it would be better to have a well-informed person with him who knows the local area well." She stared at him pleadingly.

At first he wasn't interested but then he conceded. "All right, Georgina. If you so wish, but where will we have to start, and at what time?" he asked her innocently.

"Nine o'clock at the church," she answered happily.

Chapter 2
The Preface

Georgina nervously stood back as Edward lifted the heavy iron latch on the metal-studded church door of St Andrew's at Sevenhampton, and entered just as the bell struck nine o'clock. They chose a pew at the rear of the church and briefly prayed. Georgina prayed for forgiveness because of her thoughts.

They sat quietly whist strange noises punctuated the silence as ancient oak beams creaked from the increasing warmth of the day. As he tried to accumulate in his mind everything he knew about the parish, Edward estimated that the original parts of the building were approximately seven hundred years old, which dates back to the Norman era.

Ten minutes in Georgina's life seemed like an hour in the cool of the Lord's preaching house, and her patience became thin. Edward, feeling his cousin's agitation, leaned over and whispered, "I don't think he's coming; the weather doesn't look too friendly."

Georgina had given him no indication as to what he might expect from the researcher, and he could only imagine an aged wordsmith with a long, grey beard and moustache, dressed in tweeds, sporting a deerstalker and smoking an expensive continental pipe.

As he dreamed the door's latch clunked and the noise reverberated around the solid stone walls. Both stretched their necks towards the old oak door, but were disappointed to see Mrs Denley enter, who had voluntarily looked after the church for decades, and had come to prepare the religious sanctuary for the weekend services.

The old woman thought it strange to see the two Cavner cousins, but did not utter a word as she passed quietly behind them and went into the vestry.

Georgina's frustration almost overwhelmed her but in God's house she controlled her emotions. It was Edward who suggested that they should leave, as further waiting could prove futile. Georgina agreed because it didn't seem likely that Mr Desailley would make the effort, especially as the weather had all the signs of deteriorating.

In the porch they retrieved their umbrellas as the heavens finally decided to open on St Andrew's, and it began spotting heavily with rain.

As they made their way back to the gate Georgina abruptly stopped. "He's here!" she exclaimed. "That's his horse!"

The pair looked around the graveyard and then saw a crouched figure reading epitaphs on gravestones and taking notes.

Edward could not understand what drove her enthusiasm but was soon enlightened when catching sight of the handsome man for whom they had been waiting, who was quite a contrast to the man he had imagined. Rather than walk through the wet, untended grass, Edward called out to him. "Sir! Sir!"

Stefan stood upright and stared at the couple for a few seconds before recognising the fair woman dressed colourlessly in anticipation of dour weather. He hadn't expected to see her again, and at variance to what he had been told she appeared to be with her husband. Glancing upwardly at the grey, formidable skies he made his way back through the angled headstones, pocketing his notes and tucking his pencil behind his ear.

"A little inappropriate to say so today perhaps, but nonetheless, a good morning to you, ma'am. Good morning, sir," he said as he bowed his head very slightly and tipped his leather hat with regard to their status, smiling as he did so.

"Good morning, Mr Desailley," Georgina replied, "I have brought my cousin with me so he can guide you around the two villages. Edward knows a great deal about his family estate and its history."

Edward and Stefan shook hands as they introduced themselves. "That is very kind of you, Mr Cavner. I will indeed appreciate your knowledge and assistance," Stefan told him, again dipping his head with respect. His quick mind pondered for a second that they could surely only be cousins by marriage. Cousins-in-law perhaps?

Edward gestured towards the church. "I think perhaps the first person you need to speak to is inside. Mrs Denley's family have lived here for hundreds of years, and what she knows about the local people would be precious to any historical writer. Come, let's go and find her."

Mrs Denley was a mine of information as she showed Stefan around the church, with its inbuilt epitaphs. Edward and Georgina followed, equally interested. Outside, reading the inscriptions on the tombstones, Mrs Denley explained the family names and what their place on the estate had been, whether labourers, farriers, carpenters, or herdsmen. During this time, Edward could not help noticing Georgina's inability to keep her eyes off Stefan. He began to think that he himself was only there to inhibit any gossip should the pair be seen walking around the parish alone together. Stefan, he thought, was a handsome and presumably intelligent man, whilst Georgina was a beautiful and wealthy lady. Edward would have to find out more about the stranger who had infiltrated his family circle.

The rain had come to nothing, and between the billowing clouds the sun shone brightly, which nevertheless greatly raised the temperature. Squalls were their only problem but high as they were on the Cotswold Hills their imminence was entirely foreseeable, rendering them avoidable. Shortly afterwards they left Mrs Denley to her chores.

Georgina handed Stefan some written papers that she and Edward had briefly composed the evening before, which concerned the ownership of Brockhampton Park over the centuries since its construction. They hoped it would help with his compilation of the manuscript about the upper reaches of the Coln Valley. Together, they sauntered around the two villages and the outlying district.

Long past midday they made their way back to the Cavner Arms, where Stefan had earlier that morning tied Marengo, his grey mare, during his rambling tutorial.

Stefan turned to his village guide. "Thank you for your help, Edward. I have appreciated and enjoyed your local familiarity immensely. In the next couple of days I shall begin putting it down on paper in decent handwriting. A visit to the Coln Gallery in Fairford will not go amiss, and I'll see if there are any maps of the area, new or old." He stroked his old horse and briefly scanned the back door of the public house.

Edward realised that Stefan's next desire was to go inside the alehouse and he interpreted the desperate expression on Georgina's face.

"Georgina! By all means, stay here and I will send someone down with a horse and gig to take you back to the house."

She barely threw a glance towards Edward as her eyes were firmly fixed upon Stefan. Her mind was already clear, and against her earlier disinclination about being seen in an alehouse with a stranger. Rather than allow Stefan to walk out of her life as abruptly as he had walked in, she decided to accompany him into the Cavner Arms.

"No need, Edward. I will not be long. I will take the shortcut and walk back up along the avenue and by the lake. Thank you, Edward," Georgina gently kissed her cousin on his cheek in a show of appreciation.

Edward, suddenly feeling like a gooseberry, left them to their own devices. Stefan offered Georgina some refreshment, and although completely unbecoming for a woman in her position she could not decline, and allowed herself to be ushered into the inn.

A couple of old, rheumatic-ridden men attempted to stand whilst respectfully taking off their sweaty, threadbare hats to expose furrowed brows and balding heads. Stefan politely asked them to remain as they were. Georgina had never been in the inn before even though it bore her married name and family crest. The landlord's manners became exemplary in her presence but pondered over the man who only two days before had been asking personal questions about her family. They asked for the brew from the adjoining malt house and then took a vacated table by the window, where Stefan could browse through all of his scribbled information he had gathered that morning.

Georgina watched as he studied his roughly scrawled documents. Occasionally, he stopped and re-wrote some of the manuscript. At first he was mostly taken in by what he had written and took little notice of her. She was also infatuated for entirely different reasons, and studied his features as he read his scripts. Here, sat before her, was a man of most women's dreams. He was tall, handsome, muscular, well mannered and obviously intelligent.

Eventually, he placed his pencil upon his pile of papers and apologised for his ignorance but was satisfied with his first serious day's outing along the upper reaches of the Coln Valley.

Stefan looked around the bar room and only then noticed that few people had spoken since they sat down. He smiled, thinking that they would have enough to talk about when he and Georgina left. Rumours would spread as cholera did in the Crimean War, he thought, and smiled to himself. It was only human nature.

"You have beautiful handwriting," she told him meekly, trying to begin a conversation.

"Have I?" he asked, shrugging his shoulders with a boyish look as he picked up his paperwork and sifted through it.

Georgina glimpsed at the other customers' looks and suddenly appeared concerned. "I am afraid I must go," she said quietly. "The whole estate will be talking about us."

"Mrs Cavner, please–" he began but she stopped him dead.

"Please do not call me that," she demanded as she quickly looked around to see who was listening. "Ma'am or Georgina. It is up to you. But I don't mind if you call me Georgina," she hinted.

Nothing seemed to worry Stefan. "Georgina, the people of the whole Cavner estate can say what they wish because we have not done anything, let alone done anything wrong. We can hardly be up to no good sat here in their company. Allow the people to think the worst, and when they hear the truth they might just be surprised. Please! Don't leave just yet," he smiled.

For a few seconds she said nothing.

"What made you come to the church this morning?" he asked.

At first she remained discreet but then she plucked up the courage to tell him. "On Sunday I must travel back to Shropshire. I have been here for more than a fortnight and yesterday I received a letter telling me to return."

Georgina was telling a half-truth because for some time she had known about returning to Shropshire.

Stefan was confused. "Why do you need a letter to tell you to go home?" he asked, prying. Being asked is one thing but being told has serious undertones, he thought.

"I come to Brockhampton to convalesce, and talking to you has already made me feel better. From the moment I left you by the house on Wednesday I haven't been able to keep you out of my mind, so I thought I'd come and see you for one last time. Now please, I have to go home." She spoke sullenly with a very sorrowful expression.

"When you say that you are here to convalesce, what has been wrong with you?" Stefan asked, concerned about her welfare.

She wasn't sure whether to tell him or not but it would make no difference. On Sunday she would still have to return home. "My husband beats me badly. It is all to do with alcohol. When he is sober he is a wonderful, loving husband but when he drinks too much for days on end he becomes jealous of anyone who sets eyes upon me. He doesn't take his violence out on them, who are innocent anyway; it is me who has to suffer. The letter I received was from my mother-in-law, who reassures me that my husband hasn't drank for some days now, and so I should return home. It will happen again, it always does, but his family always insist that I go back, simply to save face."

Stefan placed his hand upon hers. She didn't shy away. "I cannot imagine why any man would want to assault any woman let alone one as beautiful as you, Georgina. I am so sorry for you. What does your uncle and aunt here in Brockhampton think of all this?"

"They are on my side, especially my aunt. That is why I come here. She is so good to me. They are all on my side down here, Edward included." She stared mournfully into Stefan's eyes.

"But what about your own family. Do they not care about you?" he asked sympathetically.

"They warned me not to marry him. As far as they are concerned 'I made my bed, so I shall lie on it'. They were right, of course, but in those days I was naïve, young and self-centred." Georgina gazed out of the window. How life could have been so different had she listened to them, she thought.

"Do you have children?" Stefan queried even though he already knew the answer. He had no wish for her to think he had been asking private questions behind her back.

"Yes, a boy and a girl. Thomas and Jennifer. My husband never does anything in front of them or hurts them either, everything is taken out on me." Worried again about the time, she studied the clock's pendulum, which seemed to will her life back to Shropshire with each arc, and sat like a detainee might await transfer to prison.

"You cannot carry on your life the way it is. Give the man some kind of ultimatum," Stefan advised her, as he looked deep into her eyes. She slowly shook her head in despair.

"I am afraid I have little choice. To leave him means that I would have to give up my children, and then where would I go? I would have no financial support from either family, mine or theirs."

She stood up, visibly upset. "I should not have come here today. I knew it was a foolish thing to do."

"Please! Georgina, please sit back down. Talking to a stranger might make you feel better." Stefan genuinely wanted to help the desperate woman standing before him.

Georgina viewed the customers who had remained silent throughout, all trying to listen to their private conversation.

She sat back down and dabbed her eyes with a silk handkerchief, "I shouldn't stay. I cannot afford to mar the relationship I have with my aunt and uncle. They and Edward are the only friends I have. Oh, except for Mary, my cousin."

"Just tell them that I am only here to write about the Coln Valley, as Edward already knows. I am married as well so they should more than understand. They are obviously aware enough to take you in under their protection until everything settles down, and they must surely know what your feelings are and what is going through your obviously tortured mind. Georgina, you cannot possibly want to go back to Shropshire?" Stefan felt she needed to make some important decisions with her future, although, as he knew only too well, there were always two sides to every story in a marriage.

"It is my children. I will never be allowed to see my children if I leave. There is nothing I can do. Aunt Maria knows that. She says that if I take them away from Stokesay, Uncle Charles couldn't possibly have them here. He would have to be discreet with any matters involving his blood family. As I have already told you, I would have nowhere to go and be exempt from any financial access. He doesn't mind if I stay here alone without the children but I would never be able to divorce his nephew for fear of bringing the family name into disrepute. We are all stuck between a rock and a hard place."

"What do your in-laws think of it all?"

"Frederick, Uncle Charles' brother, says absolutely nothing. He treats me ordinarily, as if nothing is happening. As for my mother-in-law, she's the one who wants me to return, just to save face. She is embarrassed about her son but tells everyone that all of it is my fault. She believes that if we stay together then everything will appear to be all right, but it is far from the truth."

Georgina again stared out of the window. She knew that she had to return to Shropshire and once more become a prisoner in her own home.

Stefan wrote a note on a piece of paper, tore it off and handed it to her. "Here. That is my address. Should you want to write and tell me anything, do not hesitate. Is there any way that I might be able to contact you?"

She pushed it back to him. "I cannot possibly take it. God only knows the consequences if I were to be found corresponding with a stranger, especially a man."

"Georgina, you cannot carry on with your life as it is! Your husband needs to change and treat you properly. Life is too short and I can see that you are desperately unhappy. Please take it and write to me should you feel the need." Stefan was adamant that she should try and stay in touch.

"But what about your dear wife? What will she think when she sees a stranger's letters arriving on her doorstep from other parts of the country?" Georgina raised her eyebrows wondering what kind of marriage he had.

"It's not my home address but I can assure you if she did find out she would be quite all right about it." He turned Georgina's hand over, placed the note in her palm and squeezed her fingers shut. "Take it and please write."

They decided to leave. Stefan returned their empty glasses back onto the bar and looked around the room and smiled at the customers.

"Gentlemen, I trust what you have heard will travel no further than this establishment. Thank you for your discretion, and a good day to you all."

He was greeted with murmured replies.

Outside, Stefan had one last thing to say to Georgina that day.

"One mile south of here is a tiny hamlet with a ford running through it, which is aptly named Syreford. I'll come up tomorrow morning and explore the river between there and Sevenhampton. I'll tie my horse on the bridleway as close to the ford as possible. I'll be there at nine o'clock."

He drew her to him, kissed her softly on the lips and stroked her hair. "We'll make you a happy woman again one day," he said before mounting his horse and riding away.

He was around the corner of the building and out of sight in seconds, leaving Georgina standing alone with her heart beating wildly, as intrusive faces peered through windows behind her.

Throughout his return journey to Bibury, Stefan tried to formulate the beginning of his new book in his scrambled mind, but both the weather and the fate of Georgina Cavner distracted him. He arrived on the estate early in the evening and at the door of his home was greeted by Francois, his youngest son. They were pleased to see each other, and Stefan lovingly picked up his son and carried him into the kitchen, where Charity, his wife, was preparing an evening meal.

He kissed her on the neck from behind and she asked how much he had achieved that day. She listened without turning away from the sink and stove, and soon after, he retreated to have a strip wash before changing into clean, more relaxing clothes.

He returned to find dinner served, and as a caring father he chatted with all three of his children, asking what they had been doing all day. Later, after reading to them extracts from works of the noted author, Charles Dickens, they were sent to bed.

Leaving Charity crocheting by a diminishing fire he retired to his small drawing room, where he began sorting out his day's work and putting it into some semblance of order. As darkness fell he lit the two kerosene lamps that offered just enough light by which to put pen to paper.

He knew that if he could at least write some kind of introduction that evening it would give him the impetus to work on the rest of the manuscript.

With inkwell full and paper before him, he sat with pen at the ready. With his elbow poised on the leather-topped desk and his hand stroking his chin, he began.

The Coln Valley, Villages & Towns

The Coln River rises from the ground as several small springs just to the north of the picturesque village of Brockhampton, approximately five miles to the east of the stylish spa town of Cheltenham. It takes a generally southerly route and eventually joins the River Thames at the charming town of Lechlade.

As the crow flies the River Coln is eighteen miles in length, but taking into account its meanderings, the walker can expect a considerably longer journey.

It begins as a streamlet passing through Brockhampton Park but soon develops into a healthy brook further downstream before developing enough to be classified as a river.

The scenery all around and the Cotswold stone-built villages and towns through which the Coln passes are some of the most beautiful in the whole of the English countryside.

Much history has passed by over the centuries, some recorded, but the majority of tales have been handed down verbally and have inevitably become distorted. In this short book I hope the reader and/or walker can trust my accuracies of the historical accounts, which I have taken from speaking with people and local authorities of the area, as well as reading their documents.

I sincerely hope that you will enjoy walking along the Coln Valley and using its hostelries on the way.

Stefan F. Desailley

It had been a long day and Stefan was tired. He read what he had written, and thought that perhaps he had been a little presumptuous to have written a preface so soon. But at least he had made a start, he thought.

He pulled open a drawer and took out a bottle of Armagnac, and retrieved his French crystal glass, which he rarely washed, from the mantelpiece. He poured a large tot, which was more than welcome to induce a peaceful night's sleep, and reclined in his chair, rocking slowly back and forth. He would soon be in bed with Charity but his thoughts would not leave Georgina alone. Both women were beautiful in different ways but both also had serious problems of their own.

Empty of kerosene, one of the lamps began to burn out and the smoke from the dying flame began to permeate the room. He turned it off, snuffing out the acrid vapour, and did the same with the other one before making his way to the bedroom.

Two candles illuminated the bedside tables as Stefan quietly undressed, and he blew out Charity's candle and then his own before sliding between the sheets. He lay on his back for a while deep in thought, and Charity turned towards him and took his hand. They kissed briefly.

After two or three minutes it was Charity who spoke first. "Who is she?" she asked solemnly.

He sat up on an elbow. "How do you know?"

"You don't normally go out with perfume on," she replied.

Whilst still holding each other's hands Stefan told her everything that had happened over the last couple of days.

Charity knew that in the morning she would write a letter to her oldest sister, Faith, who lived in London. She would mention Stefan's possible infidelity.

Chapter 3
Sennington Barn

Georgina dismounted Eugene and tied him next to Stefan's grey mare, and they acknowledged each other with a quick thrash of tails. Her assumption was that the man she had come to see was upstream, probably tickling trout again. She followed a path that was well trodden on market days by plebeians, who trundled alongside the brook with their wares between Sevenhampton and Andoversford.

It was not far before she found him lying on the riverbank with one arm searching an underwater ledge for any signs of piscine life.

As Georgina approached he muttered a barely audible profanity whilst lifting himself up from the leaf-strewn ground. Standing tall he brushed himself off then bent down and swilled his hands and face in the murmuring water.

Something caught his eye. He turned and there stood Georgina, smiling.

It was the first time he had seen her properly smile, and it gave her an even more engaging appearance.

"I didn't expect to see you here," he told her, smiling back but this time empty-handed. "You seem more relaxed, happier perhaps," he suggested.

"It is my last day of freedom before returning north tomorrow. I thought I would make the most of it and take an early ride out and come and see you. Do you mind?" she asked, tempting him with an answer as the morning breeze swept her hair across her face.

They came together and Stefan tenderly brushed her golden hair back into place and at the same time gently touched her cheek with his thumb. They stared into each other's eyes, infatuated.

Georgina very much wanted him to take her in his arms, but he was careful. The woodland was scant and their horses were almost definitely tied up together. Rumour of yesterday's liaison in the Cavner Arms would have almost certainly spread around the parishes of Sevenhampton and Brockhampton like warm dripping on fresh bread. Georgina's life could be in peril once more despite being so far from her home.

He took a step back. "I will explore the stream as far as the end of the copse and then we will return to our horses. From there I will visit some old ruins, which, so I'm told, were formerly a part of the original village of Brockhampton. Would you like to come with me?" he asked her politely.

"Of course I would. There is little else to do today," she paused, "except pack my trunk," she added solemnly.

After catching a small trout Stefan decided to search no further. They were at the end of the sparse woodland and exposure over open ground would almost certainly have them seen together. They turned and headed back towards Syreford.

The narrow footpath allowed them to walk in single file only. Behind Stefan, Georgina tripped, quite deliberately, and Stefan spun around to see her sprawled on the ground.

"Are you all right?" he asked and helped her to her feet. She kept her balance with a hand on his forearm as he brushed the woodland debris from her long skirt.

"Yes. Yes, I am fine. A little embarrassed though."

Stefan straightened up. She ran a hand down his chest and held him by his side. Georgina's heart pounded as she waited for him to make a move.

He studied her face all over and then leaned towards her and their lips met. It was not a simple kiss but a long, lingering physical involvement. Tongues intertwined as if neither had had any sexual interaction for a long time. He gently caressed her breasts as she ran her hand down onto his groin, and Georgina swiftly activated his sexual desires. Stefan realised they could not carry on at the edge of the wood and pulled away, holding her by the shoulders at arms' length.

He studied the ground and landscape beyond the thinning woodland. "Georgina! We cannot stay here. We must go. Please! Let us find our horses." He took her hand and led her along the path back to where the Coln crossed the bridleway.

They mounted and without another word set off towards the remnants of the hamlet of Sennington.

It was a slow climb onto the higher ground of the Cotswold Hills, and as the land opened up, sheep dotted an almost treeless landscape punctuated only by small pine plantations. The fleecy ruminants were the staple diet of the people and the mainstay of a local woollen industry. Lambs were in abundance but did not venture too far from their unsuspecting mothers as a red kite fed off the carrion of a stillborn. Rooks, watching from nearby, waited for their share of the springtime feast.

Georgina ignored her hair blowing across her face as she stared at the powerful back and shoulders of Stefan, who led the way.

"Where are you leading us?" she called out but there was no reply. He guided his horse to the right along an almost disused bridleway until he caught sight of a small copse to his left.

Suddenly, he jumped off his nonchalant mount beside a clump of fir trees. He wandered around the site upon the plateau, inspecting the ground for any signs of archaeological life. Georgina remained upon Eugene, wondering what intrigued Stefan; she herself could see nothing of interest.

He went back over to her. "Yes, I can definitely see that there was a village here many years ago. Sennington was here decades before Brockhampton! Centuries ago there was a great plague that killed many of the people in Europe. Maybe that is what happened here, and it became deserted."

Georgina was confused because she understood little of the local history. "So, what are you going to do now that you have found what you were looking for, Mr Desailley? Return home to your wife?" In her question was a hint of sarcasm, which Stefan chose to ignore.

"What would you wish to do now, Georgina?" he asked her sultrily. "On your last day in the Cotswolds." She looked shyly down at a cluster of young nettles but remained silent.

Stefan led his horse over to the bridleway and onwards towards a winter barn, and Georgina urged her horse to follow. Once there, he hitched his horse to an iron ring attached to the wall. He went inside and then returned to Georgina who, unassured, remained astride Eugene.

"Would you like to come and look inside?" he asked, knowing what was troubling her. "It is entirely up to you, Georgina. It is your choice to turn away now before it's too late and revisit your nightmare, or enter the heavenly barn." He half smiled and raised his eyebrows.

Georgina stole a glance at Stefan and then surveyed the barn from the outside in the springtime sun. Obsolete and rusting farm implements lay amongst piles of Cotswold stone and old fence posts and timbers.

Tomorrow she would be going back to her private hell but what could the fortunes of a secluded barn bring? Eugene stood motionless as if he knew which decision she should make. She patted him affectionately on the side of the neck, and Stefan offered his hand to her but still Georgina hesitated.

Had she come too far or not far enough? Entering the barn would surely be stepping over a moral precipice with her life, but a life that she so desperately needed to change for the better. She thought about her husband's morals. They had taken their vows together years before when he was a descent man, but now he is an alcoholic wife beater who has no shame for the hurt he causes. Never before had she broken her dedication to their marriage, remaining stoical throughout, for better or for worse.

Eugene snorted and nodded his great head, annoyed more so with the emerging insects of springtime than Georgina's hesitancy.

Georgina made her decision and took Stefan's outstretched hand.

They kissed, at first frenetically, but then in a more relaxed and mature manner. She unbuttoned his shirt and ran her hands over his bare chest whilst he undid her jacket, untied her laced bodice and explored her perfectly formed breasts. Georgina's pink nipples began to stand erect from a combination of sexual excitement and the cool draught passing through the barn.

Stefan became sexually aroused; her beauty was irresistible. Their lips barely parted as she dropped her long skirt to the floor and he ran his hand up inside her petticoat along the inside of her thighs. She shifted her stance slightly, and beneath her silky lingerie he found and gently caressed her soft pubic hair and began massaging her organ of sexual pleasure.

Georgina gently pushed him away and freed his firm penis. Kneeling on the ground before him she ran her tongue up and down the highly activated organ whilst simultaneously tenderly stroking his testicles. His glans was bulbous and she didn't hesitate to take it in her mouth and massage it with her tongue and lips. After months of sexual abstention soon Stefan pushed her away for fear of spoiling the whole scenario by ejaculating prematurely.

Now both completely nude, they lay down on the remnants of hay in the corner of the old stone barn and he began to explore her beautiful body. He sucked and softly pinched her nipples, now hard from arousal, and kissed her, stroked her and smelled her pale, slightly perfumed feminine skin. Her blond pubic hair was as feathery as her silk handkerchiefs and his nose began to explore her genitalia. She exuded translucent femininity as her vagina produced its attractive odour, which few men would resist. He searched the fleshy crevices of her most private part and soon found its highly sensitive nerve end: her clitoris. His tongue darted in and out, gently titillating the sexual organ as she lay back with her shapely legs spread wide apart, completely exposing her womanhood. He caressed her breasts at the same time, and she urged him not to stop. She pulled at his tousled hair as if to drag him inward, together to become one.

Her breathing increased and her heart rate doubled. Never before had she felt such complete sexual satisfaction. Drugged by his masculinity her mind was in a different world. Suddenly, with her head thrown back and her eyes closed, she let out a cry of ultimate fulfilment and emotion. Stefan held her arms down until she could carry on no more and tried to fight him off but he rose above her and with his fully erect penis penetrated her, and they made love for the first time. She pulled him towards her as if she could not have enough of him. Never in her life had she had such ultimate carnal pleasure, and strangely enough with a man she had fallen in love with at first sight just days before.

Stefan hadn't had physical indulgence for a long time and his resolve was weakened mostly due to the exquisite beauty of the woman who lay beneath. Nothing could stop him from letting loose his sexual prowess and at the zenith of illicit love he released all of his pent up sexual emotions.

Soon afterwards he lay slightly breathless upon Georgina's torso as the blood drained quickly from his once proud and erect penis. He withdrew and rolled aside, holding her head close to his chest and taking long, deep breaths.

Georgina lay with her hand caressing his softening penis whilst staring through the barn door at the bright daylight. For her, tomorrow would be an entirely different scenario.

A barn owl, watching the pair's interactions with its impassive expression, had witnessed everything from a roof beam.

Later, after their goodbye embrace, Georgina stood gazing as Stefan sauntered away upon his grey mare. When he was finally out of sight she turned the mighty Eugene by the reins and led him all the way back to Brockhampton Park.

Deep thoughts raced through her mind. She felt like chasing Stefan back to Bibury, but where could she stay? When could she return to

Brockhampton without arousing suspicion? Should she go back to Shropshire and never return? Did Stefan love her or did he merely lust for her? Regardless, he was the most beautiful being who had ever entered her life.

Stefan reached Bibury in the middle of the afternoon, and made straight for the Catherine Wheel, which is his local inn. His mind was confused. Importantly, he needed to put pen to paper but nothing could stop him from dwelling over his liaison with Georgina. He thought a few ales might settle him down. And he needed to talk to someone, and who better than his great friend Lionel, the landlord's son. Lionel was also Stefan's father-in-law's butler at Bibury Court.

Fortunately, Lionel was working behind the bar and there were few other patrons around. At first, Stefan said very little and Lionel guessed that his friend's mind was troubled. Their friendship went back a long way into the depths of childhood.

"Something is wrong, Stefan. I can tell. You are acting strangely. What have you done this time?"

Stefan scrutinised everyone along the bar. "Come outside, Lionel. I will tell you there, not here."

They sat at a makeshift table made from a sliced up tree trunk, and Stefan told his friend what had happened that morning, asking for assurances that Lionel would tell no one.

Lionel smiled at him, "I'll wager you've already told Charity."

"She knows about her but not about what happened today. I haven't been home yet." Stefan answered.

Knowing of Stefan's wife's problems and the repercussions of little Frankie's difficult birth, Lionel sympathised with them both. "Are you going to tell her?" he asked carefully.

"I'm not sure. Charity may not have meant what she told me all those months ago. Perhaps she was merely testing my character." Stefan looked away towards the rookery, where the seasonal breeding activity was at its height and the chicks were very demanding. The large black birds were raucous and oblivious to the two men's sultry conversation.

"If Georgina is not back here for some considerable time then try and forget about her. It's probably just a one off incident anyway. An upper-class woman, possibly from aristocracy, with money pouring from her ears and who is miles from her husband, has a clandestine sexual encounter with someone she hardly knows and then, on returning home nothing will be said." Lionel paused to reflect. "It sounds to me you were a fortunate man in the right place at the right time. If I were you I would assume that it was a one off chance meeting. Get back home and start writing that book you've kept on about for the last three years. This woman will soon become a distant memory. Oh, and whatever you do, do not let Charity's brother find out. You know how he hates you. He'll have all the ammunition he needs to get you out of his life. The hierarchy in England have all power over the working classes. You are a mere minnow, albeit a damned fortunate one."

Lionel tried to make Stefan come to terms with what he'd done, and was resolute in what he told his friend. "Go home to Charity and begin writing; it is what you are best at. Charity may get better in time but not with you gallivanting up and down the countryside screwing around with strange women." Lionel went back inside, leaving Stefan to muse over his ale pot.

As he walked home Stefan thought of Edgar, his brother-in-law. Edgar being stationed in India meant that he was the least of his problems. For all that had happened over the last four days, Stefan was now in two minds. He wondered what his wife would say if he told her about his sexual encounter that morning.

Chapter 4
The Inquisition

Eugene was a highly adaptable horse used for country pursuits and heavy agricultural work, but on this particular day he was a carriage horse. He was an American breed and very rarely found on English soil, affordable only by the extremely rich. Paired with another strong animal they pulled the four-wheeled Brougham, with its coachman and one passenger, with utmost ease along the fresh leafy lanes towards Bibury.

Painted on each door of the carriage was the Cavner family crest of gryphons and crosslets, and seated inside was none other than Sir Charles Corbett-Cavner. Edward, his son, was the carriage driver.

They made their way down into the village and over the triple arched bridge spanning the Coln River. Their destination was Bibury Court to visit the patriarch of the Collison family, who was affectionately known as the Brigadier.

Sir Charles, a normally placid man, had come to ask him some very serious questions.

"Who the damn well is it? And why haven't they made a bloody appointment?" the old Brigadier shouted. He was sitting near to the window, and in the morning's light was trying to read a copy of The Times published three days previously. It had just arrived and he wanted to keep up with the news from the city.

The Brigadier's butler was dressed in classical attire and was not in the least bit flummoxed by the outcry.

"He says his name is Sir Charles Corbett-Cavner. He appears to be quite well to do, sir," Lionel replied with his hands clasped behind his back and his eyebrows raised almost indiscernibly.

"Charles Cavner? He owns the Brockhampton estate. What the hell does he want?" the Brigadier said, staggering to his feet. "I'll see him in the drawing room. Make sure the nurse is there, and I want you to stay by my side at all times."

Lionel handed him his carved wooden walking sticks and the old man made for the meeting place.

The drawing room was adorned with several splendid portrait paintings and ancient books and antiquities that only very few could afford. A delicate chandelier hung from the centre of the oak panelled room, which was lit by the intricate ornamental candles that the Brigadier had had especially sent over from France.

The Brigadier's demeanour changed upon accepting Sir Charles' hand and that of his son, Edward, although he never left the comfort of his armchair. They sat opposite each other.

"Sir Charles, how can I help you?" he asked quietly and politely.

Sir Charles Cavner, a rotund fellow in his mid-sixties, was straight to the point. "Who is Stefan Desailley? Apparently, he lives here in this village. Rather than go around asking the riff-raff I thought it better to come and ask you and get a more truthful answer."

Lionel turned and looked out of the window across the lawn towards the magnificent trees. Knowing the story he tried not to smile. The Brigadier's young nurse, recently recruited, also wanted to know of the handsome Stefan, having only heard about him.

"And what interest do you have in him?" the Brigadier asked, screwing up his eyes. His question was that of a man on the back foot.

With a worried expression Sir Charles glanced at both the Brigadier's butler and then his nurse. The Brigadier himself then eyed them both, wondering what was on Sir Charles' mind, but then suddenly realised. "Oh, don't worry, Sir Charles. Whatever is said in here will not go any further. Please, trust me."

Not totally assured Sir Charles carried on, and kept his eye on the butler, who seemed more than interested in what he had to say. "Is it true that this Desailley fellow is a writer? Or so he claims!"

The Brigadier puckered his lips and thought. "Yes. Yes, I believe he is an articulate writer, or so I am told. Quite an extraordinary talent, rumour has it, especially coming from a village so small. He is a rarity, I believe. Again, why do you ask?"

"What is it he is writing about?" Sir Charles asked abruptly. He was a little irate but neither man was giving anything away.

The Brigadier turned towards Lionel. "This is my butler. You may call him Lionel if you so wish. He is Mr Desailley's best friend, and as such he will probably be able to tell you."

Lionel hesitated, shrugged his shoulders and rubbed his chin. "Stefan is a keen stream and brook fisherman. In the spring and summer months he is after trout, and later in the year he will be chasing the Lady of the Stream; the beautiful silver grayling.

"For some reason, he has decided to write about the Coln River and the attractive villages that adorn its banks. He is a very emotional and romantic man at heart and there will probably be no better an author locally to write such a book. And it will be good for tourism too, I would imagine."

The Brigadier carefully watched Sir Charles' facial expressions as he glanced nervously over his shoulder towards his son, and again towards the butler and the nurse, indicating to the Brigadier that they should leave the room. The Brigadier ever so slightly nodded his head in the direction of the door and the three left courteously.

"Sir Charles, what is actually troubling you?" the Brigadier asked.

"This Stefan Desailley chap has caused some eruptions in my family and I want him taken off the streets. I now consistently receive angry letters from my brother in Shropshire, who claims that Georgina, his daughter-in-law, has a completely changed temperament since she returned there from our home in Brockhampton. He seems to think that my wife and I are to blame. All we know is that when Georgina was down here last she met this Stefan Desailley character and since returning home to Stokesay, she is apparently an entirely different woman."

"In what way has she become a different woman?" the Brigadier asked softly, trying to placate his visitor who seemed quite highly strung.

Sir Charles went very quiet. He stared down at the floor and then looked up, his face showed melancholy. "She had an argument with her husband, my nephew, and picked up the poker from by the fireplace and hit him around the side of the face with it. She broke his bloody jaw!"

"Did he deserve it?" the Brigadier asked, almost smiling and trying hard not to laugh.

"My eldest brother, Frederick, inherited the entire estate from our father. He is a very demanding man and knows something occurred when Georgina came here last. I need to clear this up or else he could quite easily oust my wife and me from the Brockhampton part of the inheritance. My brother and I have never seen eye to eye, and so it is important that I make sure that my wife and I do not end up in a lodge house next to a set of iron gates. I need to be seen to be doing something to calm him down. Eliminating this Stefan Desailley from any involvement within the family is now my priority. As it happens, Frederick is not a well man, and Fulwar, his only son and Georgina's husband, will inherit the whole estate from his father."

"What makes you think that this physical outburst has anything to do with this Desailley chap?" the Brigadier asked.

"Georgina caught him trout tickling on my land; a boy's pastime. Whatever happened she appeared to arrange a meeting with him and offered a guided tour around our two villages. She took Edward along too, but probably only as a distraction. Edward then left them together at the Cavner Arms in the afternoon, which is not a done thing for the women in our family. The next day she was up early and off on one of the horses and she did not return until after midday. Someone in the village had briefly seen them both together down near the hamlet of Syreford, and–"

The Brigadier stopped him. "What was she doing down here in Gloucestershire with you and without her husband? Do they have children? If so, why wasn't she with them?"

At this point Sir Charles faltered. He now didn't know whether to trust the man sitting in front of him.

"Sir Charles, please tell me what is exactly going on and I will try and put your mind at rest because I am equally as interested." The Brigadier called for his butler who was waiting outside the door.

"Yes, sir?"

"Lionel, please go and find Mr Desailley and bring him here."

Lionel exchanged glances between the Brigadier and then Sir Charles. "Yes, sir. I'll go straight away," he answered and left, smiling to himself.

Stefan had struggled with his conscience for three weeks. Every time he had sat down and tried to write anything about the Coln River and its first two villages at its source, his exploit with Georgina created turmoil in his mind. He knew he would have to make an effort and start writing the first chapter. Deep down he believed if he could finish it quickly his memories would cease to return to Brockhampton and Sevenhampton, and he would be able to continue with the manuscript about the villages further downstream. Charity knew that something or someone was troubling him, and had urged him to sit and write for fear of their subsidiary income drying up.

For the umpteenth time over the last days he began again a project that he had been toying with in his head over recent years. His writing had been affected badly and the waste paper basket had been emptied on several occasions. He kept telling himself to at least put the first few lines on paper and once started there would be no going back.

Sevenhampton and Brockhampton

I must first point out to the reader and/or hiker the geographical position of the source of the River Coln in relation to the first two villages closest to its head. Perhaps just half a mile north of Brockhampton and two hundred yards to the east of Winchcombe Lane lays a piece of marshy ground. Off the lane at Cotehay, behind a cottage, there is a footpath that leads you over to a tiny watercourse, which, if you follow it northward for perhaps two hundred yards, will bring you to Coln Head. Here the river begins its course south and gains its momentum from the beginnings of other infinitesimal springs supplying it from the surrounding Cotswold hillsides.

Brockhampton is ultimately the first village the Coln passes through and is the larger of two within the parish of Sevenhampton, (formerly known as Clopely), and the church of St. Andrew.

Originally in the area, approximately a mile to the north, there was Iron Age involvement and the remnants of which is now known as Roel Camp, possibly a hill fort village. The Celtic tribe known as the Dobunni were integrated under Roman rule and the village was evacuated. There is unrecorded archaeological evidence throughout the parish of such human life of that period.

The parish was first recorded in 1086 and has in the past been named as Senhampton or Sennington which used to lie a half mile to the west. By 1327, Brockhampton, now the larger of the two villages, was classed as being a different manor, with the Coln being its western boundary. There are several small hamlets and farmsteads dotted along the valley and upon the hillsides, many of which now cover old Roman sites.

In 1531, the River Coln was known as Senhampton Brook. The valley itself is formed of upper lias clay and midford sand.

Each dwelling has played its part over the centuries, inhabited by various families of many trades, businesses and serfs or farm labourers. Wool was the main trading product, as it still is today. Sheep are abundant, although a larger percentage of the surrounding land is now under tillage, with arable crops grown, such as such as turnips, wheat, oats and barley. Beef cattle are more commonly bred than in the past, and most of the villagers are employed on the numerous farms, such as cowmen, shepherds, ploughmen or general labourers.

In the Middle Ages the quarrying of stone was an important part of the economy and Brockhampton quarry supplied quality stone around the Gloucestershire area. In the early 1600s, quarry owners employed masons, named as members of the Denley family. Interestingly, some of their descendents are named on ancient gravestones in the churchyard at Sevenhampton, and some of their relatives in the villages are alive to this day.

Slate quarrying existed to the west of the villages towards Puckham Woods, and archaeological activity suggests that it thrived during Roman times. Slate diggers were recorded in the mid-1600s

Shoemakers, or cordwainers, practise their art of soft leather production to this day. A blacksmith is employed on the Brockhampton Park estate. A wheelwright/carpenter originally set up his business in Sheephouse barn, and his family name is still associated with their craft. Bread baking began on an economic scale in the late 1700s and still exists to this day. A brewery has now been built and supplies the Cavner Arms and several other local alehouses. Its chimney is a landmark in the valley.

Stefan's concentration was broken by a knock at the door. He ceased what he was doing and looked up. It was Charity.

"Lionel is here," she said sounded apologetic. "He wants to talk to you. He says it is important."

Stefan blotted his pen and paper dry and leaned back in his chair. "Send him in, sweetheart."

Lionel entered the room and closed the door behind him because he did not want Charity to hear.

"Sir Charles Cavner is here over at the house with the Brigadier. Sir Charles is angry because something has happened with that Georgina woman you fornicated with. His son Edward, who you apparently know, seems to think that she has broken her husband's jaw.

"Why are you telling me this, Lionel?" Stefan asked.

"The Brigadier asked me to come and get you. He wants an explanation. There is one other thing though." Lionel raised his eyebrows.

"What is that?"

"I don't think Sir Charles knows that you are the Brigadier's son-in-law."

The Brigadier struggled from his seat and made his way to his drinks cabinet. He brought two glasses and the remains of a bottle of Armagnac back to the table and poured generously.

"Before we locate Mr Desailley, let me tell you a rather insignificant story. Many years ago I owned a large house and small farmstead in the extreme south west of France. A French couple oversaw the property in my absence, but the wife was such an excellent cook and that I offered her a job here. They decided to emigrate and are still with me to this day. Naturally, she runs the kitchen here and Marcel, her husband, maintains the farm machinery." The Brigadier stopped and took a large gulp of brandy. "They have one son, who is my accountant and is in charge of everything on paper to do with this estate. I can assure you that he is very good at his job and is well rewarded. He was not one year old when he came here from France but soon showed that he was a very intelligent young boy. Years before my wife died we often spoke of his education, and one day I decided to finance him, and sent him to a boarding school. Between us all, we chose Wellington School in Somerset."

Sir Charles interrupted him. "Excuse me! What has he to do with all this?"

"Please, Sir Charles. Allow me to finish. The boy excelled at school, brilliant at both English and French. He turned out to be a well-rounded young man who cares a lot for other people. He often travels into Cheltenham, Gloucester or Cirencester to help with the poor people. He doesn't care much for class divide and is quite prepared to offer advice to anyone from all walks of life. Being highborn does not mean that one doesn't have any problems, be they mental or physical disabilities."

Sir Charles began to say something else but a knock at the door stopped him.

"Come in!" the Brigadier called.

Lionel opened the door. "I have Mr Desailley here, sir. Shall I show him in?" His usual courtesies were exaggerated.

The Brigadier nodded and Stefan entered the room.

"Before I introduce you both, please let me explain to you, Sir Charles, that this is Stefan Francois Desailley. He is the same young man I have been describing to you. Stefan, this is Sir Charles Corbett-Cavner. He owns Brockhampton Park and apparently has some kind of issue with you that I hope we can conclude in a gentlemanly manner." He smiled at them both and poured himself another Armagnac.

Sir Charles stood and both men shook hands and each dipped their heads with respect to each other. Sir Charles remained stone-faced whilst Stefan offered a small ironic smile.

Sir Charles detailed to Stefan what had happened between his nephew and Georgina, repeating only what Lionel had already told him, except that a fire poker had been used to inflict the damage.

"What have you done or said to her that has made her behave in such an outrageous manner?" Sir Charles asked.

Stefan glanced quickly towards the Brigadier, whose demeanour suggested that he was as equally interested to know. Stefan turned back to Sir Charles.

"Sir, I am not sure that you fully understand how much your niece loves you, your wife and Edward. She is periodically beaten up by her alcoholic husband and then sent down to you in Brockhampton to recuperate, out of sight from anyone who might know her, and into the arms of the only people she can trust. If that kind of behaviour by a husband happened in a city slum somebody would be arrested and probably imprisoned."

Sir Charles began to interrupt but Stefan cut him short. "Your nephew needs help and your brother is probably in a state of denial about his son's problems. Instead of brushing everything under the carpet trying to defend your family name, persuade your brother to help your nephew and between them gain some respect from the people on their estate. From what Georgina has told me I gather it is a case of 'like father, like son'. Georgina is a beautiful woman but I have seen her scars and listened to her traumatised mind. She is desperately in need of help and protection, which only you and your wife can provide her with. But remember, she desperately wants to remain the mother of her two children and doesn't wish to lose contact with them."

Sir Charles was bemused. "How did you see her scars?" he asked angrily.

"She has shown me recent and past injuries. Bruises which do not disappear overnight when you are in your third decade, a still disjointed collarbone, a forearm broken from being thrown to the floor, which has healed slightly bent. It is strange that there is no damage from her neck upwards for all the public to witness. I think here we are talking about a persistent wife beater! Good day, sir." Stefan made to leave.

"Those injuries are all from horse riding accidents." Sir Charles was making feeble excuses.

"Georgina is a fine horsewoman and your family have some of the best animals in Europe. Do not try and cover up the sins of your despicable nephew and his father in front of me. Had she been a poor horsewoman, with the injuries she has received, nobody would trust her on a child's rocking horse!" Stefan was furious, and walked to the door.

Sir Charles was equally infuriated. "You've had sexual contact with her, haven't you?"

Stefan turned back and looked at both men. "That last Saturday when she was here, we went up to Sennington barn, late morning I believe. We had full physical sex three times." It was a half-truth. "Ask her and see if you can believe her because you obviously don't believe how she receives her injuries, although you are more than happy to allow her to recover at Brockhampton." Stefan slammed the door on his way out.

The Brigadier again found it hard not to smile, and gulped his Armagnac. Sir Charles' glass remained untouched.

"Well, you've met the man you wished to see, and you have listened to his side of the story. What are you going to do now? Take his advice, Sir Charles?"

"Why do you employ somebody so insolent?" Sir Charles asked shaking his head.

"Do you believe that they really had sexual intercourse in that barn, which I can only assume belongs to you?" the Brigadier asked.

"Yes, I damn well do. I now have enough evidence to rid her from the family. The problem has been solved!" Sir Charles was livid but also disappointed. It was something he did not want to hear.

The Brigadier struggled to his feet and went to the window with his glass in hand. For a while he gazed across his expansive lawn.

"Whose side are you really on, Sir Charles?" he asked without turning around. "Your brother and his son, or your niece by marriage to that disgraceful nephew?

"What am I supposed to say? My brother has the upper hand with the entire estate," Sir Charles answered quietly and sadly as if he had given up all hope of staying at Brockhampton.

"If that is what you believe but if you think deep down that your brother is wrong then you must become more outspoken. This poor Georgina is being made a scapegoat. By using her and her apparent misdemeanours he has every excuse to evict you from your estate. Let me ask you an important question. When you were young would you admit to your father-in-law that you had had sex with another woman other than his daughter?"

The Brigadier turned and faced the troubled man sitting opposite his desk.

Sir Charles was completely taken aback. "God no! Should it have ever happened, I wouldn't dream of telling anyone."

The Brigadier smiled. "Well, my son-in-law has just told me that he has had sex with your niece on several occasions one morning in a barn on your estate. Now who do you believe or trust?"

Sir Charles sat with his mouth agape. "He is your son-in-law?" he eventually asked, shocked.

"Yes, Sir Charles, and a very fine one at that. He is married to my youngest daughter, Charity." He sat back down and watched as Sir Charles pondered over what to do or say next.

"Is Edward your only son? He seems a pleasant chap. Not married though, I presume?" the Brigadier asked inquisitively.

"He is my only son and there is an elder daughter who lives in America," he told him.

"What do they think of it all?" the Brigadier asked.

He mellowed and conceded. "They are both firmly on Georgina's side. You have to realise that my brother is not a well thought of man and my wife and I are more than aware of what he is like; a tyrant on his own estate. Nobody wants to work for him but the poorer people have no choice. Unfortunately, his son is turning out to be much the same. That is our problem. Our father died a year ago, and my brother will inherit the whole of the Cavner estate when the deeds are finally concluded. Now I believe he wants to try and install his son, Fulwar, down here at

Brockhampton. That would be a disaster for both villages, Brockhampton and Sevenhampton." Sir Charles was visibly irritated.

"By the sound of it, Sir Charles, I don't think you can blame Stefan or Georgina for what is going on. There is little you can do but wait for the final outcome of your father's will." The Brigadier tried to reassure him but knew Sir Charles would leave Bibury an anxious man.

Sir Charles made as if to stand with the intention of returning to Brockhampton but then stopped. "I have just remembered another reason why I came here. The letter I received from Frederick suggests that they might send Georgina to us long-term. He implied in the letter that unless her attitude changes in favour of his son, this is what they will do. He also asked how I felt about it, but so far I haven't replied. Thank you for your time, sir. I will see myself out." He stood up, gulped down his Armagnac and weakly shook the Brigadier's hand before turning away and abruptly leaving.

The Brigadier watched from the window as Sir Charles' Brougham drew away. He then hobbled to the entrance hall, where both Lionel and Stefan were talking. He looked Stefan straight in the eyes. "Did you really make love to that woman three times that Saturday afternoon?"

Stefan hesitated. "No, sir."

"I'm glad to hear it!"

"It was only once. And it was in the morning."

All three men went back to the drawing room to discuss the repercussions of the morning's events. Stefan didn't stay long. He knew Georgina's story and he had things to do.

"Does Charity know what has happened?" the Brigadier asked his trusted butler.

"Probably. It was her decision to let Stefan loose as long as he didn't leave her. He has stayed by her through thick and thin." Lionel waited for the Brigadier to add something.

"It's a pity. I'm glad that we don't have to go through childbirth, especially when it is such a difficult one." He mused over his daughter's problems and then asked if the nurse was still about.

"Yes, sir. Do you want me to go and fetch her?"

The Brigadier indicated to the cupboard and Lionel retrieved another bottle of Armagnac.

"I'm going to have another couple of drinks first, now that I've started this early in the morning, and then I'll retire back to bed. Make sure she's around, and you can take the rest of the day off. But go and find Stefan and find out what he's really thinking; he is worrying me, and we cannot afford to lose him."

Lionel corked the bottle and left it with the ailing old man.

Lionel went to the Gatehouse to find Stefan. Charity hadn't seen him but he stayed for a short while out of respect, and asked how they were faring. She divulged little. Afterwards he strode up the hill to the Catherine Wheel, which was his father's alehouse.

"Dad, have you seen Stefan?" he asked, concerned.

"He came in a little while ago, bought a beer and sat in the corner. He didn't stay long. Curious though, I gave him a letter that was addressed to him but was delivered here. He read it, drank his beer and then left. Something is on his mind." Lionel's father said no more and turned to serve someone.

Lionel could only think that he had gone to the Swan Hotel. He trundled back down the hill and across the Coln, finding his friend sitting alone near to the window. He had the letter in his hand and appeared to be contemplating its contents.

"Tell me what's wrong," Lionel said, placing two beers on the table.

Stefan dragged one of the beers towards him and pushed the letter towards his friend, who read it and then scrutinised the address on the envelope.

"Why did she send this to the Catherine Wheel?"

"It is the address I gave her; any letters were always going to be safe in your father's hands. I thought it better Charity doesn't know too much?" Stefan said, and waited to hear what Lionel had to say.

Lionel read the letter again before sliding it back across the table to Stefan. "She definitely wants to get her claws into you. Are you going to meet her?"

Stefan gazed out of the window. In the street an old man whom he knew limped by. For all the years he had known the old fellow he could not remember him having a wife. A life without a woman did not bear thinking about.

He looked back at Lionel. "I love Charity deeply. She is so pretty and a good mother, cook and housewife."

He stared back out of the window as a lady with a young child walked over the bridge. "Lionel, you obviously know that I haven't been able to touch Charity since she gave birth to little Francois, and he is now over three years old. I have stayed with her in the hope that one day she will change and become the full woman she once was. She has told me to go and find sexual gratification where I can, as long as I do not leave her."

Stefan nodded towards the letter on the table in front of him. "Georgina and I met quite by accident. Turn the clock back or forth two or three hours and she and I would never have met. For me this would have only been a dream, but it really happened, and now that letter has arrived it has confirmed that it is still happening."

"So, she's coming down from the Midlands and staying the night in Fairford at the Bull Hotel before going onto Brockhampton. She's going out of her way, isn't she? There must be a far shorter route."

"It has something to do with those newfangled trains. Cirencester is currently the end of the line. She will then take a horse and carriage the remainder of the way to Fairford."

"Are you going to pay her a visit?" Lionel sat back and raised his eyebrows, knowing that his friend was considering another liaison with the beautiful, aristocratic Georgina Corbett-Cavner.

"There is something I have to tell you that the Brigadier asked me to broach," he said, watching the expression change on Stefan's face. "Edgar has resigned his commission in the army and will be back home by the autumn, but possibly even sooner. If he finds out that you are having an affair behind Charity's back, what do you think the repercussions will be? He hates your guts enough as it is."

Stefan had no answer, and Lionel could only stare down at the remains in the bottom of his pewter mug. Stefan had enough on his mind as it was but now Edgar, his detested brother-in-law, was coming home.

"Did he mention whether Charity's two other sisters know that their brother is coming home?" he asked.

"The Brigadier didn't elaborate any further but when Edgar does arrive home I suggest you watch your back." Lionel drank the residue of his beer and went for some refills.

Chapter 5
The Bull Hotel

"You are just using me, Stefan. If the Brigadier finds out what you are up to he will not be amused." Lionel had been reluctant to accompany Stefan but solidarity had prevailed.

Stefan held the reins of the buggy. "It's market day in Fairford, so just enjoy it. Buy something or other for the kitchen or flowers for the windowsills, and have a beer. You might meet the woman I keep telling you about. Relax, Georgina might not be there anyway." He eagerly shooed the horse onwards.

They tied up their buggy near to the Walnut Field and walked along through the Croft to the Market Place, which was teeming with people bartering for the best prices from the wily stallholders.

The pair wandered around, mingling with the hordes of people, many of whom were poor and buying gizzards and intestines from the cheap butchers to make their humble pies. Others had been sent by their middle-class employers to secure some of the best cuts of meat for the family dinner. Filthy children from hopeless families tugged on coat tails of moneyed people in the hope of a farthing, but few were obliged. A juggler performed his act, much to the amusement of many, and several passers-by tossed coins into his upturned top hat.

Stefan was not interested in the clamour of market day; he was on the look out for Georgina. Lionel followed him, inspecting the stalls with the knowledge that they had to take something back to Bibury to prove where they had been that day.

They sidled slowly up to the top end of the street near to the church, where elderly men and their sons bartered for cattle, pigs and sheep. A little further on horses were for sale, mostly by the gypsies, who naturally followed the markets.

Suddenly, a pretty, well-dressed woman pulled Lionel's sleeve and asked him if he wanted sex for a sixpence.

Lionel pulled his sleeve away and stood back. "Certainly not! Go away!" He was embarrassed to have been asked.

Being a woman of no great height she tugged on his arm and moved close up to him.

"The lady your friend is seeking is taking tea in the Bull Hotel," she said quietly.

Stefan was already eyeing the young woman up and down from the other end of a cake stall. "She says Georgina's in the Bull," Lionel said to his friend, shrugging his shoulders.

Stefan immediately headed off into the crowd, and as Lionel went to follow the determined young woman held him back. "I'm sure they will be all right on their own for now," she smiled. "Come on, let's wander around. You don't need to be afraid," she said, provocatively, and tucked her arm inside Lionel's and ushered him back down towards the lower Market Place.

"How long have you known Stefan?" she asked as they walked. "You two seem to be very good friends."

"Before you start asking questions, who are you?" he asked.

"Mary Buchanan. I am Georgina's cousin. She asked me to be her escort for a week. As I have never been this way before, I thought it a good idea to take the chance and come with her." She smiled up at Lionel's suspicious face.

"Are you really a lady of the night?" Lionel asked. He believed she was dressed more so in keeping with an aristocratic family to whom she probably belonged.

"No, but I needed to attract your attention – and it worked, didn't it?" She smiled at him again with her full red lips and white teeth shining.

As they came to know each other a little better, they wandered around the market stalls and then decided to stroll over to the river towards the oxen pens, and they chatted amiably, mostly about themselves than anything else.

Appearing resplendent in her blue patterned dress, and with her hair held up at the back with a ribbon of the same colour, Georgina was sitting in a corner of the tearoom beside a window. She was reading a copy of the Daily Telegraph and sipping chinese green tea.

When her concentration was broken she looked up. Stefan stood before her appearing every bit the man she had so desperately hoped to see again.

"Please, sit down" she invited him with a warm smile. "How good it is to see you again. I didn't expect that you would bother to come, thinking that perhaps your conscience would get the better of you."

"Why shouldn't I? I received your correspondence and felt it was an opportunity too good to ignore." Stefan slid a chair out from beneath the table and sat down opposite Georgina.

"You're a married man with three children, and you're the son-in-law of the owner of the Bibury Court estate. You must be on dangerous ground here in Fairford. A little too close to home, perhaps? Might it be that you are being watched?" Georgina kept her eyes on his, never faltering.

Stefan glanced around the room. "Not in here this morning. I don't recognise anybody. How long have you come down for?" he asked quietly, desperate to know.

"Just a week. It is good to be here with no bruises for once." She could feel his desire for her but there were questions she wanted to ask. "Stefan, I don't want to be the one to drive a wedge between you and your wife because I am told that she is a lovely woman. Maybe it is best we don't take our association any further. What do you think? Perhaps it will be the best idea for both of us?"

"Someone has been doing their homework. Do I take it that you have been receiving information from Sir Charles?" Stefan asked.

"Aunt Maria, actually. They both already know quite a lot about you now." Georgina seemed a little sad. Deep down she yearned to hold the man seated before for her and never let him go but she didn't want to ruin someone's marriage because of her own personal whims.

"What happened with you and your husband? I understand his jaw was broken," Stefan said, looking at her sympathetically and hoping to hear her side of the story.

Georgina was quick to the point. "I bought him a bottle of whisky. Quite naturally, he drank most of it and, as usual, his temper flared. This time I stood up for myself and hit him with a fire poker. I am not at all in favour now at Stokesay or Cavner Arms." She turned and stared out across the busy market square, wondering what was ever to become of her.

"Has it changed him? Is he a better man now?" Stefan was interested as to how her marriage was holding up under the circumstances. More to the point, he wanted to know whether Georgina's attraction for him had dwindled or risen.

Georgina held her hand over her mouth. She was close to tears. "I cannot honestly say. We have hardly spoken since it happened, and his injury has obviously not helped. The atmosphere has changed completely. People who were on my side are now afraid to speak to me for fear of reprisals, and I am now a victim of my own actions."

"What about the children? What are they thinking? Do they say anything to you?" Stefan's thoughts were those of consternation.

"After what I did to my husband they are now kept well out of my way and I rarely see them. A nanny attends to them." She gently blew her nose on a white-laced handkerchief.

Stefan tried to touch her hand but she recoiled. "We cannot stay here. I am going upstairs." She looked at the clock on the wall. "Someone is picking Mary, my cousin, and me up at three o'clock. Please come back in thirty minutes. I'll be in room Thirteen." Georgina stood and left, drawing little attention to herself.

Stefan ambled around to the nearby White Hart Inn, and time could not go any slower for him. Each minute was an eternity as he sat staring out of the window with his hand curled around a beer. When Lionel sauntered past with Georgina's escort and entered the Bull Hotel by the back door, he almost decided to join them, but then thought better of it. Both of them seemed to be enjoying each other's company, and were laughing and joking. Whoever she was, she clung tightly to his friend's arm.

Stefan passed unnoticed into the residents' quarters at the turn of the porter's back. Room thirteen was at the very top of the stairs. He tapped on the misshapen elm door and was enticed through by Georgina's quiet, sultry voice.

She was lying face down on the four-poster bed with her legs slightly apart, and a white cotton sheet lay across her lower half. A large wall mirror, discreetly positioned, reflected her torso from another angle, which made the beautiful temptress even more alluring. The tiny window offered little light and one gas lamp lit up her soft, pale skin. A faint fragrance of perfume hung in the warm, airless room, which further stirred Stefan's passion.

Georgina turned slightly and exposed a breast as he closed the door, and she stretched out an inviting hand.

Stefan approached the bed and kissed her tenderly on her neck and cheek and ran his hand gently down her back and between her buttocks.

Georgina took a long, quivering breath and turned over onto her back. She undid his shirt as he explored her body and ran his tongue around her soft nipples, which began to respond to his attention, and he caressed the blond hair surrounding her genitalia.

Stefan rose above her and stripped off his clothes, exposing his bulbous erection, and with no misgivings Georgina slowly performed oral sex on her illicit lover, who in her imagination had the body of a young Greek god.

Stefan turned his attention to the aphrodisiac secretions exuding from her vagina and manoeuvred himself so that he could lay his head between her widely spread legs.

For some time they lay exploring each other's genitals until she could take no more and suddenly exploded into a sexual climax, which took Stefan by surprise. An indescribable tingling sensation erupted over her whole body and she arched her back violently, squirming with carnal pleasure and bursts of ecstasy. She tried to push him away but he continued to stimulate her tiny organ with his tongue whilst exploring within her with his index and middle fingers until her whole body culminated again with sexual excitement, and she had a second, longer orgasm that lingered for some time.

Eventually, Stefan rolled away and Georgina climbed over him, straddling his thighs whilst masturbating his firm penis and simultaneously titillating his testicles. He played with her fully erect nipples as her beautiful breasts were suspended before him

She was incredibly alluring, especially with her golden hair flowing over her shoulders and face, and soon he was close to having his own ultimate orgasm. He pulled her delicate hands away and coaxed her closer. He gently rubbed her pubic hair and held his penis upright, tempting her to allow full penetration into her moist, demanding opening. She duly obliged him by engulfing him within her, and was forced to suck in deep breaths as Stefan's sexual organ invaded almost the last vestige of her physical privacy.

The two were now one and they bodily drove each other towards a final climax. Georgina cried out with satisfaction as Stefan struggled to hold back his convulsive orgasm and ejaculation. He drew her down on top of himself, and with a final flourish of rhythmic contractions climaxed with Georgina; the definitive sexual achievement for two lovers

Now inactive but still in the same position, Georgina felt the blood ebbing from Stefan's penis. As he gently massaged her back she ran her hands through the hairs on his head and chest and kissed him gently and meaningfully, conceding to her love for Stefan. Eventually she moved over and lay down close to him, still caressing his powerful torso.

With eyes closed and with sleep near, she remembered a visit to an art museum in Paris when she was a young girl. The painting that had preyed on her mind ever since was that of Eros flying away with the woman he loved, both seemingly very content. She remembered her father explaining to her the ancient Greek myth, and naming the painting as *The Abduction of Psyche*. Georgina compared Stefan with Eros, whose love was spiritual as well as physical, and who had founded the love of beauty, healing and freedom. Stefan, by accidental design, was a beautiful lover who had come to reconcile her tortured mind and offer her liberty from a disastrous marriage.

She opened her eyes and scolded herself for being so selfish.

"Are you happy, Stefan?" she suddenly asked after minutes of silence.

"Do you think that anyone making love to a beautiful woman like yourself would not be happy?" he replied quietly.

"It doesn't work like that though, does it? My husband is not happy, even less so now than he once was. He obviously doesn't see me like you do, and I don't think other people see me that way either. Anyway, that wasn't what I meant. If you are content with your home life why do you need me?" Something was wrong in Stefan's marriage and Georgina wanted to know because she felt that she wasn't helping.

He turned his head towards her and stretched to kiss her. "It's a sad story, and one that you don't need to know."

"If it is a sad story then you must only be unhappy. Please tell me what is troubling you, Stefan. Please." She tugged at his arm.

Stefan studied the cracks in the ceiling and remained quiet for some time. His thoughts about his marriage were deep and he was well aware that Georgina wasn't the cure. She affected him profoundly sexually but Charity also affected him, but much more in a marital way. He decided to tell Georgina where his anxieties stemmed from.

"I knew Charity when we were growing up on the estate as children. She was always a pretty, jovial girl. My mother and father are French and worked for Charity's father. They still do, in fact. They once maintained the Brigadier's smallholding in southern France, especially in his absence. When he inherited the Bibury Court estate he sold the property in France, and my parents, gracious for the opportunity, moved here to continue to work for the Brigadier. I was not even a year old at the time."

"The Brigadier has a son, Edgar, who is quite a lot older than me, and when the Brigadier paid for my education, Edgar was furious. He hated me in the first place, because of jealousy I think. I always seemed to get along with his three sisters though, which annoyed him all the more. Charity, being the youngest, is five years younger than me, and when I finished my education at boarding school and returned home, Edgar had joined the army, apparently against his own wishes."

"Is their mother still alive?" Georgina asked sympathetically.

"No, she died when Charity was about nine or ten years old."

"Is it Edgar who worries you?" she asked.

"Please, let me continue, Georgina," he said gently. "Edgar didn't want us to marry and made it plain to his father, citing it would be a disaster for the family. The Brigadier, which is what we all call my wife's father affectionately, apparently asked his son why he didn't want us to marry, but Edgar refused to answer. When we did marry, Edgar never attended our wedding."

Georgina asked him again why he needed her when he had Charity.

"We have three children. The last one born was Francois, but we call him little Frankie. He was an extremely difficult birth and Charity suffered badly over many hours but eventually he was delivered by a very patient midwife under the supervision of an eminent physician rushed down from a Cheltenham hospital." He turned towards Georgina. "Money is not an obstacle to the Brigadier." He paused in thought for a moment before continuing. "Whatever happened that day changed our lives. Charity's attitude altered. At first, she rejected Frankie but we persuaded her to become the good mother we all knew she was. She still is. Ever since though, for some reason, she hasn't let me touch her. Frankie is three years old now and I haven't been able to have any sexual contact with her since his birth. Please believe me, Georgina, when you came along you were a godsend to me. In different ways our problems are almost equal. I don't want to use you, Georgina, but after three years of a sexual sabbatical and frustration you are a dream come true."

"And what if Charity finds out?" she asked him.

"We have both had this discussion on several occasions. She has agreed that I can have liaisons with other women as long as she doesn't know who they are and never meets them. She will be content as long as I leave her alone physically but stay with her in our marital home, 'for better or for worse and till death us do part'."

He watched Georgina's face. "The same as you, I suppose."

Georgina thought about what he said. "But what does her father think? Does he know?"

"He knows that there is something wrong with Charity but he doesn't know exactly what, but then nor does anyone else. As long as I stay with her he seems perfectly at ease as to what I do. He knows that you and I made love in the barn near Sennington."

Georgina sat bolt upright, holding the sheet across her breasts. "What! You told him? Uncle Charles will find out!"

Stefan eased her back down beside him. "I believe that your uncle already knows." He didn't explain as to how her uncle found out.

She remained quiet for some time as she pored over her sexual exploitations in her mind. "Do her sisters know about Charity's problems?"

"Yes, but they never elaborate as to what might be the cause. They both put it down to a difficult childbirth and are very protective towards her. They are still very devoted towards me, and we all have a good relationship."

Stefan relaxed but the odour of Georgina's body began to arouse him again and she didn't resist his advances. Laying side by side their lips met and their free hands caressed each other's bodies.

Stefan gently pushed Georgina onto her back and stroked the inside of her thighs. He ran his tongue around her nipples and slowly she spread her legs and closed her eyes. His hand slid down to her vagina and with his gentle fingers rubbing its fleshy opening he began to stimulate the woman he was falling in love with. Georgina simultaneously masturbated the man she had fallen in love with. She dreamed of spending the rest of her life with her beautiful lover, never imagining that age would one day bring them down to earth.

Her breathing deepened as Stefan concentrated on her clitoris, occasionally penetrating her damp vagina with his finger and allowing it to loiter. He pulled her hand away from his bulbous penis so as not to spoil their lovemaking and sucked one of her hardened nipples.

Suddenly, she burst into another orgasm and breathed heavily with her head thrust back into the pillow, her mind drowning in a sea of euphoria.

Georgina rolled back onto her side and raised a leg over his thigh pulling his penis towards her and inviting its penetration. Stefan found the temptation unavoidable once again and any thoughts of both of their marriages drifted out through the window.

Afterwards, they again lay together talking and Georgina broached the subject of how they first met. "How is your book coming along? Have you written much yet?"

"I started writing it but my concentration is poor. One day my pen was flowing but then I was summoned to the Brigadier because your uncle had turned up. We had a stormy but brief confrontation. The Brigadier made him see where his problem lay, although that day it stemmed from you and me in the barn. It gave me the impression that something else was bothering Sir Charles. Exactly what, I do not know. Anyway, the answer to your question about my writing is that it is not proceeding very well at the moment, but I will shortly begin again in earnest, if only I can keep you out of my mind."

There came a delicate knock at the door. Surprised to be disturbed, the couple remained silent, but the knock came again.

"Who is it?" Georgina called out.

"It's me, Mary. Edward is already here and says he needs to return home straight away. He's pacing up and down in the foyer." She waited for a reply but there was none.

"Georgina! Speak to me. Edward is here. He doesn't look very patient," she added a little louder.

"Answer her, you have to go. I'll find another way out." Stefan kissed her whole-heartedly on her lips and climbed out of the bed to dress.

Georgina went to the door and cracked it open. "Give me half an hour. Whatever you do, don't let him up here to help with the luggage."

Mary felt trapped as well. "But I have the same problem with Lionel, Stefan's friend."

Stefan saw the comical side of the situation, and thought of Lionel cavorting with Georgina's companion. But he had to be decisive. "Listen, just throw your things together and leave. Sort them out when you reach Brockhampton. Tell him you didn't have time to do your hair. Go on. Just go!"

He watched as Georgina dressed herself, and hated to see her hide her body away, a body he might not see or touch for some time, if ever again. Stefan helped her with her luggage onto the landing, where the porter now stood, and she handed him a good reward to say nothing about her lover, and he acknowledged that he would duly oblige.

Both women were soon on their way and Edward was apparently none the wiser.

As they drank their ale in the Plough Inn, Lionel asked Stefan if he had had a good time in Fairford so far.

"Probably as good a time as you had by the sound of it." Stefan said, smiling at his friend.

Shortly before reaching Bibury Georgina tapped at the front window of the Brougham to gain Edward's attention. He pulled up, turned and asked what she wanted. "Can we stop and browse around the shops and village?"

"My father wants us back as soon as possible," he told her.

"Half an hour will not make any difference," she replied, hoping Edward's normally pleasant nature would give way.

He turned back and with a thrash of the reins urged the horses on. Soon they were parked beside the river in Bibury, and Edward helped his two well-dressed passengers from the carriage. "He's not here, you know," he said to Georgina sardonically.

Georgina glowered at him. "I didn't imagine he would be but how do you know?"

"I saw a buggy tied up in Fairford, and forgive me if I am mistaken, but Stefan's grey mare was leading it. Georgina, if you want my father and mother on your side, then please do not use them to your advantage. They have a lot of time for you but just remember that you are not a blood relation to my father. I'll give you half an hour and no more!" Edward was resolute.

Both women set off around the village, peered through the black iron gates of Bibury Court, admired the quaint cottages of Arlington Row, and walked up and down either side of the river before returning to the impatient Edward.

As they were about to board the Brougham a woman with a young boy at her side called out. "Ma'am! Ma'am! I think this is yours."

Georgina turned back to see a well-dressed woman approaching them.

"Frankie saw you drop your handkerchief," she smiled.

Georgina accepted the silk handkerchief with the initials *G.B.C.C.* embroidered in the corner. "Thank you very much," she said, bending down and shaking the little boy's hand. "Well done, young man. You were very observant." She nodded in appreciation to the boy's mother, and they went on their separate ways.

Chapter 6
Uncle Charles and Aunt Maria

"So, what are you going to say to Georgina when she arrives here, Charles?" Maria was naturally anxious about their niece's welfare.

With hands clasped behind his back Sir Charles mused over the question his wife had put forward as he stared out of the window across to Whitehill and its woodlands.

"The first thing is to find out from her how Frederick's illness is; Georgina must see him every day. His health is pivotal in all of this." Nervously he scratched his head and turned towards his wife. "We need him to live at least another year so we'll have more time to resolve our situation. It's ironic that he may not live to see the will concluded, but we still may be better off with him ailing but alive than with Fulwar."

"Are you going to be angry with her?" Maria asked with trepidation.

"I don't think so," he replied, recalling the Brigadier's words. "It's hardly any fault of hers. In fact, she's as much a scapegoat as we are."

"Why did she stay in Fairford last night and not come straight here?"

Sir Charles studied his wife's face and was unsure whether he should tell her what was on his mind, or indeed what he thought he knew. After some consideration he decided to be up front. "I believe that she is having an affair with that chap she met somewhere here in Brockhampton, the one I told you about who lives in Bibury. He is a writer and an intelligent man. I think she may have become infatuated with him. I met him briefly at the Brigadier's place, and Edward also knows him because she asked him to be her escort when they met here whilst he was doing some research for a book that he is apparently writing." He looked meekly at Maria. "I'm afraid it is rather more complicated than meets the eye. He is married to the Brigadier's youngest daughter and I had the impression that the Brigadier doesn't particularly mind how he behaves."

Maria looked worried but remained positive. She actually knew more than she let on. "Charles, we have to keep her on our side. Georgina is our only insight into what is going on in the minds of your loathsome brother and his equally contemptible son. Just remember that Georgina is a member of my family, the Buchanans."

"That is providing she doesn't come to stay here permanently," Charles said with a resigned expression on his face. He thought that if she has fallen in love with the so-called writer her permanent residence at Brockhampton Park would almost be inevitable.

"Do you think that it is a physical affair?"

"Possibly, but oddly enough he doesn't seem to worry that his father-in-law knows."

"What do you mean?" Maria asked, perplexed.

"It was just something he said before storming out. He may have said it sarcastically, but maybe not. I do think that perhaps he was exaggerating."

Unbeknown to Sir Charles, his wife had been kept very much informed by their son.

The sound of the gravel crunching in front of the house drew Maria out of her chair and to the window. "She's here," she called excitedly. "Oh, and Mary is with her! We could be having some fun this week."

Chapter 7
Faith, Hope and Charity

A woman sat at an ornate white-enamelled cast iron table that was placed conveniently in the centre of a large immaculately tended lawn. Although alone she was expecting a visitor and kept far enough away from the main house where they would be out of earshot from her staff.

The birds in the surrounding trees were frenetic as the early summer sun burst through the slowly moving cotton wool clouds. She sat patiently reading, awaiting the arrival of her elder sister.

The butler ushered a splendidly dressed lady through the house and onto the veranda. He pointed in the direction of his mistress and told her he would presently bring them both tea and cakes.

The two women greeted each other and kissed with all the mannerisms of the southern French. They hadn't seen each other for some time, and Faith Havrincourt had travelled from London, the centre of empire, to see her sister. Faith was the eldest of the Brigadier's three daughters and was a wily but fun loving woman. She was slightly overweight and quite plain in her looks but was forever good company, especially amongst her husband's social circles in London. Hope, on the other hand, was quite the opposite. The second eldest daughter was tall, slim and graceful, but always appeared firm and quietly in control.

"Faith, my darling. How are you?" Hope asked.

"I am fine, although a little tired after the journey." She smiled, so pleased to see her sister after such a length of time.

After the usual exchanges and personal enquiries they sat to discuss the reason of Faith's visit; the troubling subject of their brother, Edgar.

Hope stared into her sister's eyes and her expression was one of despair. "God only knows what will happen when Edgar comes home. I don't look forward to him being here at all, let alone what may be passing through poor Charity's mind."

"I came straight here to Chedworth because I thought it better I spoke to you first before going on to see Charity in Bibury. How is she?" Both women had much consideration for their younger sister.

"Just of late she has become very withdrawn. I think she suffers more whilst alone but when she has company she concentrates better. We hate Edgar, but Charity, poor soul, despises him even more than we do. If only Mother was still alive. Things might be so much better."

The butler and maid crossed the lawn to deliver the ladies' tea. Before leaving, the butler asked if anything else was required but the ladies politely declined his offer, and waited for the pair to return to the house before continuing.

"What does Stefan think of all this?" Faith asked.

"He has been so patient since Frankie was born, and Charity has refused any physical contact with him since the birth. They sleep in the same bed together but that is as far as it goes." Hope felt sorry for her brother-in-law.

"Poor Stefan. He is such a handsome and intelligent man. Neither of them deserves this."

"I wonder how he feels about Edgar's imminent return," Faith wondered aloud."

"There is an unexpected turn of events to all this, Faith, which Charity seems to be more than content to allow to carry on. I must tell you something, Faith. If I don't tell you, you would find out sooner or later," Hope said, not knowing if she was going to shock or disgust her sister "Stefan has been having an affair with a woman from the Brockhampton estate. It is apparently an on-off relationship."

Faith remained passive and sat thinking about the information she had just heard.

"Who is the woman?" she asked her sister after a few moments musing over any possible outcomes to the affair, "someone who works on the estate?"

"No, far from it. She is married into the Cavner family. She is aristocracy, Faith. Her husband is the heir to a vast family fortune."

Hope went on and explained the story as much as she knew. She had initially heard it from rumour but then directly from Charity, although Charity had no clue who Stefan's mistress was. She spoke to her sister of the woman's awful husband and the beatings he bestows upon her. She told Faith that as long as Charity never met the woman, and Stefan remained in the family home, Charity would allow him to take his sexual gratification wherever he could. Their children, Charity had told Stefan, needed their father.

Faith stood up and walked away. She studied the passing clouds in thought. Three buzzards circled high in the sky above her, mewing for each other's attention. She stopped, turned back to her sister and retook her seat. She said little at first but then cocked her head to one side, resigned to the fact that something had to be said or, more importantly, done about the impending situation.

"Actually, Hope, I did know something was going on and you have just confirmed the situation. Charity sent me a letter some time ago that suggested there was another woman involved. From what you have told me at least now I can find out who she really is.

"I'll be staying at Father's tonight but I have to be back in London by the end of the week. I'll have a long talk with him and find out if he knows anything. Edgar is an issue but I will have to broach that subject very carefully. As you well know, it would be impossible for Edgar to run the estate without Stefan, but Edgar hates him. I will, of course, speak to Charity and Stefan, together and then on their own." Faith paused again and seemed to study the tealeaves in her cup before looking up. "Isn't it strange how two families attached to two estates have become involved at the same time because of an illicit affair? And both estates have unwanted heirs."

"What can we do about it though? Edgar will inevitably gain possession here when Father dies. We will just have to do as he says." Hope did not sound optimistic.

"I'll think of something. Being a lawyer, Gerard, my dear husband has access to some of the best legal minds in London. We will work something out. Believe me." Faith suddenly felt more confident that the Bibury estate would fall into secure hands.

After walking around the garden and discussing all matters that concerned the family the two sisters bade each other farewell and Faith, the stalwart, began making her way to see their younger sister, Charity, and subsequently their father, the 'Brigadier'.

Faith reached the Gatehouse at Bibury Court and decided that it would be impolite not to stop off, albeit briefly, and chat with Charity and Stefan.

Charity answered the door. Stefan was not at home, and upon seeing Faith Charity immediately immersed herself in tears. She could hardly utter a word as Faith held her distraught young sister tightly before ushering her back into the house before even attempting to calm her down.

Little Frankie was curious, and watched the scene unfold from behind a long drape curtain as his mother slowly regained her senses. He had no idea who the other woman was, but the pair spoke for quite some time, and all Frankie could hear was the word *Edgar* repeated time after time.

He eventually approached his mother and pulled at her skirt, and Faith exchanged some words of encouragement and admiration with him before deciding it would be better to leave.

She left Charity in tears but her resolve told her that it was better to be forceful now rather than to regret any inaction later.

Dinner that evening was scheduled for eight o'clock. Having bathed and dressed with the assistance of her chaperone, Faith descended the stairs to meet her father. Stefan was waiting at the bottom of the stairs, and they briefly took to a side room and chatted until Lionel alerted them to the presence of the Brigadier.

In the dining room father and daughter warmly met for the first time in two years, although both regularly corresponded.

Over dinner they discussed the business of the estate, the tally of the winter shooting season and Faith's social life in London amongst the educated elite. Edgar was not mentioned once during the meal. Afterwards, they retired to the drawing room, where the Brigadier felt most comfortable, and Armagnac was served. The conversation soon became mellow and Stefan decided it best to leave for the sake of Charity and their children. He courteously bowed out, leaving his father-in-law and sister-in-law alone.

Faith stared at the portrait painting of her mother on the wall and wondered what she was thinking. She appeared to be smiling lovingly at Faith's father but her eyes suggested that Faith should be careful what her father would say to her. One of her mother's eyebrows suddenly seemed to be very slightly cocked. It was surreal, and Faith questioned the amount of alcohol she had consumed. Was her mother's spirit living on?

Suddenly, Faith snapped out of her dream. "What will happen when Edgar returns to Bibury, Father?" It was a burning question for her, but was one that had to be asked and, better still, answered.

The Brigadier knew an interrogation would soon come. He appeared sullen. "I know you three girls have never seen eye to eye with Edgar but bear in mind your age difference."

Faith looked away. Her father, she believed, did not understand, and she wondered how much was actually folded away in his ageing mind. She faced him again. "That was not my question, Father. What is he going to do when he arrives back here? Help the labourers?" she asked sarcastically. Her brother had never laid a finger to anything work related in his life, and was very good at upsetting anyone who stood below him in status.

"Faith, my dear, he has been twenty plus years as an officer in the army. He will be a different man when he finally comes home." The Brigadier wasn't entirely convinced himself. His son had still only achieved the rank of captain after many years in service. Personal finance had kept Edgar in his comfortable position in India for most of those years but his father had also supported him financially.

"Can't you find him a position somewhere else in the empire where he can languish lazily in a job which might suit him?" she asked hopefully.

The Brigadier sat thinking, gazing into his glass of Armagnac. He suddenly looked up at his daughter. "There is something you don't know, Faith, which I am duty bound to tell you. You won't be happy about this, but last year Edgar decided to marry a woman from a well thought of family within the empire. Her previous husband died of a mysterious disease." He sat wondering what his daughter's reaction would be to the awkward revelation.

At first Faith said nothing but continued to study her mother's picture on the wall. In Faith's mind past events began to add up. "Carry on, Father. Tell me what else there is I might wish or need to know."

"She has three children," he almost stuttered.

Faith said nothing, expecting her father to continue but he merely waited for her next question. The Brigadier knew that by the end of the evening all of the cards would be on the table.

"Boys? Girls?" she asked in a matter of fact manner.

"Three girls," he answered sheepishly.

Faith was tired from a long journey but her eloquence never faltered as she stared over the top of her glass at her father. Again she glanced up at her mother who now had an expression of disdain on her face as if there was a deep-rooted problem.

"Do I take it that Edgar's wife is Indian by birth?"

"They are moneyed people, Faith. Moneyed people, I'm led to believe. She is from a powerful business family on the Indian sub-continent. They are well thought of by the British too, so I understand."

He went to carry on but Faith cut him short. "And the whole family will be coming back to live in Bibury, I take it?"

"Edgar is the heir to the estate," the Brigadier answered meekly.

Faith was furious. "Have you any idea what everyone will think? It will be preposterous to have an Indian mistress as the head of the household, let alone Edgar trying to run the estate. She is probably a lovely woman and has beautiful children but most of all the whole of England will undoubtedly shun our family. As for them being a well thought of family it is obvious that they are simply puppets of the British Empire. Father, why can you not get it into your head that Edgar is a fool? He only ever attempts to upset people and get under their skin like a homeless bed louse. I have no doubt that he did not resign his commission but was told to because of this marriage to an Indian widow. Edgar is not wanted by the army or wanted back here either!"

Faith stood up and walked across the room. She was adamant. She could visualise the estate in the future losing money by poor management. Everything would be squandered or lost, and the whole village would be affected. Edgar was not the answer. There was also the question of Stefan. Her brief conversation with him yielded little information. She would speak with him privately first thing in the morning, as he was the most important factor in the affairs of the Bibury estate.

She turned to her father. "I am going to retire to bed, Father. It has been a very long day," she said and kissed him on his forehead.

The Brigadier was glad that his daughter was retiring and asked her to send the nurse in on her way out. She duly obliged.

In the hallway Faith spoke quietly but briefly with Lionel before he escorted her to her bedroom. Upon reaching her door, she questioned him. "Did you do as I asked?"

"Yes, I did as you asked, ma'am," he answered.

"Well, are you coming in?"

At first, Lionel was a little reluctant but he soon conceded. Inside he had prepared a bottle of claret, and soon they sat in opposite armchairs talking about the future of Bibury Court. They concluded that the future didn't bode well and that something would have to be done to prevent its demise.

When the wine was finished Faith invited Lionel into her bed. He told her he couldn't stay long but she didn't mind. It wouldn't take long, she thought.

The pair had been childhood friends and companions during their youth, and Lionel had lost his virginity to her, although he couldn't say that she had lost hers to him.

They kissed each other gently and began to explore each other's bodies. The perfume from the bathwater lingered all over her. Not since the day he had met Mary in Fairford had he had any kind of sexual encounter, and Faith was difficult to resist. She tried to hold him back, and after brief oral sex she allowed him to have intercourse with her. After weeks of abstinence Lionel's resistance was low and he suffered a pre-ejaculation.

Lying on top of her he quietly apologised in her ear. She smiled and squeezed him tight. It didn't matter.

For a while they lay together and he told her about Mary and her relationship with Georgina. As Faith lay with her head on his chest and gently stroking his stomach, she could not help thinking about the two women she had not yet met. In the morning she would find out from Stefan the full story from Shropshire and try and put a plan into her mind.

Some kind of action needed to be taken.

Stefan and Faith strolled around the village early the next morning. They eventually sat by the bridge and stared into the water. The ducks eyed them, expecting to be fed, whilst he told her everything he knew. Likewise, she told him everything *she* knew or, at least what she thought she knew. He had no idea what was really going through her mind.

"I need to speak to your friend, Georgina. Have you an address where I might contact her?" she asked him nonchalantly.

Stefan was flabbergasted. "What do you want her for? She has nothing to do with Bibury Court."

"Perhaps not but what is her ultimate aim? Surely not living with that tyrant for the rest of her life. Hasn't she told you what she plans to do?" she asked him, expecting a truthful answer.

Stefan was submissive. "She believes that she is caught between a rock and a hard place because of her children. I am afraid that our society is not for women; they are almost classed as the disadvantaged."

"Which then are you, Stefan? The rock or the hard place?" Faith asked, staring into her brother-in-law's eyes.

She had put him on the spot. He had a wife who lived a decent life, but who was sexually benign, and a lover who was quite the opposite. He looked at Faith without knowing if she understood what he was going through. "I would like to think that I was a soft spot. I never wanted it this way and I still love your sister dearly. If only I could have her back in her entirety. She is beautiful, and a good wife and mother. As for Georgina, she would probably be a good mother too, if she were allowed to be. Sexually, she is what any man would ask for. She is a lovely woman, Faith, but all she wants from life is someone to love her and treat her with respect."

"Tell me, Stefan, if Charity did return to normality, would you give up Georgina for good?" Faith wanted to know how deep his feelings ran for Georgina.

"Yes, I would, and Georgina knows that. We have spoken about it. She is more or less resigned to the fact that one day our relationship will end." Stefan looked at Faith almost pleadingly. "I wouldn't want anything to happen to Georgina though, no matter what. She deserves much better."

"Nothing will happen to her if you just tell me somewhere where I can contact her."

Stefan was far from sure what Faith was planning but he knew that she had something up her sleeve. He agreed to write down an address for her when they returned to the gatehouse. She then proceeded to ask every explicit detail about Georgina's family, especially about the man she was married to. He could see that she was deep in thought as he told her everything he knew. Eventually, she had heard enough and took him by the hand. They walked back along the river footpath to see Charity.

On the way she told Stefan about being in bed with Lionel the night before, if only to make Stefan feel at ease. "What is good for the goose is good for the gander", she told him, smiling.

The next day Lionel escorted Faith to Brockhampton and he waited outside whilst she spoke with Sir Charles for the best part of an hour. Lionel never asked why she was going there or queried the reasons of the meeting. Whatever had been said Faith was quietly pleased with herself.

Later, Lionel spent all evening with Faith at Bibury Court. He was on call all night.

Chapter 8

The Invitation List

Lionel sat in his father's alehouse waiting for Stefan. It had been a fortnight since Faith had returned to London, and he still pondered over her carefree attitude to sex and extra-marital affairs. He knew Gerard to be a wealthy man with an excellent position as a partner in a London law firm. He was always genuinely pleasant and never put upon any of his servants. Fortunately for Lionel, due to Gerard's commitments, he didn't often come down to Bibury any more, and after fornicating with his wife the chances of meeting him face to face were negligible, thus avoiding any shameful encounters.

Stefan entered the bar, and asked Lionel with his thumb and forefinger tipping towards his mouth if he wanted another drink. Cider was his preference on that stifling early summer evening.

At the table Lionel took a letter from his back pocket and passed it over. "This was delivered here but it's for you. Father kept it behind the bar."

The handwriting was easily recognised as Georgina's, and Stefan quickly slid his thumb through the envelope and withdrew the letter. He read it at the window and when he had finished he passed it to Lionel and allowed his friend to peruse its contents. Lionel smiled. Mary was coming to Brockhampton with Georgina.

"Our troubles are only just beginning, Lionel, so it's no good smiling." Stefan looked seriously at his friend. "They are coming down on the Thursday in a fortnight's time for a few days. That is the weekend of the Summer Ball at the Court, when most people can go. They are sure to invite themselves. Besides, I think that they may already have."

"What makes you think that?" Lionel asked.

"This afternoon I overheard the Brigadier talking to his nurse. She was confirming his list of invitees to the Ball, and Sir Charles and his wife were mentioned. It is almost certain that this is why the women are also coming down the same weekend."

"That shouldn't be a problem. Well, not for me, anyhow." Lionel was hopeful.

"Don't bank on it. I have just left Charity with Hope and her husband. Faith and Gerard are coming down as well. Oh, and Edgar will also be there. He is back in England, although he apparently still has some time to serve in the army before he faces demobilisation. Afterwards, he has to spend time to try and extricate his wife and her children from India. There are family problems in India because they don't want them to leave and come to England." Stefan held his hands up. "That's all I've been told."

Both men were flummoxed as what to do but there was very little they could do. They kept imagining a London theatre comedy act as they all tried to avoid each other at the Ball, and not be noticed whilst doing so. The evening was going to be quite laughable, if one had the opportunity of looking from the outside in.

Chapter 9
Charity

"Charity darling, how are you feeling?" Hope held both of her sister's hands and asked sympathetically of her well-being.

"Hello, Hope. Hello James," Charity said, greeting her sister and brother-in-law timidly. She appeared jaded and disinterested, and was slow to react, staring at the floor and then out of the open door. The evening sun was low and bright and reflected back off the flagstones onto her tired, grey face. Premature wrinkles had appeared and she had lost weight.

"Come, sit down. You don't seem well at all. I'm sure the children will be fine on their own for a while. We saw Stefan on his way out as we were coming here. He said you had been unwell, Hope said compassionately.

"Some days I feel fine but others I am not so good, but I'm sure it will pass." She looked away as if ashamed of herself but suddenly she turned back, "Hope, what are we going to do when Edgar comes back here? I don't want to see him; he is so horrid. Life has been so good since he went away, and now everything will be spoiled."

"I know, Charity. We all think the same way. We're trying desperately to persuade Father to tell him to live in London, or at least somewhere away from here. I'm afraid that whatever happens, Edgar will one day inherit the estate and nothing will stop him from doing what he wants to do." Hope stroked the back of her sister's hand to show her that everything would be all right.

"Charity, I want you to listen to me carefully," James said calmly. "If you want to help keep Edgar away from Bibury, I need you to do us all a favour."

Charity nodded her head very slowly and waited in anticipation to what she might be asked to do.

"Do you remember Stefan's thirtieth birthday party, when his father gave him that beautifully carved box?"

"Yes."

"May I please borrow it? But whatever you do, do not tell Stefan that I have it, or anyone else for that matter."

Charity retrieved the box from a wardrobe upstairs and handed it to James. It was made from the finest cherry wood, intricately sculptured and inlaid with a gold-leaf pattern. James carefully opened it and smiled in admiration at its contents. He closed the lid and nodded satisfactorily towards Hope. "Will Stefan notice that it is missing?"

"No. I doubt it very much. It has been kept under a pile of bedclothes in the bottom of the wardrobe away from the children. He rarely goes there."

Hope scrutinised her sister. "Only us three know about this, Charity. Please do not say anything to anyone." Charity nodded her head slowly, assuring Hope that nothing would pass her lips.

The couple stayed with Charity for another half hour, gently trying to coax from her what was causing her upsets. But it was to no avail; Charity's mind was firmly locked in.

Chapter 10
The Summer Ball

On the Friday evening prior to Bibury village summer fete and evening ball, dinner was served promptly at eight o'clock at Bibury Court. In attendance were local dignitaries, friends of the Brigadier and his immediate family.

Lionel, as ever, butler exemplary, stood by the side door that led from the dining room into the kitchen, waiting in anticipation for the young waitresses to bring forth the first course; fresh summer asparagus soup.

Everyone was comfortably seated with a glass of wine of their choosing. The conversations were informal, and various subjects could be heard around the table. Only Faith remained quiet as she made a conscious effort to hear what Edgar was telling their father.

Edgar was dressed resplendently in his service dinner jacket and he spoke passionately to his father about his future at the Court. Faith, however, had other ideas. She had given her sisters and brothers-in-law strict advice not to broach the subject of Bibury Court that weekend with Edgar whilst he was in the company of the Brigadier.

Edgar's army service would be completed in a little over two months, and he was hopeful that his new wife and her children would be able to join him shortly after his official demobilisation.

His father listened with both interest and disdain. He could not understand why his only son would marry a woman with three children, thus jeopardising the lineage of their English family name. Faith was unaware of her father's deep-seated feelings.

After dinner the guests mingled in the main hall and the Brigadier took to his wheelchair, aided by his young nurse. Both Faith and Hope conversed reluctantly with their brother as he had only one outlook;

himself. He talked about his future and what he would do with Bibury Court when he officially returned, which disregarded anyone else who might have something important to offer. Stefan avoided him, although they had acknowledged each other very briefly earlier in the evening. He decided instead to help clear up, thus avoiding any confrontation with the man who loathed him for some unexplained reason.

As the evening wore on it was Gerard and James who mostly spoke with Edgar, under orders from Faith to find out as much as possible about their brother-in-law and his future ambitions.

Apart from the concealed disaffection within the Collison family the evening went very well. Eventually, only family remained in the drawing room and Stefan excused himself for Charity's sake. The remaining family members had a nightcap before retiring to bed.

Tomorrow was going to be a long and hot day.

Stefan arrived at Bibury Court early the next morning to find it a hive of activity

"Have you seen Lionel?" Stefan asked one of the maids rushing past carrying a box.

"He is upstairs, sir. One of the bedrooms has sprung a water leak, on the day of the Summer Ball of all days," she sighed and then shouted after him as he ran up the steps. "Sir, along on the left!"

Stefan found his father with Lionel mending a broken tap. "Ah, Stefan. *Comment allez-vous?*"

"*Je suis très bien, papa, merci beaucoup.*" Stefan said, patting his father on the back as he shot a serious glance at his friend. "Lionel, come with me, I need to tell you something."

They went onto the landing at the top of the stairs out of earshot from anyone.

"I've just had a message sent down from Brockhampton. Georgina has her husband with her. They're coming here today, along with Mary and Sir Charles and his wife."

"Stefan, we'll just have to play it by ear,' Lionel replied, almost smiling. The afternoon and evening were going to involve family politics, intrigue and avoidance, and someone might just say the wrong thing in front of the wrong person. "You know which subjects may arise, so we will be careful who we talk to, Stefan."

"Why *we*?" Stefan asked. "I'm the only one who could be in trouble."

"Don't worry for now. Let's just get through the weekend and talk about it afterwards."

Stefan's father approached them along the hallway, smiling and wiping his hands on a towel. He had fixed the tap.

As the three men went their separate ways a bedroom door that had been slightly ajar closed quietly behind them.

Edgar chose to push his father around the village in his wheelchair quite some time before the midday sun would make it unbearably hot for his ailing father. There would be many visitors to Bibury that day and most householders were on the streets with something to sell, from homegrown vegetables and handmade knitwear to rabbits, poached locally. The Brigadier traditionally turned a blind eye to poaching before the fete, as he knew all of the local reprobates and their families by their first names, and didn't mind as long as he didn't see venison or out of season pheasants or partridges hanging up.

They passed women laying out knitwear; blankets, pullovers and cardigans, and beautiful, ornately sewn items could be found adorning the little tables in front of some of the cottages.

The cobbler and his son advertised their trade on the pavement. '*Heeled & Soled, only Thruppence*' their sign announced.

The smell of fresh bread from the bakery wafted down the street and a queue had already formed up to the side door in fear of missing out on their daily quota. For these tradesmen it would be the busiest day of the year, especially the demand for Mr Gray's jam and sugar doughnuts.

Every household, shop or artisan in the village would try to take advantage of the day's events before the main fete began in earnest on the Brigadier's estate. The atmosphere in the village was buzzing and the drinking hostelries were already at full capacity.

Maurice, the town crier, patrolled the streets extolling the order of procedure at the top of his voice

"Oh Yea! Oh Yea! Visit Bibury Court this afternoon! Beginning at one o'clock with a display of falconry! Put your money on the cock fighting in the stables! A fun dog show followed by terrier racing at three! Put your team in the tug o' war and win two gallons of beer! Flower, plant and vegetable show with good prizes! Fancy dress for the children and Tommy O'Brien's One Man Travelling Circus! Fun for all the family! Lots and lots of side stalls. Beer, cider and spirits are being sold in the old stone barn! Don't miss it, all starting at one o'clock today. Oh Yea! Oh! Yea!"

Edgar began to edge back along towards the Court. Delighted faces often tipped their hats towards the old, popular Brigadier but tended to ignore his son or some even threw sarcastic jibes towards him. The old man couldn't understand why or how his son had made himself unpopular during his long absence from the village; which seemed more so now than when he had originally left and joined the army.

Soon he was being helped up the steps into the front of the house with his young nurse at his side, and after being settled into his favourite chair in the drawing room, he dismissed Edgar.

As his nurse tidied the room he asked for an Armagnac. She deftly poured a large one and placed it into his ailing hand, clasping his fingers and thumb around the glass for him.

"Thank you, my dear," he said, glancing at the nearest clock. "Nobody – family nor friends – are allowed to disturb me until one o'clock. I have some local guests arriving in the early afternoon and I will need to be ready at two o'clock. Please ask the maid to prepare my clothes and bath previously," he sighed and took a large gulp of Armagnac. "Today will be interestingly long, and I envisage a few domestic discoveries," he mumbled.

Before she left him in his chair, his young nurse, slightly bemused, adjusted the cushion behind his back and topped up his glass.

Stefan and Lionel stood watching as the young women manoeuvred the Brigadier into his summer attire, casually dressing him to his own liking in a cream three-piece suit with a shirt and cravat. Socks and sandals were chosen to keep his swollen feet cool in the intense heat.

"Stefan! Don't put a foot wrong today," his father-in-law called. "You are married to my daughter and that is the way it will remain. This evening you take her to the Ball."

Stefan tried to interrupt but the Brigadier was having none of it. "Shut up and do as I say. "He quickly turned on Lionel. "Make sure everything around me is in order. By ten o'clock I want to be back here away from the marquee and alone. Whatever you do, stay at the Court tonight. I am expecting shenanigans." The Brigadier raised one eyebrow back towards Stefan. "You take Charity home after the Ball, and you stay there. I mean it." He could visualise Stefan's thwarted sexual prowess creating him a lot of trouble.

The Brigadier dismissed them both. The Ball was now a chore in his old age, and the heat of the day disgruntled him.

He turned to his maid. "Go and find Faith. I want to speak to her immediately," he told her, unusually without manners, and she scurried off.

Faith soon entered the room. With a nod of his head the dress maids scuttled out of the door with their pinafores pulled up. "Well? Is everything going to plan?" he asked his daughter.

"As far as I know, Edward and Mary are coming this afternoon."

"Mary. Who is Mary?" the Brigadier butted in.

"She is Georgina's cousin. We can't really leave her back at Brockhampton on her own. The pair of them are coming down for the fete as well as the Summer Ball." Faith half expected her father to say something.

He held his hand up to his forehead and waved for her to carry on as he tried to perceive who was who.

"Sir Charles and his wife, and Georgina and her husband are coming later, perhaps about seven o'clock,' Faith said, explaining the proceedings to her father as simply as she could. "They will have a drink here with us before going over to the marquee."

"What about the bedrooms? Are they all ready?"

"Yes, two double rooms have both been prepared."

"What about Edward and Mary? Where are they staying?"

"Edward is returning to Brockhampton quite early whilst there is a little light left in the sky, and as for Mary," she hesitated, "well, you've asked Lionel to stay over tonight, have you not?"

The Brigadier looked dumfounded. "Please don't tell me they're both at it as well." he stopped and thought about it. "My God! Surely you must have a vested interest in that relationship?" he spun his wheelchair around to face the window and shook his head slowly. "What type of household do people think I run here? It is a bloody den of iniquity." He went quiet.

"Father, I think the less said the better."

He spun back round. "What is that supposed to mean?"

Faith smiled at him. "Stories about you and your nurse are rife. I believe the saying 'those in glass houses should not throw stones' is applicable here," she said before turning on her heel and leaving the room.

Faith left her father speechless, and for a long time afterwards he sat wondering what people were thinking of him and his formerly respectable family name and home.

The fete was a success after being very well organised and presided over by several senior villagers from along the Coln Valley and surrounding districts. No inter-rivalry skirmishes were reported, and after the Grand Finale of the tug o' war people dedicated to sobriety began to slowly drift homewards whilst the disappointed and the jubilant alike headed towards the drinking establishments.

Edward and Mary stayed close for most of the afternoon, although Mary had been warned that Lionel was officially at work that day and not to interfere with him.

Billowing clouds, snow white on the sunward side, burst upwards and dissipated as enormous cotton fluff balls that drifted along with the prevailing winds, but few on the ground noticed their continual metamorphosis.

Lionel and Stefan began to organise a general clear up. Guests and local dignitaries would begin to arrive within the hour, and in two hours the Summer Ball would be in its ascendancy.

The dance band had set up at the far end of the marquee, and they were practising a few lines. Makeshift tables and chairs filled the other end with a drinks bar in the corner. Waiters had prepared the wine, spirits and glasses, and those preferring cool beer or cider could fetch it from the stone barn. There were still plenty of people around who were willing to help and as soon as everything was ready, Lionel and Stefan went to change.

There was a knock on the drawing room door and Lionel showed his face. "Sir Charles and his wife are here, sir."

The Brigadier adjusted himself. "Show them in, please."

Sir Charles introduced his wife, Maria, his nephew, Fulwar, and his daughter-in-law, Georgina. Lionel served them all drinks. Mary soon appeared and cheerfully pecked Georgina, Sir Charles and her Aunt Maria on their cheeks. She ignored Fulwar. The Brigadier discreetly eyed Georgina up and down. It was understandable what attracted his son-in-law to her, he thought. She was an exceptionally beautiful woman.

He suddenly wished he was sixty years younger. She made the old man think about his youngest daughter. Would she realise what had been going on between the alluring Georgina Cavner and Stefan?

Shortly afterwards Edgar entered the room along with his two sisters, Faith and Hope, and their husbands.

They all talked generally about how the day had fared so far, and there was a little banter about some of the acts and competitions.

The room suddenly went quiet when Stefan ushered Charity through the door. The poor woman didn't seem too sure of herself but Faith, her forever-confident sister, took her by the hand and made the point of introducing her to Sir Charles and his family.

Everyone present had been made aware of Charity's unexplained problems and discreetly acted as if there was nothing wrong at all. With a drink Charity appeared a little more relaxed.

The Brigadier, Sir Charles and Fulwar began discussing the estate and the position of agriculture in the British economy, but Fulwar's real interest was the Brigadier's Armagnac, of which he had an ample supply. After setting the rural industry to rights they were soon heading towards the marquee, where a long table had been reserved for the family and their guests.

It was some time after the music had begun before one couple raised enough courage and rose to their feet to dance, after which it wasn't long until they were far from alone on the makeshift wooden floor.

Faith drew a reluctant Gerard from his seat, and Hope followed suit with James. Once the audience saw the majority of the Bibury Court family participating, most eased themselves from their rickety chairs and began earnestly joining in.

Stefan leaned across his seat and whispered into Charity's ear but she wasn't in the mood, making the feeble excuse that the music was too fast. He instead tried to gain eye contact with Georgina but she sensibly remained completely aloof. Frustration crept into his divided heart.

Finishing her dance, Mary, perhaps astute, came across and began talking to the couple, and asked Charity what it felt like to be the mother of three children, and telling of her hope of one day having her own family.

Disinterested, Stefan left them to their maternal conversation and went outside. He was soon seated upon an old milking stool with a jar of cider in the stone barn. It wasn't long until his father came in and sat next to him. He spoke English to his son but with a strong French accent.

"Your mother is with the children. They are in safe hands, of course. Tell me, what is wrong, Stefan?" His father, Monsieur Desailley, raised his eyebrows in anticipation of his son telling him the truth.

Stefan said nothing but faintly shook his head. There was little he could divulge to his father.

Monsieur Desailley spoke again but more determinedly. "My son! Listen to me. The beautiful woman you yearned for when you were such a young man will one day be well again. A little more time and everything will come together. This weekend is not a pleasant time for you both. Please Stefan, persevere. I assure you that everything will one day come right. Stefan, you are still a young man."

Monsieur Desailley lifted himself off his seat with the help of his son's shoulder. "Charity is my daughter-in-law. Please do not desert her now when she desperately needs you by her side. The time is not right."

Alone again, Stefan sat and pondered his extraordinary situation but he had no answer. How much did his father know – and then, of course, his mother. With another cider he reluctantly made his way back to the marquee, or as he described it in his mind, the amphitheatre, where everyone would be watching.

The table was sparse of people. Only the Brigadier remained seated in his wheelchair. Even Charity was missing. The music was that of Irish dance songs. Stefan sat down beside his father-in-law who, half smiling, pointed towards Charity. She was dancing to some bizarre song and being tutored by Georgina and Mary. Stefan and the Brigadier watched, both quietly pleased that the distraught wife and daughter had seemed to find some comfort.

A small break for the musicians brought everyone back to the tables, and it was suddenly apparent that Fulwar was becoming very drunk, and Edgar's attentions were turning towards Georgina. Faith watched intensively, and Hope sat with Fulwar and broached the subject of the Cavner estate.

Fulwar's voice was slurred. "It is a sore subject, especially with Uncle Charles sitting over there." He gestured slovenly with his head and rolling eyes.

Hope asked no more awkward questions and sipped her wine but briefly made eye contact with Faith. Stefan watched their silent interaction as the band struck up some slower music and several couples took to the floor, and he took Charity by the hand and gently coaxed her onto the floor as Fulwar politely asked James if he could have the hand of his wife.

James duly obliged as he and Gerard were engaged in a long conversation about London and its industries.

Edgar, without polite permission, asked Georgina if she wished to dance. She accepted, smiling and he took her hand and led her onto the floor. Faith remained with her father, watching as Sir Charles and Maria headed for the floor.

"That Fulwar chap is beginning to look rather worse for wear," the Brigadier observed. He was not wrong, and Faith watched as her sister tried to dance and talk to Fulwar at the same time. Fulwar had little etiquette whilst dancing with his two left feet. Perhaps it was just the drink, she thought, although Edgar appeared to be a complete officer and gentleman in Georgina's company.

Faith wondered what Fulwar would say or do if he saw his wife dancing with Edgar. Edward, Georgina's close ally, had left at least an hour earlier, and Faith thought that it would have been far better if he had taken Fulwar back to Brockhampton with him.

Mary returned from a dance exuberant. All the young single males had wanted to dance with her, and one by one she had duly obliged them. Lionel could only stand and watch from the marquee entrance, barely controlling his deep frustration from afar. He hoped the Brigadier would retreat back to the house so he could relax more and perhaps join in, although he still had to involve himself in organising the clearing up.

Fulwar returned to the table with Hope. Georgina was missing and he had seen her talking to Edgar in between pieces of music. The band struck up again and the guests continued to dance. Fulwar suddenly went strangely quiet, prompting Faith to move across and sit next to him. The two sisters were now propping him up on each of his shoulders, as he was definitely the worse for wear because of his alcohol over indulgence.

"Are you all right, Fulwar? You don't look very well," Faith asked kindly. He muttered something that she didn't understand, and so she asked him again. There was still no discernible reply.

Stefan was watching carefully from the dance floor. His and the Brigadier's eyes met, and Stefan slowly shook his head. Seeing this, Georgina realised that there was a problem with her husband, and she decided to return to the table.

Once seated, Fulwar began to say something to his wife but Faith butted in and tried to keep him from talking to her. The last thing she wanted was for him to set a scene.

The Brigadier summoned Lionel over and discussed with him what to do about Fulwar.

Lionel looked towards the ailing guest and nodded. He approached the drunken man from behind, bent down and spoke in his ear. "Mr Cavner, the Brigadier wondered if you would like to join him in the drawing room for a glass or two of Armagnac Special Reserve. You could both chat about your businesses, perhaps." Fulwar did not reply.

"He would be very disappointed if you don't accept his offer," Lionel added with irony, speaking childishly as if to a little boy.

Fulwar agreed to go and Faith suggested she would join them. As Lionel pushed the Brigadier's chair across to the house, Faith followed arm in arm with a staggering Fulwar.

In the drawing room Lionel poured the men a large Armagnac each, and Faith sipped a small glass of red wine.

The Brigadier shifted across into his armchair, glad to be away from the noise of the band but not happy that he now had unwanted company sitting on his chaise longue.

"I'll be outside if you need me," Lionel told them, a little peeved that he could not yet return to join the entertainment in the marquee.

Lionel wasn't disappointed for long. Faith soon reappeared from the drawing room.

"Fulwar's asleep," she said quietly. "We'll cover him up and he can stay in the drawing room tonight. All we have to do before going back across to the Ball is help my father into bed.

With the Brigadier firmly tucked up in bed, Faith and Lionel lingered quietly outside the drawing room. "Come on," she whispered. "Let's go and see if Fulwar's all right before we go back."

Lionel shook his head. He wasn't interested, but Faith took his hand and they crept through the door.

Fulwar was thoroughly drunk and very soundly asleep. Faith suddenly rounded on Lionel. "Come on. Let's make love." She pulled Lionel towards her and planted her painted lips against his. Lionel tried to resist but feared waking the almost comatose Fulwar, but shook his head in desperation. Faith soon had her hand on his groin and Lionel began to raise an erection. "Come on, Lionel. I haven't any underwear on." She leaned back across her father's leather-topped desk with her legs apart, and her femininity oozed into the warm sultry atmosphere through her flimsy summer outfit.

As in the past, Faith was overpowering and Lionel soon began to make love to her. He held her ankles and stood on the floor thrusting into her as she lay back across the edge of the desk. The stationery fluttered away as her arms flailed in ecstasy. An empty inkbottle hit the wooden floor and Fulwar moaned.

Lionel stopped, and they both turned to see the drunk turn over and fall back to sleep. The brief interlude gave Lionel his second wind and he continued, eventually satisfying both himself and Faith in their illicit sexual activity.

With both desires satiated, Lionel pulled Faith up towards him and they kissed passionately as his blood flow ebbed away inside her.

At the end of their sexual liaison there was a knock at the door. After little readjustment Faith stood over the drunken Fulwar, and Lionel, dressed himself correctly and opened the door.

It was Gerard.

The three walked back across to the marquee. Stefan had recently returned after escorting Charity back to the gatehouse, against the Brigadier's wishes, and was sitting at the table alongside James. He found it extremely difficult to keep his eyes from wandering towards Georgina because he so desperately wanted to touch her or dance with her, but that evening he had to exercise all of his will power. What made it worse was Georgina plying her whole attention onto Edgar who, in turn, couldn't leave her alone but was being the perfect regimental gentleman.

Faith went across and whispered into Georgina's ear. "Your husband is asleep in the drawing room. He should be safe there for the night."

Sir Charles and his wife indicated their intention to retire to bed, and Stefan escorted them back to the house. Other people were also slowly drifting home, although the band still played.

Lionel took his chance and danced with Mary, who was soon smitten with him, and they were laughing, joking and genuinely enjoying each other's company.

Faith and Hope persuaded their husbands up onto the dance floor for one last time. A wonderful day was coming to an end with a series of waltzes, and nobody other than Faith noticed Georgina leave alone, but she was then discreetly followed shortly afterwards by Edgar.

The pair met outside and walked over to the house together. Stefan watched from the darkness of the dining room as they ascended the staircase arm in arm as quiet as church mice.

He returned to the marquee feeling helpless. The music ceased and the remaining dancers returned to their seats. Many began finishing their drinks and leaving for home, some in carriages or on horseback but most on foot. A few responsible people stayed behind to help clear up the mess.

"What's wrong? Faith asked Stefan, clutching his arm. "You look like you've seen a ghost."

"Nothing. It doesn't matter," he replied.

"Stefan if you are worried about Georgina, then don't be. She can handle herself. She can't be seen with you this weekend so she is just using Edgar as a decoy. If Fulwar thinks something is going on, then Edgar will get the blame and not you. Do you understand me? She is doing it for you." Faith tried to be philosophical with him. "Don't forget that you will always have Charity to go back to. Georgina has an awful husband and everyone knows it."

Stefan nodded his head slightly. He realised Faith was right and that there was little he could do about it.

Georgina crept along the landing from Edgar's bedroom. She thought her husband was bad enough but Edgar was the worst sexual encounter she had ever had. He handled her roughly and was only concerned for his own satisfaction.

Distraught, she made her way back to her bedroom and collapsed alone on the bed. She felt terribly unclean but it was a function she had had to fulfil to get Edgar eating out of her hand. She found it difficult to wait for the morning, when she could have a bath and rid herself of Edgar's bodily fluids and odours. Strangely, she felt she couldn't wait to get back to Shropshire.

Lying alone and feeling disgusted with herself, Georgina sincerely hoped she wouldn't meet Stefan before she left, as she was so ashamed of what had happened and couldn't possibly face him. Alone, she turned onto her side with her knees tucked up and cried herself to sleep.

Chapter 11
Azamgarh

"Please go and find Staff Sergeant Starbury," the Rautara, Arjun Singh, pleaded with his son. "I need to speak to him before he returns to England next week. It is important. Hurry, Azim. Hurry."

The forty degree heat from the afternoon sun was unbearable and the British soldiers on duty at the barracks just outside the town of Azamgarh took shelter wherever possible. Staff sergeant Starbury was no different. He had taken refuge in the cool of the ammunition shed, a dusty stone building nestling among other larger structures.

Azim found him sitting quietly, and relayed the message to him from the head Rautara, the richest landowner for miles around. Together, the two men walked back across the town to Arjun Singh's palatial home.

"Thank you for coming, Mr Starbury," he said, and then turned to his son. "Thank you, Azim. That will be all for now." Azim nodded and closed the door behind him.

"So, how can I help you, Mr Singh, bearing in mind that I only have six days left before I return home to England?" Starbury was matter of fact and could not wait for his embarkation day.

"What are you planning to do when you arrive back in England? Do you have a job?" The Rautara now spoke in English but with a heavy northern Indian accent.

"I don't know yet. It will be worrying times, although I am told in certain areas of Great Britain there is much work. Whether or not that work suits me remains to be seen. Besides that, I am not sure if my wife and I could afford to relocate elsewhere." The staff sergeant was suddenly puzzled. "Why are you asking?"

Arjun Singh didn't answer his question. "How much do you earn in the army, Mr Starbury?"

"Forty-two pounds a year. Please tell me what this is all about?" The staff sergeant tried not to show his impatience.

"What I tell you now must not go beyond these walls, whether you decide to go along with my proposal or not," he told him, expecting complete secrecy.

The staff sergeant hesitated but then answered with a shake of his head. "I promise that whatever you say will not go beyond these four walls."

"Do you know of Captain Collison? He left this year and returned to England," the Rautara said, fidgeting in his seat. "The captain that nobody liked."

"Yes."

'Well, as you must know, your chaplain married him to our daughter behind our backs. He married them as Christians, but she is a Muslim. There is little we can do about it here, under British rule, but now that he is trying to arrange for her and our three grandchildren to immigrate to England to be with him, my wife is distraught. She says that she will never see them again, and I believe that she is right. We do not want them to leave India, and seeing my wife so distressed has prompted me to do something about it. That is why I have asked you here."

Staff sergeant Starbury shrugged his shoulders in simple resignation. "I can do nothing. It's completely beyond my control. I grant you that everyone hated him but soon he too will be out of the army and he will be able to do as he wishes."

"I will pay you to assassinate him," Mr Singh told him abruptly, and calmly watched the reaction on the staff sergeant's face.

There was a look of astonishment on the soldier's face as he considered the request and the repercussions.

"I don't mind killing people in the name of the British Army to defend the crown against its enemies, but I am not a murderer. I am sorry, but you have chosen the wrong man to be standing in front of you." He turned towards the door shaking his head in disbelief at such a request.

"I will pay you two years' wages for your services."

Starbury swung sharply around and looked at one of the richest Muslim men in India hard in the eyes. Since the attempted Indian rebellion and mutiny, the leading Rautara was kept on the payroll of the

British. Money was not an object to Arjun Singh but, if Starbury himself were caught, spending the rest of his own life in a Victorian prison or ending up on the gallows were not options. The money might set him up for life but was it enough? All manner of ideas went quickly through his mind.

Mr Singh could see the man's hesitancy. "I will pay you one year's wages in British pounds before you leave India, and then through my agent in London, you will be paid one year's wages when the assassination is successful. You can contact him before you eliminate him to reassure yourself that I am genuine. Please, Mr Starbury, you don't understand how desperate we are to have Mr Collison dispatched as soon as possible."

Starbury remained hesitant. Life in prison or even execution kept entering his head.

The old Rautara made his mind up for him. "I will also buy you a small home of your choice anywhere you might need to live. I am afraid it is my final offer. If you refuse I trust that nothing will be said beyond these walls. I can tell you that I will deny ever speaking to you, and will find someone else who will carry out the task."

Staff Sergeant Starbury stood easily. It was an offer he couldn't refuse. With the money he could even afford to pay someone else to carry out the murder. "All right. I will arrange his liquidation on those terms but you had better tell me everything I have to know."

The old Rautara smiled. He stood and shook the man's hand, thanking him profusely. "As you already know him, there is little I can tell you except that I have found out that he is going to live in a small village called Bibury. Come back tomorrow for your initial payment and I will tell you everything. The one thing I will ask is that I am informed that your task is completed before my daughter and grandchildren leave for England."

The two men bade each other a farewell, and Staff Sergeant Starbury left for the barracks a worried man.

His superior officers allowed him to leave three days earlier than previously arranged after he had planned a new route home via rail and ship aiming for the Mediterranean. He would avoid the journey onboard a stifling troop ship and cut out the arduous trip around the Horn of Africa taking weeks off his journey time.

With his major belongings following at a later date, and despite a toilsome journey, it was not long before the former staff sergeant set foot on English soil.

Chapter 12
The Ladies' Liaison

Faith tapped softly on the panelled bedroom door. There was no answer and not wanting to make any louder noise to wake the household she tried the handle.

The door was unlocked.

She pushed her head inside and saw Georgina, still fully clothed, lying asleep on the bed. She hadn't even attempted to get under the bedclothes. She was clutching a pillow to her bosom, and tears had yet to dry on her face.

Faith let herself in and quietly closed the door behind her. At first she went to the adjoining washroom and began filling the cast iron bath, knowing full well when the rest of the guests had the same idea, there would be little hot water left.

Back in the bedroom she gently rocked Georgina's shoulder. She initially stirred but then suddenly sat bolt upright.

"Fulwar!" she shouted.

"No. It's me," Faith said soothingly. "Come on, wake up and have a bath before he gets here." Faith spoke as assured as a hospital matron, stroking Georgina's hair away from her face and helping her from the bed.

In the washroom Georgina slowly took off her clothes with Faith's assistance.

With Georgina in the bath Faith sponged her down and helped her to wash her hair with water from a white enamel jug. Afterwards, Georgina was helped to stand on the bathroom rug, and little was said as Faith towelled her down. Georgina was clearly still very upset.

Faith softly dried her breasts and then began to tenderly dry between her legs. Dropping the towelling at Georgina's feet she began to caress her vagina.

The two women suddenly kissed and Faith fondled Georgina's breasts and sexual organ, and Georgina held her head back and began taking deep breaths as Faith softly manipulated her body. Her nipples stood erect and Faith soothingly sucked one, which was as comforting to Georgina as to a weaning baby.

Her vagina dampened and soon her clitoris conceded to a sexual orgasm, and all her dire memories of the night before became diminutive. Faith was a better physical lover than both her husband or Edgar. Besides, she suddenly felt that Faith probably cared more for her than the pair put together.

Faith helped fashion Georgina's hair and prepare her for the journey back to Brockhampton as the women spoke of the days to come, and how they would keep in touch. A meeting in London between them was imperative but the timing had to be right and the arrangement perfect. Deep down, Georgina was distraught but knew exactly what part she had to play. She smiled and then hugged Faith.

The bedroom door suddenly crashed open and Fulwar stumbled in. He was angry and confused, and he began to confront Georgina before realising that Faith was in her company standing by the fireplace.

Faith remained calm but damning. "There is still warm water in the bath tub. Make the most of it because you need it! Breakfast will be served in the dining room in half an hour. Your carriage back to Brockhampton will be one hour after that." Stern though she was and staring back over her shoulder at the drunk, Faith escorted Georgina from the bedroom to take her down to the dining room.

Chapter 13
A Private Confession

Stefan had written only a few pages of the manuscript regarding the Coln Valley. His concentration as a writer over the past months had dwindled to almost nothing and his life had entered a crisis. He needed physical love of a kind he could trust. His circumstances were strange but he was a patient, virulent man whose life desperately needed to change.

He walked around the back of the Court and entered the churchyard through the rear gate in the old stone wall that separated both buildings. He quietly and carefully trod the stone slabs leading to the south door, and as he lifted the great cast-iron latch a feeling of guilt and trespass came over him as if someone from above told him he should not be on such consecrated ground. Undeterred, he crossed the threshold into the ancient church, devoted to St Mary the Virgin.

For all the years he had lived in Bibury he had only set foot inside the resplendent antiquated structure for very special occasions, such as weddings and funerals. The Church of England did not welcome Roman Catholics.

He wandered around reading the dedications on the floor and walls, and browsed the large black Bible, which read so similarly to the one his mother used to quote to him many years before. Stefan smiled. The ceiling struck him as being an awesome design and he admired the long since deceased carpenters who had laboured on its construction for several years.

He sat down on an elm pew and contemplated his own life, but most of all those of his immediate family and friends. Never once did he pray for his own forgiveness.

From the vestry peered the vicar, the Reverend Henry Snow. He had watched Stefan from the moment he had entered the church. Silently the revered figure descended the steps and from behind approached his disconsolate visitor. He placed a hand on Stefan's shoulder. Stefan never flinched.

"How is your book of the Coln Valley proceeding, my son?" he asked.

"With difficulty, Rector. I have too many things on my mind." Stefan refused to look up.

"Stefan, you are welcome to pray here anytime you wish but your problems are only for you to answer. You have a beautiful wife and three equally beautiful children. They must come first, at all cost. You married 'for better or for worse'." The vicar knew more than he was letting on.

"Do you think I am wrong what I have been doing or thinking?" Stefan asked the learned scholar, still afraid to look into his eyes.

"In the beliefs of any Christian church, yes, but without being hypocritical just remember who instigated the breakaway Church of England from Catholicism; Henry VIII. And for what reason? Divorce. Stefan, we also practise forgiveness. A time will come and you will be glad of Charity's company once again. Have faith. Do not let Charity down."

Stefan was politely left alone so he could ponder his future and perhaps pray. He stared up at the altar with his mind in turmoil.

Chapter 14
Writers Block

Seated at his desk for the last hour, Stefan continually fidgeted. He simply couldn't concentrate. His friends and family had tried to persuade him to take his mind off things by writing, something at which he was strongest. To have such a talent, they told him, should never go to waste. He kept staring down at where he had left off all those days ago when he was interrupted by the visit of Sir Charles. Over the months his only contribution was to visit the villages of Andoversford and Withington to carry out some research.

He knew deep down that he had to make another start, and when he did perhaps the words would flow as they once did. As it was, he would pick up his pen and then put it down again, or rise from his seat and walk to the window and stare through it. Or he would leave the study and walk to the kitchen and back, or to the sitting room and drawing room, or perhaps all three.

Suddenly, Stefan appeared to have an inspiration and looked down at the last words he had written. He read the last paragraph, dipped his pen into the inkwell, and stared thoughtfully for a while before finally touching his pen to the page.

The Brockhampton estate began to develop in the mid-17th century by local landowner, Paul Peart. He instigated the building of the original house, which has since been extended in various architectural styles. The present incumbents are Sir Charles Corbett-Cavner and his dear wife, Lady Maria Corbett-Cavner.

To the traveller and the discerning eye, Brockhampton and Sevenhampton are a pleasure to visit, and Sir Charles and Lady Maria own most of the buildings in both villages and are the largest employers in the area, maintaining the estate in an orderly and pleasant manner. Lady Maria has benevolently laid down the funding towards the opening and upkeep of the new schoolroom in Brockhampton, and she currently manages both the day and Sunday school.

The local alehouse holds the family name and its sign is that of the family crest depicting a gryphon and crosslets, which may also be found on the cast-iron rainwater heads of their stately home.

The beautifully crafted Cotswold stone houses and cottages of the two villages takes one back into their historical past. Set at the head of the valley of the Coln River, the magnificent rolling countryside is an artist's dream. Wildlife abounds, and deer graze at the edge of the woods, red kites and buzzards grace the skies, grey partridge and pheasants scour the arable lands, and corncrakes scuttle along its edges. In the springtime, hares box for a female partner as the rabbits nibble away unconcerned. In the summertime, the magical wheatears appear on the windswept hilltops. From whence they came, no one knows. All kinds of wayside flowers bloom, at their designated time of year, attracting various butterflies and insects.

The hardworking folk from the parish are very friendly and the alehouses welcoming. Brockhampton and Sevenhampton are well worth a visit, just five miles east of the spa town of Cheltenham, a day trip should not be avoided.

Stefan put his pen down, unsure whether he had written enough about the two villages. He stood up and paced around the room. If he finished it there he didn't have to think about the villages any more and he could concentrate downriver on the village of Andoversford and onwards towards Withington.

"Move on," he told himself.

He went back to his desk and filed away his incomplete manuscript, thinking that perhaps Georgina would now not come to mind so much. Glancing at the clock, he pondered over what to do next. The Catherine Wheel would soon be opening, and an early evening drink suddenly seemed very desirable.

On his way out he told Charity he would return at eight for dinner.

Chapter 15
The Stranger

"The fellow you need to speak to lives in the gatehouse. Stefan Desailley is his name. He is the man who makes the final decision when it comes to hiring labour, especially seasonal labour. There is an estate owner but Stefan runs the financial side of the business."

The barman gave the stranger in the Swan Hotel directions to Stefan's house. "It is harvest time and they should be taking on workers right now," he added.

The stranger thanked him for his advice and rose from his seat. He drank the dregs from his pint pot and pulled from the floor a shabby knapsack containing the whole of his belongings. He ran his fingers through his long, greyish beard and flicked his hair back over his shoulders. The wrinkles around his tanned face gave a false impression, as his bright blue eyes implied that he was a healthy individual.

Walking across the road and then alongside the river towards Bibury Court, he stopped briefly and stared at the paddling mallards, wondering when the shooting season might start. It had been many years since the taste of wild duck had passed over his tongue. Again he set off following the barman's simple instruction and soon he approached a large iron double gate and knocked meaningfully on the open door of the adjacent house.

A young boy appeared at the threshold and with no exchange of words scurried off to find his mother.

She came to the door, wiping her hands in her apron. "Hello. How can I help you?" she asked warily.

"Ma'am, I am looking for gainful employment and was told to come here and ask for a Mr Desailley. Please, might he be available?" The stranger's manners and speech were above his tramp-like appearance, and he had no particular accent.

Charity eyed her visitor up and down. It was a request for Stefan to decide upon. "Frankie, go over to the house and ask your father to come home. Tell him someone wants to speak to him. Go on please! Be quick!"

As the child obediently ran off, with the stranger thinking that the boy was too young to be sent on such a task, Charity turned her attention back to the newcomer. Her hospitality was unremitting. "Can I get you a drink? I don't think he'll be very long, my husband's meeting with the Brigadier should be over by now."

"Ma'am, it would be most appreciated. Thank you kindly."

Charity ushered him into the kitchen and began making a pot of Chinese green tea; an aphrodisiac, she had been told. Stefan's opinion of the drink differed.

"Sir, what can I do for you?" Stefan asked the man sitting comfortably at his kitchen table.

"I need work, sir. I am from the north but wish to move here to the south, where the working environment is much healthier. I want an outdoor life full of fresh air and away from the grimy factories. I have a wife and children but want to keep them away from the grease, the oil and the stifling chimney pots. Is there any way that you might be able to help me, sir?" he pleaded.

Stefan eyed him up and down. The man's hair and beard were long but well kept, clean and tidy, and his physique was that of a man who thought well of himself. Stefan needed labour but in a capacity probably below that of the itinerant's competence.

"What are you capable of?" he asked.

"Hard work, sir. Just give me a chance and I will prove to you that I am worthy of every penny. Anything you ask of me and I will do to the best of my ability, sir," he answered persuasively.

Stefan thought for a while and then, as Charity poured the tea, he turned to the stranger. "What are you like working with machinery?" he asked, mindful of his father's age. Marcel Desailley was coming to the point in life where he needed help.

"Most of my life I have worked mechanically but I must admit not with farm machinery. I am still prepared to learn, sir."

Stefan looked at Charity. "I won't be long. I'm going to speak with your father," he turned back to his visitor, "I might have something for you but

I will have to confirm it with the Brigadier first. Wait here, I'll be back as soon as possible." Stefan left the stranger with his wife.

"So, is your father the owner of the estate?" the stranger asked Charity.

"Yes, he is." It was all she said.

"What is his name, if you don't mind my asking?"

"Collison. Stanley Richard Collison. He is known as the Brigadier but it is just a nickname he was given when he lived in France as a young man, and he has been proud to use it ever since. Don't be afraid to call him that should you come to meet him."

"Thank you. I will remember that."

"And yourself? What is your name?"

He hesitated as he turned over the name *Collison* in his head. "Portlock, ma'am. Neil Portlock," he replied.

In Stefan's absence they talked about their children, although Charity estimated that at least one of his children was now of working age, far from being a child more so a youth.

Shortly afterwards Stefan returned. "You can work with my father, Marcel. He is getting old now and needs permanent help. If you require somewhere to stay, which I assume you do, there is the Catherine Wheel, or I hear that Mrs Bicknell on Arlington Row is looking for a lodger. Let's go and find my father and explain the situation to him, and then I'll take you to find lodgings."

Neil Portlock was in luck. He had found a job almost straight away and in the village of his choice. Stefan wrote his name and address down and both men left Charity to her chores as they went in search of Stefan's father.

Marcel sat with Neil at the back of the repair shop-cum-barn and explained what his job would entail; the maintenance of all the estate's mechanical equipment. Stefan allowed them to talk alone, trusting his father's instincts. He leaned on the wall outside watching the birds flying around the treetops. Shortly afterwards, Neil and Marcel emerged from the barn and a very slight nod from Stefan's father confirmed Neil's employment. From there they visited the Catherine Wheel, and by early evening Neil Portlock was fully ensconced in a room of his own and had a job to start the day after next.

Chapter 16
Maidenhead

Georgina crept into the main hall in Stokesay Castle. Fulwar slouched in his armchair by the large open fire. As usual, he had drunk himself to sleep. The remaining whisky he had in his glass was spilled down his trousers, giving the impression that he had suffered a bout of incontinence. One arm hung limply over the side of the chair and a letter, addressed to Georgina, lay on the floor beneath his fingers. She quietly picked it up and took it to the window seat, where she read it and absorbed its contents. After acquiring some free tickets, Faith had invited her and Mary up to London for the opening night of the New Theatre Royal in Holborn.

Georgina sat gazing thoughtfully out of the window. She knew what the trip would entail and it wouldn't just be going to the theatre. She looked across to her husband, who would already know about the invitation.

Fulwar read all letters received at their home, regardless of whom they were addressed, such was his overwhelming jealousy. She had very little privacy and would often take the dogs for an early morning walk, not for health reasons but simply to intercept the postman.

Having Stefan as company at some time during the same weekend was an idea that excited her, and she contrived in her mind the ways in which she could meet her lover. Georgina replaced the letter on the floor close to Fulwar's hand and went upstairs to concoct some secret correspondence of her own.

Stefan went searching for Lionel and found him helping his father in the Catherine Wheel.

"Lionel, can we have a chat, please? It's important." With drinks in hand they sat in the corner and Stefan was quick to the point.

"This morning I received a letter at home from a publisher in Maidenhead. They are interested in putting part of the manuscript for my book about the Coln River into print because they specialise in travellers' guides and maps." Stefan carefully watched the expression on Lionel's face.

"Well done! That's good," he commended, genuinely pleased for his friend. "Maybe they'll pay you up front, or give you a commission, perhaps?"

"Perhaps," Stefan smiled.

"And it might inspire you to get on and finish writing it as well," Lionel laughed.

Stefan retrieved the letter from his pocket. "Here, read it before you get too excited."

After he had finished it Lionel looked up. "That's interesting. You must take up their offer, especially if they are going to pay for your hotel stay. You should at least make an effort and find out what it's all about."

"But don't you understand what is suspicious, Lionel?" he asked.

Lionel looked at the letter again and slowly shook his head. "No. What?"

"They are supposed to be a publishing company but the letter is entirely handwritten. This day and age it would surely be printed on headed notepaper." Stefan was flummoxed.

Lionel thought about his observations. "That is true but maybe they have just started their business and don't yet have it quite up and running, and that's why they are looking for people like yourself."

"Lionel! Who in Maidenhead would know that I am writing a book about the Coln River? No one, surely." Stefan looked around him, aware that he might have been overheard.

"Besides, one cannot start up a publishing business when one doesn't have a printer," he said with less volume, waving the letter at Lionel. "It's akin to having a plumbing business but possessing no tools."

"Stefan, just go there anyway because you have absolutely nothing to lose. They are paying for your food, drink and a night at the hotel. If they don't turn up for the breakfast meeting, so be it. Take a day or two off and enjoy yourself." Lionel was emphatic that his friend should take his chance.

The amiable pair sat drinking and talking, and were soon joined by Neil Portlock for the rest of the evening. Between the three of them they played cribbage, where the loser stepped aside each time but had the dubious task of drinking a large whisky down in one.

Much laughter came from their corner long into the evening.

The train chugged into Maidenhead station, spewing smoke across the town. It was late afternoon and raining as Stefan alighted onto the platform. Outside the station Stefan took a carriage to Redroofs Hotel, where his meeting was to take place the next morning at nine o'clock. Having given his name to the receptionist she checked the booking and summoned the porter, who guided him upstairs to his room.

Although small his room's plush furnishings were contrary to the exterior facade the building portrayed. He settled himself in and after a bath and rest on the four-poster bed, he decided to go downstairs and sample the hospitality. Disappointed that the hotel did not have a bar, he sat near to the window with a copy of The Times, noting that it had that day's date, such was the proximity of Maidenhead to London.

Having browsed through the paper he neatly refolded it and placed it back on the table. Before leaving to walk into the town centre he wandered across the back lawn to the riverbank, where there were boats moored, mostly pleasure craft but there were some for the keen anglers. Stefan kicked himself for not thinking to bring his rod and line. He could have tried some grayling fishing, but alas it was not meant to be.

He turned back and as he passed through the hotel he could not help wondering whether he could lease fishing apparatus in town to use after his meeting in the morning.

The hotel receptionist suddenly came out and called after him. "Mr Desailley, there is a message for you," she said, handing him a note, and he thanked her.

Stefan began reading it as he walked along the street but he suddenly stopped. He studied the note and then gazed back towards his hotel. Stefan returned and questioned the receptionist. "Can you please tell me who delivered this note?"

"A young man, not very old. I would say he was a hotel porter by the way he was dressed."

Stefan studied the note once again. It implied that he was to be in the Grenfell Arms at eight o'clock and to be discreet. It also insisted that he should not be there before that particular time. The clock on the wall told him he had just over one hour. He again thanked the young lady and went back out onto the street with the intention of asking someone where he could find the Grenfell Arms.

Stefan found the Portland Arms in West Street, where a patron told him that it was a mere five-minute walk to his rendezvous. He stood at the bar nervously drinking and then, due to his query, a conversation broke out about the Grenfell. Apparently, it was an expensive establishment designed purely for the upper-classes. Definitely not for the 'hoi polloi in life' as one elderly drinker remarked whilst eyeing Stefan up and down. The customers laughed.

After two pints of Nicholson's, a local brew, and a dram of the best whisky to calm his nerves, Stefan left the Portland feeling much more mellow and with a settled stomach. It was becoming dark but he found the Grenfell quite easily. His fellow drinkers at the Portland had been right; the clientele were from a different society, but definitely not one he wasn't used to.

It was mostly waiter service but he bought a drink and stayed near to the bar. No one approached him and he began to think that his being there was a complete hoax, and all manner of ideas passed through his head as to why.

Half an hour went by and still nothing had happened, and he was about to leave. He hadn't noticed a woman enter from a back room and sit down at a reserved table in a far corner. A waiter attended to her and she ordered a bottle of fine red wine with two glasses.

She sat staring into Stefan's back with the hope of gaining his attention but he still faced the wrong way. The waiter returned and placed the wine on her table, and the woman raised herself off her seat and whispered something to him whilst gesturing towards Stefan. He looked over his shoulder and then nodded.

Back behind the bar the waiter referred Stefan to the lady in the corner. Surprised, he turned and there sat Georgina. His heart pounded and he went over to join her.

Georgina stood briefly and they lightly kissed as if they were brother and sister. She was so pleased to see him; as he was to see her.

"Why all the secrecy, Georgina? Who might find us here, in Maidenhead of all places?"

Georgina stared briefly down into her glass. "Didn't you want to see me?" she asked sullenly.

"Yes, of course but why make up the story about a publisher?" He looked suspiciously at her." I assume that it was you who sent that letter?"

She gently nodded. "Yes. I wanted Charity to believe it to be genuine. Had I posted it to the Catherine Wheel and she somehow had read the letter, she would have thought it a cock and bull story. I'm sorry, I shouldn't have sent it, but I was just so anxious to see you." Georgina made to get up and leave but Stefan took her hand and they stared into each other's eyes.

"No! Please stay." He caught the attention of the waiter and beckoned him over. "Let's order food and then we can talk."

Dinner was ample, and they said little as they ate. Afterwards, Stefan made the first move, stroking the back of Georgina's hand. "Tell me, please. What *is* going on?"

Georgina was wary of what she could say or how much Stefan should know but she told him of the letter Faith had sent regarding the theatre tickets. "Believe me, Stefan, I wanted to be with you so much that I concocted the story and arranged for us to be here. I have a tiny room behind here rented for the night in case you didn't wish to come. Every day I think of you and just want to be in your arms. My life is awful without you."

Stefan stopped her. "I know what you might be going through but please compare your life with so many others'. Just remember all those who haven't any fresh water and sanitation or healthy diets. They live shoulder to shoulder in the back streets of our cities and towns. Education for their children is non-existent and those poor souls fall into the same trap, as did their destitute parents. Believe me, Georgina, all you have to do is rid yourself of self-pity and try and piece together a new life without Fulwar. Money or no money, someone will love you and work hard in return for your love. That man is out there somewhere."

Georgina remained quiet as the waiter removed the plates and cutlery. "Stefan, do you love me?" she asked when he left.

Stefan was restrained. He had to choose his words carefully. "If it is possible to love two women at the same time, then my answer is yes. Georgina, at the moment we both need each other to satisfy our physical souls, and then one day we will be able to walk the earth with our heads held high. You organised this sojourn here, and had I known it was you I still would have come. I do love you but, more importantly, I want you to be happy and free."

Georgina visually scoured the wall beside her, her thoughts elsewhere. She turned her beautiful head and gazed at Stefan up and down. The candle flickered its light over his masculine face, and her eyes reflected the candle's flame. She wanted to say something but refrained.

It was the waiter who brought them both back to reality. "Sir, madam. May I serve you something else?"

"Yes, please," Stefan replied. "A bottle of the same wine we have been drinking, thank you."

They waited for him to return. Georgina paid the entire bill, including her night stop at the Grenfell. She paid a handsome tip for the waiter's discretion.

"Do you want to be with me tonight, Stefan?" she asked.

He nodded. "Of course I do."

Georgina was straight to the point. "Then listen carefully! I think I am being followed by at least one of Fulwar's spies. When you leave here, go straight back to your hotel and I will arrive possibly a half an hour later. I'll stay the night. Tomorrow morning, Faith's husband's company carriage will come here and pick up all of my luggage and then drive to Redroofs. For fear of being seen I will board without hesitation and then set off for London, leaving you to return to Bibury. Please drink up, Stefan, and believe me that I need you now more than I have ever needed anyone."

Stefan was unsure. He felt that there was more to all the proceedings than Georgina was saying. He desperately wanted to take her to bed, but deep down his stomach told him that there was something amiss; something he did not yet know about, but his sexual inclinations were too powerful.

For now he decided to do what he was told.

They drank most of the wine and Stefan left the Grenfell, apparently the worse for wear. He noticed two men, whose faces were difficult to discern, talking quietly under a gas lamp on the other side of the street. As he crossed over he heard them bid each other a goodnight, and he heard footsteps follow him as he weaved along the pavement.

Being drunk was one thing but acting drunk was entirely different. Stefan turned onto the main thoroughfare, and with only the full moon breaking through the clouds to light his way, he staggered into the wall of a house, and the man following suddenly offered assistance. "Come, take hold of my arm before you do yourself some damage, old chap."

"No! No, sir! I'll be fine thank you," Stefan answered, slurring.

"Please. I insist," he said, taking Stefan's arm "Where are you going? I hope it isn't far," he chortled.

Stefan was reluctant to tell him but as he was most likely going to be helped all of the way, he conceded. "Redroofs," he answered.

Outside the door he thanked his mysterious assistant for his help and went inside. Free from his pretence he quickly climbed the stairs and entered his room, where he peered through the curtains to see if his Good Samaritan was loitering outside. It was too dark to be sure but there was no one in sight.

As he lay on the bed dreaming about Georgina his loins began to stir. He kept imagining all the things he wanted to do with her. He remembered the first time in the barn at Sennington, where he explored her beautiful body all over. Then there was the time at the Bull in Fairford. He recalled the disappointing time at the Summer Ball, when she had totally ignored him but seemed to have attracted Edgar's attention. His penis was now firm. He couldn't wait for the knock on the door.

The handle quietly turned and Georgina stepped into the candlelit room. He raised himself up onto his elbows, and she could see from beneath the sheets what was on his mind.

She closed the door and went to him, sliding her hand down to his groin and grasping his blood-driven organ. She pulled back the sheet and began gently masturbating him whilst stroking his testicles. Her soft lips and tongue began to tantalise his glans. He lay back and closed his eyes as she continued to stimulate his sexual prowess and then sucked his hardening nipples. She kissed his toned body all over and could sense his orgasm arising and so temporarily released her grip, only to torment him for a few seconds and then continue.

Stefan stretched and ran his hand up inside her thigh and then inside her underwear, gently fingering the moisture exuded by her genitalia. Eventually her massaging brought him to a head and he began to take deep breaths and his chest heaved up and down as she masturbated his penis to its final conclusion, spraying semen across his muscular torso. She continued until he could stand no more, and he took her by the wrist and pulled her hand away.

Georgina took off her clothes and stood in front of the dress mirror. Stefan returned from the bathroom and from the angle where he stood could see her naked body in its entirety, back and front. She had perfectly formed breasts, a slim waistline and well-proportioned buttocks. Her legs were long, slender and shapely, and her golden hair hung down her back to her waist. With her beautiful facial features, she was every man's dream. Equally, Stefan's muscular frame reflected back to Georgina and his tanned French features and tousled hair would be difficult for most women to resist. He approached her from behind and began exploring her body as she stood before the long mirror. He kissed her neck and gently caressed her breasts, and his hand ran across her stomach and down between her legs and stroked her soft pubic hair. Georgina reached behind and caressed Stefan's flaccid penis and testicles, and he responded to her touch. His finger found her clitoris and began massaging her sexual organ, slowly at first but she stepped her legs apart and urged him on.

With her eyes closed she could now only visualise the man standing behind her, and her breathing began to crescendo. Her vagina was wet from sexual excitement and easily penetrable but Stefan was not yet back to complete readiness and continued to titillate her 'little hill'.

Suddenly, she threw her head back into his chest and her breathing became heavier and heavier, and with each breath she began to let out cries of pleasure. An inescapable vibrant sensation began to erupt through her body. Her fantasies were coming to fruition, and she cried out louder and louder and began to scream with every breath as every nerve tingled and the feeling of ultimate orgasm was inexorable.

Stefan watched her in the mirror, more than satisfied that he had brought the beautiful Georgina to a supreme climax. Her breathing finally slowed and her cries became little more than whimpers, and after some time she opened her eyes.

She turned to face her real, live dream and they kissed passionately. They climbed onto the bed and he began exploring her body once more with his mouth and tongue. Her nipples stood firm as his tongue searched every crevice, and with her lying on her back with her elegant legs wide apart he again found her clitoris. Soon she began to squirm with pleasure once more but Georgina pushed him away and she turned over onto her knees. He penetrated her with two fingers whilst caressing her breasts, and then began exploring and penetrating her sexual organ with his tongue. Her breathing was heavy and she shrieked with the utmost pleasure, demanding for him to penetrate her.

Fully erect again, he rose up and mounted her from behind. She pushed back hard into him over and over, but then she withdrew his penis, reached between her legs and guided it into her anus; an entirely new experience for Stefan, and one that had always eluded him.

She took his hand and placed it on her vagina and he simultaneously had anal intercourse whilst stimulating her clitoris. Soon she could feel that he was about to orgasm and again she pulled away and turned over. From under the pillow she procured a beautifully carved wooden dildo and pushed it inside her, gesturing for Stefan to use it whilst having anal sex.

She moved to the edge of the bed as Stefan stood on the floor. His penis again infiltrated her anus whilst he rhythmically manipulated the dildo in and out of her demanding vagina.

He had never seen a woman orgasm so many times before but he soon spoiled her continuing desires with a powerful release of all of his own sexual desires. For some time Stefan stood over Georgina's stunning body as the blood ebbed away from his spent penis once again.

He wondered why anyone would ever want to hurt such a beautiful woman.

Georgina lay admiring the magnificent male body that stood holding onto her hips, and she couldn't imagine why Charity could not be sexually excited by him. Stefan bent down and kissed Georgina gently on the lips and then they shifted back onto the bed, both completely satisfied. Until the next time.

After sponging and caressing each other's bodies in a large cast iron bath, they climbed back into bed in the early hours of the morning, close to exhaustion. They had said little, such was the intensity and longevity of their lovemaking.

Stefan stared up at the ceiling, and Georgina studied the reflection of a picture on the wall through the mirror on the wardrobe. Tired as they were, sleep was difficult. It was Georgina who spoke first.

"As I told you earlier, there is a carriage that will pick up my belongings at the Grenfell first thing in the morning before coming here. I then have to make a quick exit because I do not want to be seen." Stefan went to say something but Georgina placed her finger on his lips. "Please. Don't get involved. It is important that when I leave, you stay here. As much as I would like to stay with you, it is impossible. I have to go to London. Stefan, please go to sleep."

He did what she asked and never felt her tears gently running down his chest.

A carriage was heard to pull up outside Redroofs as the sun was just beginning to light the early morning sky, and Georgina discreetly peered through the curtains. Along the road she could see two men loitering near to the river. Below, a veiled woman dressed in a bright red and white costume was helped from the carriage and onto the pavement, where she was ushered into the hotel. Stefan still slept.

Georgina held the door open and Faith walked in. "Hurry," she whispered with her forefinger over her lips.

Faith removed her outer clothing and Georgina proceeded to put it on.

Stefan suddenly woke and sat up, wondering what in hell was going on. Faith told him to keep quiet, and he lay on the edge of the bed watching the two women. When Georgina was fully dressed she hugged Faith, kissed Stefan wholeheartedly, pulled the veil over her face and went out of the door.

On the street below Georgina was helped into the carriage and they set off towards London. On the opposite side of the road the two men were puzzled but nonetheless maintained their vigil on the hotel.

"What is going on, Faith? For Christ's sake tell me!" Stefan was confused. His sister-in-law was standing before him in just her underwear and he was sitting on the edge of the bed completely nude.

Faith sat down next to him. "Do you really want to know, Stefan?" She placed her hand on his inner thigh. "Come on, let's make love and then I'll tell you everything you need to know."

He flinched. "Don't be ridiculous, Faith. I'm married to your sister."

Faith looked at him and said wryly. "She needn't know," as she slipped her underwear off. "Besides, you didn't mind getting into my knickers before you married her," she laughed. "Do you remember those times?"

Stefan remembered vividly, and Faith slipped into bed with him. Stefan conceded and made love to his sister-in-law, although not with the same passion as he had with Georgina. Faith had always been a good lover and friend and he knew she would say nothing to her younger sister.

Afterwards, when he asked her again what was going on, Faith had emphatically changed her mind.

"Please don't ask. All I will say is that tomorrow I am going to the theatre with Gerard, Mary and Georgina." She never mentioned Edgar.

Stefan and Faith left the hotel arm in arm, making a point to walk to the station quite brazenly in front of the two sleuths, who watched from a distance. She wore Georgina's clothes.

The two men were completely confused. They seemed to have mistaken the couple in the hotel. One followed them to the station whilst the other went to the hotel and bribed the receptionist to find out who had paid the bill.

He was told that a Captain Edgar Collison paid the bill in cash.

Chapter 17
The Castle Tavern, Holborn

Faith lived with her husband Gerard in Leather Lane, Holborn. It was an old but modest house with three floors and a basement. From the pavement there were four steps up to the front door, and decorative iron railings prevented anyone falling from the street into the basement yard below.

It was Friday and Mary had joined Faith and Georgina, and the three women sat at the dining table discussing the weekend ahead and awaiting the arrival of Gerard from his workplace in the city. It was to be frightful for Georgina and none of them dared to guess the outcome.

"Georgina, are you sure you want to go through with this?" Faith asked. She was naturally perturbed for the troubled woman.

"I have to now. After what you have told me. I cannot let you down."

Mary took her cousin's hand. "Try not to think about it, my darling. We'll go out to dinner tonight and have a relaxing time. Tomorrow is going to be a long day."

Gerard eventually arrived and quickly went to change into something less formal. He had arranged to meet some friends and colleagues at the Castle Tavern at seven o'clock. He wasn't long and soon they were all leaving the house.

Well within walking distance from their home the Castle Tavern on the corner of Castle Street and Furnival Street was far from being a restaurant. It was an entertainment pub. Upon arrival Gerard introduced his colleagues, and the party found a long pine table with equally long wooden benches and captain's chairs at either end. The parquet floor, although brushed and scrubbed every day, was black from trodden in spilt drink and tobacco ash.

Although still only early in the evening, grey blue smoke hung head high throughout the bar because of the venue's poor ventilation. Loud conversation and banter already filled the room, as most of the clientele hadn't been home from work. In another hour the custom would change as Friday night revellers began their tour of duty throughout Holborn's many pubs. In one corner a trio of bandsmen began tuning up for an evening of music and merriment. The filthy, stained panelled walls were adorned with maps and paintings of Holborn and its surrounding district. Each had layers of nicotine sticking to the glass, making reading nigh on impossible.

Gerard handed money over at the bar and offered to settle the final bill before they left. Waitress service was a part of his deal, and warm London Pride beer from Fuller's brewery was soon brought over by buxom wenches who carried six handled pots at a time. They all drank, even the women. Wine was not available. Mary, the good time girl, was in her element and her excitement was there for all to see.

Plates of food appeared on the table, and a tea towel was thrown at them. Roasted chicken legs with potatoes, a hock of ham and pork chops. The Castle was no place for table manners, and they all ate heartily, and shared the towel to wipe the grease from their chins.

Conversation dried up as they ate but soon returned as the band struck up. The music hall songs were second rate but more than satisfactory amongst the appreciative crowd of half intoxicated local people.

When they finished eating, belching discreetly, Gerard invited the prying eyes from outside his entourage to devour the remains of the food. It wasn't long before all they were left with was a pile of bones and many contented stomachs.

When a bottle of whisky appeared on the table beside a jug of water, Georgina stared at it and shook her head, and Mary saw her change of mood.

"Come on, Georgina. Let's dance," she said, pulling her reluctant cousin onto the temporary dance floor. Georgina soon felt better because Mary always made her feel that way. When they returned to the table the whisky bottle had been discreetly removed from the table and port and gin had taken its place.

The band slowed down and all sorts of people intermingled. The atmosphere was one of ambience and good nature, and Mary made a beeline for the happy drunks, who were more than pleased to be in her company, and Faith danced with one of her husband's colleagues.

Gerard asked Georgina to dance but she quietly shook her head. Instead, he sat down beside her. "How was Stefan last night? Does he suspect anything?"

She looked Gerard in the eyes. "He was beautiful. We actually hardly spoke. Stefan is such an understanding man, but when we were back in his hotel I can barely remember speaking to him."

Gerard, an astute lawyer, understood her problem. "But do you think he knows anything?"

"He is suspicious but of what I don't know. When Faith turned up in Maidenhead this morning he was confused but he is far from stupid. When Faith and I swapped clothes it was to do with my husband's creeps watching us. Hopefully, Stefan will not have been implicated. We worked everything out carefully. You know that all this will end up in tears, don't you, Gerard?"

He pursed his lips and gently nodded his head, "Yes, Georgina. But believe me when I say that we will take care of you." He asked her once again to dance with him and this time she obliged his offer.

The night soon became raucous but it was typical London entertainment.

Sadly, the evening came to an end and the customers spilled out onto the streets. Gerard's party made their way back to his home where the wine rack was full. They drank and talked into the early hours of the morning until what had been a good evening all the way through naturally came to an end.

Chapter 18
The Theatre Royal

After a late breakfast-cum-lunch, which would suffice until after the play, it was decided that they would take a walk down to the Embankment and along the riverside. Gerard declined the exercise, however, and only the ladies participated.

Dressed casually they set off towards Newfetter Lane. They had orders to be back in time to change clothes accordingly and leave the house no later than five o'clock. The new Theatre Royal was within walking distance but Gerard had arranged a stop off point on the way.

Gerard sat in his armchair, barely concentrating on a copy of the Daily Telegraph. He read a summing up of the Tea Race that had taken place earlier in the year, and tried to compare it with the French grape growers vying to be the first to bring the fresh wine to Paris restaurants. A smile spread across his face at the thought of competition in business making the world go around.

His maid tapped on the door and she put her head around inquisitively. "There is a gentleman to see you, sir. A Mr Collison, I believe."

"Thank you. Please show him in."

Edgar Collison strutted into the room.

Gerard, a consummate professional, greeted his brother-in-law warmly. "Edgar!" he exclaimed, as if pleased to see him. "How are you? It's good to see you. You look well, considering you're out of the Indian sun and back here in rain-sodden London," Gerard laughed.

"Thank you, Gerard. Yes! I am well. I have a few problems trying to get my wife and children back here into England, but I am managing."

"Ah! Now you mention it, may I ask how the situation is with your wife and children?" The subject had become important to Gerard and the three Collison sisters, let alone their brother.

"I am afraid that someone somewhere seems to be objecting along the line. Whether it is here in England or over in India I don't know, but it is terribly frustrating." Edgar had a disappointed look on his face, one of almost despair.

"Perhaps my company can be of help? We hire some of the best judicial brains in the country, especially when it comes to international law." Gerard's offer of help was almost on the table.

"What has international law anything to do with it?" he asked. "India is a part of the British Empire."

"We would have to delve into it. There are certain treaties within the empire that we have a duty to abide by. Maybe one of them is thwarting your efforts to have a favourable decision made. How many children has she?" Gerard needed as much information as possible to proceed with any inquiry.

"We have three, and they are all under twelve."

"Boys or girls?" Gerard asked.

"Girls. They are all girls," Edgar replied, smiling sheepishly, and Gerard was suddenly sceptical.

"I'll try and find out as much as possible, Edgar. I'll take down some details before you leave tomorrow and we'll look into it during the week, but just remember that these things do often take time."

Both men remained quiet for a time but Gerard broke the ice by offering Edgar a whisky, which he didn't refuse. "Tell me, Edgar. When are you officially leaving the army?"

"Friday the ninth of November, in just a few weeks time. I only found out the date this week, and I have sent the Brigadier a letter telling him I will be home permanently the week following after tying up a few other minor problems."

"Are you looking forward to returning to Bibury after so many years away?"

"Yes. Very much so."

"But what are you intending to do when you move there?" Gerard was concerned but his face showed no emotion. Edgar's return after so many years didn't bode well in the family.

"The Brigadier is getting old now so I'll return and take over the running of the estate. It could do with some fresh blood. Let's just say that a new brush sweeps clean."

Gerard was astonished but his professionalism kept him quite calm. "But I was under the impression that the estate functions perfectly well as it is. Why alter something which works without a glitch?"

"I believe the business could do better and should show profits of ten to fifteen per cent more than it currently does. There is no reason that I can see why it shouldn't." With his eyebrows raised confidently, Edgar was adamant.

"How are you going to achieve this rise in profits?" Gerard asked him, fearing the worst.

"Cut back the labour force for a start. I am convinced that there are too many working there and, might I say, not working hard enough. It could operate profitably with a reduction of a quarter of the workforce." Edgar seemed quite pleased with his belief and what he had divulged to Gerard.

Although Gerard didn't show any emotions he was far from happy. "Have you considered where these labour cuts might begin?"

"I've done nothing but consider it," Edgar said smugly. "First of all, old Marcel can retire, as well as several other farm labourers of the same era. What with the new machinery coming of age we simply don't need them any more, as you must agree." Edgar raised his eyebrows at Gerard, believing that his brother-in-law would hold the same opinion.

"What about Stefan? Where does he fit into your plans?"

"I will work alongside him until I understand fully how the business is run and then I'll take over his job. I'll find something else for him to do on the estate until the Brigadier dies. When that happens, which will be sooner rather than later, Stefan, will have to find work elsewhere."

The sound of women's voices ended their conversation. Gerard wasn't sure if it was a good or bad idea that they had returned. Whichever, he thought, there wasn't going to be a favourable outcome at Bibury with Edgar's long-term intentions.

Faith entered the front room and saw her brother.

"Edgar!" she exclaimed, hugging him. "How lovely it is to see you." She stepped back and eyed him up and down "You look so well in your theatre dress!" she laughed and hugged him again.

In the hallway Georgina and Mary heard the greetings. Mary squeezed her cousin's hand.

"Sweet Georgina, the time has come for the greatest act on earth." She squeezed her hand more tightly and led her into the front room.

Mary latched onto Edgar as if pleased to see him. Georgina initially stood back but Edgar's eyes were upon her. When Mary stepped aside Georgina appeared more than delighted to see Edgar. They embraced and kissed.

Gerard excused himself from the room, and Faith stopped him in the hallway. "Gerard, please don't let us down," she said quietly, concerned that her husband had become much too involved.

"From what I've just heard, it won't be me letting you down." He kissed his wife on the cheek. "Come on. Let's prepare ourselves for the theatre. We have to look our most splendid."

A gentlemen smoking a pipe stood across the road from the High Holborn entrance to the Theatre Royal, waiting and watching. He occasionally strolled to his left and then returned the other way. To the immense theatre crowd mingling outside eager to attend on the opening night, he was nothing more than a fellow awaiting a companion.

A man suddenly stepped from the shadows. "They are coming now, sir. Look to your left. There are three women and two men, and Mrs Cavner is the very good-looking one on the arm of the tall, well-dressed chap. Now I must disappear. If she sees me she'll realise that her husband has his eyes on her." They acknowledged each other and he walked off.

The gentleman turned away and through the reflection of the shop window watched Gerard and his small entourage join the queue for the privileged and eventually enter the theatre away from the agitated throng. He would wait laboriously for them and after the final curtain follow them back to wherever they were staying. He envisaged another long, tiring evening of cat and mouse, made more difficult by the enormous crowds combined with autumn darkness.

In the foyer of the new theatre stood its proud owner, Mr Sefton Parry. The architects and the owners of the various businesses relevant to the different trades who took part in the theatre's construction accompanied him.

Mr Parry welcomed everyone as they slowly filed past. Gerard, a friend of the owner, briefly spoke to him before entering the auditorium, and congratulated him on his achievement because the theatre had taken just six months to build.

An usherette guided them to their box seats, where they made themselves comfortable. Their conversation turned to the interior décor of the horseshoe shaped auditorium adorned in pink, salmon and white with gold relief. The ceiling was panelled and had ample ventilation. Decorative gas lamps adorned the walls.

The theatre audience settled down as they prepared to listen to a brief opening speech by Mr Parry, who thanked all those involved with the construction work and wished everyone a pleasant evening's entertainment.

The evening began with a short farce written by Mr TJ Williams called Larkin's Love Letters. It was a comical, often absurd play that went down well with an appreciative audience. The interlude was taken up by another, longer speech by Mr Parry, who comically lamented the spending of his life's savings to build the theatre. He was an entertainer in his own right.

The National Anthem played before the main event, and everyone gave a hearty rendition, which was followed by a drama written especially for the theatre's opening by Dion Boucicault.

The Flying Scud, also known as The Four Legged Fortune was an excellent play of four acts about the horseracing world, and previews had drawn the attention of sporting journalists from all over Britain. They were seated comfortably in a special box, a clever advertising ploy by the wily Sefton Parry for his new theatre. Both performances went down very well, and a standing ovation lasted ten minutes.

As most of the audience spilled out onto the street the three women went to the powder room. Georgina and Mary chattered incessantly about the evening's entertainment as they readjusted their faces, but it was Faith who brought them both back down to earth.

"You'll be glad to know, Georgina, that Edgar has to be back in Woolwich Barracks first thing in the morning. Your ordeal won't last until Monday unless you choose to go to Woolwich with him," she said, trying to reassure her.

Georgina's mood suddenly became sombre. "It won't. I have already told him I am returning to Shropshire tomorrow. I lied but I can't bear the thought of him pawing over me for any longer than I have to. This won't end tomorrow anyway. When Fulwar finds out, which he inevitably will, I'll be in worse trouble. I suppose having sexual intercourse with someone you don't like is better than ending up in hospital after being badly beaten up by someone who is supposed to be your loving husband. Whichever way, I'll be the loser." She finished preparing her face and snapped her make-up bag shut. "Come on. It's too late to go back now, so let's get on with it."

They found Edgar and Gerard standing amidst dissipating crowds, and Georgina openly kissed Edgar on the cheek as he helped her into a waiting Hackney carriage.

"Dolly's, please," Gerard shouted up to the driver. "Queen's Head Passage." They pulled away. Edgar and Georgina sat very close together, and opposite were Faith, Gerard and Mary. Only Faith and Gerard talked but merely discussed the opening of the new theatre and the quality of the actors and actresses.

"Follow that carriage, please!" The private detective needed to stay on Georgina's trail. It was important that he found out where she was staying that night, but it was more important that he discovered whom she was staying with.

They stopped at Paternoster Row and he and Fulwar's employee watched as their quarry was helped down onto the pavement. Gerard paid their man and the five walked into Dolly's Restaurant'.

"Do you mind that we wait here, please?" the detective asked, "I'll pay you the extra." The driver had no qualms; for him and his horse it was easy money.

Two hours later, after midnight, Gerard's party left the restaurant and had obviously decided to walk home.

The inquisitive pair hurriedly paid off a very contented driver, and they both set off in pursuit on foot. They raced along back lanes to close the distance; losing them was not an option. Soon they were on their trail. It was obvious that Georgina and Edgar were behaving as lovers. Finally, the entourage turned into Leather Lane and entered Faith and Gerard's house halfway along on the left.

The two sleuths had no option but to wait and see what might happen. For them, it was going to be another long, cold night on the street.

Gerard poured some wine and whisky, and suggested playing a game of poker but none of them could conclude how they could play the card game for fun. They opted for Canasta.

Georgina drank heavily, and Mary and Faith pretended not to notice. Edgar wasn't ignoring the port bottle either and both women thought that it might just be Georgina's saving grace.

"Excuse me. If you don't mind I need to retire to bed," Mary announced. She was tired but wanted to stay relatively astute. Georgina was Mary's cousin and great friend, and she didn't want to see any harm come to her. Georgina was, after all, the sacrificial lamb for the evening.

After short embraces Mary left the room.

"I think I'll do the same," Gerard said, also conceding that going to bed was a good idea. "Besides, there's a church service in St Paul's tomorrow morning that I would like to attend."

"I'll come with you, darling." Faith said. "To bed! Not to the church service!" she interjected and smiled at Georgina, Edgar and her husband. She kissed Georgina and Edgar and followed Gerard out of the room and up the stairs.

Georgina poured a large port into Edgar's tumbler, unsure whether his intoxication would prolong her nightmare or end it quickly.

"Come on! Drink that up and let's go to bed," she said. "It's rude to stay downstairs when the hosts are not here."

Georgina took her time in the bathroom whilst Edgar hopped around the bedroom struggling to take off his pantaloons. When she finally climbed into the bed next to him it was she who made the first move. She caressed his penis but he just lay on his back. Once he tried to kiss her and caress her breasts but he just fell on his side and began to fall into a deep sleep. His partial erection came and went. She attempted to straddle him but to no avail. Georgina turned away, satisfied at not being satisfied but at least she had tried. She didn't cry herself to sleep on this occasion. With the port sleep came naturally.

"Edgar, wake up! Come on, wake up!" Faith tried hard to arouse her brother because outside a carriage was waiting for him.

He slowly began to come around and then realised where he was. He tried to focus on the clock on the mantelpiece and when he saw the time he sat bolt upright.

"My God! I have to be at the parade ground by ten o'clock," he cried, stumbling out of bed.

Georgina maintained her pretence of sleep throughout his scramble for clothes, and soon Edgar kissed her lightly on the cheek.

"Goodbye my lovely. I'll be in touch."

The front door slammed and horse's hooves clopped up the street. Edgar was gone! A great sigh of relief came over Georgina.

Faith crept back into the bedroom. "Are you all right? How did your night go?"

"Nothing happened. He was too drunk. I tried but whether he will remember is another thing. At least I stayed the night with him." Georgina said with a sense of achievement.

"Do you think he has fallen in love with you?" Faith asked.

"Yes, to a point but he still talks of his wife and children in India." Georgina lay back with her hands behind her head, staring at the chandelier. Her breasts were bare, and in the cool autumn air her nipples stood erect. She felt clean, untouched.

Faith stretched across the bed and took one of Georgina's nipples in her mouth and gently sucked and caressed it with her tongue.

Relieved at not being with Edgar, Georgina responded and persuaded Faith to remove her nightwear. They kissed passionately and stroked each other's breasts, and soon were head to toe, exploring their vaginas with pulsating fingers and tongues. Delving deeper inside searching for an erogenous zone as the scent of warm sexual secretion aroused them further and they gently embrocated each other's clitoris until both reached orgasms simultaneously.

Their engagement had lasted for some time, culminating in satisfying sexual euphoria, and neither woman heard the bedroom door gently click closed.

Mary stood on the landing with her back against the wall. She shook her head disbelievingly as if trying to rid the image of her cousin entwined in a lesbian embrace with a partner she barely knew.

Bewildered, she retreated along the landing, wondering what the coming months might bring.

Georgina produced her beautiful wooden dildo, carved for complete sexual satisfaction, and inserted it into Faith, who lay back with her eyes closed and her legs wide open with her knees almost touching her large breasts. As Georgina manipulated the sexual substitute back and forth, she gently sucked and caressed Faith's nipples. Muscle spasms increased as blood pumped into her pelvic region until she eventually reached another orgasm. Faith then repeated a similar erotic act with Georgina upon her knees.

Faith approached the sensual woman from behind, and she soon experienced an intense feeling of pleasure throughout her whole body, and violently pushed back into Faith as if she would never receive anything similar again. With a final flourish and shrieks of ecstasy Georgina attained her consummate achievement and climaxed at the hands of her secret lover, or so she thought.

Afterwards the unlikely pair lay next to each other holding hands. Speaking quietly, Faith reassured Georgina of the coming months, the possible traumas and impending problems, but emphasised that no stone would be left unturned. They faced each other in the bed and kissed lips to lips with immense emotion. Both knew what they had to go through, Georgina especially.

"May I ask you a question, Georgina?" Faith asked after a moment's pause.

Georgina was lying on her back, contemplating future events with her eyes closed. "Why not. I am not sure if I will be able to answer though."

"When we were sexually engaged with each other, who were you thinking of, who was going through your mind? Me or somebody else?" Faith waited for a reply from the beautiful creature lying next to her.

Georgina breathed slowly and surely. Eventually she turned her head towards Faith and kissed her gently. "Your brother-in-law. Who were you thinking of? Me?" Georgina answered, nearly smiling.

Faith leaned across and kissed Georgina. "Sorry, I should never have asked." Faith climbed out of the bed with a yearning for the very same man; Stefan Desailley, her brother-in-law.

Chapter 19

The Report

"I am afraid to say that the last few days have been very confusing. First of all, I did what you asked of me. You told me that your wife was travelling to London by train. Your chap wasn't much good to me because your wife knows him and he so had to remain out of sight for most of the time. Fortunately, she travelled first class and remained at the front of the train, whereas we stayed at the back in third class."

Fulwar Cavner stopped his private detective. "Was there anyone else on the train with her?"

"No. She appeared to be completely alone. The first thing that was completely odd was that she left the train at Maidenhead. With her luggage she took a short carriage trip to a bed and breakfast-cum-restaurant called the Grenfell Arms. We thought she must have been fed up with the travelling and wanted a stopover for the night. Anyhow, we kept watch on the place. Most of the people going in and out were in pairs or groups but one single fellow went in when it was dark at about eight o'clock, unfortunately we depended on silhouettes only. Later he left alone, appearing to be quite drunk. Your operative helped him to where he was staying; a hotel called Redroofs, before returning back to the Grenfell. Shortly afterwards, your wife left the Grenfell accompanied by who we thought was one of the waiters. Again, it was very dark and difficult to see and we depended on the lighting from within the restaurant when the door was opened. She also went to Redroofs, and her attendant left her at the door."

Fulwar was becoming impatient because the detective was taking too much time. "Come on! So, what did you conclude?"

"You'll have to wait until I explain, sir," the detective replied, annoyed at the interruption and thinking that his paymaster was being irrational.

"I'm sorry, please continue," Fulwar apologised.

"It was at this point that I was not sure whether or not she was having an affair, or at least meeting somebody. We waited all night outside of Redroofs Hotel, taking it in turns to stay awake. At first light a carriage pulled up and a woman dressed in a veiled, bright red and white dress alighted onto the pavement. She was in the hotel for no longer than ten minutes and then she reappeared and left in the waiting carriage. We don't know her identity or whether she has any connection with your wife at all. We waited for probably half an hour and then the drunken chap whom your man helped back to Redroofs the evening before came out arm in arm with a woman. He had hardly any luggage, just a briefcase. We haven't a clue who he was, or her for that matter, but she certainly wasn't your wife. Your operative followed them both to the station and he went westward towards Bristol while she embarked on the London train. We never saw him again all weekend. I went inside and bribed the receptionist, and she told me the room he'd occupied was booked under the name of Edgar Collison. Your wife, presuming it was your wife the night before, by that time was nowhere to be seen."

Fulwar held his hand up. "Wait a minute. I know that name from somewhere," he said scratching his head. He paced up and down for a while studying the floor, and then asked the detective to carry on.

"The next day, Saturday, we waited across the road from the theatre in Holborn. As arranged, your wife appeared. I am afraid to say that she was arm in arm with a tall gentleman, and they seemed quite comfortable together. Importantly, they were with another couple and a single woman. The female partner of the other couple was none other than the woman who we saw leaving the hotel in Maidenhead the morning before and went on to catch the London bound train." He waited for Fulwar to say something.

Fulwar tried to fathom it out. "She might be the woman called Faith who invited Georgina down to London to go to the theatre. I read her letter. It's coming back to me now. Collison is the Brigadier's surname in Bibury. We went to their Summer Ball. I think who you saw Georgina with on Saturday at the theatre is perhaps the Brigadier's son, Edgar. Faith could possibly be his sister. I don't know her married name but I vaguely remember her escorting me over to the main house on the night of the Ball. I was introduced to them all earlier that evening but there were too many people to recall who was who." Fulwar's voice began to sound serious. His alcohol problem exacerbated his memory loss. He could see the people in his mind but could not put names to faces.

"Excuse me, Mr Cavner. You could well be right. Let me carry on a minute please. After the theatre they all took a carriage and went to a back street restaurant called Dolly's. Some time later they left on foot and eventually entered a house in Leather Lane, presumably the home of Faith and her husband.

"After some considerable time the lights went out and we assumed that they had all retired to bed. It was cold and we hired a carriage in which to sit at the end of the street so we could watch the house all night. Just after nine in the morning a carriage pulled up and a very flustered man who you believe to be Mr Collison left the house. Your operative followed his carriage early that Sunday morning back to Woolwich Barracks. When the gentleman had departed inside your man questioned his driver, and asked the name of his last passenger. He was told that it was a Captain Edgar Collison. Not only that, he told him the name of the person who owned the house from where he had been picked up in Leather Lane and who had paid the fare. A Mr Gerard Havrincourt. Though one strange thing is, why was Edgar Collison's name on the hotel register in Maidenhead when he was nowhere to be seen? If we can relate the names Collison and Havrincourt, especially by family, then there could be a good case of adultery within your marriage." Other than that the detective was puzzled.

"In which case why was the woman named Faith in Maidenhead, and who was she with when she left the hotel? And where did my wife disappear to when you can positively say that you saw her in Maidenhead?" Fulwar was angry. "And what did he look like? I mean that chap Faith was cavorting with."

"He was at least six foot tall and a very powerful man. He was muscular and he had a moustache and dark tousled hair. He was a good looking fellow, and I am sure he would be popular with many women."

Fulwar couldn't recall anyone of that description at the Summer Ball. "I don't remember. There were quite a lot of people there that night. That other girl you saw Georgina with at the weekend, was she quite short but pretty?"

"Yes. That fits her description. Why? Who might she be?" asked the detective.

"Mary Buchanan, my wife's cousin. The pair of them are good friends. She lives just outside London." Fulwar wondered what she was doing there. Both of them were up to no good. "I'm going to ask you if you could visit Brockhampton and Bibury and see what else you might be able to find out. I'll pay you now for the weekend and some money up front for your trip south. Is that all right with you?"

"Yes, thank you. This time I will go alone. Your man can be a hindrance because your wife knows him. One question though, is your wife back home?" the detective asked.

Fulwar nodded. "Yes, she arrived yesterday evening."

As the detective left the castle Fulwar went to the drinks cabinet and poured himself a large scotch. He sat down in his armchair by the fire, brooding over the information he had just acquired.

Chapter 20
The Backlash

"Edward, I think you had better go and find your father. Persuade him to return here immediately, please," Maria said to her son as she tightly held a letter in her lap, and her hands visibly shook as he left the room. She stood and paced the room waiting for her husband, occasionally gazing at the message in disbelief. She shook her head and held a hand over her mouth, trying to hold back the tears.

Sir Charles walked into the room followed by Edward, and saw his wife quite distraught.

"My darling! What is the matter?"

Maria held the letter out before him, and most reluctantly he took it from her unsteady hand. Near the window in brighter light he read what had affected his wife.

"The man is an animal!" he shouted after reading the letter, which he screwed up tightly in his fist. "He cannot be allowed to carry on like this. We'll have to somehow put a stop to his abhorrent behaviour!"

Edward took the letter from his father's hand, straightened it out and then slowly read it, shaking his head incredulously. "Poor Georgina," he said sadly. "She must be in such a bad way that a nurse has had to put pen on paper for her."

"And by the sound of that letter she won't be coming out of hospital for some time, it will take weeks for those injuries to heal," Sir Charles bemoaned.

"Why doesn't Frederick do anything about him? Why does he just turn a blind eye?" Maria asked her husband.

Sir Charles' face wore a grim expression. "Frederick was almost as bad as his son at the same age, and that is why Isabella also says nothing. Frederick will almost certainly take sides with Fulwar." He went quiet but then a sense of realisation came over him. "I suppose Georgina will have to come down here to recuperate, but what happens when she is well again? And that depends on whether she makes a full recovery," he added.

"Edward, when she is able to leave hospital you'll have to go and escort her because it will be impossible for her to travel here on her own," his mother said. "I'll reply to the letter and ask when she will be fit enough to leave the infirmary. Also, we ought to try and get those children down here. It can't be doing them an iota of good seeing their mother being beaten up so often." Maria's concern was all too apparent but she knew bringing the children to Brockhampton would be a dangerous and divisive move within the family, which could cost them their own home and livelihood.

"I think we will have to consider the children in the future," Sir Charles noted with pragmatism. "First of all we need to stabilise Georgina but we'll have to wait and see what the reply is to the letter you send."

"I will reply immediately, and will keep it short and sweet." Maria left her husband and son to muse over the dire situation.

The next morning Edward left Brockhampton alone on horseback. He headed south towards a village with which he was unfamiliar. It was a journey he had no wish to make as the cold early October wind had already begun to blow hard from the northeast. The remaining leaves on the trees fluttered across his path, and sporadic rain showers slashed his face and reddening his cheeks as he made his way to the village of Chedworth nestling on the side of a steep inclination amongst mixed woodland.

The fieldfares and redwings had made their way from the cold north, returning to the high ground and feeding off the residue of the autumn harvest.

Edward followed the Coln River until he reached the tiny hamlet of Woodbridge, where he guided his mount to the right, upwards through the dense hillside forest, keeping to the main bridleway. It was steep but his powerful steed plodded onwards until they reached the plain at the top. From there they veered left and entered the upper slopes of Chedworth Village. Passing below the ancient walls of a church, and then with the Seven Tuns on his right, he soon found the house for which he had been given directions.

"Can you help me, please? I am interested in speaking privately to Mrs Hope Ronssoy," Edward spoke quietly but was perfectly polite.

"Who might I say is enquiring, sir?" the maid asked, equally well mannered.

"Edward Corbett-Cavner, young lady. Please tell her that it is important and I need to speak with her."

Sceptically, the sweet girl turned and went into the house, only for the butler to quickly return and usher Edward off the doorstep. "Come this way, please."

Edward followed, as might an obedient dog. In a side room he was introduced to Hope by her butler, who then left them to talk of the reasons for Edward's sudden appearance. He refused an offer of tea. Hope sat down and courteously asked him to take the chair opposite but Edward was nervous, "No! Please! Read this," he said, and he gave Hope the letter his parents had received the day before.

Hope read it. "This is going too far," she told him passively and handed it back.

"You need to explain that to your sister. I personally do not know what is happening but Faith is involved somewhere along the line. Georgina has been beaten badly again. She is hospitalised. This surely has to stop, Mrs Ronssoy. Faith has to avoid aggravating Fulwar before he kills his wife. Georgina is my cousin, for Christ's sake. Stefan must also have a hand in all this."

Hope turned on Edward. "How dare you say that! He knows nothing. Like yourself, the less Stefan knows the better."

Hope rose from her chair and placed her hand on the mantelpiece with her head resting on her forearm. At first she stared down at the embers smouldering in the grate and then she glanced over her shoulder at Edward.

"I will write to Faith and speak of Georgina's incapacity," she said calmly. "You are right, this must stop but just remember, Edward, the Cavners are not our family. I did know that Georgina and Faith were in London together recently. They enjoyed a visit to the theatre, I gather." Hope approached the concerned Edward. "Tell me, what will now happen to your poor beleaguered cousin?"

"She will almost certainly have to take refuge at Brockhampton. Mother and Father have already sanctioned her respite there. Time will tell. I have come here on orders from Georgina herself from some time ago because she asked me that if anything goes wrong I should come here and tell you. Why, I do not know but please remember that she is related to me and I am quite fond of her. I will see myself out." Edward, not often forthright, turned and left, leaving Hope standing alone in the middle of the room.

Hope, deep in thought went straight to her writing desk. She needed to let Faith know what had happened. She kept thinking of poor Georgina. Hope was involved with a woman she barely knew, having met her only once, and even then had hardly spoken to her. Faith would have to deal with the problem.

Hope began to write.

Edward headed in the opposite direction from Brockhampton; further southwest towards Bibury. The weather had changed for the worse, with the wind blowing even harder and the rain incessant, making him wish he'd driven the carriage. Fortunately he had brought with him a full-length oilskin coat and a leather wide brimmed hat.

He rode down into the village from Ablington and veered right over the bridge and up the hill towards the Catherine Wheel. Inside there was a roaring log fire, and he hung his coat and hat nearby before discreetly asking to talk with the landlord in private.

Edward was ushered into the passageway behind the bar. "I desperately need to speak to Mr Desailley but I can only do so away from his house. Is it possible to get a message to him and tell him I am here?"

"I take it that you mean Stefan Desailley, the Brigadier's son-in-law, and not his father, Marcel?"

Edward nodded.

"Who do I say wants to speak to him?" he asked.

"Edward Cavner. He knows me. I have some important news for him but I cannot stay long." Edward needed to return to Brockhampton as soon as possible. The weather was inclement enough and showing all signs of worsening.

"I'll send someone right away. Go back into the bar and warm yourself by the fire," Lionel's father told him, then summoned the girl who helped in the kitchen and cleaned the rooms. He asked her to find Stefan and tell him of Edward's presence but to be very discreet. She set off immediately as Edward waited, shivering by the fire with a large whisky in hand.

Stefan arrived, eager to hear what Edward had to say, and they shook hands and sat down in the window seat out of earshot from anyone.

"I am afraid Georgina has been beaten up badly. She has broken ribs, arm, collarbone and nose, let alone extensive bruising. Here read this."

Stefan read the letter shaking his head throughout. He finished it and passed it back to Edward. "Stefan, I think something is going on between her and your two sisters-in-law. Probably Mary is involved as well. Why would they all suddenly go to the theatre together when they barely know each other? Georgina asked me some time ago if anything went badly wrong I should go and tell Mrs Ronssoy. It seems strange. Why would she want me to tell Hope? Let alone Faith." Edward was sincerely uneasy about Georgina but felt whatever the women were up to was exacerbating Fulwar's mood swings.

"How did you know they went to the theatre?" Stefan asked him.

"Mary sent us a letter telling us before they went. Why she did, I don't know. It all seems so very odd." Edward was at a complete loss as to what was going on.

Stefan wasn't sure if he should tell Edward about his trip to Maidenhead and the women swapping their clothes in the morning. That was all also very odd. "Do I take it that Georgina will be coming down to Brockhampton?" he asked.

"Yes, probably, but I don't know how long for. It might be permanent because she can't carry on with her life in that abominable fashion." Edward turned and gazed out of the window at the falling rain and swirling leaves.

"What would happen to the children if that were the case?" Stefan was interested to know.

"There is no possibility that Fulwar would allow them to leave the estate. They would stay with him and their grandparents." Edward shrugged his shoulders, to him that matter was closed.

"How old are they?" Stefan asked him.

"The boy is ten and the girl is probably eight now." He wasn't completely sure. "I am sorry, Stefan, but I have to ride back to Brockhampton. It was bad enough coming down here. What I've told you is between us both but those women are definitely planning something. We need to find out what. If you hear something, please let me know because they might be inadvertently putting our estate in a perilous position, let alone Georgina's life." Edward stood up and retrieved his coat and hat, which were still very damp. He reluctantly donned them both, took another look out of the window, shook Stefan's hand and went back out into the wet and cold.

Many times during the last few months Stefan had stared through the same window whilst deep in thought, and today was no exception.

A woman he had a deep respect for lay injured in an infirmary far away. Every day he dreamed of her, and during the night he awoke thinking of her. As he lay next to his sleeping wife with her mental frigidity his sexual exploits with Georgina were foremost in his mind. He wondered whether he was chained to the woman he was married to now or to the woman he had originally married.

"Wake up! Come on!" The words shocked Stefan, and two beers slammed down on the table. "Your mind is wandering off again," Lionel said, smiling. "What were you thinking about this time? Drink up, you fool. Here have another beer." Lionel slid a pint of frothing ale towards Stefan.

"Why are you so happy?" Stefan asked and then reverted his eyes back out of the window. "Christmas is far away."

Lionel smiled. "Mary sent me a letter this morning. She is coming down to stay a few days in Bibury. The Brigadier says she can use one of the small bedrooms."

Stefan was flabbergasted. "The Brigadier says it is all right?" It was an observation and also a question.

"Yes. He knows that we have been writing to each other for some time now. Anyhow, why would he object?" Lionel studied Stefan's face.

Nothing added up to Stefan. Mary was coming to Bibury; Georgina could be going to stay at Brockhampton; in the near past there had been an odd theatre trip to London; and Edward Cavner had today visited Hope. Where was all this leading? Then there was Maidenhead. Faith was definitely involved there. The change of clothing between the women at the hotel was still unexplained. He shouldn't have had sexual intercourse with Faith because now he could only remain resolutely quiet. Would Faith tell Charity? He had been a fool, and now he couldn't ask any questions for fear of Charity finding out. Why didn't they want him to know?

He looked across to Lionel. "Does the Brigadier ever say anything about the Cavner family? Anything inappropriate or detrimental?"

"No. I've never heard him. He says very little about them." Lionel spoke as how he understood the situation. He himself was preoccupied with Mary coming to stay.

"Has he been receiving any excess post lately or over the last few months?" Stefan asked.

Lionel thought back. "He has but it's mostly from Faith. I can tell from her handwriting. She is worried about her father's health, I presume. As his butler I am not privy to the contents of his letters."

Both men decided to meet together in the Swan early that evening and after a couple more beers went their separate ways.

Chapter 21

Infidelity Exposed

"What is the matter, Stefan? What is grieving you?" Charity asked, sensing the tension in Stefan's mind. "Your mood has changed. Is it the woman who is affecting you? Something has happened, hasn't it? Something serious. You can tell me if you want."

Stefan glanced at the clock on the wall as its pendulum swung methodically, slowly ticking away the seconds. He was to meet Lionel at six o'clock and had only twenty minutes before leaving.

Stefan suddenly made a momentous decision. "Sit down, Charity. I will tell you the whole story because I need someone I can trust."

Stefan told his wife everything from his original meeting with Georgina and his first sexual exploit with her in Sennington barn. He explained to Charity her problems with Fulwar and the beatings he gave her during his alcoholic rages. Stefan never minced his words. Avoiding the details Charity heard about the Bull Inn at Fairford, his meeting in Maidenhead but avoided telling her of his liaison with Faith. He told her he was suspicious about the Summer Ball and about Georgina cavorting with Edgar. There was also her visit to the theatre in London with Faith, and Mary was connected at both events. He again mentioned Edward Cavner and his meeting with Hope that day, and then his own subsequent meeting with him in the Catherine Wheel, where he was told about Georgina's current hospitalisation. He tried to explain how Edward believed that all four women were contriving something or other but he didn't know what.

Stefan looked at the clock. "I have to go, Charity. I am meeting Lionel soon. I've told you all there is I know. I am not holding anything back." He rose from his seat with the intention of leaving.

"Before you go there is one thing I'd like to know," she said as she stared sullenly into his eyes.

He almost knew what she was going to ask. "What is that?"

"Have you fallen in love with Georgina?" Charity wasn't sure if she really wanted to know but if he had, she herself felt mostly to blame.

Stefan hesitated. "I don't see her very often, although she is on my mind a lot. I physically lust for her because she is a beautiful woman. She doesn't deserve to be assaulted and humiliated. When she first told me, all I could think of was to try to help her in any way I could, and not in my wildest dreams did I imagine having an affair with somebody else's wife."

"You still haven't answered my question." Charity continued to stare into his eyes.

"Charity, I think your biggest problem would be whether she has fallen in love with me." He shrugged his shoulders and glanced once more at the clock, "I'm going up the Swan." Without another word he turned and left.

The children soon came in from playing outside, which diverted Charity's mind away from her marital problems.

Sitting in the Swan with Lionel, Stefan told him of Edward's unexpected visit and their brief discussion of the letter. He had not intended to say anything to him but, after careful consideration, felt it better that Lionel knew, especially as he and Mary seemed to be very happy together in each other's company. He then went on and told him of his heart to heart with Charity and that he had divulged everything to her.

Lionel looked at his soul-mate and shook his head. "Stefan, if you are not careful you are going to dig yourself into a hole that you won't be able to climb out of. I know Charity has problems but you must consider your position on the estate. Apart from having a good job, you have a home that you don't pay anything for. Don't ruin your life for the sake of sexual satisfaction with a woman you might never be able to have. And if it does come to that, both of you will, in all likelihood, be penniless and out on the streets."

"I probably will be anyway when Edgar gets back here. Everyone knows what he thinks of me, and I still wonder why, all those years ago, he was so angry with the Brigadier when he was informed that Charity and I were going to marry." Stefan could only visualise problems on the horizon.

Lionel decided to go off on another tack. "When Mary comes down to Bibury soon for a week, maybe she'll be able to tell us something."

Stefan was surprised. "If what Edward believes is true then she'll be under strict instructions to remain silent on the matter. None of these women are giving anything away."

The two men sat in silent contemplation for several moments before Stefan thought of something. "Was there any mention of Georgina being beaten up in that letter you received this morning from Mary?"

"Nothing at all. In fact, there was no mention of her at all."

"But why–"

At that moment the door opened and Neil Portlock entered the bar on his way back to the Catherine Wheel from work, and the conversation between the two came to halt.

Neil could sense that there was something wrong or something he was not supposed to hear but, nevertheless, bought a round of beers and they sat talking about what to do the following day.

As Stefan and Neil had time off work the next day, he suggested taking him along the river and teaching him the art of grayling fishing, weather permitting. They agreed that it was the best idea and Stefan proceeded to explain the methodology of fly-fishing; one of his favourite pastimes.

Lionel sat back, disinterested; he had heard it all before. Some time afterwards all three drank their beer and left the Swan to continue their soirée at the Catherine Wheel.

Stefan and Neil left Bibury on foot at first light the following morning, with Stefan deciding to fish the river between Bibury and the pretty hamlet of Coln St Aldwyns. With its open stretches of water and having few trees or bushes in which to entangle a beginner's line it would suit Neil.

Shortly after Stefan had left, Charity asked Elizabeth, their eldest daughter, to go and organise a carriage to take them all to Chedworth. One of the estate's employees pulled up in a carriage soon after, picked up Charity and her children and set off on their journey to visit Hope.

She didn't have much time because she knew only too well that as soon as the alehouses were open in the morning Stefan would be one of the first sitting drinking. With his new found friend it would be an inevitable fact.

Neil took to fishing like a duck to water, and in no time his casts were quite accurate. His only setback was trying to remember which artificial nymphs, flies or larvae to use on the river, and the season they should be introduced.

"The fish are not stupid," Stefan persistently told him.

They took a brief rest and sat on the bank eating bread with cheese and beetroot. Stefan had brought a costrel of cider, which they shared; that was an indication as to how the day would develop. There was little wind, ideal for fishing, but the clouds showed no signs of lifting.

"How are you getting along with my father?" Stefan asked.

"Fine. He is an interesting old fellow and talks a lot about the Napoleonic wars, but I listen as a good student does." He laughed, spluttering food into the river. "He has to be careful what he says because sometimes he sides for Napoleon and other times he sides for Wellington."

"I'm afraid if you give him the chance he will sit and talk about European wars all day. It is a passion he has. Still, at least he's not out there participating. He always used to quote an old saying, 'it is pointless going to war unless there is love'. When you think about it, it is true. You fight for something for which you have a passion but if there is no passion or love to fight for, it is murder." Stefan went quiet.

Neil watched him swilling the remains of the cider around, mulling something over, and Neil wanted to ask him whom he intended to fight for, Charity or Georgina, but then thought better of it. His information came from rumour only, and he was on dangerous ground. The less said the better.

Stefan suddenly jumped up, drank the remaining cider and looked down at Neil. "Let's fish for another hour and then I'll take you to a little pub in Coln St Aldwyns. From there I'll arrange a lift back to Bibury."

Neil did not disagree and eased himself off the ground.

Charity stayed talking with Hope for more than an hour whilst her children played on the expansive lawn. Their conversation was serious and Hope agreed that she should write to Faith for the second time in as many days and update her on all that was happening.

Charity's instincts were to be proved correct later on in the day. Stefan had indeed made it to an alehouse, and she and her children arrived back at Bibury before her husband returned from his so-called fishing trip.

Chapter 22
The Set Up

"I have to tell you this, Edgar. The government will do little to assist you in bringing your wife and three daughters from India to England," Gerard announced with mock sympathy." From the powers that be, their attitude is that when you officially leave the army you have to make your own strides towards arranging their immigration papers, financially and bureaucratically. Our company can, of course, help but the financing will have to come from you." He was lying but for Edgar to instigate an Indian woman and her three young daughters as possible inheritors of the Bibury Court estate was completely out of the question. He needed to stall Edgar and he had most of the Collison family on his side.

Edgar paced around the room, clearly disappointed. He had hoped that when he returned to Bibury his wife and family would be on their way to England.

"Another thing, Faith has asked me to tell you that Georgina has been badly hurt."

"How? How badly?" Edgar asked, concerned.

Gerard thought it strange that one moment Edgar could be so anxious about his wife in India and then the next moment be anxious about Georgina.

"Well, it's not life threatening by any means but she is severely injured nonetheless, and she is in on the mend in an infirmary." Gerard told Edgar everything that Hope had written in the letter to Faith.

"Damn the man! Something has to be done about him. He needs to be put down like a rabid dog." Edgar was incredibly angry.

Gerard couldn't agree more. "There is little you can do. The authorities will not step in. They consider it a marital problem, and only the two parties can sort it out between themselves"

"I'll take some leave and go and see her," Edgar said, nodding his head as if he'd made his mind up.

"What are you going to do if you meet her husband?" Gerard asked.

"I cannot imagine a coward would do something like that to his wife and then go and pay her a courtesy visit. No, I'll leave tomorrow. She needs help." Edgar was determined to visit the stricken woman.

Gerard arrived home from work and Faith greeted him in the hallway. "Well! What happened?" she asked.

"He's doing exactly what you wanted, and sooner than you expected. Tomorrow he is travelling to Ludlow to see Georgina." Gerard was sceptical about the whole affair but wouldn't say anything against his wife. If Fulwar found out that Edgar was at Ludlow visiting Georgina, at least she would be safe in the hospital, he thought.

Chapter 23
Marcel Desailley

Every Tuesday evening Stefan took his family to his parents' home for dinner. His mother's cooking was distinctively French, subject to the availability of the ingredients, and it was her natural talent and the preferred tastes of the Brigadier that kept her gainfully employed at the estate. Her grandchildren in particular enjoyed *coq au vin*, which was sitting steaming hot in the centre of the table when they arrived. Vegetables accompanied the tasty dish, and a short prayer was said before they all began to eat. Each child was allowed a small glass of wine to wash down the dinner; a French custom that Frankie turned his nose up at in disgust.

A pudding was soon served, and the children squabbled over the size of their allotted portions. Charity divided them equally and they fell into silence as they ate with eyes aglow.

Afterwards, Stefan sat with his father drinking brandy. "So, how do you find Mr Portlock, Papa?"

Marcel answered in his accented English. "He is a hard working man and is good at his job, but I don't think he learnt his trade in the factories of northern England."

"Where then? He did admit to not knowing much about the agricultural trade." Stefan was interested.

"I think he was in the army. As you know, many of our recent ancestors fought in the Napoleonic wars, and the lucky ones who returned always told stories of those times. Fortunately, I was too young to fight." Marcel smiled.

Stefan thought for a while. "Why wouldn't anyone admit to being in the army, especially if you had spent most of your working life there? He must be in his early forties."

"You ask him. You took him fishing the other day. What did you talk about?" Marcel asked, thinking it strange that Stefan hadn't been a bit more candid with his new employee.

"He did say he wants to move his family here to the south but only when he knows he has guaranteed employment." Stefan knew little else about him.

"Did he tell you that he wants to buy a house first?" Marcel knew more about Neil Portlock than his son obviously did. "Where would he have got the money to finance such a move? A loan?"

Stefan was surprised with what his father had told him. "Impossible! Who would possibly lend him the money on his wages? Even on army wages he hasn't a chance of buying, especially around here."

"I think you'll find that he has the money to buy outright. He either has a benefactor or has married into a wealthy family, which is similar, in fact, to someone sitting quite close to me now," Marcel said smiling. "Many things are possible, Stefan, and it is not in our nature to persecute people without knowing all of the facts."

"But why would a man come to a place such as this and take up a paltry job on a farm if he was wealthy? That is ridiculous, especially if he is as intelligent as you imply. I can appreciate that he wants to bring his wife and children to a healthier environment but for him to labour for the rest of his life as a moneyed man seems quite odd."

Stefan was perplexed. Neil Portlock seemed to be a decent enough fellow who was easy to get along with and Stefan would call him a friend one day, providing he stayed around that long.

"Another thing you might like to know then," Marcel mused. "He is forever asking about the Collison family, particularly Edgar. Obviously, rumour has it that there will be wholesale changes on the estate, almost definitely when the Brigadier dies. Perhaps he is simply interested to know what the difference will be when Edgar returns here and eventually owns all the assets."

Stefan's father's words struck a chord. What was going on? Could Neil Portlock also be involved? But why would he be so interested in Edgar? The man apparently has money, or so his father was telling him.

Stefan suddenly stood up. "Papa, can you help me? Do not upset Neil but try to find out as much as you can about him because I need to know what is going on here at Bibury."

"What is on your mind, Stefan? Something has been troubling you. Your mother notices that you are behaving differently." Marcel was naturally worried about his only son.

"Nothing, Papa. It is nothing. Please, just find out from Neil as much information as possible."

Marcel poured another brandy, and Stefan sat back down.

"I don't want to scare him off, Stefan; he is good for me. He is strong and knowledgeable, and if you ask too many questions with people like Neil they disappear into the night. It will be our loss, especially mine."

Stefan knew that Marcel was ageing and but there were still questions to be asked.

Stefan walked home with his wife and children, and soon after was sitting at his desk with a restless mind that refused to allow him to write a single word. Instead, he drank Armagnac and re-shuffled his world time and time again but came to no conclusions, and the more Armagnac he consumed the likelihood grew less and less that he would.

The one definite thing that disturbed him was that Edgar would soon return to Bibury Court. Might his return be the excuse to extract himself from a cold and dispassionate marriage? He knew that it would be a disaster for Charity, but the one person who came to mind every hour of every day was Georgina. He lusted for her but was hopelessly unable to do anything about it.

In his confusion he began to fall asleep. Tomorrow, he told himself, would be a different day with changeable consequences.

Chapter 24
Ludlow Infirmary

Jennifer, an innocent eight-year-old girl, happily skipped along the hospital corridor, and was restrained only by the hand of her elder brother.

At the swing doors a nursing sister crouched down and quietly explained to them how they should behave whilst in her ward. There was to be no shouting, no dancing around and, above all, they must show respect for the other patients.

The little blue-eyed girl smiled and nodded her head, and her brother followed suit. Satisfied, the sister stood and ushered them through the doors.

Contrary to what she had been told, the little girl pulled free and ran to her mother's bed.

"Mammy, Mammy," she shouted, and the boy followed her solemnly, apologising quietly to everyone for his little sister's excitable behaviour. The patients smiled with difficulty, wishing only to be their age once again.

Georgina stretched out her good arm and tried in vain to pull her daughter towards her whilst her son stopped in his tracks when nearing the bed. He couldn't believe that the woman before him was his mother. She was heavily bandaged, both her eyes were blackened and nose misshapen. Never before had he seen her in such a bad condition. He was older now and beginning to realise his father's poor mentality.

Thomas moved towards his mother and leaned over to delicately kiss a ravaged and swollen face, and at the same time he slipped a letter under her pillow. When asked how she was his dear mother claimed to be all right, which she was clearly not. Talking was difficult for her, and her internal bleeding was not visible to the two innocent children.

In great pain, Georgina spoke softly with her children but it wasn't long before the ward sister politely asked them to leave for fear of tiring their mother.

Jennifer didn't wish to go but Thomas coaxed his sister away from the bed and out through the swing doors. The poor child cried so much that their mother could hear her wailings echoing along the corridor.

Georgina lay staring at the ceiling for several minutes, and silent tears spilled onto her pillow. She eventually drifted off to sleep. Time was a great healer.

She was suddenly awoken by a soft kiss on the cheek. Edgar stood beside her with a doctor who tried to explain her internal injuries. Shortly the unconcerned physician left them together.

Edgar grasped her free hand. "My dear Georgina, you can't carry on like this. I implore you to leave that reprehensible coward before he kills you. You would be a great loss to me."

"But where could I go?" she asked. "I would be homeless. Destitute."

"You would be more than welcome at Bibury Court. I will be returning there very shortly, and everything will work out perfectly for us both." Edgar sounded very confident that she would agree.

"What would happen to your wife in India? You just can't ignore her demands," Georgina asked.

"I am not yet sure that she will be allowed to come here, but she is Indian and will recognise that there may be more than one wife in the household." Edgar didn't sound very convincing.

The last thing Georgina wanted was to be shared. "I'm not sure it will work out, Edgar. Not the two of us sharing your bed."

"Georgina, just say yes and I'll arrange with Gerard that my wife cannot come to England. It is as simple as that. We can work something out." Edgar's hopes were now high.

"There is still the question of my two children. If I did as you have asked I would never see them again and I cannot live without them," Georgina said, for once with conviction. This would surely test Edgar's resolve, and she could find out how much he really wanted her to live with him.

"I'll speak with Gerard. He'll know what the legal situation will be, but I am more than sure that we can come to an arrangement. Please, Georgina, everything will turn out fine. I can assure you of that." Edgar gently squeezed her hand.

The sister approached and urged Edgar to leave, and he quickly bent and gently kissed Georgina's swollen face before dutifully obeying the request.

The letter Thomas placed under his mother's pillow remained unread. It was from Charity Desailley.

"Has anybody been in to see her today, other than her children?" Georgina's mother-in-law, Isabella Cavner, asked a young nurse.

"Only her brother," the nurse replied.

"It is strange you should say that because Georgina Cavner does not have a brother," Isabella said vehemently, pushing her way into the ward.

Her visit was also brief, and the two women spoke only of Georgina's intended destination when she was discharged from the infirmary. Georgina, however, was in no position to think about decisions that would affect her future. The only respite she had from the pain and turmoil was the morphine injections which sent her to sleep for long periods of time.

Chapter 25
The Private Detective

Sir Charles was irate because a gentleman he didn't know wished to talk to him without the courtesy of making an appointment. Edward had informed his father that the gentleman had something to do with Fulwar Cavner, and Sir Charles sat impatiently waiting for his son to show the man through.

The door opened and he rose from his chair to be introduced to Mr Willie Greyffos.

"Please, sit down. How can I help you?" Sir Charles asked, being as polite as possible.

Mr Greyffos glanced at Edward, expecting him to leave the room but he remained by the fireplace. "Mr Fulwar Cavner from Stokesay Castle has asked me to investigate his wife, and I understand that she often stays here with your good selves."

Sir Charles stopped him dead. He looked across to Edward, "Edward, please go and find your mother. She will want to hear this."

"Please, no. It is probably best that your good lady is not present," Mr Greyffos suggested out of politeness.

"I am sorry but Georgina is my wife's godchild and blood relative. My wife will definitely want to hear what you have to say. Please, Edward. Go and fetch her."

As they waited Sir Charles curiously asked Mr Greyffos the derivation of his surname.

"When my grandfather arrived in Liverpool from Ireland he couldn't read or write, and the authorities could barely understand his accent. After repeatedly asking him his name, they eventually wrote it down as

Greyffos. Years later his brother came looking for him and finally found him working in the docklands. My family name was actually Dreyfus but by then it was too late and he retained his new name, of which he was actually proud." The story still amused Willie Greyffos and he smiled.

Edward returned with his mother and Sir Charles asked him to begin explaining again the reason for his visit.

"Mr Fulwar Cavner believes that your niece, his wife, has been having an affair but with whom he does not know. At the end of September I followed her to London, where she went to the theatre with various individuals. On the way down to London, the previous night, she stopped off for a sojourn in Maidenhead." Mr Greyffos continued telling the same story he had told Fulwar Cavner, and all three listened intently.

He eventually finished. "This is all I have ascertained thus far, and I was hoping that you could elaborate further, or give any information about the people with whom she had been cavorting.

Maria was livid. Sir Charles went to say something but she raised her hand and he went eerily quiet. Edward tried to thwart his mother from attacking the man who stood impudently before them in their own front room, but she went over to Mr Greyffos and spat in his face.

With the cuff of his sleeve he wiped the saliva from his face in disgust. Never had Sir Charles or Edward seen her seething in such a rage before.

"So, you snoop on the poor woman and then go back and tell your paymaster what you think has happened when you know absolutely nothing," Maria yelled and then suddenly attempted to swipe the visitor around the face, but Edward managed to hold his mother back.

"Did that paranoid alcoholic tell you what he has done to her over the years? He has been the greatest wife beater in the whole of bloody Shropshire. She has been thrashed more times than a bare-knuckle boxer. Would you like to guess where she is now?" she shouted into his face. "No? Well, she has spent the last twelve days in Ludlow Infirmary. And all because of what you suspected. Not knew! Merely suspected!"

"I can assure–"

"Did you actually see her being fucked?" Maria shouted, and gasps from her husband and son were audible.

She waited for an answer but to no avail. "No! No, of course you didn't, and now she lies in a hospital bed struggling like a cripple because you told her husband that she *might* be having an affair. Supposition, you damned worthless idiot! Supposition! You are no better than the useless cretin who employs you."

"Madam, Mr Cavner has employed me to find out what his wife does behind his back, and that is what I do is for a living."

"Surely you have a soul. If you thought that there was something seriously wrong would you not back away and tell him there is nothing proven. What swirls around in Fulwar Cavner's alcoholic mind is relentless. He will pay you to say his wife is immoral and he then feels he is completely vindicated by beating her. He'll then go and drink another bottle of whisky, convince himself that he is the innocent party, beat her up and blame his failing marriage on his wife's apparent misbehaviour. Fulwar Cavner needs to be in an asylum or, better still, hung!" Maria stood back.

"I am afraid, Mr Greyffos, that as much as you are being well paid, I fear that you have taken the side of the devil," Sir Charles said quietly, watching the reaction of the man sat before him.

"You must know that Georgina, my cousin, is a beautiful woman," Edward said in a calm manner. "Perhaps there is little wonder why she looks for alternative love whilst in such a dire marriage. Please believe me. Seek her out and talk to her. She does not deserve what is being physically and mentally bestowed upon her. The man who pays your wages is worse than how my father and mother have portrayed him, and your professional judgement could well be in jeopardy."

"Do you also realise that there are two children involved?" Maria asked, still on edge but she had calmed down considerably. "You must consider them in your findings. Where might they end up? Under the control of a raging alcoholic father?" She hoped Mr Greyffos had understood their family point of view.

"As usual, Georgina will come to recuperate here," Sir Charles added. "Although we don't know how long it will take this time. She is quite ill. Edward is going to escort her here; she is unable to travel alone. I am afraid, Mr Greyffos, that it is far from being the first time this has happened, although this is the worst it has ever been. I hope you understand our predicament."

Edward suggested that he and Mr Greyffos take a walk around the grounds, and Maria couldn't think of a better idea to get him out of her sight.

Edward showed his dubious guest around the stunning gardens with their mature trees and a beautifully kept, man-made lake. Amid the manicured lawns were fine examples of topiary and box hedges. They strolled up the driveway and turned and looked back towards the house.

Edward explained its beginnings in the seventeenth century and how it came into his family's possession. As they walked back they detoured to the orchard and kitchen garden and sat down on a bench seat.

"I am afraid to say it, Mr Greyffos, but you are taking the wrong side with this issue. The more information you pass back to Fulwar Cavner, whether true or false, will only incense him even more. He is a very unstable man and I honestly believe that he will one day instigate her murder. If Georgina is having an affair outside of her marriage then he has only himself to blame." Edward went quiet. He desperately wanted Greyffos to refrain and report Georgina's innocence even though he knew deep down that it wasn't the case.

Mr Greyffos stared out across the garden. He never looked across at Edward. "So you think he'll have her killed off at some point?"

"I do, but I don't know what other people might be thinking. You wouldn't want your name linked with anyone's death, would you? Or is that in your line of work as well?"

For some time Willie Greyffos said nothing, he just watched the wood pigeons foraging in the cabbage patch. Eventually he turned towards Edward. "Normally, my line of work involves catching murderers, and sometimes there is a large reward for such successes."

They spoke for some considerable time, and the private detective told Edward his side of the story.

"Tonight I will be staying in the Cavner Arms and tomorrow I will be taking a coach to Bibury. Is there anything else you would like to tell me before I leave? Anything I might need to know?"

"On the way to Bibury stop at Chedworth and speak to Hope Ronssoy. She is one of three Collison sisters, and they all dislike their own brother, Edgar. From what you have told me you know him and the elder sister, Faith. The sisters are up to something but I don't know what. Hope is worth talking to. There is a problem with the younger sister, Charity. There are strange goings on in her mind. All I will say is that I think that there is a link between Hope and Fulwar Cavner's wife but I'll leave that for you to find out."

Edward said no more other than to recommend the Catherine Wheel in Bibury as a place to stay should he eventually arrive there.

The next morning at first light Edward reluctantly set off for Bibury. He needed to speak to Stefan and then leave the village before Mr Greyffos arrived. He trotted, galloped and walked Eugene. The exercise would do the animal good. In just over an hour he knocked on the gatehouse door and Charity answered looking sullen.

"Hello. How can I help?" she asked submissively.

"Mrs Desailley, I wish to speak to your husband please," he tried to soften his urgency, "I'll wait outside," he added.

Stefan came to the door and was surprised to see Edward. At first he thought he was the bearer of bad news. They spoke briefly and he went back inside to don his boots.

Away from the house Edward questioned him. "One morning, at the end of September, you were seen coming out of a hotel in Maidenhead with, I can only presume, Faith. Is that true?"

"Yes." Stefan couldn't deny it. "How do you know?"

"Was Georgina there that night? Someone seems to think she was."

"Who does? Fulwar?" Stefan asked.

"I'll tell you who if you tell me the truth. Was she there or not?" Edward sounded a little irate.

"Yes, she was." Stefan went on to tell him his side of the story that night from the very beginning until Faith arrived and they swapped their clothes. He didn't mention the sexual intercourse with Faith.

"Why didn't you tell me this the last time we met?" Edward asked.

"What good would it have done? Besides, how *do* you know about all of this?"

"Do you know who paid your bill in the hotel?"

"Well, it wasn't the imaginary publishers so I presume it could only have been Georgina." Stefan thought that it was a strange question.

"No. It was your brother-in-law, Edgar Collison. That was the name the receptionist gave when asked." Edward watched the expression on Stefan's face change dramatically.

"What!" Stefan was dumbfounded. "Come on, Edward. Who told you all of this? It is completely bizarre."

"The person who saw you leave the hotel that morning also saw you stumble back to it the night before. And that person paid my family a visit yesterday. He is a private detective working for Fulwar, and he is on his way here to Bibury today. He will undoubtedly want to find out the identity of who was with Faith that morning, because he knows it wasn't Edgar who paid the bill." Edward wanted to tell him about the theatre trip and Edgar's presence on that particular night but he remembered what Hope had told him, 'Stefan must not know what is happening', he would let him find out for himself.

"So, what's he going to do when he arrives here? Ask a few questions and then what?" Stefan shrugged his shoulders. "He can't prove anything?"

"No, but anything this private detective does find out he'll go back and tell Fulwar, which will make him go off on one of his rages again. Fortunately, Georgina will hopefully be out of the firing range for the time being. I gave him Hope's address and told him to talk with her before coming here. We need to get him on our side, and perhaps he will come over if Hope verifies what Georgina has been going through."

"I am going to have to speak to this so-called detective. What do I care when he finds out who I am? I'll just tell him what I think in no uncertain terms. He can't upset Charity because she knows everything anyway."

Edward stopped him. "What! She knows about you and Georgina?"

"Yes. She has done for a while. What is the man's name anyway?" Stefan asked, adamant that he could not lose by talking to the detective.

"Willie Greyffos, or so he tells me. I recommended the Catherine Wheel, so if he does stay in Bibury you'll probably find him there."

Suddenly, a woman shouting from a window to someone in the grounds of the main house broke their conversation.

"Who is that?" Edward asked.

"I thought you would know. It's Mary Buchanan. She is down here for a week to see Lionel. I'm surprised you haven't been told about them," Stefan smiled "Relax, she's good for him."

"I'd better go and see her before I head back," Edward said, and the two men parted. Edward headed towards the main house whilst Stefan went to find his father.

"Papa, where is Neil? I need to speak to him," Stefan said, sounding as if it was urgent.

"A ploughshare has broken. He is up near Knoll Barn. If you need him badly go and find him, otherwise they are trying to bring the plough back here for repair. What is the matter, Stefan? You don't seem yourself." Marcel was still anxious about his son.

"Please, when he gets back tell him to come and find me. It might be important. I'll be at home."

A little later Stefan ushered Neil Portlock into his study. "Sit down, Neil. Would you fancy a glass of Armagnac? Only the best." Neil did not refuse. "I'm going to ask you a favour but first there is something I want to know".

"Is it about your father's health?" Neil interjected.

"No. Why do you ask that?" Stefan queried.

"He is definitely unwell. I've tried to persuade him to see a doctor but he just says that there is nothing wrong with him. There is little I can do but it would be best if you or even the Brigadier said something to him." Stefan stared at a picture on the wall before turning back to Neil. "I'm obviously missing something. I'll go and speak to my mother and find out what she knows." Stefan felt guilty because of his own preoccupation with Georgina.

"The reason why I've asked you here was not about my father. What is your interest in Edgar Collison? You apparently keep asking questions about him."

Neil was taken aback. He didn't realise that he had been so noticeable, but he was quick to make an excuse. "I understand he'll be back here in a couple of weeks to take over the running of the estate from his father, and I was only wondering what the man was like and what were my chances of remaining here. A new brush sweeps clean, so to speak. There's a lot being said about him and none of it is complimentary, if you don't mind my saying so."

"Not at all. I'm afraid Edgar's unpopularity might go a lot deeper than you think. We'll have to wait and see. How long were you in the army?" Stefan watched the response on Neil's face.

Neil felt if he admitted being in the army Stefan might find a link between himself and Edgar, although generally the chances were slight. "I was in the Northumberland's; an infantry regiment. I left years ago." He lied.

Stefan had said enough on the subject to put pressure on Neil Portlock. "You have to realise that it might be in both of our interests that Edgar Collison doesn't return here, or at least not for long. I want you to do something for me. Probably staying at the Catherine Wheel tonight will be a gentleman named Willie Greyffos. He is investigating a woman who has been having an extra-marital affair."

Neil stopped him, "Is this the woman village rumours say you have been involved with?"

Stefan had to concede. "Yes. I want you to find out all he knows, if you can. Tell him the man he needs to speak to is me and, say that you'll arrange for him to meet me here at, let's say, ten o'clock tomorrow morning. Stefan didn't want to confront Mr Greyffos in the Catherine Wheel, especially under the influence of alcohol. "Will you do that?" Neil agreed and Stefan proceeded to tell him everything he knew from the very beginning.

As Neil walked back to work he wondered if he could reciprocate and also trust Stefan, and tell him the truth about his real motives for being at Bibury.

"No one stayed at the Catherine Wheel last night, nor was there anyone in the bar I didn't know," Neil said, shrugging his shoulders. There was nothing more he could say.

Stefan saddled up his horse and rode to Chedworth at a pace that suited his old mare. Hope greeted him but when he questioned her about Mr Greyffos she denied having any visitors the day before. Maybe she was lying and didn't want to tell Stefan anything because it had been agreed that it would be left to Faith to divulge snippets of information as time went on.

Stefan rode slowly back towards Bibury, still mystified. Had Edward been lying to throw him of the scent? Was he also a part of the conspiracy? He decided to stop in Fossebridge at the Lord Chedworth Arms on his way home. The local clientele still retained the original name despite it being registered as The Fossebridge Inn.

Here he met some old acquaintances and overstayed his welcome. His dependence on Marengo was urgent, and a single word in her ear – "Bibury" – set her off independently with Stefan slumped on her back.

She went no further than the Catherine Wheel.

Chapter 26
Faith and Gerard

"So, where are you going from here? Is your jigsaw puzzle coming together?" Gerard asked his wife.

"Georgina is leaving hospital this week, and Edward is going to Ludlow to help her because she is still quite poorly. At first she will spend some time recuperating at Brockhampton but she won't be able to stay there forever. Sir Charles doesn't want to be seen favouring her on a permanent basis. Hope, however, says that she can stay with her at Chedworth. Her house is more than adequate, it is secluded and it is ideally situated between Bibury and Brockhampton. If all goes well very few people will know she is there, especially her husband."

"And then what?" Gerard asked.

"When Edgar's back at Bibury we'll tell him where Georgina is staying and he'll be on to her like a fly on a summer cow pat. It might even keep him away from the estate, which is what we all want," Faith concluded with a half-hearted smile. She was playing a dangerous game.

Gerard shook his head. He wasn't sure everything would work out. "What will happen if Fulwar finds out where she is?"

"That is ultimately what we want to happen but first we must rescue Georgina's children. They are the trump card in all this. Georgina is going to persuade Edgar to organise removing them from their school and taking them down to Chedworth. The boy doesn't want to stay with his father anyway, so it might be an easier task than we think. But we're jumping ahead. The first thing is to have Georgina healthy and settled."

"I can't see Stefan being at all happy with the arrangement, especially when he finds out Georgina has been cavorting with Edgar."

"He's bound to find out one way or another but the longer he doesn't find out, the better it will be for us all. You know what he's like, Gerard; he'll never agree to the final outcome. For the time being we have to keep Stefan and Edgar apart, and let's hope their paths don't cross in Chedworth because if they do all of hell will be let loose. After Charity's recent visit to Hope she now knows what we're planning. Hope seems to think that she is a lot better, which is a relief. Charity can keep an eye out for Stefan and make sure he doesn't visit Georgina when Edgar is calling. We'll have to wait and see."

Faith had thought deeply about her father's estate and nothing was going to stop her from making sure it ended up in the right hands. "The week Edgar returns to Bibury I will be going there to sort out a few things, and Georgina will hopefully be at Brockhampton by then."

"You have only one chance at this, Faith my dear, so make sure you get it right," Gerard said, and kissed her affectionately.

Chapter 27
A Painful Journey

Every time the train jolted or came to a sudden stop Georgina winced from the bruising and damaged ribs that had not completely healed. Her internal bleeding had ceased but doctors were not privy to the actual degree of harm done during Fulwar's terrible beating.

Edward, sitting opposite, could see the stress on her swollen face. Fulwar had assaulted her above the neckline for the first time. Her eyes were yellowed and her nose was slightly disjointed, although the wounds were slowly healing. Edward thought how could anyone hurt a woman in such a way, let alone one so beautiful? Again he was ashamed to have such a beast as a cousin.

Edward took out his watch. "There's about fifteen minutes before we reach Cheltenham, and then, if we are lucky, it'll be no more than another half an hour before we'll be at Brockhampton."

Georgina smiled wanly.

"I'm afraid that it will be a rough carriage ride because the tracks are badly rutted from the rain, and have since dried out. We'll go slowly but you'll just have to grin and bear it."

Georgina tried again to smile but not only was she in pain, her mood was also very low. She imagined that she would never see her children again, or at least never see them growing up.

"When we get back you can stay in the main house for now, and we have hired a nurse to care for you until you have fully recovered. Your room is on the ground floor so you won't have to negotiate the stairs. Father has the builders and decorators in, and when they have finished, you will be able to live in the annexe. It will give you some independence and privacy."

"Thank you, Edward. You are so kind to me." Georgina told him abjectly.

Unknown to Edward she had other ideas but had left it in the hands of Faith. She was sure that Faith would turn up at the house as soon as she knew she was back in Brockhampton. As much as she appreciated Sir Charles and Aunt Maria's help there were other things on her mind that she couldn't divulge. Firstly, she needed to try and extricate her children from Fulwar's custody. There were going to be difficult times ahead, but at least she wouldn't be beaten up any more. Despite this, an air of guilt hung over her because she was using the people who cared for her most.

Edward helped her step uneasily down onto the platform, and the waiting driver took her valise as they made their way outside the station.

Inside the town the roads were relatively smooth but soon they were driving on little more than improvised bridleways that, as Edward had predicted, exacerbated Georgina's pain. The driver did his best to avoid the holes and ruts but many were not negotiable.

They eventually arrived at the iron gates of Brockhampton Court and turned into the driveway. Maria soon emerged through the great oaken doors to greet her son and niece on the stone steps of the entrance.

Sir Charles watched the arrival from inside the house, and couldn't help but wonder what grief his niece by marriage would bestow upon his household, especially if she permanently chose to stay away from Stokesay.

There was a lot of doubt in his mind.

Chapter 28

Brockhampton Visited

There had been an air of disquiet on the Brigadier's estate for more than a week. Murmurings were rife and all directed at the imminent return of Edgar. Indeed, the unpopular son seemed to affect the whole village and the surrounding district.

Faith had recently arrived and was sitting with her father, again deliberating over the estate's future. She told him of the conversation Gerard had had with Edgar the day that she, Georgina and Mary had gone to the theatre.

The Brigadier was not amused. "I can assure you that Edgar will not be in charge of this place whilst I am still alive, and Stefan will still be the estate manager. He is the lynchpin to the successful management of this business. There simply is no possible way that Edgar could do Stefan's job; he is arithmetically inept and wouldn't understand the facts and figures. When he arrives here in two days' time we will sit down and analyse the economical side of the business and try and work out a way forward for the future. With this sudden onset of mechanisation agriculture was becoming a fast-moving commercial enterprise. It is a pity that Gerard won't be here with his legal mind because there are some things I would like to consult with him."

Faith informed her father of her itinerary. "Tomorrow I am travelling to Brockhampton, and on the way back I am going to visit Hope and James because there are some things I need to sort out–"

He stopped her in her tracks. "Such as what? What has Brockhampton to do with all of this?" he asked.

Faith realised straight away she shouldn't have mentioned the place. "I have to deliver some paperwork to Sir Charles from Gerard," she countered. "I think he needs to sign a document or something or other."

The Brigadier stared at his daughter through narrowed eyes. He didn't believe her. Since when had Gerard any dealings with Sir Charles and what could they be about? There were plenty of able solicitors and lawyers in Cheltenham that were much closer and less expensive than those in London.

With Stefan for company Faith travelled to Brockhampton in her father's Landau, which was driven by one of the farm workers. The weather made the journey onerous; it was the middle of November and raining heavily. The horses struggled to pull the carriage along the heavily rutted country lanes, and the leafless trees and bushes swayed frantically in the northwesterly wind, rendering little or no protection against the elements and thus multiplying the journey time.

Hardly a word was spoken between them because nearly everything had been discussed before leaving, though Faith did make one extra point in particular.

"There is something I must ask you, Stefan. I will need to spend five or ten minutes alone with Georgina and it's about her possible divorce from her husband. Gerard is going to deal with it but there is some private business he needs to know. I am going to ask her outright if divorcing him is what she really wants but for obvious reasons I am more than sure she won't answer when you're in the room. I'll need to speak to Sir Charles and his wife as well because I want a clear picture from all concerned."

Stefan didn't reply but he certainly wanted to be the spider on the wall when the pair had their conversation. He was sure that they were not going to deliberate over divorce proceedings until Georgina knew what might happen to her children. It was a ruse to keep him out of the way whilst the real reasons for the visit were discussed, which he was still not privy too. He tried to put it out of his mind so as not to spoil anything. Seeing Georgina was paramount to whatever else was happening around him.

The carriage rolled on slowly and he knew they were close when they crossed the babbling stream at Syreford.

Georgina was still delicate but had improved enough to occupy the annexe of the house. Neither Sir Charles nor Maria said anything against Stefan's presence. They seemed almost resigned to the idea that Georgina would never return to Stokesay and so little mattered any more.

As Stefan spent time alone with Georgina, Faith spoke earnestly with Sir Charles and Maria. She reiterated her former written requests to keep Georgina at Brockhampton for as long as need be, and not succumb to her mother-in-law's begging to have her sent back to Stokesay.

Sir Charles explained the situation at Brockhampton to Faith. If Frederick died then Fulwar would inherit everything. Sir Charles had to keep his nose clean, and as much as he wanted to protect Georgina he couldn't be seen to take sides. If he did then Fulwar would one day almost certainly take his revenge.

Faith confronted Sir Charles and Maria. "Hopefully, in the not too distant future, I am going to ask you to send a letter to your despicable nephew, but don't worry, it will give him the impression that you are on his side. It will be quite simply be an admission of fact. If you both want an end to this terrible ongoing saga then it would really be better if you do as I ask but, I can only leave that for you to judge. I cannot envisage any problems arising from such a simple communication but if it does, my husband will use all of his considerable expertise as a lawyer to placate any repercussions. He will not charge you." Faith watched the couple's faces because she didn't know how they would react, and she perhaps needed to give them time together to dwell over the situation.

"What is in this for you?" Maria asked with scepticism. "Georgina is not even related to you, nor you to us for that matter."

"You must realise that Stefan and Georgina have been having an affair. I do not condone what has happened but his own marriage with my youngest sister has reached a nadir for him sexually. Our family want them back together as a normal happily married couple. He has been a rock but he has to have his physical passion like any other man." Faith made her excuse sound simple.

"But what about your brother?" Sir Charles asked knowingly. "He is now involved with Georgina, or so we have been reliably informed."

Faith knew that she had to be careful. "We all went to the theatre together in Holborn, and then they both stayed at our home for the night, but as far as I know they did not sleep together."

Sir Charles and Maria looked at each other, and Faith knew that neither trusted what she was telling them.

"Having spoken to the Brigadier," she continued, "he told me about your plight here. Gerard seems to think that there are ways around the inheritance of the estate whereby you will have tenancy rights here for years to come at a peppercorn rent. Not only that, his company will look back into all the deeds available and see if there is any way you could be ousted from your position in the foreseeable future. This might take years but it is up to you."

Both had little option but to believe that there was more to it than met the eye. It was Maria who took up the reins, although she had the feeling that they were being blackmailed. "All right. We will do as you ask, and you will let us know, of course, when you want the letter sent and what its contents should be"

"Hopefully, the ball will begin to roll in the next few days and I will send communication to you from London. Please, whatever happens, help Georgina make a full recovery." Faith kissed them both, wished them a good day and then went to speak with Georgina.

One look from Faith and Stefan realised that his time was up. "I'll be five minutes," she told him.

Stefan gently squeezed Georgina, pecked her on the cheek and went to sit in the Landau like a disobedient and impatient schoolboy.

"When do you think you'll be ready, sweetheart?" Faith asked Georgina.

Georgina sat demoralised in an armchair staring down at a Persian carpet with her feet crossed and her hands tucked between her thighs.

"Take your time, Georgina. Take your time," Faith said when she realised how distressed the poor woman was. "I am sorry but I never imagined that Fulwar would go this far. Please believe me that it will not happen again, and be thankful that the beatings are over."

Faith thought deeply about Georgina's health – physical and emotional – and bent over the poor girl and gently hugged her and stroked her hair. "Write to me when you feel ready and able for the move and I will arrange a date and time. I won't tell you right now where you are going but you will be completely safe and well provided for, and you will not be alone."

Georgina grasped Faith's bustle and wept quietly with her head on Faith's stomach for a few moments before pushing herself away and blowing her nose as tears freely ran down her cheeks.

She looked up at Faith. "When can I see my children? I so desperately want them with me."

"We will do our best. When you next see Edgar, tell him that this is what you want most in the world, and when he mentions it to Hope she will insist that he does something about Thomas and Jennifer. We are more than sure that he will."

Faith was confident that her brother had fallen for the beaten woman who sat before her. Most men would.

At Hope and James' home in Chedworth, James poured the first of the autumn cider from a large stone jar. Faith and Stefan had recently arrived, and James and Stefan sat drinking and talking politics at a pine table, mostly about the effects of the civil war in America, whilst the two sisters were in the sitting room quietly discussing Georgina and Edgar.

"Georgina is going to let us know when she is well enough to abscond from Brockhampton," Faith said to Hope. "You will have to arrange to pick her up, and it all has to be undertaken in secrecy. No one from the Cavner family must know that she will be here. Only Edgar can know but we will have to tell him at the right opportunity, but he must also be sworn to secrecy."

Faith's timings had to be perfect.

They drove along the highway back from Chedworth. The rain still pelted down but ran off the steep slopes just as fast. Stefan had mellowed considerably after drinking James' potent homemade apple concoction, and Faith moved across and sat next to him. She placed an arm around his stomach and rested her head against his chest.

"Come on, Stefan. Play with me."

"Don't be ridiculous, Faith. Not here, or anywhere for that matter." He tried pushing her away but she clung on.

"I can tell you now that you won't be having any sexual intercourse with Georgina for months to come. She is too ill so you had just as well try with me. Come on. I haven't anything on underneath."

"You never have, have you?"

"The carriage driver can't see us," Faith said, kissing him on his cheek and smiling, knowing that he wouldn't be able to resist for long. She exposed his hardening penis and took it in her mouth, stimulating it until he was ready for action.

As they bumped along the road they made love in the most comfortable position that they could find in the circumstances.

The carriage's suspension often helped Stefan's forward thrusts, making Faith gasp, but other times he would slip out and struggle to find the target again. Little mattered, however, because Faith had achieved what she had to do that day.

She was wrong, however, about the carriage driver's line of sight.

Chapter 29
Lionel's Revelations

"Why have we come here?" Stefan asked Lionel. The pair were sitting in the New Inn at Coln St Aldwyns and the effects of James' cider still hadn't worn off, and Stefan was about to start drinking again.

"I didn't want anyone from Bibury to hear the things I am about to tell you, and there's one person in particular who would almost certainly come and sit with us if we saw him in Bibury." Lionel rubbed his hands together, eager to tell his story.

Stefan was becoming impetuous "Well, start talking." He wanted to get back to Bibury before the alcohol overcame him.

"It's about Neil Portlock. My father told me this morning that Neil was in the Catherine Wheel last night and he was quite unusually drinking heavily. There was a stranger in the Wheel drinking with him. The two seemed to get along quite well together. It appeared that they both came from around the same area; Liverpool. They spoke affectionately about the city and seemed to know most of the old drinking haunts, dance halls and streets, let alone the city's landmarks."

Stefan sat wondering what Lionel had to say that might be of importance.

"By the sound of the conversation my father was sure that he heard Neil say that he'd been in the army for some considerable time and had only left a couple of months ago. There was a mention of a Lancashire regiment but he didn't quite hear which one."

Stefan suddenly took interest in what his Lionel had to say.

"Anyway, the stranger asked Neil what he was doing in Bibury and he told him that he worked on the estate. Apparently, it was at that point the stranger became more than interested, and started plying Neil with drinks."

"Who was the stranger? Where was he staying?" Stefan asked eagerly.

"The only thing that my father found out about him was that he was booked into a hotel in Cirencester and he had a carriage waiting for him outside. Anyway, let me finish. Neil became more and more drunk and the stranger kept asking questions. The subject of Edgar kept coming up and Neil, who by this time was badly slurring, began telling him how everybody hated Edgar. My father seemed to think that Neil knew more about Edgar than most people. Here's the bombshell. Father couldn't believe what he heard. Neil tried to whisper in his drinking partner's ear that he was really in Bibury to, and I quote, 'eliminate Edgar from the world'."

"My God!" Stefan retorted.

"Indeed. Even the stranger was shocked, and he then turned and realised that Father had overheard what Neil had disclosed. Neil was very drunk by that time but from the gist of what he'd said, he is here in Bibury to kill Edgar Collison." Lionel leaned back in his chair and looked at his great friend, wondering what he might say on the subject.

"We're going to have to confront Neil over this. Not wanting Edgar around is a good reason but killing him to have your way is entirely another entity," Stefan said, shaking his head disbelievingly. "But why would he want him murdered? He must have a damn good reason." He wondered when all of the innuendos and talk behind people's backs would end so that everything would return to normal.

"You are going to confront him, not me. Are you going to sack him?" Lionel asked, almost amused at the revelation.

"We don't know if what he said is true or if he really means it, do we? He was very drunk from what your father has described. I'll talk to him tomorrow but we'll stay out of his way tonight in case the wrong subject is broached." Stefan was rather bemused.

"I suppose though, if you have to dismiss him it still might not stop him from wanting to kill Edgar," Lionel said, shrugging his shoulders. Neither knew Neil Portlock's true motives.

Stefan wanted to return to Bibury before it began to rain again, and urged Lionel to drink up.

"There is something I want to ask you before we go," Lionel said.

"What's that? Come on, hurry up!" Stefan asked without thinking, gesturing to him to empty his pot.

"Will you be the best man at mine and Mary's wedding?" Lionel asked, unable not to smile.

It took a few seconds for the news to sink in but then Stefan stretched across the table and slapped Lionel's cheeks. "After all these years and now you decide to get married? I am really happy for you, Lionel. Yes, of course I will. It will be a great honour. Now don't rush that beer; we'll have another one here and then get back and celebrate."

A worried look appeared on Lionel's face. Stefan was the only one who he had told about his forthcoming marriage and was suddenly concerned that the whole of Bibury might find out before his parents.

Chapter 30
Stefan's Nightmare

Stefan tossed over and over in his bed. His dreams were vivid, and all sorts of scenarios visited him. He almost made love to his wife but Faith was watching them through a window. Grayling fishing with Neil Portlock was spoiled by Lionel coming to tell him of Georgina's demise. Standing face to face with Edgar in a gunfight, pistols at the ready, was interrupted by being arrested by the local judiciary.

He uttered unintelligible words as his mind attempted to decipher what was happening. Withdrawal from an excess of alcohol and lack of bodily fluid exacerbated his partial unconsciousness. Parts of his pillow suddenly seemed hot and in his sleep he turned it over to find a cooler spot.

Another dream materialised. Little Frankie kept running between the horse's legs as a carriage was driven by. He couldn't stop him; Frankie wouldn't listen. Stefan saved his son at the expense of being run over.

The woman in the carriage laughed as they passed by, and he looked closer to see that she was Georgina, and her chaperone was Edgar. They were going to the Brigadier's funeral. He waved, but there was nothing he could do other than lay helpless in the gutter.

Faith walked by but ignored him, and then Hope smiled at him. 'You were always so naïve,' she said. Charity stopped and stared down at him as he lay unable to move. She shook her head and told him that Georgina was a bad mistake as sweat ran from his forehead and chest.

His agitation grew worse and he scratched his arms and tucked his knees up into his chest as a child would with stomach cramps. Fulwar Cavner suddenly dragged him from his stinking refuge as the Bibury people mocked him for being such a fool. 'Work for me!' Fulwar demanded. 'Work for me!'

Stefan turned onto his back with a full bladder and slowly regained some of his senses, but all too soon he drifted back into his darkened world of misrepresented thought.

With his hands suddenly tied behind his back he was powerless, useless and unable to do anything about his disability. He had the capacity but not the ability to move or do something about it. He cried for help but there were no utterances. The louder he shouted the less he was heard. Tied into the world of the deaf and dumb forever.

His sight was suddenly impaired, obscured. Trapped forever, he was unable to escape back to the reality he once knew. He fought to relinquish himself from his imprisonment, and shook his head violently but he was still gripped by an unknown fear. His whole body poured perspiration.

Edgar suddenly entered the unknown room, and in his hand he held a stiletto. He lunged at Stefan. 'Your life here is over,' he shouted as he plunged the blade into him. 'You're not wanted here anymore, you adulterous bastard.'

Stefan sat bolt upright in bed breathing heavily and sweating profusely. Charity mopped his brow. "What is the matter?" she asked. "What were you dreaming about?"

Stefan lay back down and tried to bring his breathing under control. He was scared but of what he did not know. He rose from the bed and went to the bathroom.

Chapter 31
Neil Portlock, The Truth

"Papa, where is Neil? I need to speak to him urgently," Stefan sounded very much on edge.

"He is around the side of the barn fixing the seed drill. Why? What has he done this time?" Marcel sensed that there was something wrong by the tone of his son's voice.

"Nothing," Stefan hesitated, "at least not yet anyway".

Neil was lying on his back partly under the seed drill and shouting profanities at some nuts and bolts that had rusted badly and were difficult to loosen.

"Neil! Please stop what you're doing, I want to talk with you."

Neil crawled out from beneath the ageing machine, unaware of what Stefan was about to ask.

"Come on! Let's go somewhere quiet," Stefan said, and turned and walked away.

Neil reluctantly followed, wiping his filthy hands on an old sack.

Stefan stopped at a dilapidated wooden gate overlooking a winter crop field. He rested his elbow upon it as if he was relaxed but this was far from the truth.

Neil stood close by. "So, what is it you want?" he asked warily.

"I'm not quite sure where to start," concluded Stefan "How many years did you spend in the army?" he asked.

"What makes you think I was ever in the army?" Neil replied.

"Two evenings ago you were talking to someone in the Catherine Wheel. A stranger. That is what you apparently told him. You said that you had only recently been demobilised." Stefan cocked his head slightly, wondering if he would receive a veritable answer.

Neil was in trouble. He couldn't recall much about that night but vaguely remembered having a conversation with someone and waking up the next morning feeling foolish, as if he was guilty of something.

"Is that what I said? I was pretty drunk, which is unusual for me." He still didn't admit about his long career in the British army.

"You and the stranger were apparently very interested in a member of the Collison family, and I am going to find out why."

"I'm not sure we were that interested. If I remember rightly the conversation came up because the Collison family are who I work for. It was as innocent as that." Neil shrugged his shoulders and briefly shook his head.

"Then why was the main topic of conversation mostly about Edgar Collison, a man you have supposedly never met?" Stefan began to become agitated. He sensed Neil was hiding something.

"Let's be fair, Stefan. Everyone talks about your brother-in-law. He is the main topic of conversation in the whole village right now. He is a hate figure here in Bibury, and you must surely know why, but I don't." Neil held his hands up in resignation.

"Is that why you want to murder him? At least that is what you told your acquaintance the other night. You are only here to murder Edgar Collison. If you don't know Edgar, who has put you up to it and what is the motive? Nobody would go to the extreme lengths to kill someone like you might because anybody else would catch him alone and unaware, kill him and then disappear." Stefan expected a dubious reply.

"Of all people Stefan, from what I can gather, you are the one man who would really want him dead. He hates you because he is completely jealous of you. If he gains tenure of the estate you will be out on the street, married to his sister or not."

"So, what was overheard was true?" Stefan suggested.

Neil decided to concede. "You recently trusted me with private matters, despite knowing the dangers of me being privy to such delicate information. Well, now it's my turn to trust you."

Neil told Stefan the whole story, and when he had finished, Stefan, with his elbows on the wooden gate and rubbing his hands over his face and through his hair, could not believe what he had just been told.

"So what were you going to do with him?"

"I don't know. I obviously wouldn't want the blame. Perhaps I could make it appear like an accident. The offer I have been made is too good to refuse. I've already been paid almost half of it, the rest would set me and my wife up for life."

"But it seems like you will need to act quickly because of Edgar's wife in India."

"But not if you turn me in. What *are* you going to do with me? Hand me over to the police? Let me leave?" He tested Stefan.

"If I let you leave it will not necessarily mean that you still won't try to murder Edgar," Stefan said, pondering the situation. He didn't visualise Neil as a dangerous man but his promise of payment from a powerful Indian for a contract killing was tempting indeed. The equivalent of two years' army salary and a comfortable home paid for as a bonus.

Stefan believed that if Edgar could be kept out of the way, perhaps in London or somewhere, the estate could run smoothly. But all the signs were that Edgar was returning to Bibury that afternoon or the next day.

He looked sternly at Neil. "Stay with my father. He has a lot of respect for you and believes you to be an honest man who has an underlying problem. At least I know what that problem is. I'll trust you for now but please do not become so drunk again, like an off duty soldier, and spout your mouth off in the wrong places." Stefan turned to leave.

"And what if Edgar recognises me when he gets here?" Neil asked.

Stefan turned back to him. "Keep out of his way. In all probability he will not come and talk to the proletariats, which currently includes you. I'll speak with my father."

Stefan turned to leave but stopped. "Oh, by the way, I suggest that you do not get rid of your disguise."

Stefan sat at his kitchen table agitated that there was too much swimming around in his head. He continually tapped his fingers on the pine top and his right knee oscillated up and down with nervous speed, both of which were beginning to annoy Charity.

Tomorrow his brother-in-law would be back, which would undoubtedly make things a lot worse. He had a man in his employment who wanted to kill Edgar, and they knew each other. From what Neil had told him, Edgar was also a hated figure amongst the British soldiers and the local Indians. How can a man become so abhorrent? There must be a good reason.

Charity sat down at the opposite end of the table. She stared at him sympathetically, feeling that most of his problems were caused by her own poor health. "Tell me what is troubling you, Stefan. You are not normally in such a negative mood."

Stefan looked at his anxious wife, and knew instantly that he could trust her. "I have unknowingly employed a man who has been hired to assassinate your brother."

Charity suddenly stood up, and the sound of her chair scraping across the flagstone floor mingled with her scream. She clapped her hand over her mouth. "No! No he can't. Don't let him."

Stefan never imagined Charity's emotional response. He couldn't believe that his wife, of all people, would not want her detested brother dead. He stared at her, speechless.

"Who?" she asked.

"Neil Portlock; the chap who came here looking for a job," he told her.

"Stay here! Don't move!" She quickly left and ran across the gravel drive, scrunching as she went.

Lionel heard her coming and confronted her at the door of the main house. "Charity, please calm down. What's the matter?" he asked, having not seen her so agitated for a long while.

"Faith! I need to speak to Faith! Please go and find her. I'll wait here."

Obediently, Lionel disappeared back inside the house and returned shortly afterwards with Charity's bewildered sister. Charity grabbed her sister's arm and guided her away from the house. Out of hearing range she stopped and told Faith what she had just heard from Stefan.

Lionel watched both women shaking or nodding their heads. Their voices were almost frantic but then suddenly they set off back to the Gatehouse. Once there, Stefan verified what he had told Charity.

Faith was livid. "Where can I find this Neil Portlock? I want to talk to him now."

"Of all the venomous comments you have made about Edgar over the years, why is it that suddenly you want to keep him alive? Why has he become so valuable? Neil Portlock has actually offered you a deal that you cannot refuse. Not that I condone his would-be actions but you are acting very strangely." Stefan glanced at his wife. "You too, Charity. And I suppose Hope is involved in your plans as well," he said, resignedly raising his eyebrows.

Faith softened her tone. "Stefan, where is this Neil Portlock? I want to talk with him. It is important that I talk to him alone. Please! Where can I find him?" she almost pleaded.

"What are you going to do with him? My father thinks that he is a good worker and I am sure Neil will tell you the same story as he told me. I am beginning to believe Neil is telling the truth. We can make him shave, tidy him up, and present him to Edgar, who will make an instant recognition of the man, providing he is not lying. On the other hand, he may be an impostor who told me a cock and bull story to throw me off his scent, or he may be employed by locals to get rid of your brother. Neil may still be lying but you don't know who is employing him, or why. If he is operating on his own, has he ever been in the army? Is he really from the northwest? Does he have a family? If so, why has he a notion to eliminate your brother? And for what reason?"

Stefan suddenly wondered where Mr Greyffos had disappeared to, never arriving in Bibury, and wondered whether he was the man talking to Neil Portlock two evenings ago.

Flummoxed, Stefan held his hands out at the two sisters. "If you must talk to him, Neil Portlock is with my father, but I'm not sure he'll tell you anything more than I have already told you."

Saying nothing else Faith left to find the intruder.

"So, what is she up to, Charity? You're obviously privy to the scheme. I tell you everything so how about telling me what's going on?" Stefan asked his wife calmly, hoping to receive an honest answer.

"We're just hoping we can keep Edgar away from here. It is Faith who is organising it, you'll have to ask her." Charity had no intention of elaborating any further, even with her husband.

Stefan glanced up at the clock. "When Faith returns tell her I will be in the Swan."

The barman served Stefan and then went back to his morning chores. Stefan picked up an old copy of The Times and tried to read it but he couldn't concentrate. Instead he paced up and down in the bar resting intermittently to take large gulps of beer. Sometimes he stopped and peered out of the window up towards the Catherine Wheel or he kicked the logs by the fire. Soon he ordered another beer, assuming that waiting for Faith was probably going to take some time. He was alone in the bar and was glad not to have to talk with someone. Even the barman avoided him, sensing his mood.

After nearly an hour the door swung open and in swept Faith. With another beer and a pot of Ceylon tea they sat at the window. She said nothing as she stirred the contents of the pot and then strained it into her cup. She then looked up at her handsome but mystified brother-in-law.

"I'm sorry I've been a while but I have been talking to Charity." She smiled at him, recognising the impatience on his face.

"What did he tell you? Anything different?" he asked.

"Mr Portlock is going back home immediately."

Before she could utter another word Stefan almost jumped down her throat. "What! You've sacked him! I can't believe you've done that. He's a potential bloody murderer! He ought to be reported, not sent home like a scolded schoolboy. Faith, do you know what you are doing? This is all getting out of hand. He will just as likely murder your brother in some other fashion."

Just then a movement out of the window caught Stefan's eye. Neil was walking over the bridge on his way up to the Catherine Wheel. "There he is now! I'm going to stop him!" Stefan went to get up but Faith pulled him back down by his arm.

"Don't! Let him go. Now sit down and just listen." Other customers had arrived and she toned her voice down. "He is coming back in a week."

Stefan buried his head in his arms. "I can't believe you have just said that." He looked up, "Do you really think that he is going to come back after what he has just told you? Can't you get into your head that he was going to murder your brother, for Christ's sake?"

Stefan was dumbfounded but Faith was calm. "He is having a week off to see his family and then he is coming back. It is better that he is out of Edgar's way at first until we find out how Edgar's day pattern will work out. I don't want Neil getting too close to Edgar or he'll suspect something is wrong, especially if Edgar realises Mr Portlock's identity. While he is away he is going to try and find Mr Greyffos in Liverpool. I need his postal address so that I can correspond with him."

Stefan sat shaking his head. "What does this Greyffos chap have anything to do with all of this?"

"To put it crudely, he is paid to report back to Fulwar Cavner names of people who he thinks have been screwing his wife. You are a culprit and Greyffos has been hired to find out if there is anyone else. At the moment he can't prove anything but this won't matter to Georgina's husband; he'll beat her up at the mention of anyone's name. When we left the hotel in Maidenhead together I can only assume that Greyffos was one of the two men who stood across the street pretending to be in morning conversation. I have never met him, and I imagine nor have you, but we now know someone who has. Mr Portlock. Believe me, we need Greyffos on our side and I think he might come over, especially now that he realises what Fulwar Cavner's character is like." Faith manipulated her top lip whilst her eyes were fixed on Stefan. She didn't know what he would ask next. He was far from stupid but she couldn't have him interfering.

After gazing out of the window he turned to Faith. "How long are you going to keep up this spoof?"

"Stefan, this is no spoof; it is deadly serious. I cannot have you involved. Believe me. What Hope and I want is for you and Charity to be happy, so please have patience."

Faith stood up and went to the bar and returned with a key, and scanned the bar to see who might be listening, "Give me five minutes. I'll be upstairs in room four."

Stefan looked astonished at his sister-in-law. "No! I am not going up there with you. Don't blackmail me. This has gone too far. Your sister is less than half a mile up the road."

Faith bent over towards him. "Do you want your marriage saved, Stefan? Or is it Georgina you want more?" She turned and headed for the stairs.

For some time Stefan pondered why Faith would want to complicate his life further. He knew that she would never say anything, but why would she one moment ask if he wanted to save his marriage and then the next moment insist on having sexual intercourse with him? He looked at the clock, stood up and finished his remaining beer.

On the way to the door at the bottom of the stairs he placed the pot on the bar and then went to find Faith in room four.

Stefan quietly knocked on the door but he didn't really know why. There was no answer and so he entered to find Faith lying under the eiderdown on the bed to his left. Her eyes were closed and he could see that her legs were spread and she was gently masturbating herself. Her breathing was steady and Stefan simply stood and watched, wondering whom she might be dreaming of, someone she had an obsession with perhaps.

Faith had no idea that Stefan had entered the bedroom. She thought that he hadn't taken up her offer and had simply gone home. She carried on stimulating herself whilst dreaming. Stefan was the man she thought of, and she imagined his nude, muscular body and large, erect penis.

In her erotic dream he came down on the bed and began caressing the inside of her thighs with his lips. She dreamed that he kissed her vagina, at first gently, but then he began exploring with his searching tongue. He found her wanting clitoris and methodically played over the sensitive sexual organ.

Stefan stood and watched as her breathing became heavier and heavier as she neared a climax. In turn, Stefan became aroused.

Faith threw her head back as she reached her orgasm whilst imagining Stefan penetrating inside her up to the hilt, back and forth, back and forth. It lasted for several seconds and then she began slowly decreasing her momentum. Her breathing was deep but slowing down.

Stefan watched as she finally finished stroking her genitals. Turning towards the door and opening her eyes she saw Stefan standing there.

She gasped. "I thought you had gone home. How long have you been here?"

"Long enough," he answered.

Faith threw back the eiderdown, revealing her ample torso. From the warmth of the bed the aphrodisiacs from her vaginal secretions permeated the cool room. "Come on. I know you want to." She hoped she could tempt him.

Stefan didn't resist. They began making love as if they were man and wife, nothing robust, a lot of kissing and closeness. Her nipples rose upon her generous breasts as he gently tweaked them between finger and thumb. They lay side by side and Faith stretched her leg across him and he finally penetrated her. He stroked the hair from her face and their tongues enacted a strange dance, as two exotic snakes might before mating.

Their lovemaking was relaxed and methodical, Stefan stopped occasionally and they lay, still engaged, and his blood pumping. Refraining from biting his neck, she pulled him tighter into her and dug her nails into his back as her second orgasm that morning wracked her body. Suddenly, Faith's breathing exceeded normality and she reached another sexual climax whilst gripping his earlobe between her teeth, and Stefan ejaculated in time with her convulsions.

For a while they lay there dreaming before Stefan naturally shrank away. He lay on his back looking at the ceiling and wondering where his life was leading. Faith wasn't helping, Charity was ill and Georgina was a beaten woman. Worst of all, Edgar Collison was home for good tomorrow.

Faith rubbed his masculine chest, and raised herself up on her elbow to look at his face. "Don't worry about Edgar. He will be dealt with," she said and kissed him affectionately before laying back down.

Stefan rolled his head slightly towards her. "And how are you going to do that?"

"Please don't ask me. It is important that the less you know the better it will be. Act as if your life is normal, and please don't ask questions. Hopefully, everything will come good for you and Charity, but that's if you want her back." Faith went quiet, waiting for him to say something.

Finally he did. "Faith, are you going to murder your brother?"

"No, not at all. You must know that I couldn't do a thing like that. It's not in my nature," she answered, but he did not see her smile.

As Stefan dressed a little later he looked out of the bedroom window and saw Neil Portlock boarding the Cheltenham carriage on the other side of the bridge, and wondered if it was going to be the last time he would ever set eyes on him. Or perhaps he would see him again at his murder trial.

Chapter 32
The Return of Edgar Collison

A hired stagecoach pulled up to a halt outside the entrance of Bibury Court, and the noise of gravel being crushed beneath wheels and hooves suddenly ceased. Six tired and agitated animals threw their heads back and forth before settling down. A carriage immediately pulled in alongside the coach, and the driver stood down, opened the door and ushered Edgar Collison to the ground. He was back at the Court permanently for the first time in more than two decades.

Lionel, forever a professional, greeted him at the steps. He had organised labourers to unload most of Edgar's worldly belongings from the coach, a task they immediately went about but keeping their personal views to themselves.

Although known to them as a recent visitor the kitchen staff and housemaids stood prim and proper on the steps, and for Edgar's official homecoming each smiled and curtsied as Lionel introduced them to the Brigadier's son. Edgar found it difficult to acknowledge them or smile back because of his superiority complex. To him they were mere subordinates. Arrogance exuded from him.

The Brigadier watched the proceedings solemnly from the drawing room window, and Faith stood just behind his shoulder. Neither had looked forward to this day. The talking and letter writing over the past months was no longer necessary; the issue had arrived on the doorstep.

A light knock at the door preceded Lionel's entrance, and Edgar was introduced as a matter of course.

"Father! How good to see you. How are you?" he asked, beaming.

They shook hands. "I am fine, Edgar. Fine, thank you." He did not ask the same of his son.

"Faith, I didn't expect to see you here?" Edgar said, kissing her on the cheek and then eyeing her up and down. "You look well, I must say. Gerard must be looking after you."

"How was your journey?" she asked. "Not too cumbersome, I hope?"

"A little tiring but after the skivvies unpack my cases I'll have a bath and feel much better. Then it will be about time for dinner," he said, continuing to smile, unaware that both the Brigadier and Faith had cringed at the use of the word *skivvies*.

"I'll leave you two to your men talk, and I will see you in the dining room at seven," Faith said, pouting her lips at them. She took a bottle of brandy and two glasses from the cupboard and placed them on the Brigadier's desk. "Here, that should mellow you both. Now don't start arguing," she laughed.

The Brigadier settled in his chair as Edgar poured two stiff drinks. "I have some good suggestions for the estate, Father, and tomorrow I'll sit down with you and we can discuss them in full detail. I am more than sure that you will appreciate them. I've spent a long time thinking about this place in the last couple of months and now it's time to put some good ideas into practice.

"Let's not be too hasty, Edgar. The estate is operating perfectly well. We don't want to upset the apple cart. Besides, it is now mid-November and winter is very much on its way. It is definitely not the time to begin to make changes."

The Brigadier was emphatic towards his son. Old as he was, as long as he was alive he would be the forceful character on his own estate. Time, however, was running out, and the old man was well aware of his own ailing health.

Edgar remained silent, appearing thoughtful, but suddenly he directed his eyes at his father. "Who will be at dinner this evening?" he asked.

"With us there will be Faith, Hope, James and perhaps some of their friends, providing the weather holds up." He glanced out of the window and grimaced." Oh, and Charity and Stefan, of course. It is mostly family this evening, Edgar. Mostly family." The Brigadier leaned back in his chair, held his brandy aloft and contemplated the difficult months ahead whilst viewing a discoloured, distorted room through the cut glass and Armagnac.

The horse and carriage had set off from Chedworth early because of Hope's need to speak with Faith. Neither James nor Hope relished meeting

Edgar, but they were very much aware that protocol prevailed on family occasions.

As their carriage pulled up at the main house, Charity sat waiting for Stefan in the gatehouse. She was splendidly dressed, and looked very attractive. It was her mood that spoiled the occasion, caused by the return of her abhorrent brother.

Stefan descended the staircase, adjusted himself slightly and took Charity's hand. He kissed her gently on the forehead. "Come on, sweetheart. We won't stay long." Charity felt that her husband didn't sound particularly convincing, and rose hesitantly from the chair with her nerves fraught.

There was a short walk to her father's front door and on arrival in the foyer they saw Faith and Hope indulging in an orchestrated meeting. Both greeted their younger sister and attempted to lift her spirits with little success.

Charity took a deep breath and entered the dining room. The Brigadier had thoughtfully insisted that she sat next to him on his left. Edgar sat on his right. Close as her brother was, Charity didn't have to look directly at him. Faith was next to Charity and Stefan sat opposite. Hope had two old school friends and their spouses sitting with her and her husband.

They began the evening with Barsac, a French wine that came highly recommended by Mrs Desailley.

Conversations varied around the table but died away when the first course was served, Mrs Desailley's winter vegetable potage. Charity struggled. The poor woman's shaking hands were uncontrollable and her father whispered in her ear for her to drink some more wine. She left the soup to avoid embarrassment and the wine made no difference, as she needed two hands to hold the glass.

The atmosphere in the room was sullen, and no one braved the subject of Charity's illness in her presence. Half way through the main course Charity, now visibly upset, wiped her mouth with a napkin and stood to leave. She apologised and Stefan made to go with her but the Brigadier intervened.

"Stay where you are, Stefan. Lionel, please walk back around to the gatehouse with Charity. My nurse is there looking after the children. Please ask her to stay until Stefan arrives home. Thank you, Lionel."

Charity kissed her father and left with Lionel.

The interruption produced an embarrassing silence which Edgar eventually broke.

"Charity is still not well then?" he asked, ignorant of what caused her distress.

The Brigadier gestured towards Stefan. "He's the man to ask, your brother-in-law. Stefan is more than aware of your youngest sister's problems."

Edgar reluctantly directed his eyes towards Stefan wishing he had never asked the question.

Stefan duly obliged. "Some time ago we took her to a reputable physician in Bristol who specialises in psychiatry. He was with her alone for a long time, and his conclusion was that whatever is affecting her happened in her childhood. She may have fallen from a tree or haystack and banged her head, or fallen into a river or pond and nearly drowned. It could well have occurred when no one was close to her and any incident went unnoticed."

"But I thought this all began when your little boy was born?" Edgar asked.

"It did, but the psychiatrist seemed to think that any one thing can ignite the symptoms. He has seen many soldiers who begin behaving unnaturally years after a war but the war is generally the sole cause of the mental illness incurred. He had the opinion that her illness might just disappear as quickly as it was so unfortunately bestowed upon her." Stefan didn't particularly want to talk about the subject any more.

"Illness. What do you mean? Surely it's not an illness." Edgar hadn't realised his sister was genuinely ill.

It was Hope who stepped in. She stared at her misinformed brother. "Yes, Edgar, she is ill. Do you ever remember anything happening to her in the past that may have frightened her?"

Edgar puckered his lips and shook his head slowly. It was a long time ago since he had left Bibury. Hope went to say something else but Edgar stopped her. "Odd that you should mention haystacks. I remember we were playing in Knoll Barn one afternoon when she fell out from the top. She didn't hurt herself because she landed on all the old hay from the year before which had been thrown outside as waste. She was, however, distraught, and it took me quite a while to stop her crying. Perhaps that has caused her problems."

Faith and Hope stole a glance at each other. Hope was about to ask something else but Stefan stepped in. "Please. If you don't mind can we perhaps talk about another subject? I am confronted with dear Charity's illness daily but now is not the time and place to discuss the matter."

The Brigadier agreed and broached the subject of the aftermath of the American civil war, a topical issue. Dessert was soon served and everyone else left father and son to their own conversation.

Stefan retired early and the Brigadier's nurse returned. Hope and James had to travel back to Chedworth, and when they departed so did their friends, leaving just the Brigadier, Edgar and Faith, who between themselves discussed irrelevant subjects as the kitchen maids cleared the table.

When they were once more alone and a few glasses of wine and Armagnac had been imbibed, the Brigadier decided he would retire to bed, knowing full well that Faith wanted to talk to her brother.

The nurse helped the old man out of his chair, and he bade them both goodnight before being escorted to his bedroom. Lionel took up an unobtrusive position by the door lest they need anything.

Little was said between Edgar and Faith for some time, and Faith studied his face whilst he sipped Armagnac.

"Please can you leave us alone, Lionel," she said over her shoulder, and she heard the door close behind him. As much as she trusted Lionel, appearing in charge in her brother's company was important.

"Edgar, I want to talk to you about Georgina." Faith gained her brother's attention immediately. "You probably know that she is at Brockhampton at the moment. Whatever you do, please do not go there. She is recovering, and until she is well enough to move it is better she stays uninterrupted."

Edgar tried to say something but Faith lifted her hand.

"We are moving her but no one must know where. I can tell you where, but only if you promise not to divulge her whereabouts to anyone else. Georgina would only allow the move if we told you where we were taking her. She never stops talking about you." Faith watched her brother sternly.

Edgar examined his sister. "Why all the secrecy?" he asked.

"Edgar, don't be a fool! Her husband nearly killed her. There are some things you do not understand. If she stays with her uncle and aunt then Fulwar will almost certainly demand her return to Stokesay. There, her problems will begin all over again. More mental abuse, more beatings. Is that what you want for her?" Faith asked in a scolding manner.

Edgar looked away and then back at his sister. "No, of course not," he answered, looking embarrassed.

"She needs help, Edgar. She is a beautiful woman. Will you help her?" Faith leaned back hoping her brother would say something positive.

Slightly drunk, he tried to work out a way around things in his mind. "Where is she being moved to?" he finally asked.

Faith thought he would never ask. "Hope and James' home in Chedworth, where Fulwar will never find her. There is more than enough room."

Edgar thought about what his sister had said. "Why have you all suddenly become interested in Georgina? How did you actually come to know her in the first place?"

Faith had to think quickly. She couldn't mention Stefan's involvement or Sir Charles' visit to the Brigadier. "Originally, it was Hope who first met her at a funeral service in Withington. Afterwards, as women do, they had a long conversation and more or less became friends. One day I met her as well and we've all been quite friendly and have kept in touch ever since," she expertly lied. "When Georgina does finally divorce Fulwar then Gerard's law firm will take charge, although she doesn't stand much chance of receiving anything, but that doesn't matter to her. What she wants so desperately is to have her children by her side. Thomas, the boy wants to be with her now but Sir Charles will not have them at Brockhampton for fear of losing his half of the estate. That is why Georgina is disappearing to Chedworth. If she can kidnap her own children and have them there it will be seen as no fault of Sir Charles and his wife. I'm afraid poor Georgina is in dire straights whichever way she turns."

"I must go and see her. She needs somebody she can trust." Edgar said pensively.

"You must not visit her until she has moved to Hope's. If their family know a male Collison has been seeing her then they will almost certainly put two and two together. Another thing you need to know concerns her long-term health. She has to avoid any physical handling for the time being. The doctors say her internal injuries will take some months to heal so she has to abstain from any sexual activity for the foreseeable future. Not a subject I wanted to broach but she asked me to tell you that so you've been forewarned." At least Georgina didn't have to have sex with him.

"But I can't wait to see her. Let me know as soon as she arrives at Chedworth, won't you? I'll try and sort her children out for her. I am sure she misses them terribly."

It was the very words that Faith wanted to hear. "Of course I will. If you could bring them to Chedworth without her husband finding out it will be a godsend for Georgina. She would never let you forget, I'm sure."

Both brother and sister felt it had been a long day and decided to retire for the night. In the grand hallway they went their separate ways.

In the west wing, Faith lay wondering whether she was still moving in the right direction. Funnelling Edgar in the direction she wanted might prove to be more difficult than she had anticipated.

In the east wing, Edgar continually paced around in his large bedroom trying to fathom out what to do with his wife and her children in India. "They might become a hindrance," he mumbled to himself.

Chapter 33
Liverpool

Neil Portlock walked down Copperas Hill and then crossed into Ranelagh Street. A short walk took him to the junction with Bold Street and somewhere nearby stood house number twenty-three, which had been given to him by the clerk of the court in the centre of the city. The odd numbers were on his left and he soon found the building he was looking for. Surprisingly, it was a drapers shop.

As he entered a tingling bell rang and a young smiling assistant came through a draped curtain from a back room.

"Sir, how may I help you?" the fresh-faced lad asked.

"I am looking for a gentleman by the name of Mr Greyffos, and I was told that he had an office at this address." Neil glanced around believing he had been sent to the wrong place.

The shop assistant looked at the clock. It was twelve thirty. "He'll be back about two o'clock. What is it in connection with? May I be of assistance?"

"I have an assignment for him." Neil was reluctant to say much more, especially not knowing to whom he was talking.

"Rest assured, sir. You can tell me because I am his son, Aaron Greyffos. I run this shop but also act as his secretary. All letters and messages are sent here because we have a small office upstairs. Maybe I'll be able to advise you?" The young man seemed quite genuine.

"The trouble is, Aaron, it is quite a complicated subject and it would be better if I spoke to your father directly. It is about a case he has already been working on near Cheltenham and Cirencester but for a client in Shropshire." Neil wondered if the son might know anything about it.

"Yes, he was down in Cirencester last week and made a brief visit to a small village nearby. There were some very interesting revelations, if I remember rightly." Aaron raised his eyebrows and smiled exposing his well-kept teeth.

"I think that might have been me he was talking to." Neil told him guiltily. "Listen, I'll come back at two o'clock, it's better that your father and I talk. No disrespect to yourself, young man, but I would prefer it that way." Neil went to leave but Aaron followed him to the door and placed his hand on his shoulder.

"Walk along Ranelagh Street," he said, pointing down the street, "and you will find a pub called The Commercial. He'll almost certainly be in there." Neil thanked him and they shook hands. "It is possible that I'll be seeing you again," he told Neil, still smiling, and they bade each other farewell.

The pub was highly attractive externally and internally. Inside there were many etched mirrors and glasswork. The fireplaces were made of beautiful green Connemara marble, and dark stained oak wainscot adorned the walls. The seats were padded green leather, which matched the inlaid tables with cast iron patterned legs.

It was a bustling enterprise as its name suggested, frequented lunchtimes mostly by businessmen who sounded to Neil from their conversations that they were in the shipping industry.

Willie Greyffos was chatting and drinking with a friend at the bar. As a typical sleuth he watched everyone coming and going through one of the many mirrors behind the bar, and he didn't fail to miss Neil.

He suddenly went quiet and his drinking partner realised that something was wrong and glimpsed over his shoulder to see who had drawn his attention.

"You see the chap with the beard and long hair? I was chatting to him only last week in eastern Gloucestershire. He must be looking for me because it's too much of a coincidence that he has walked in here. I imagine he'll have been around the draper store and spoken to Aaron." He watched through the mirror as Neil bought a drink.

"Landlord! I'll pay for that." Willie's friend took the bull by the horns.

Neil tried to pay but the landlord directed him along the bar. Willie tipped his hat and smiled, and Neil carefully shuffled amongst the throng and reached his benefactor. "Thank my friend, Oswald, for your beer," Willie said. "I'm sorry but I didn't quite catch your name the other evening."

"Neil. Neil Portlock. Pleased to meet you... again."

"No, I meant your real name," Willie replied, smiling again and studying Neil's face knowingly.

"For now, let's leave it as it is. We can all use pseudonyms, can't we?" he asked, raising his eyebrows slightly.

"Fair enough. So how can I help you? You've obviously come searching me out for a reason."

"I need to speak with you alone."

They apologised and left Oswald at the bar and found a seat in the corner.

"You have recently spoken to Hope Ronssoy. Well, it's her sister who wants to speak to you. Faith Havrincourt. She wants you to, sort of, swap sides. What she is suggesting is that you continue to apparently work for Mr Cavner but secretly work for her family. They will pay you as well. Faith Havrincourt wants to talk with you directly and seems to think that you know where in London she lives. It is better that you go and visit her and she'll explain what is required of you. She'll pay for your fare and time to travel to London. I have her address here and one of the pub she frequents." Neil produced a scruffy piece of paper with which Willie could contact Faith and arrange what sounded like a spurious encounter.

Willie Greyffos pondered over which direction to take. What he couldn't comprehend was why the sisters wanted him on both sides. It was only last week that Neil told him that he intended to murder the women's brother. The story was more interesting than he had imagined.

He pondered over the note that confirmed her address in his mind and then nodded. "I will pay a visit to Mrs Havrincourt in London and arrange a date and time as soon as I return to the office. Come! Let's go back to the bar."

Nothing else was said about the subject and after relocating Oswald the three stood drinking and reminiscing about the bustling city of Liverpool.

As Willie walked back along Ranelagh Street he considered several permutations as to why Faith Havrincourt wanted him to change sides. He would have to remain very clear headed over the next few days so as not to upset the wrong people. In any case, he couldn't lose by just talking to the woman.

Chapter 34
Eugene

"There goes Georgina with young Ginette," Sir Charles said to his wife from the window as he watched the two women ride away. "She seems much better lately, and she rides out on the horses more often, although I'm relieved that she is always accompanied."

"The poor girl still has problems internally, although she is much improved. Her face seems better now and she is much more confident and talkative." Maria was resigned to wait and see what would happen to Georgina in the long-term. No one knew whether she would stay at Brockhampton or return to Stokesay for her children's sake, and it would take a brave woman to go back to her husband after what she had been through.

Sir Charles gazed upwards at the sky. "They had better not ride out too far; the weather looks as if it will soon deteriorate. Besides, it will begin to darken in just over two hours." He turned and sat back down beside the roaring fire.

Sir Charles and Maria had spent some time organising the Christmas party beside the fire, and Maria had written a list of things to be done beforehand as well as whom to invite. It was to be held on the Saturday before Christmas Day in the main hall, which was only three and a half weeks away. All of the estate workers and their families would be attending, and an appropriate coniferous tree had already been chosen from the estate to take centre stage, and it would be decorated with edible items for the children. As usual, Sir Charles was looking forward to donning the festive costume and becoming Father Christmas.

As twilight gave way to darkness, Maria's list was ready, and everything was practically organised but only on paper. The conversation had turned to what the New Year would bring when a light knock on the door was followed by Edward's entrance.

"Ginette has returned without Georgina. The last she saw of her was at Andoversford. It began raining and she started back with Georgina apparently following. Ginette rode out of sight and never saw Georgina again. By then it was sleeting hard and almost pitch black." Edward shrugged his shoulders, his face said it all, perplexed and worried.

Sir Charles went to the window. The rain was blowing hard against the glass. "No one can go out in that now, it is too dangerous. They would lose their way. We'll just have to wait and see, and hope that she'll sensibly take shelter somewhere."

That night the whole of the estate was put on vigil. Georgina was well thought of by everyone, and word had quickly spread of her disappearance. At least one member of every household kept a seat by a window with the notion that she could quickly be given assistance when she did finally reappear.

Night began to turn into day, and Edward continually roamed the house from room to room in order to look out of the windows, but Georgina was never in view. The herdsmen had been working for some hours but even they still had no sign of Georgina's or Eugene's whereabouts. The estate had to operate at its capacity, and everyone took to his or her tasks undeterred as the gale force winds and lashing rain beat down relentlessly. He could only imagine that they were both down towards Andoversford, where Ginette had last seen them.

Suddenly decisive, Edward ordered the Brougham to be hitched up. He was a very good all-round horseman, and not wishing to put any of his workforce in jeopardy, he drove the carriage himself.

His relationship with Georgina was becoming personal and he frantically wanted to find her or, if need be, rescue her. He set off into the storm, and the north-westerly rain stung the side of his face, and he had the feeling that the aggravated steeds were of the same disposition as they ploughed on through the wintry weather.

It soon began to sleet but although Andoversford was not far away, he felt that if he could make it to the village, at least he would have some respite from the elements.

It was mid-morning when Edward drove down into the village. He saw no one on the way and very few were on the windswept main street, as he gathered that most people were sensibly indoors.

Having pulled up outside a greengrocer's he jumped down to question the proprietor. "Sir!" he shouted. "Have you by any chance seen a woman, a stranger, riding a magnificent horse? She has been missing all night and was last seen here late yesterday afternoon."

"Two women wandered up and down about that time, both on horseback. I didn't recognise either of them. We watched from the window and they headed up towards the Sevenhampton bridle path, but we never saw them again." He held his hands out and shrugged his shoulders. It was as much as he could say.

"One of them actually returned to Brockhampton but I'm afraid the other didn't make it, and we don't know why. Thank you anyway! I'll keep searching." Edward left, scratching his head. He tried the butcher's shop, and a tiny lady told him she had seen an unfamiliar horse tied up outside the Royal Oak pub not far up the street. Edward knew the hostelry, and with his heart pounding he went off to investigate in the atrocious weather.

With an intense sigh of relief he came across Eugene tethered up outside the alehouse with his head bent into the wind. He stroked him and checked the animal over but he appeared to be perfectly healthy. Edward could only assume that Georgina had taken refuge inside the Royal Oak during the night and looked around for access.

"Is that your horse, young man?" a voice shouted from an upstairs window, startling Edward.

Edward glanced up to the interested party and then back at Eugene. "Do you mind my asking where Georgina Cavner, his rider, might be?" he asked.

"We haven't seen anyone. The young woman who works here for me met the horse wandering around alone on the bridleway halfway between here and Syreford, where she lives. It was about eleven o'clock last evening, and in the rain and dark she managed to bring him under control and tether him to a fencepost. She left him, thinking whoever he belonged to would be looking for him. On her way to work this morning no one had come to claim him and so, with the goodness of her heart, she led him here so he could be safe until his owner could be found. Lucky you, eh? He's an impressive beast."

Edward stared into Eugene's face. "Where has she gone, Eugene? To where has Georgina disappeared? This isn't like her." Edward was completely mystified. Surely Fulwar hadn't had her abducted or even murdered. Georgina's situation was becoming dire.

He faced back up to the landlord. "Please thank your young lady for me. Her help has been much appreciated." He took a silver sixpence from his pocket and placed it on a windowsill. "This is payment for her kind heartedness."

Edward left the village with the intention of scouring the bridleway between Andoversford and Syreford. He rode the carriage slowly, especially now that he had Eugene tied alongside, but found nothing untoward. Many tracks had become waterlogged and by now other vehicles and horses had passed the same way. Edward decided to return home in case she had made it back there on foot or with help from someone.

Everyone on the estate was put on alert for Georgina, bad weather or not, and only the most important tradesmen or women were kept at their workplace.

Maria scoured Georgina's annexe. Nothing seemed to be missing. As Ginette described the day before, the only possessions she had with her were the clothes on her back. There was no sign of her as darkness fell that second day, and Georgina had become a worrying problem.

Edward set off to Cheltenham to inform the judiciary the next day, and two days later a pair of men arrived on the estate to make inquiries. Afterwards, they had formed the opinion that Georgina was a difficult wife and created her own life of debauchery and idleness. She seemed, they suggested, a little loose and had a flagrant disregard for married life.

Edward was livid, and stepped up nose to nose with the senior of the two men.

"Georgina is not the whore that you imply. She is a well-respected woman who married into our Cavner family. Perhaps you should spend some money and time and go and visit her husband in Shropshire and his private detective. Between them you might make some headway towards uncovering Georgina's whereabouts. I wager they won't mention her perpetual beatings from that dastardly husband, my cousin, because I am sure they will both be in cahoots during this anxious time. Can't you get it into your heads that Georgina Corbett-Cavner has been abducted?"

Georgina had disappeared from the Brockhampton estate, and only Eugene knew the truth.

Chapter 35
Chedworth

James guided the buggy upward through Withington woods with great difficulty. The rain lashed down and he was entirely dependent on his plough horse to see their way. The human eye was useless that early evening, especially amongst the deep woodland.

The bridleway at this point was bare of soil, and such was the poor visibility he could hear but not see his steed struggling to grip the Cotswold stone hill.

Georgina sat beside him. She was soaked through to the skin but he was confident that they would make it back to Chedworth manor. The hill was the most difficult part of the six mile journey, and once ascended they would have a free run back to the manor and the comfort of James' home.

Everyone in Hope and James' household had been lectured about the guest who was coming to stay, and no one was to mention anything about her outside the manor walls. Instant dismissal faced any culprit talking about the strange woman in the village or beyond. They had been told that her name was Anna, short for Annabel, and were welcome to address her by that name.

Expecting her husband and Georgina at any moment, Hope watched for their arrival through the window. The maids were preparing two baths, fresh clothes had been set aside for Georgina (a whole new wardrobe had been purchased in advance of her arrival), a late dinner was being prepared in the kitchen, and the stable lads were on hand to disengage and bed down the horse and then put away the buggy for the night.

Everything had to operate secretly and strictly to plan.

A single oil lamp could be seen flickering outside the Seven Tuns as James negotiated the steep downward corner and leftward turn into the entrance of Chedworth Manor, and soon they were parked and the horse held under control.

They stepped down from the saturated buggy and were escorted into the house. After a brief embrace between Hope and Georgina, the housekeeper led her away whilst the butler directed James to his bathroom.

Clean, dressed and carrying an umbrella, James made his evening sojourn across to the Seven Tuns, just fifty yards from his front door. If missed, the village drinking fraternity would wonder why, such was his popularity. He fulfilled his evening quota and left for a late evening dinner.

At the dining table Hope and Georgina seemed resplendent in James' eyes, and they all ate, drank and talked naturally. Georgina seemed to have escaped from her prisons in Shropshire and Brockhampton, and conversed as if there had never been a problem, although she would be even more cocooned in security for the time being.

Before retiring to bed James paced his dining room with a glass of wine in hand. His mind was set on the near future.

Chapter 36
Edgar and Georgina

"Are you sure you're ready to see him?" Hope asked Georgina. "I don't want to tell him anything if you're not yet willing. Your health and state of mind are of utmost importance to us all and we don't want to see you make yourself any worse than what you already are. You've been through a bad time." Hope was not sure Georgina could cope with meeting Edgar just yet.

"Hope, my dear, I shall be fine. We have to get this episode over and done with and then perhaps we can eventually finalise the story and we will all live happily ever after. Yes, I am ready. Go and speak to him and tell him I am here, but suggest that I am not yet well enough for physical contact." The thought of having sexual intercourse or any physical encounter with Edgar made poor Georgina cringe.

Hope tapped on the door of Edgar's east wing at Bibury Court. He called for her to enter and she duly obliged.

Inside his main room they greeted each other as if they hadn't met for years. He showed Hope the entire apartment, where everything was immaculate and well organised. Two decades in the army, especially much of it in India, had at least taught him cleanliness and good housekeeping. Oil paintings of battles on the Asian sub-continent adorned the walls, and military souvenirs were spread over the furniture. A photograph of a beautiful Indian woman with three young girls sat pride of place on his mantelpiece. Hope studied it briefly and then turned away, saying nothing.

"Let's sit down. I've come with some news for you." She indicated towards the two armchairs by the log fire, and both settled down.

"Georgina is staying with myself and James. She has been with us now for three days and has asked me to come here because she desperately wants to see you." Edgar tried to say something but Hope demanded she let him finish. "She is now much improved, but still far from right. At the moment she has no intention of returning to Stokesay but whether she changes her mind when she feels better we do not know. One issue that might sway her decision is her children; Thomas and Jennifer. She says she cannot live without them but the chances of them moving here are negligible. Nobody knows that she is now living with us, except Faith, Gerard and now yourself."

Edgar was very pleased that Georgina wished to see him. "I'll come over as soon as possible. I'm sure she wants to see me and I certainly do wish to see her. We'll have a long chat about the future and see what can be done about her children. Her husband needs putting in his place once and for all."

"In three days time I will be going to Cirencester to see some friends. I will be leaving home at ten o'clock and returning about three. There is an art exhibition there and we are having lunch at the Fleece Hotel. I will tell Georgina that you are coming. Oh, and by the way, her name is Annabel. Whatever you do, only use the name Annabel or Anna; we do not want the staff talking. Another thing she has mentioned is her physical well-being. I don't know if you have been told but her husband internally damaged her quite badly. Whatever you do, don't contemplate getting into bed with her. You must give her more time. I shouldn't be telling you this but it's better coming from me than from her." Hope stared at her brother straight in the eyes and he conceded to the information, puckering his lips and slightly nodding his head in agreement.

"As for her children, I will find out from Georgina exactly where they attend school. Only then can I plan how to extricate them from Shropshire and do everything in my power to bring them here." Edgar sounded confident that he could make it happen.

Hope looked at her brother unflinchingly and without emotion, despite his assurances being exactly what she wanted to hear from him. She was satisfied that Edgar had shown more than enough interest in Georgina and the welfare of her two children

Both ended their conversation and Hope went off to briefly discuss the forthcoming Christmas festivities with their father before she began her journey back to Chedworth on horseback alone.

There wasn't a cloud in the sky and the sun hung low and bright on the horizon behind Edgar's right shoulder. The cold wind from the northeast whistled its wintry song through the leafless trees and hedgerows as Edgar made his way towards Chedworth, crossing the Fosseway and heading down towards the village through Denfurlong Farm. He knew he was moments away from the home of his sister and brother-in-law when the church tower of St Andrew's came into sight.

Georgina greeted him at her door and thanked the maid, who scurried away. The door closed behind them before they spoke.

"Edgar, It's been such a long time. How was your journey? Difficult, I imagine."

Ignoring her question, Edgar pulled her to him, she winced and he apologised.

"You look much better than when I last saw you last in Ludlow. How are you feeling?"

She ushered Edgar to the sofa and gestured for him to sit down. "Oh, physically I am much better, but some days I feel so depressed. Other days I am fine but I do miss my children. I really do." Georgina sounded meek.

"The children are something I want to talk to you about. If it makes you feel so much happier when they are with you then I will try and do something about it and bring them here. What do you think about that?" Edgar asked, raising his eyebrows.

"Oh, Edgar! If only you could, but Fulwar would never allow them to live down here with me. It would be impossible."

"He doesn't know where you are so how could he find your children if they were with you?" Edgar was confident he could secure Georgina's love if he could deliver her children to Chedworth.

Georgina shook her head. "It would be wonderful, Edgar, but somehow I cannot ever see it happening."

"Tell me where they attend school, where they live, and anything else that will help to secure their release from their father's hold. I have associates in the army who will perhaps help us. Please believe me, Georgina." Edgar was determined to win Georgina's love once and for all, and although he had no friends to help him, he felt better with Georgina believing the contrary.

"They both go to St Michael's College near Tenbury Well, and he makes them stay as boarders when I am not at home. He has little time for them because of his drinking habits. Not only that but he thinks it is healthier for them when he is out of their sight in a drunken stupor. He is right; the less they see him in such a condition the better they will be." It saddened Georgina to talk about her children.

Edgar held her hand and tried to console her. "Don't worry. I'll rescue them for you and you can be happy again."

Georgina pulled him towards her and placed an arm around his neck. "Oh, thank you, Edgar. You are so kind to me," she kissed him softly on the cheek. "Come, let's go and walk around the grounds before lunch."

The pair sauntered around the well-kept garden. Its maintenance was one of Hope's enjoyable activities, and even during the winter and bitter cold she still worked hard on its upkeep. They talked about numerous topics as they walked, but the subject of Georgina's children always returned.

"Oh no," Georgina suddenly gasped, and a look of disappointment engulfed her face. "My children finish school for Christmas soon, and the only chance of rescuing them will be from the school. Otherwise, I'll have to wait until the New Year. Do you think that it is possible to have them here for Christmas?" she begged.

"Don't worry. I'll begin putting together a plan first thing tomorrow. I will need to know some dates and times concerning the school term, but I am sure that they will finish earlier than usual on the last day. That may be to our advantage, we'll have to see."

Edgar suddenly wondered how Georgina would feel about him if he could rescue her children before Christmas.

They ate lunch alone, and a table bell summoned the butler when required. Georgina broke the ice after a while. "What is happening with your wife and children in India?"

Edgar had hoped the subject would not be broached. "I'm not sure. Gerard is delving into the legalities of the marriage. Apparently, a Muslim cannot simply swap religion and become a Christian. There is a debate taking place, and if it is proven that the marriage is illegal, she and her children will not be able to travel to England."

"Oh, Edgar. Will you be disappointed?"

He remained quiet for a few moments, gazing into his wine glass, but then looked into Georgina's searching eyes. "But I have you, Georgina."

Georgina became uncomfortable. At first she turned away but then looked back with a slight smile and placed her hand on the back of his. "Of course you have, Edgar. Of course you have."

They spent the rest of their liaison discussing what their future together might hold. Laughing and joking, they discussed where they might live. Bibury Court was the eventual place to settle after the Brigadier's death. Edgar showed a great interest in Georgina's children, and promised to be a model stepfather.

The clock ticked down and, keeping his promise to his sister, Edgar prepared to leave by three o'clock. His horse was brought to the front door, and they kissed gently lips to lips before Georgina wished him a safe journey back to Bibury. He reluctantly set off, and Georgina continued to wave as he rode the length of the drive.

When he was out of sight she went back inside, slammed the front door shut and leaned against the great oak structure. She looked up at the beautiful corniced ceiling and began to cry.

A maid soon took her by her arm, bringing her back to reality. "Leave me, please. Don't touch me." She breathed heavily and then ran up the stairs to her bedroom, where she fell on the bed sobbing.

Later, Hope woke her and asked what had happened. Georgina explained everything. Although it was a step in the right direction she had hated every minute of his visit. "My God, Hope! It's no wonder all three of you hate him. He is such a creep. He'll do anything to have his own way. I feel so sorry for that poor Indian woman he has married, who must believe she is going to have a better life."

Hope stared out of the window as Georgina sobbed in her arms, and she wished that it could all end now.

Chapter 37
Willie Greyffos

After arranging a morning meeting with his client in the hope that he would be sober enough to hear what he had to tell him, Willie Greyffos arrived on time at Stokesay at ten o'clock in the morning, and was escorted to the door of Fulwar Cavner's study.

Willie tapped lightly and opened the door to find his client half asleep in a swivel chair with a practically empty brandy glass in his hand, which rested on a bloated stomach, and his feet rested upon a leather-topped walnut pedestal desk. Willie noted his client's sallow skin, which was surely a sign of a struggling liver, and he was under no allusions that the man was slowly killing himself.

Willie observed him for perhaps two minutes, wondering why he had come to help the monster lying before him, before awaking him.

"Mr Cavner, I am here at your request. How can I help you?" he asked politely yet professionally.

Fulwar awoke with an audible start, and the remnants of his glass spilled down his trousers. He cursed and then apologised. "I'm sorry, I was miles away. Yes! Please sit down." He indicated to the chair on the opposite side of the desk.

Willie dragged the chair over and stared into Fulwar Cavner's face. "What is it you want? Your letter was a little confusing."

"My wife has disappeared and I want you to find her. She went to live in Brockhampton but has mysteriously left there. She didn't take any clothes with her or anything else when she disappeared, and no one knows where she is." Fulwar actually seemed quite uneasy about his wife's disappearance, which surprised Willie.

"But you have always given me the impression that what you have always wanted is for her to get out of your life. What more could you ask for?" Willie shrugged his shoulders slightly, not expecting a sensible answer from the ailing alcoholic.

"The children want her to come back. They miss her," Fulwar replied, omitting the fact that he dreaded the thought of her having a peaceful and enjoyable lifestyle in the company of someone else, as well as the thought of her having intercourse with another man.

"Where might she have gone? Have you any ideas yourself?" Willie asked.

Fulwar shook his head. "The first place to ask is at my uncle's home in Brockhampton. It was where she was staying when she disappeared, and near to where she was last seen. Her horse was found wandering nearby."

"So, she may have been abducted or even murdered?" Willie asked without pulling any punches.

"I don't know. I really don't know. All I want is for you to find her. Please, for the sake of the children." Fulwar held his head in his hands and scratched his scalp whilst his elbows remained on the desk. Willie thought it quite apparent that his client's mental health was degenerating by the week, and an early death would be inevitable if he did not change his ways.

"I am afraid that I must increase my fee," said bluntly. "I don't mind working for you but there are a lot of travelling costs. Also, fifty per cent up front would very much be appreciated. If you agree, I can begin my investigations tomorrow. I have a meeting in London this evening but I can be in Brockhampton some time tomorrow afternoon."

Fulwar agreed and drew a preliminary sum from the desk drawer, and as Willie closed the door behind him, hiding his smile, he heard the crystal clink of decanter meeting glass.

It was early evening in Holborn and already freezing cold but dry, at least. Numerous gas lamps lit the main street and the small shops and businesses were vying for pre-Christmas customers. Willie Greyffos was looking for the Castle Tavern on Furnival Street. He had sent a letter to Faith Havrincourt three days before and had decided to take a chance that she would have received it by now, and would hopefully meet him at a pub recommended to him by the intriguing man who called himself Neil Portlock.

Faith was already in the bar talking to some neighbours as Willie lumbered in with his small suitcase. They recognised each other from his past surveillance work in Maidenhead, and they greeted in a businesslike manner, and soon were sitting down, drinks in hand.

"So, Mrs Havrincourt. How can I help you?" he asked.

"Please, call me Faith. May I will call you Willie?" He had no qualms about her taking the reins as she might end up as his paymaster, and so nodded in agreement. "You've spoken to Mr Portlock about the proposed arrangement. Have you come to any conclusion?"

"Not that long ago I had a confrontation with a Mrs Maria Cavner. In no uncertain terms she explained to me what my client was really like. Mr Portlock told me that you would like me to change sides without telling my client. However, I'm afraid that this would go against my professional ethics. However, if–"

Faith cut him short. "No. You don't have to stop working for him, just start working for us as well. You can tell him everything that I tell you, and before you ask, yes, there *will* be more than an element of truth in everything you hear from me. This means that you can retain your professional integrity, and he can then make his own mind up what he wants to do about the situation. He is paying you and we will be paying you. What more could you wish for?"

Willie was unsure whether or not to trust her. The circumstances were unprecedented. "Will you tell me exactly what is going on? I will need to know."

"Are you actually working for him now because if so, what has he asked you to do?" Faith countered. She could only imagine his answer.

"Fulwar Cavner simply asked me to find the whereabouts of his wife this morning. Tomorrow I begin at Brockhampton. It is all he has asked from me, nothing else." Willie knew full well Faith was deeply involved in Georgina's disappearance but before he openly committed himself he needed as much information as possible.

"As far as we are concerned, you can carry on with your work, and you can take back to Stokesay any evidence you may gather from us. That is how we want it," she smiled. "Tell me, do you want to be in our pay as well?"

Willie had financial problems, and double earnings were irresistible, despite his ethics. "Yes, I believe that we can come to an arrangement, but let us first talk about remuneration, and then we can talk about your intentions and where you want me to be in the full picture."

After an hour both parties had come to a general agreement, and Faith wined and dined her new recruit. By the time they departed company Willie Greyffos was well aware of his double role and Faith felt confident that he would not backtrack.

Late that evening Willie Greyffos made his way to Paddington and booked himself into a dingy hotel. His intention was to be on the first train in the morning, with his first destination being the Cavner Arms in Brockhampton. He did not sleep well.

Faith arrived back home feeling jovial, and Gerard questioned her over a glass of wine. From what he could gather, another part of his wife's jigsaw puzzle had been slotted into place.

When the bottle had been drunk he had to coax her from the armchair to their bed.

Chapter 38
Lionel and Stefan

"What do you think has happened to her, Lionel? And what does Mary think?" Stefan asked in his anguish. "They are supposed to be the best of friends, for Christ's sake." The local Gloucestershire journals had written about Georgina's unexplained disappearance, and some had even suggested that her demise was certain.

"Believe me, Stefan, Mary is as worried as we are. Georgina has never been out of contact like this before, and her godmother and aunt is of the same opinion. It is completely out character for her. You'll be able to talk to Mary soon because she's coming here for Christmas, but Georgina will have turned up safely before then anyway."

Lionel was just as distraught as Stefan. Indeed Georgina's absence was beginning to affect quite a number of people. "Why don't we take a day off tomorrow and go and visit Sir Charles and his wife. We can perhaps retrace Georgina's last known steps. We probably won't find her but at least it will give us something different to do, and a few drinks wouldn't go amiss either."

Stefan agreed with him. "Yes, let's go. It's worth a try." For Stefan the trip was already instilling hope within him, but if they did find Georgina it would be a godsend.

Having decided the evening before to follow the Coln River Valley, both men set out before first light. It wasn't the fastest route to travel to their destination but it would certainly be the most appealing.

The morning slowly illuminated around them, and when the sun emerged from behind the eastern Cotswold Hills, it revealed an impressive mid-December hoar frost, with only the most sheltered woodland spots avoiding the wintry glaze.

The men rode beside frozen water meadows and watched mallards slide their way between the clumps of bog grass in search of any morsel of food. The Coln, undeterred by the ice-bound pastures, bubbled towards its confluence with the great River Thames.

The horsemen kept to the valley floor on their outward journey, riding below the level of Chedworth village, but had the intention of paying a visit to Hope's home on their return later that day.

Along Monarch's Way they were surrounded on both sides by leafless woodland but soon they were back into the open heading towards the tiny village of Withington. From there they followed the footpath towards the village of Andoversford. The sun cast its dawn rays across the hills, creating lengthy shadows in a westerly direction, but neither man appreciated its warmth as they travelled beside the brook.

Onward they strove and they eventually reached Brockhampton Park; the last known residence of the woman they had come to find. They approached by the rear entrance and tied their mounts to railings. At the back door a young maid confronted them politely, and asked of their business.

"We wish to speak with Sir Charles. Could you apologise for our unexpected call but please tell him it is Stefan Desailley? Thank you."

She turned and left. Shortly afterwards the butler came to the door and accepted their presence and showed them into the kitchen. "Gentlemen, please have some tea to warm yourselves. Sir Charles will see you in fifteen minutes," he said with a warm laugh. "You've caught him unawares."

Lionel and Stefan appreciated the offer and drank the tea whilst they thawed before a great cast iron kitchen stove. Shortly afterwards they were called through.

Sir Charles was in the company of his wife and son, and they were all hoping that the two men had brought some good news. They all acknowledged each other graciously.

Stefan was straight to the point. "We've come in the hope that you can give us some clues as to the whereabouts of Georgina, such as where was she last seen or how she was just before her disappearance. Anything you can tell us about her, sir, would be much appreciated."

It was Edward who spoke, out of turn, and they looked across to him.

"Georgina was recovering from her beating, and was becoming healthier by the day. For some reason she was determined to begin riding horses as soon as possible. Before that, she took long walks around the park and then up onto the hills before plucking up enough courage to ride. It was obvious to us that it hurt her to do so but she was resolute. We gave her the submissive Eugene to ride. He is as safe as any mount you could imagine. Besides, we always believed that they loved each other.

"On the fateful day Georgina had become more and more confident, riding out further, but never alone. Ginette went with her the day she disappeared, and the pair rode down to Andoversford. The weather deteriorated quickly, and they turned back. At Syreford a shallow part of the stream crosses the bridleway on a meander, and Ginette, who was leading the way, carried on without looking back, assuming Georgina was following. I'm afraid that it was the last anybody saw of her."

Stefan knew very well of where Edward spoke. He and Georgina had crossed that point in the river. "Please, is there any chance I may be able to speak to Ginette? There are some things I would like to ask her."

Shortly afterwards Maria returned with the bashful young horsewoman and Stefan told her not to be afraid before questioning her.

"How was Georgina's behaviour that day? Was it odd?"

Ginette glanced at all those around her, reluctant to answer for upsetting one of the people in the room. "Tell him what you think, Ginette. Whatever has happened is not your fault." Maria spoke softly and calmed the poor girl's nerves.

"She was always intending to go to Andoversford because she said she had never been there before. I didn't mind but by the time we arrived it was late and we had to ride back. We looked around the village quickly and I suggested that we hurry. Mrs Cavner didn't seem that perturbed when she was following me out of the village. It had begun to rain quite hard and I just rode for home with my head down, assuming she was behind. After the tiny ford at Syreford I never saw her again. I really believed she was following not far behind." Ginette felt guilty but they all assured her that she was not to blame for anything.

"Georgina is alive." Lionel said quietly.

Everyone stared at him silently after his sudden assumption, and Maria broke the impasse. "Hopefully, you are right but what makes you think that?"

"Ginette suggested that Georgina seemed to want to go to Andoversford that day, as if it were a plan, perhaps. And she was slow to follow Ginette home, despite the rain, as if she had an ulterior motive. If someone had unlawfully abducted her then why didn't the culprit bother with Ginette?" Lionel shrugged his shoulders "I personally believe that Georgina's disappearance had been planned, possibly with her knowledge, but by whom I have no clue. That is why I sincerely believe she is alive."

"You believe that her departure might be her own doing?" Sir Charles asked Lionel.

"Yes, that is a possibility but it might not have been orchestrated entirely by herself. Someone is shielding her; someone she knows well enough to trust. No remains have been found and from what I gathered from reading the local journals there was an extensive search throughout the locality. She has left the area without her horse or any means of transport, but how? Someone has picked her up in a carriage or provided another horse. A rapist and murderer wouldn't take her miles away. They would do their awful deed in the vicinity and simply leave the body. Yes, I do believe that she is still alive." Lionel was convinced with his theory.

"You need to speak to Albert Moss, the hurdle maker." On hearing Ginette's meek voice all attention turned back to her.

"Why?" Maria asked.

"There is a story about a carriage being in Andoversford at around the same time or just after we had left, and Andoversford is where Albert lives." Ginette was very self-conscious in the room but her suggestion seemed quite viable to Lionel.

Sir Charles looked across to his son. "Edward, if you know where Mossy is can you go and bring him here, please?"

"I'll go, sir," Ginette said quietly, and looking like she couldn't wait to leave the room. "I know where he can be found." Sir Charles nodded, giving her permission for her to find the man they needed to speak to.

Albert was introduced to Stefan and Lionel a short while later, and was then asked what he knew of Georgina's mysterious disappearance.

"I don't actually know much at all, sir, but there is a story in Andoversford about a horse and carriage in the village that very same evening when the woman went missing. It was just about dark and this particular horse and carriage was seen to come down the Gloucester road before turning left up towards Syreford. About ten or fifteen minutes later it was seen to return and go back up the Gloucester road but no one knows where to." It was all Albert knew.

"What makes you think it had anything to do with Mrs Cavner's disappearance?" Stefan asked.

"There were no other carriages about at that time, sir, and it passed the spot where the horse was found. It then turned around and went back the way it had come. Doesn't that seem odd to you, sir?"

Stefan stopped him. "What makes you think it turned around rather than there being another one coming in the opposite direction?"

"It went up as far as where the road splits left to Whittington and right to Sevenhampton. There's a large patch of triangular ground at that junction, and you can clearly see where it turned around in the mud. Since then the ground has more or less been frozen and the wheel tracks can still be seen. I pass by there twice a day, and can't stop myself from wondering about that carriage turning around at the same time Mrs Cavner disappeared. Everyone talks about it, sir, especially in the pubs. The wheelwright in the village even reckons that a person would be able to find out which make of carriage it was if you went and measured the axle length, which is the distance between the wheels, sir. Each carriage maker has their own specifications, he says." Albert raised his eyebrows, and was unable to add anything else to his revelation.

Sir Charles thanked him and he left. "You could well be right, Lionel. What Albert has just disclosed makes your theory quite feasible. What we have to find out now is where the vehicle was travelling. It could have been towards one of many destinations."

They spent another half an hour discussing the repercussions of the mystery before Stefan and Lionel decided to visit the Cavner Arms, but after gathering no further information at the hostelry they headed back towards Andoversford. On the way they stopped at a fork in the road and confirmed what Albert Moss had told them about the cart tracks, and Stefan absent-mindedly wondered how he could get his hands on an accurate measuring stick.

They soon rode on to the Royal Oak in the village, where the landlord told them the same story they had recently heard, but most of it seemed like village gossip.

After two beers they rode onward to Chedworth.

The two men tied their horses up outside the manor house, and as they opened the gate a large bell rang in the trees, warning the household of any intruders or visitors. Both men thought it very unusual; it was the first time Stefan had ever heard a bell ring at his sister-in-law's home. A maid greeted them at the door and they went inside to talk with Hope. While each sipped a glass of brandy to warm their hearts, they told Hope of their visit to Brockhampton and the mystery of the carriage at

Andoversford. She was of the same opinion as Lionel and believed that Georgina was probably still alive but she couldn't fathom out what had happened to her and why. Hope asked if they had considered that Georgina's husband could be involved, and the looks on their faces suggested that they had.

Both men left, none the wiser. At the gate the bell rang again, heralding their departure, and they decided to try the ale in the Seven Tuns across the lane.

Neither saw the face watching them from the manor house bedroom window.

"Have you just come from across the road, boys? The house with the bell? Well, you're not welcome!" The barman laughed.

"Why do you ask?" was the retort from Stefan, protective of his sister-in-law's privacy.

"Oh, nothing, sir. Nothing," he backed down "What can I get you, gentlemen?" he asked, almost apologetically.

They both decided cider would go down well and sat either side of the log fire. The cider was chilled and almost tasteless, and Lionel laid the poker in the glowing embers. When it was cherry red he plunged it into his drink, and then Stefan did the same. Their simple action produced a better taste to the apple brew.

The mystery that surrounded Georgina was their topic of conversation, and with the bar area being small the barman, also the landlord, listened intently. When Stefan rose from his stool and entered the washroom the innkeeper sat on Stefan's stool and whilst stacking the fire with more logs. He whispered to Lionel.

"I didn't mean to upset your friend earlier, but that annoying bell over there has only just been installed," he said over his shoulder. "And the gates are always kept closed so if anyone enters, the household know about it. Rumour has it they're covering something up. The owner drinks in here every evening but he gives no inclination as to what might be going on over there, I must say." The noise of the latch made him stand and return to his former position behind the bar. Stefan retook his seat and warmed his hands by the fire whilst they discussed where they should go next.

They left after another cider, and Lionel stared towards the house whilst unleashing their horses. He walked over to the gate and pushed it open and then pulled it closed, sounding the bell. Through the trees Lionel saw a side door of the house open and a figure emerge and the two men stood looking at each other. Could there be a link? All the way back he said nothing to Stefan about what he had been told. Mary was coming for Christmas very soon. He would speak with her.

Home in Bibury later that evening, Lionel and Stefan became notoriously drunk, and Lionel's father assured their safety and a reasonable night's rest, albeit in the same bed.

Willie Greyffos turned up at Brockhampton Park later that same afternoon but there was no mention to him of the visit that morning by Lionel and Stefan.

Chapter 39
The Abduction

The Brigadier quietly discussed the estate's affairs with Stefan but in the middle of a conversation about finances the old man changed the subject. "You had a few drinks the other night, didn't you?"

"Yes, sir. I can't deny it. It's not often these days but sometimes I let myself go."

"Stefan, I am going to warn you only once, so listen to me." The Brigadier sipped his Armagnac. "We need you to keep your wits about you. The estate depends on your knowledge so don't be hasty with your decisions. I am sure that if you keep your head straight in these uncertain times then everything will work out for the best in the future. You have three sisters on your side and one of them, of course, is your wife. Please don't let them down. Other women also firmly favour you, and don't let them down either. Believe me, Stefan. Just be patient. Whatever is going on between you and Charity, time will be the great healer."

Stefan said nothing. How often had he heard those same words or similar? He just tried to take in what the Brigadier said and meant. Little made sense to him at the current time but maybe, just maybe the Brigadier was the only one reading correctly between the lines.

"How have you been getting along with Edgar? Are you speaking to each other?" the Brigadier asked him studiously.

Stefan cocked his head to one side. As If the Brigadier doesn't know, he thought. "I hardly see him but when we do meet, although it is not my intention, he completely ignores me and walks past as if I were less than an apparition. I have tried to speak with him but he turns the other way as if admiring a view. Your son, I am afraid to say, has a problem within himself that only he can resolve." Stefan regretted telling his father-in-law his thoughts but knew he would understand.

"Did you know that Edgar left for Shropshire yesterday? He claimed he had some business there." The Brigadier wanted to know how well informed his son-in-law was.

His question made Stefan suddenly pay attention. "May I ask what part of Shropshire?"

"A small town called Tenbury Wells. Quite insignificant, I believe. He has gone for a few days but for what reason he didn't exactly elaborate." The Brigadier watched the expression on Stefan's face. It was anguished. He realised that the woman, Georgina Cavner, meant a lot to Stefan, but if Edgar was now cavorting with her the whole situation on the estate could rapidly change.

"Perhaps it is to do with some ex-army colleagues or matters of that kind?" Stefan ventured without conviction.

"We will have to wait and see," the Brigadier said, pouring himself another drink.

Stefan went home and pulled out some charts and maps. On one he found Tenbury Wells. It was close to Ludlow, which was not that far from Stokesay. He was confused and went back to the main house.

Lionel was in the hall trying to organise the layout of the Christmas party that was taking place the following weekend. Stefan approached him and took him aside.

"Did Edgar mention to you that he was going to Shropshire?" he asked, not wanting to be overheard.

Lionel shook his head. "Not at all. Why?"

Stefan walked around in a circle, rubbing the back of his head. "I think he knows something about Georgina. I'm positive now that all this began at the Summer Ball."

Lionel thought back, adding things up in his head. He too thought that Edgar was involved.

Edgar Collison booked himself into the King's Head inn, a nondescript alehouse in Tenbury Wells. It would be a foolish mistake to bring too much attention to himself. He bore an English army officer's accent, and he hardly dressed ordinarily.

It was Monday afternoon and he had little time but needed to visit St Michael's College first thing in the morning. That evening he ate and drank alone. His only pre-organisation was a carriage picking him up at nine promptly the next morning. He was nervous and that night he slept very little, thinking only of his nefarious task ahead.

In the morning his transport arrived as requested and they left for the college. It was a mere mile from the main street of Tenbury Wells. The building was relatively new with many gables and towers forming sharply pitched roofs. It was built from locally mined stone but gave an appearance of a religious structure, such as a monastery. On arrival Edgar asked his driver to wait, telling him he would be handsomely rewarded for doing so.

Inside at the reception desk a polite secretary asked him of his needs. "Madam, my name is Edgar Collison, I am passing through fleetingly on business but need to speak to someone regarding the education of my three children. Would there be any possibility I might be able to have a brief word before I carry on?"

. "One moment, sir," she said, glancing at her diary." I shall enquire." She disappeared through a side door and quickly returned. "Please follow me," she said, indicating towards the door behind her desk.

Edgar was introduced to a matronly woman who announced herself as the deputy headmistress. "How can I help you, Mr Collison?" she asked, smiling.

"My family and I are moving to the area and your school has been recommended to us with regards to our children's education, more probably at the beginning of the next academic year. However, we thought it would be better if my wife and I would now probe into all scholarly possibilities. If you, by any chance, have any information or paperwork about your school that I may take back to my dear wife it would be much appreciated," Edgar implored.

"Sir, thank you for coming. All I can ask of you for now is to send us a letter of your wishes for your children. Our school is in such demand and we have to consider all applicants. Deciding next year's intake is some way off but we do take considerable time to assess each child individually." She smiled again as she eyed Edgar up and down wondering if he came from a moneyed family.

"I will do so. Have you by any chance a letter heading or an envelope by which I can take back with me that has the school's address on?"

"Of course, Mr Collison." She delved into the drawer beneath her desk and produced both.

Exactly what he needed. "What time do you break for Christmas on Friday?" he asked.

"Thursday, Mr Collison. We break on Thursday at two o'clock prompt," she informed him, smiling.

"Then I shall ensure the letter is with you before then."

They bade farewell and Edgar left. He had everything he wanted. Soon he was back at the King's Head and writing a letter. As soon as he had finished, he went out and posted it.

He had a day and a half to prepare. Firstly, he pre-paid for a high quality carriage to take him to St Michael's College by two-fifteen o'clock precisely on Thursday, when the school term ended for the Christmas break. Secondly, he hired a nanny to safeguard the children's well-being from the school and travel to their eventual train destination at Cheltenham. She was also pre-paid with a promised gratuity on safe delivery. They were to meet at one o'clock outside the King's Head in Cross Street, where Edgar was staying, on Thursday afternoon. Edgar then arranged an outing for the following day to the Newtown area near Stokesay Castle, and on his return he would pay a visit to Ludlow, a popular Shropshire town.

A letter arrived at Stokesay Castle from St Michael's college. It was addressed to Mr and Mrs FJ C Cavner. The butler took it to Fulwar who, partially inebriated lying on his chaise longue asked the butler to read it out aloud.

"It is from your children's school, sir. It reads, 'Due to a repeat of the highly successful nativity play, the school term will now end at three-thirty p.m. and not at two p.m. on Thursday, as was previously perceived'."

Fulwar waved his arm. "Tell the driver. He'll have to leave later."

"Yes, sir. I will inform him." The butler placed the letter on the table and left to warn the staff at the stable yard of the rearranged agenda.

Edgar was tense. The driver loaded his luggage into the back of the carriage whilst he paid his bill at the King's Head. The nanny stood by as he fumbled with the ink pen before signing the cheque. They were soon on their way to St Michael's College. Edgar had arranged to arrive at two-fifteen, hoping most of the children would have left and the two remaining would be Thomas and Jennifer. He was almost right although several carriages still remained on the driveway and quite a few children were milling around.

Edgar reminded the nanny before she went to find them. "Should anyone ask, their names are Thomas and Jennifer Corbett-Cavner. Their mother's name is Georgina and their father's name is Fulwar."

The nanny stepped out of the carriage and walked towards the front door, where the remaining children waited surrounded by schoolteachers and maids. The nanny approached one of the younger maids. Speaking eloquently, she asked, "I have been acquired to escort Thomas and Jennifer Cavner back to Stokesay Castle. Can you tell me where I might find them?"

The young woman searched the throng. "Yes, there they are." She pointed towards the two children waiting patiently by the entrance.

Edgar watched nervously from inside the carriage as the nanny approached the children and spoke to the boy. Thomas looked across to the maroon carriage.

"How do I know who you are?" he asked sensibly.

"I am a good friend of your mother's. We grew up together. She wrote me a letter asking to pick you up at the end of the school term and make sure you are safe. Come on! We haven't much time." She took the little girl's suitcase, held her hand and escorted them to the carriage. Thomas followed reluctantly, looking despairingly over his shoulder and hoping someone would come to their rescue. No one did; everything seemed quite innocent.

The carriage wheels scrunched on the gravel as the horses did a sharp turn in front of the school, and they set off to Leominster. Edgar's aim was to catch the three-thirty train to Cheltenham.

A carriage with the Cavner family crest adorned on either door arrived at three-thirty outside the entrance of St Michael's College. Perplexed, the school secretary and bursar both came out and asked the driver for whom he was waiting. After some enquiries within the school it became apparent that the children had been abducted. The driver turned away and headed back to Stokesay Castle.

At Leominster station Edgar tipped his driver with a fine remuneration as nothing was to be said. They touched hats in acknowledgement. Young Thomas was agitated and the nanny took both of the children aside and sat them on a bench. "Please believe me that we are taking you to see your mother. I will be travelling as far as Cheltenham with you, and then you will be met by friends of Mr Collison. It will be a long journey late into the evening but I am more than sure you will be safe."

Thomas' face was distrusting but to reassure his sister, who clung tightly to his shoulder, he squeezed her hand. The poor boy was tired, scared and wanted to cry, but he tried to put on a brave face. "Where *is* my mother? Tell me or I'll scream the place down." Thomas meant what he said.

The nanny did not know where Thomas' mother was but to avoid an incident she beckoned Edgar over. He spoke to the boy firmly. "Please listen to me. I have known your mother for some time now and she desperately wants to see you both," he smiled, trying to be the father he could never be "Please reassure Jennifer that she is safe, and later tonight you will both meet your mother. I am sure that is what you want most."

"But where? Where are we going?" Thomas was astute. "Tell me where exactly and at least then I will know."

"A place called Chedworth. Your mother is perfectly safe there and you both will be as well." Edgar's encouragement was not beholden.

At the mention of the name Chedworth Thomas looked across at the nanny. She raised her eyebrows at him. Thomas trusted no one but his sister's safety was his first priority.

A train pulled into the station and the four embarked. They were in the warmth of first class travel and soon Jennifer was asleep up against the nanny. Thomas, however, remained awake at the side of Edgar, fearful of going to sleep and never waking up.

Darkness soon fell and the winter scenery rushing by was slowly replaced by the reflection of the gas lamps within the train. Few words were spoken but Thomas often glanced at Edgar, who had his pencil in hand although failing even to start The Times crossword.

Edgar continually eyed the sleeping Jennifer over the top of his journal, and the train rattled on.

After two changes they reached Cheltenham station. Thomas stood next to the nanny as she accepted a large reward from Edgar. She bent down and kissed Jennifer goodbye. "You will be safe," she told her. She took Thomas by the hand, smiled and whispered in his ear, "I heard where he is taking you and I will not forget."

The nanny waved them off from the station. A horse and carriage had been organised by Edgar. She then turned to find the high-class hotel into which Edgar had booked for her night in Cheltenham.

The journey back to Chedworth was harsh. It took great dexterity to control the horses in the dark, and unknown to Hope and James, Edgar was arriving with Georgina's children. No one knew what was about to happen, including Georgina.

The driver negotiated the hill down into Chedworth with great skill and horsemanship. He turned left sharply towards the front of the manor house gates and halted. Edgar jumped out and pushed them open ringing the bell in the trees as if proclaiming a monarchic procession, and a door opened at the house shedding light onto the paved step.

The carriage pulled up towards the side door and Edgar closed the gates behind him and walked the final few yards in a show of personal triumph. There in the half-light he recognised his sister and brother-in-law, plus several staff all standing bemused.

With help the children vacated the carriage. They were completely lost and afraid but Georgina appeared on the doorstep looking over everyone's shoulders at the unannounced spectacle, and in the dim light she recognised her children.

"Thomas! Jennifer!" she screamed and fell to her knees as they ran towards her. She cried uncontrollably as they all hugged each other as if it was to be their last act in the world, and everyone else stood around watching the wonderful scene. It was James who coaxed Georgina to her feet and persuaded her to enter the house. Soon everyone was back indoors and out of sight from prying neighbours.

Georgina hugged Edgar. "Oh, thank you, Edgar. Thank you so much. I simply cannot thank you enough. Oh, I love you so much."

Edgar smiled at her. "I think you had better take them upstairs," he said as he crouched down and kissed them both with real warmth. "They will need a bath, something to eat and then a good night's rest. They have had such a long day."

Instead of replying she kissed him passionately before turning and leading the children upstairs to her bedroom. He was Georgina's hero, or so he thought.

James took Edgar aside. "Well done. You've certainly made Georgina very happy. What are you going to do next?"

"As much as I would like to stay for a while I must take the carriage back to Bibury tonight, so I will leave shortly. It is a treacherous route in the dark."

"I fully understand," agreed James.

"James, please allow the children to settle down with their mother over the Christmas period, and in the New Year we shall relocate them at a local school. I will be in touch."

James could not help but wonder at how remarkably fatherly Edgar was. "Goodnight, Edgar," he called as his brother-in-law climbed into the waiting carriage.

Thomas and Jennifer spent their first night at Chedworth manor, where neither slept at all well.

Chapter 40
The Search Begins

"He is not in a good mood," Mrs Cavner said as she stared at Willie Greyffos, seemingly implying that everything was his fault.

"I am sorry, Madam, but may I ask one simple question? Is he sober?" Willie raised a suspicious eyebrow.

"Go and see for yourself," she replied, and she turned and walked away, knowing that Willie knew which door to approach.

Rather than bothering to knock, he simply walked straight in to find Fulwar sleeping on the hearthrug with his crystal glass on its side next to him.

Unconcerned, he kicked his paymaster hard on the back of his thigh. Fulwar awoke abruptly, and his face was reddened and blotched by the heat from the fire, exacerbated by his alcohol intake.

"Sorry," Willie said. "It was difficult to wake you."

Fulwar crawled onto the chaise longue and sat upright. There were dregs left in the whisky bottle, which he emptied into his glass before eyeing Willie up and down. "What have you found out? Anything useful?" he asked with a gravely voice.

"I have someone working in the area who has given me a name." Willie lied.

"Who is it?" Fulwar demanded.

"He has been mentioned before, and is someone you should know." Willie glanced at the empty whisky bottle. Fulwar Cavner remembered very little.

"Edgar Collison. Rumour has it around Bibury that he has been and still is heavily involved with your wife."

Fulwar stood up and walked uneasily to the fireplace. He rested his elbow on the mantelpiece and rubbed his hair whilst in deep thought. Slowly he shook his head and then suddenly looked up.

"Three days ago my children were abducted from school. A woman came in a carriage and persuaded them to leave with her and we haven't heard from them or seen them since. I am anxious to have them back as soon as possible, especially for Christmas."

"Christmas Day is on Tuesday, and today is already Sunday. If they could be found it would take more than a day to bring them back here, and no trains or coaches will run on Christmas day. I think you will have to put the idea of them being with you for Christmas out of your head. Besides that, who has taken them and where? They are not necessarily with their mother, and even if they are, we do not know where she is." Willie couldn't see anything being done about it until later in the week or even in the New Year.

"My father and mother are concerned. They are their only grandchildren. After me, Thomas is the heir to the whole estate," Fulwar said, agitated. "Something has to be done."

Willie looked at the forlorn figure hanging on the mantelpiece and then again at his empty whisky bottle. "Maybe if you could control your alcohol consumption none of this would be happening. It is not for me to tell you how to run your life, far from it, but perhaps if you steered clear of the dreaded drink the situation might resolve itself. Do you really want your children brought up by a father such as you? What do you think goes through their young minds when they see you as you are now?"

Fulwar avoided the subject. "This Edgar Collison, his name crops up all the time. Go and investigate him, and try and find out if he was at the school or had anything to do with the abduction of my children. It sounds to me that he is the man behind all this."

"I'll go but don't expect any results this side of Christmas or even the New Year. I will go to the school first thing in the morning, and on Wednesday or Thursday I'll head south and see what else I can find out." Willie pointed at the empty whisky bottle. "Stay off that stuff and you might start thinking clearly, especially if you want your family back once and for all."

Willie left Fulwar feeling very despondent for himself, and as he walked out of the building he couldn't help thinking how an intelligent man with so much at his feet could have allowed himself to become so ill.

St Michael's College was completely silent. Willie cupped his hands around his face and stared through several windows. The inside was as equally devoid of life. He was about to walk away when he heard a voice shout across to him. "Hello! Can I help you?"

He turned and there stood a middle-aged man with a broom in his hand. They approached each other. "I've come to investigate the disappearance of Thomas and Jennifer Cavner," Willie told him.

"Strange circumstances, that. The police were here but their attitude was simply 'find their mother and you'll probably find the children'. Marriage problems, apparently. They were reluctant to get involved. Aristocracy, that's why. Too many repercussions if anything untoward turns up."

"Did anyone recognise the people who came to pick them up?"

"The receptionist wasn't completely sure but she thought the gentleman sitting inside the carriage was the same one who came enquiring about the school two or three days before. She had a fleeting view of him but it all happened so quickly. I don't know his name. She might know."

"Where can I find her? Does she live locally?" Willie asked.

"I am afraid that she is away visiting relatives for Christmas."

Willie thought deeply. If it *was* Edgar Collison and he was here last Monday or Tuesday, he would never have travelled back to Bibury and returned on the Thursday. He must have stayed here somewhere.

"Where is the nearest place I can book a room for the night?"

"That'll be the King's Head in Tenbury. It's the only place close to here."

Willie thanked him and turned back to his waiting carriage. He had a momentary conversation with his driver and set off for his next destination, the village of Tenbury.

Inside the King's Head he spoke briefly with the landlady. With her information in mind he booked a room for two nights, which included Christmas Day, and then went outside and dismissed his driver whom he had hired from Ludlow. After settling in his room Willie decided that a walk around the village would enlighten his comprehension of the area. His first objective was to find the owner of the carriage that apparently took Edgar to the college and subsequently picked up the children on Thursday afternoon. Boraston Lane was the address across the river that his landlady had given him. He was the only man in Tenbury who had such a business.

He crossed the arched medieval Teme Bridge, which took him into the village of Burford on the north side of the river, and he soon came across what he had hoped to find; a horse and carriage parked outside a cottage. Willie rapped hard on the brass doorknocker, and a middle-aged man answered. He was chewing and wiping his mouth simultaneously, and Willie waited for him to swallow his food.

"I beg your pardon, sir. How can I help you? Do you need to travel somewhere?" He glanced back at the clock in the tiny hallway, "There isn't much time today, sir. It's Christmas Eve."

"No thank you. I will be quick and to the point. I believe you picked those two missing children up last Thursday from school. Where did you take them?" The driver was reluctant to say anything. Willie produced his wallet and he soon began to talk when seeing the money.

"Leominster train station. We only just made it in time. The bloke who took them was after catching the three-thirty to Cheltenham, I believe. I wasn't involved after that. Nothing to do with me, anyway, I was just hired as a driver. You would be better off speaking to Maggie Plunkett."

"Why? Is she the woman who was with you that day?" Willie asked.

The carriage owner gestured towards Willie's wallet, and Willie offered him a half crown, which he took without hesitating. "That payment includes a lift for me to Leominster train station as well, first thing Wednesday morning."

It loosened his tongue. "Yes, Maggie was with us and I'm sure for the correct remuneration she will probably tell you exactly where their destination was." He explained to Willie where she lived.

"Please be at the King's Head on Wednesday at first light." Willie left him on the doorstep and headed back to Tenbury.

He passed the strangely designed pump rooms as he tried to find the address he'd been given. Tenbury had become a mineral water town, and The Round Market resembled a giant dovecot.

He soon found the address he had been given. Mrs Plunkett's house was thoroughly decorated for the festivities, and when she opened the door Willie saw that the interior was as equally adorned as the exterior. He smiled. Such was Christmas, he thought.

"Come in!" She said without hesitation. "Come in! Don't stand out there, it's Christmas." Willie entered the modest house. The front room had a tree surrounded with presents.

"I have seventeen grandchildren and they will all be around tomorrow morning. Wrapping them all is so time consuming, and the children keep knocking on the door or peering through the window. So excited are they. Oh! I love children, especially when they are so happy. But I can't stop, I must keep going."

"Actually, Mrs Plunkett, it is children I have come to ask you about." Willie raised his eyebrows, wondering how she might behave.

She stopped what she was doing and looked him coldly in the eyes. "You are going to ask about the two children at St Michael's College, aren't you?"

"Yes, ma'am. It is important we find them. Safe and sound, hopefully," he added after a few seconds.

"I shouldn't have become involved but he paid so well. From what I gathered he was taking the two little souls to their mother. When we reached Cheltenham my job was finished. He had a carriage waiting at the station. He even funded my overnight stay in a posh hotel. Money was no object. The very next morning I returned here. Without him we wouldn't be having such a good Christmas." Maggie gestured towards all the presents and decorations.

"Can you verify what his name was at all, and where he was heading?"

"Collison. I saw his name on the cheque when he wrote it out in the King's Head. He told the boy he was being taken to a place called Chedworth. I have never heard of it but I do hope they are both safe. I didn't trust him; he was always staring at the little girl."

Mrs Plunkett had said enough.

Willie reassured her. "I am sure they will be safe, although he does have an underlying motive. Don't fret and have a jolly Christmas with your dear grandchildren. I will see myself out."

As he walked back to the King's Head he kept thinking of Georgina and her children staying at Hope Ronssoy's house in Chedworth. But he asked himself over and over why they would stay there? And what will Fulwar Cavner do about it when he finds out? If he finds out.

His landlady confirmed that it was Edgar Collison who had stayed at the King's Head but Willie couldn't understand why the police didn't go through the trouble of making the same enquiries as he had done.

Chapter 41
Christmas Day, 1866

Christmas Dinner was a very traditional affair at Bibury Court, and it took place in the great hall simply because the dining room was far from expansive enough. There would be three sittings. The Brigadier's family and their invited friends and relations would sit to eat and drink first, followed by the estate workers whilst the men and guests from the Brigadier's entourage temporarily retired into the dining room; their ladies always then helped in the kitchen or acted as waitresses.

The milking parlour men would be fed early because they would later have to go and relieve the anxious cows of their frothy white liquid. Finally everyone who worked inside the house would have their opportunity to sit down and deservedly enjoy their dinner.

Ultimately, Marcel Desailley and and his wife Mrs Desailley would sit together at the kitchen table to eat their dinner. The preparations had begun some time ago and the dear Mrs Desailley would undoubtedly be extremely tired having toiled through most of the night to make sure everything went to order. Faith, Hope and Charity, as they did every year with some volunteers from the second shift, would wash up and put away the spent dishes and cutlery in earnest under the watchful eyes of the respected French woman. They would not cease until every pot, pan and utensil were hanging back on the walls, the great stoves were scrubbed until pristine and every square inch of the floor mopped with disinfectant.

The Brigadier allowed one of his guests to lead a prayer and soon afterwards they were consuming some of the finest Christmas food in Gloucestershire. Mrs Desailley's reputation went far and wide.

After a while Gerard asked, "Where is Edgar? I haven't seen him since lunchtime yesterday. His first Christmas back home for years and he doesn't attend dinner? That is most strange."

The Brigadier sat back in his chair, wiped his mouth and took a sip of Armagnac. "He has contacted some old army colleagues. They wrote back inviting him to an ex-officer's get together in Cheltenham. His opinion was that he shouldn't ignore the invitation. He left some time yesterday afternoon and will be back this evening." He watched with amusement at his guest's suspicious looks and sideward glances.

Gerard still thought it very odd. Hope carried on eating but said nothing, as if oblivious to the conversation. Charity said nothing either but was more than happy that Edgar was not in attendance.

It was James who spoke next. "How is he settling in here? It must be quite a change after all those years in the services. Much less disciplined, I assume."

"He seems a little agitated. Something is on his mind, probably his family in India," the Brigadier looked across to Gerard, "can we have a chat about that this afternoon?" Gerard could only nod because his mouth was full.

"He isn't aware yet but after Christmas we have one of the farms being vacated," the Brigadier announced, "and so I am going to suggest to him that he can manage that to see how he gets on. That should keep his mind off things. Stefan will show him the ropes regarding the paperwork. It will do Edgar good and perhaps get him into some sort of groove."

"Which farm is that, Father?" Faith asked, more than interested, hoping it wouldn't interfere with her plans.

"Kilkenny's. The tenants have been good to us over many years but now wish to retire. I'm letting them have one of the cottages close by. Mr Kilkenny will be staying on for a couple of months to help Edgar and teach him the art and management of Cotswold farming." The Brigadier smiled at the thought, wondering if it was possible.

"What if he says no? Then what is he going to do?" Hope was just as interested as the rest of them. The sooner Georgina vacated her household the better and any repercussions would be diverted elsewhere. The Kilkenny farm vacancy might just be a godsend.

"His options will be stark. Start somewhere or there is nothing for him. It would be better for him and his family out there although I'm not sure what local people will say when they find out he has an Indian wife with three children who, through no fault of their own, are not his. It is a large, beautifully structured house ideal for a family, and the farm buildings are more than adequate. Over the years it has been a well-run enterprise, and the staff up there are excellent. I'll be sorry to see Mr and Mrs Kilkenny leave." The Brigadier was sceptical but he had to do something with his undesirable son.

Someone changed the subject, it was too easy to sit around a table and talk behind a man's back. They finished their meal. The children were, as every Christmas, over excited and went to view the presents under the Christmas tree. The men stood and moved into the adjacent dining room still talking and drinking, and the three sisters and two friends went to help in the kitchen. Top of the agenda was the emigration of Edgar's family. Stefan declined to offer an opinion, even though he had one.

In the main hall the second sitting went with few mishaps, and everyone was having a jolly time. There was much banter and joking, and as each individual finished their meal they graciously left the table to allow the housekeepers to deservedly take their place. The congregation by the makeshift bar grew larger and larger.

Lionel and Mary took their place opposite each other at the end of one of the long tables. Mary could have sat with the Brigadier's family and friends but chose instead to be with her man. To anyone looking on, they were in love. As they waited for their plum pudding Lionel pulled from his jacket pocket a tiny box covered in velvet and placed it on the table in front of him. Someone further along the table noticed his almost ceremonious act, and it soon spread around the great hall. The joviality died down and all eyes were directed towards Lionel and Mary. Oblivious, Mary looked around at everyone's smiling faces.

Lionel opened the box gently and took out a beautiful gold and diamond engagement ring. Stretching across the table he took Mary's left hand. By that point word had reached the kitchen and then the dining room, and their occupants excitedly spilled out into the main hall just in time. It went eerily quiet.

Lionel smiled at Mary. "Will you marry me?"

She made him wait a little while as she tried to imagine how her hand would seem bejewelled with such a charming engagement ring. "It would be the best Christmas present a woman could ask for. Of course I will, Lionel. Of course I will."

Before sliding the ring over her finger he smiled again. "Only for a sixpence, I hope."

She nodded her head and agreed. "Only for a sixpence."

The whole hall erupted with cheering and shouting as Lionel pushed the ring into place, and the couple stood and strained across the table holding each other's hands. They gave each other a lingering kiss that saluted the first progression towards a long and happy marriage. Lionel had asked her to marry him some time before, but now it was official and the ring was firmly in place. They smiled at each other and sat back down.

Someone at the back began singing "For he's a jolly good fellow" and soon everyone joined in. There were scenes of amiable rowdiness and country dancing supported by several types of musical instruments, along with excessive celebratory drinking.

The Christmas party had truly begun. Children ran between the adults' legs, playing their imaginary games, and Santa Claus would soon arrive and hand out all of the presents under the large tree in the corner.

Sir Charles's Christmas lunch was a much more sullen affair than that of Bibury Court. They had dinner with just a few friends from the surrounding villages. The dinner was as equally sumptuous and there was much fine port available from several of the best Portuguese vineyards, but the conversation brought no good tidings.

"Have you heard anything about Georgina?" David Webb asked. He was a Highworth businessman who owned Hawling Manor.

"Nothing. She has well and truly disappeared. She can't be local because she would have been seen wandering about. It is a mystery. She has no money or clothes with her, so somebody is either keeping her or she has passed away somehow or other, but it is fortunate that no body has yet turned up." As much as Sir Charles wished she was alive and well, deep down he was glad that she was off his estate.

"And what has apparently happened to the children? You mentioned the other day that there was a serious problem with them but you didn't elaborate." David Webb still showed concern although he did have an ulterior motive when asking, he owned an insurance company.

"I can tell you now the message we received on Sunday was dour. Both the children were abducted from school on the last day of term before Christmas. They haven't been seen or heard of since. I don't know what more to say." Sir Charles was truly worried about them.

"They will turn up, if someone wished to murder them they would have just shot them on the spot. Why take them somewhere else when they could be murdered and then disposed of." Maria whimpered at the thought, and David apologised profusely, not intending to sound so basic, "I think, at the most that a ransom note will arrive stating the demands."

"Georgina disappeared nearly a month ago now and there has been no ransom note for her," Edward said. He had his own opinions but, similar to everyone else, no answers. Rhetoric was commonly used to allay the fears of the concerned. "We'll just have to wait and see," he added.

Sir Charles' party spent the rest of the afternoon drinking, joking, playing card games or billiards and discussing less stressful subjects.

Just three people sat at the end of the banqueting table in Stokesay Castle; Frederick and Isabella Cavner and their son, Fulwar. They were accompanied by two deerhounds lying lazily in front of the hearth.

Not a word was said between the three of them. The starter requested by Fulwar was a thin cock-a-leekie soup, which was presented by equally silent servants.

Freshly baked brown bread supplemented the well-balanced soup. For Fulwar it was easy to digest. His mother watched him carefully as she supped from her soup spoon. For every spoonful her son swallowed, he took a sip of whisky. Unseen by Fulwar, she very slightly shook her head in despair as every mother would, watching her son slowly killing himself.

As the dishes were cleared away Fulwar excused himself, and Isabella turned to her husband, who was reading a week old copy of the Telegraph. "You have to do something about him. He cannot carry on like this. He'll be dead within a year."

Isabella's remark wasn't what annoyed Frederick; it was because she stopped him from reading the newspaper. He stared angrily back at her.

"And what do you want me to do with him? Spank him! Send him upstairs to bed! He is an adult, Isabella, and he can do as he wishes. Perhaps I'll send him down to Charles. He'll know how to look after him," he laughed arrogantly.

"Move him there and that half of the estate will be bankrupt as well. Everyone is leaving here because they so despise you both. They can earn more money in a Birmingham factory nowadays – and be treated better. Who can blame them? Fulwar has lost his wife, who is such a lovely woman, and now his children, who are our grandchildren, I might add. He doesn't know where they have gone but, worryingly, he doesn't understand why they have left him. You think he does no wrong but that's because you were exactly the same until you became too old to beat me up. You were just as big a bastard to me as he has been to Georgina, and neither of you can see that you have ever done anything wrong. You are suffering from denial, Frederick Cavner, and it's catching up on you. That is why none of our invited guests have turned up. Quite simply, you two have brought the estate to its knees because of your pig headed, abhorrent attitudes towards other people. It's not only the lesser people either; you've upset the aristocracy as well. Even they won't come here unless they have to."

The main course arrived, and Frederick stood and glared down at his wife of over forty years. "I am not staying here eating next to a selfish bitch such as you!" He looked at the servants. "Lay me a plate and deliver it to the drawing room." With no manners he grabbed the newspaper and stormed out. Both dogs craned their necks to see what the fuss was about as the poor maid ran out of the room to oblige Mr Cavner's order.

Isabella held her head in her hands despairingly. Fulwar didn't return and she ate alone.

It was late at Bibury Court and most people were still dancing, although the beer had run out. Lionel and Stefan sat talking; they were quite drunk.

"Why isn't Edgar here? His first year back?" Lionel slurred as he asked the important question. "

"He's gone to meet some old comrades in Cheltenham. Apparently, he went yesterday afternoon and will be back some time this evening," Stefan replied, thinking that it would satisfy his friend's curiosity.

"This morning, you mean," Lionel replied almost incoherently.

"No, the Brigadier said he left yesterday afternoon. Why would he lie?"

"Sorry but you are wrong, my friend. He left this morning just as it was getting light. Mary and I saw him from the window when he left. It's true." Lionel dropped his drink down his front and cursed.

Stefan left him to it and staggered over to Mary, who was jigging around on her own, and spoke in her ear. The last thing Lionel remembered that evening was that she was nodding as if what he had told Stefan was the truth. Stefan didn't return to the table. The little piece of information had already begun to torment his mind, and he went home without saying goodbye to anyone.

Chapter 42
Greyffos in Bibury

"Just wait here a moment, will you please?" Willie Greyffos asked his driver. Willie needed to secure a bed for the night before being left stranded in a remote Cotswold village in wintertime. Lionel's father recognised him and discreetly offered him the only room left, which was one he didn't normally let. Willie didn't refuse, as long as the bed was clean and dry, and went back outside, retrieved his luggage and paid his driver. It was late, and having thrown his belongings on the bed he was soon back downstairs drinking a beer. Shortly afterwards he made his way down to the Swan, and luckily found the man he wanted to talk with, but he was in company.

Neil Portlock, who had returned from his home in the north that day after the Christmas festivities, couldn't believe Willie Greyffos would walk into a bar in Bibury so brazenly.

"Gentlemen, may I buy you all a drink?" Willie spoke as if he knew everyone. Neil went to stand but Willie pushed him back down into his seat. "No! Honestly, it is my pleasure. Please allow me."

While he was at the bar Neil explained who the stranger was. Stefan didn't take his eyes off him and Lionel could see the tension building up in Stefan's afflicted mind.

Soon the unexpected visitor brought back two beers and went to fetch another two before realising that there were others missing at the table. Lionel gestured behind him and he turned, there stood Faith with Mary

"Mrs Havrincourt and Ms Buchanan! Please, I beg your pardon. Let me buy you both a drink." They accepted his kind offer and he again returned to the bar.

Willie eventually settled himself in. "Do I take it you all had a pleasant Christmas Day?"

None of them could deny that they had. He then went on to describe his long and uncomfortable journey down to Bibury. Neil explained that he had travelled much further that same day but had arrived somewhat earlier.

"So, what brings you here to Bibury? Especially so soon after Christmas." Faith had to ask him although she could only imagine that he had been told to come searching for Georgina and her children.

As he spoke Willie stared straight at Faith. "As you all probably know quite well, Mrs Cavner disappeared some time ago but the abduction of her children is rather a more serious matter." All eyes directed onto Faith as if she had an inclination as to their whereabouts. Neil knew of Georgina's mysterious departure but had not heard of the disappearance of her children. Willie quickly explained to him what had happened, prompting Neil to look at Faith. He could only imagine that the woman sitting opposite was the instigator of such a despicable kidnap. Willie finished what he had to say. "Basically, I have been sent here to find Fulwar Cavner's children."

"What makes you think that they are down this way?" Faith asked maintaining the pretence.

"I don't even know if the three are all together but what better place to start searching. If I can find their mother then I can probably locate her children. Mrs Cavner was known to you." Willie took a sly glance at Stefan, who remained resolutely quiet although underneath he was seething, perceiving that anyone working for Fulwar Cavner was a threat to Georgina's life. "She is obviously not with Sir Charles and his wife. Her own family don't want her because she married Mr Cavner and had been forewarned of the repercussions."

He turned to Mary, "Ma'am, you are her good friend and cousin, have you any inkling as to where she might be? It is important for her children's sake. Is there anyone else in your family who might take her in and offer refuge?"

Mary shook her head. "Not at all. Nobody in our family has heard from her. Not even her parents, I'm afraid. We all fear the worst." Mary gripped Lionel's hand, and he tried to reassure her that she would turn up in the not so distant future.

Willie was disappointed but he had a trump card up his sleeve. "I shouldn't be telling you this but if I don't instil a sense of urgency into you all, this matter might take a turn for the worse." He quickly stole glances around the table and carried on. "Last Sunday I was with Fulwar Cavner and he appeared seriously depressed. Naturally, he wants his children back as soon as possible and will do anything to achieve that goal. Unfortunately, it is how far he is prepared to go to have them back permanently."

"And how far is that, Mr Greyffos?" Faith asked slowly and solemnly, knowing exactly what he was about to say next.

"He asked me if I knew anyone who might be prepared to assassinate Mrs Cavner – at any price."

Willie Greyffos provoked an angry reaction from Stefan. He tried to stand up and voice his own opinion in no uncertain terms but Lionel pulled him back into his chair and told him to calm down.

Under great self-control Stefan confronted the man he had been hearing about. "My God, what impertinence you possess to come here and tell us that the imbecile who employs you now wants to have his wife murdered. Why didn't you go straight to the police and warn them?"

"Mr Desailley, you tell me where I can find Mrs Cavner and then I'll know which county judiciary to notify. Not only that but no county police force will act upon hearsay. Nothing has so far happened and nothing has been written down to suggest that it might." Willie raised his eyebrows waiting for Stefan to reply. It was obvious to Willie that Stefan didn't have a clue of Georgina's whereabouts, and it was frustrating him deeply. "I doubt very much that Mr Cavner meant what he said, and it might seem a ridiculous thing to say but in his current state I don't think he could even organise a hooley in a malthouse.

Neil smiled to himself, quite sure that except for Willie no one else at the table knew what a *hooley* was.

Faith made a move. "I must go. Gerard is returning back to London first thing tomorrow, and I'd better make sure he has everything ready."

"Mrs Havrincourt, I will walk along to the house with you. It is dark and it might be safer with an escort." Faith accepted the offer.

In the black of night Faith took Willie's arm. "You know where they are, don't you?" Faith asked.

"I think I know where the children went after being taken from the school, but I can only assume that their mother is with them."

"What are you going to do next?" Faith asked, worried that Willie would remain only in the pay of Fulwar Cavner.

"I am waiting for your command, Mrs Havrincourt. This situation will have to come to a head eventually. It cannot possibly drag on for ever."

"We'll be sending off the first letter very shortly now that the children are more or less secure, and hopefully they will settle in and we won't have to move them again until everything is resolved." Faith didn't sound entirely convincing that everything would work to plan.

"What will be in the first letter you send? Something that might incense Fulwar Cavner, I assume?" Willie was interested to know.

"More or less. Maria, Sir Charles' wife, will send it. It has to be worded carefully because we want to give him an address where Georgina might be but not the children. Somewhere locally has become available, and it will make an ideal location." She smiled in the darkness. Kilkenny Farm was bestowed upon her by pure luck.

"Where?" Willie asked.

"It's better you don't know just yet. We cannot afford things to move too fast. The last thing we want is for it all to end in just a pub brawl. It has to be much more serious."

"If you tell me where Georgina will be operating from, I can always return to Stokesay and confirm what is in the letter. Fulwar will then be more than convinced that that is where his troubles are stemming from, especially if your brother is involved. Be careful, Faith. Make sure that wherever she will be staying, Mrs Cavner is well protected. I wasn't telling the truth this evening, but it is possible that murdering her is going through his fractured mind, and then only he can have custody of the children."

The unlikely pair stopped at the Court gates and Faith kissed Willie passionately on the cheek. "I'll write to you as soon as I know more. Please do not let us down," she pleaded and then turned and entered the Court grounds.

Only when he had turned into the wind and felt the cold down one side of his face did Willie Greyffos realise that Faith had been weeping. With his cuff he wiped his cheek dry and carried on back towards the Catherine Wheel to find Neil Portlock.

Chapter 43
The Brigadier's Offer

"Don't argue with me, Edgar. Kilkenny Farm is my final offer. Take it or leave it. You will not be fully involved on the estate as long as I am still alive." The Brigadier was adamant.

Faith couldn't believe that Edgar was being so stubborn. Although she remained tight-lipped her frustration boiled within her.

"Please, Father. I don't wish to be out on an isolated farm away from the main business. I would be much more useful here." Edgar pleaded for his father to change his mind.

"Edgar you don't even know the cost of a bushel of grain or the price of lamb per pound. Indeed, you wouldn't even know how to start to gather in the wheat, let alone slaughter an animal in preparation for the market. No, I am sorry but it is my final offer. You go there and learn about the farming industry on a small scale and then, perhaps, you will one day be able to take on the estate as a whole. Mr Kilkenny will remain with you for two or three months and will be just down the lane should you need any advice. Stefan will advise you on the money side of things and the paperwork. Had you not been so damn lazy when you were a young man, this wouldn't be happening now."

Edgar stopped the Brigadier dead in his tracks. "I am sorry but there is no possible way that Desailley will be participating with anything I am involved in."

"Well, as you are not involved in anything at the moment, that will not present a problem. Believe me, Edgar. I suggest you take this opportunity because I already have someone very interested in taking over Mr and Mrs Kilkenny's tenancy, and he has the deposit at the ready." The Brigadier wondered if his disclosure might move him.

There was a worried look on Faith's face. "That's rather sudden, Father, especially as you haven't even put it on the market. Who is it?"

"That chap working for Marcel. Portlock, isn't it? He's expressed an interest. Hard working fellow and a fast learner, so Marcel says." The Brigadier saw the look of shock on his daughter's face. "What is the matter? What have I said?"

"Nothing, Father. It's nothing," Faith turned to Edgar, "Edgar, why don't we both go and have a good look at the farm. Don't be irrational; it may be just what you want at the moment. We can go up there this afternoon as the weather is clear and have a tour around."

The Brigadier thought it odd that Faith would try to persuade her brother, whom he knew she hated, to take over Kilkenny Farm. He could only surmise that she had a concealed reason. He watched both son and daughter and waited for Edgar to respond.

Edgar was staring out across the lawn, not wanting to make any immediate decision.

Suddenly, he turned around. "All right, we'll go up there this afternoon," he finally said and left the room without another word.

His mind was not on the overall picture, Faith thought, and he was going to take some persuading.

Neil Portlock was working by himself repairing a horse carriage with a broken axle. It was parked inside a large stone shed with double doors that were closed against the weather. Up against the wall at the back of the building was an old cast iron stove, and beside the stove was an old sofa where he and Marcel would often drink their tea debating Anglo-French politics or current affairs.

Faith entered by a side door. "Mr Portlock, may I have a quiet word?" Faith's voice startled Neil. He had been concentrating on his task in hand.

"Of course, ma'am."

Faith discreetly looked around the shed. "Where is Marcel?" she asked quietly.

With an old rag he wiped the dirt and grease from his hands and then washed them in a bucket of cold soapy water. " He is unwell and having a day off. What can I do for you, ma'am?" he asked warily.

She refused his offer of tea. "Father told me you have made an offer for the tenancy of Kilkenny Farm. Do I assume that this is true?" Faith was calm even though it had been the last thing she wanted to hear.

"For me and my family it is a good opportunity. I have known for some weeks now that Mr Kilkenny intended to retire, so when I was home this Christmas I broached the subject with my wife, and she doesn't seem to mind. We discussed it in detail and she agreed to go ahead and put forward our application, which I did. The air here is clean and farming seems a healthy way of life and it should be good for our children. We haven't put our hopes up as we're sure there will be other interested parties and so we'll have to wait and see. The Brigadier's word will obviously be final."

"Did you know that my father is trying to persuade Edgar to take over Kilkenny Farm? He has offered him one chance to prove himself prior to eventually taking over the whole estate." Faith watched Neil carefully. She knew why he had originally come to Bibury and he could have done his treacherous deed long ago and moved away but he had put it aside on her request, and remained working at the estate. He now had another reason to kill her brother and she had to keep the man standing before her under some sort of control for the time being.

"In which case, ma'am, along with yourself I will have to be a little more patient. I'm sure that everything will work out fine in the future for the both of us," he smiled wryly, knowing her own ultimate intentions.

As Faith walked away she considered her position. She wondered whether she had put her trust in too many people? What if Neil Portlock decided to blow the whistle? There was no real proof why Neil was here at Bibury. Everything would be in the open and nothing could be done about it. Edgar would inherit the estate and she would be utterly humiliated. She suddenly stopped and thought again about the entire situation. What Neil Portlock did or, more importantly, didn't do in the immediate future was pivotal in the whole exercise. Faith walked back towards the shed.

"Mr Portlock." He looked up, surprised to see her again. "If you remain discreet over the next few weeks then I can assure you that you will gain the tenancy of Kilkenny Farm. You might possibly find my brother managing it in the very near future, but I can guarantee you that for him it will only be a temporary arrangement."

Neil said nothing. He just nodded his head in agreement and then went to go back about his work.

Faith hadn't finished and her next question surprised him. "How many years did you spend in India, Neil?"

He pondered over the question and then answered. "Five. Why do you want to know?"

"So, what did you do for five years without your wife being there? Were you celibate?" she asked, moving close to him.

"Prostitutes," he told her quite plainly.

"So you don't mind who you go with?" she asked, moving even closer.

"The more money you spend the better quality you get," was his simple reply, knowing that she was coming on to him.

"When will you see your wife next then? One month? Maybe two?" she asked, now within touching distance.

Faith's reputation was well known on the estate and he had often thought about her but had always decided to keep his nose clean. This time was different though; they both needed each other.

Neil was straight to the point. "You want me to fuck you, don't you?" he asked in basic soldier language.

"Yes, please," she answered simply and stretched her arm out and took hold of his long, greying hair and pulled him towards her. Neil was in no position to resist and their lips met, at first lovingly but then she began caressing his body under his worn leather waistcoat. She could feel his strength. He had the solidity of a well-trained soldier.

She began to undo his shirt buttons and then run her hand over his chest. There was no resistance as she suckled Neil's nipples whist sliding her hands down over his diaphragm and into his trousers.

He was stirring, a little slowly in the circumstances but stirring nonetheless.

He backed up against the carriage door, partially sitting on the entrance step, and Faith dropped his trousers and underwear to his ankles and began gently stroking his testicles, and stimulating his penis even more. He undid the bodice of her upper garment and exposed her fulsome breasts and kissed them fervently. She breathed slowly but surely and took his hand and guided it beneath her skirt, where all of the rumours were answered and he found that she wore no underwear.

They kissed as they explored each other's genitals and then Faith ran her tongue down Neil's body, slowly dropping to her knees and taking his penis in her mouth. The soft creature still hadn't attained its full capacity but as she titillated his testicles it began to stand to attention like an obedient private.

With her mouth over his glans she simulated the entrance to her vagina. As one hand gently masturbated him and her other stroked his scrotum, Neil began to rise and harden as his heart pumped faster. It became too much and before ejaculating he dragged her back on her feet. He kicked off his boots, left his trousers on the floor and pushed Faith onto the sofa by the stove. She lay up against the back of the sofa with her legs wide open. She pulled up her dress and beckoned Neil to satisfy her moistened organ.

Under the dim lights of the oil lamps, reminding him of the Indian whorehouses, Faith's wanting vagina was too good to resist. On his knees his tongue searched the insides of her thighs as a snake's tongue searches for its prey. Her sexual secretion was irresistible and he soon found her vagina and the ultimate prize – her clitoris.

Neil's tongue darted in and out as he played with one of her nipples at the same time, and soon, as she began to orgasm, she pulled Neil towards her by his greying hair, willing him to climb inside her. Her deep breathing gave way to pleasurable shrieks as her orgasm began to crescendo, and she pulled Neil off the floor, imploring him to penetrate her. He duly obliged and within moments it was all over for them both.

They both dressed and bade each other goodbye. Another job done, Faith thought smugly as she made her way back to the main house.

Neither had seen the silhouette of a man watching from the doorway, who had sidled away as they dressed.

Kilkenny Farm farmhouse was a beautiful three-storey stone building of ample size. Mrs Kilkenny showed Edgar and Faith around. Faith was impressed but Edgar said very little. Afterwards Edgar toured the farm with Mr Kilkenny, who gave him a basic idea of what the farm produced and how it operated. After an hour and a half the siblings left to return to Bibury.

"Edgar, you must take up Father's offer. I don't know what is going through your mind but I can imagine that it is all too confusing. Your wife in India will need somewhere to stay, Kilkenny Farm would be ideal, even if it is temporary." Faith hoped for a reply but he remained quiet, staring out of the window of the Brougham. "Is it Georgina you are thinking about? Have you asked her what she wants to do? She can't stay at Hope's home forever. When she is well she will have to move somewhere. If you discussed it with her I am more than sure that she wouldn't say no to such an offer at Kilkenny Farm. She would feel safe there with her children. You can explain her presence by telling Father that you have employed a housekeeper. He's hardly going to come up to the farm and meet her in his condition."

Edgar turned to his sister. "I will have to travel to London in the next couple of weeks to try and resolve the issue of my marriage to Charusheela. In the meantime I will ask Georgina if she would wish to move in at the farm with me."

Inwardly Faith smiled. "I am sure Georgina will not refuse, but you'll have to wait a while until she is fully recovered. She will want to make sure her children attend school. There are many things to think about, Edgar, but it will all work out with a happy ending."

The carriage trundled into Bibury Court, and Edgar retired to the annexe whilst Faith went to tell her father of Edgar's probable decision to take on Kilkenny Farm. She didn't tell him why he might have changed his mind.

Rumours of Edgar's move went around the estate like wildfire. The only people not pleased to hear the news were Mr Kilkenny's workforce and Neil Portlock, who pondered over what his own next move could possibly be.

Chapter 44
The Ladies of the Stream

Faith held her hand over her yawning mouth and then apologised to Charity for her bad manners. Having spent most of the evening before writing genuine letters or concocting fictitious notes to be sent on other people's behalf, her tiredness was showing in the lines of her face.

The sisters were journeying to Chedworth to meet Hope and Georgina, and the carriage jolted uncomfortably along the bridleway. As much as Charity had always said she didn't want to knowingly meet Georgina face to face, it was always felt that the time would eventually come, and now was that time. Charity was understandably nervous, and her illness wasn't helping her to confront the woman with whom Stefan was having an affair. At least her two sisters would be close at hand for support.

There was a lot to discuss that morning and all the meticulous planning had to be put in place. Faith was hardly in the mood for talking either. She had made a decision to invite Maria down from Brockhampton and was beginning to doubt whether it was a sensible idea.

Although James was taking Georgina's children to the morning market at Cirencester, Maria would inevitably meet Georgina but at least she would find out that her niece was safe and well. To Maria the children were to remain a mystery and any indication that they were staying with Hope in Chedworth would be meticulously removed. As for their disappearance, should Maria ask – and as their great aunt she naturally would – it had been agreed that the blame should lie firmly at Fulwar's door. Neither the three sisters nor Georgina were to elaborate in case their opinions differed.

As the Brougham turned down the steep slope and into the driveway entrance, they were suddenly forced to a halt. A carriage was returning up the drive, and at the reins was Edward. He had delivered his mother and was off elsewhere for a couple of hours. Soon, the three sisters and Maria would be chatting around the fire in the lounge with tea and biscuits. Georgina was waiting in her upstairs rooms.

Before they settled, the butler put his head around the door. "Mrs Cavner will see you now. Mrs Desailley, if you would like to follow me."

Charity self-consciously rose from her seat, spurning Faith's offer of support, and was led up the staircase lined with beautiful oak wainscot, upon which hung several large oil paintings.

One painting caught her eye, and she stopped to study it. A woman on horseback stared back at Charity almost apologetically. The resemblance between Charity and the woman portrayed was apparent. If only mother were alive today, she thought before continuing up the staircase and into a spacious living room, where the butler introduced her to Georgina before withdrawing.

They faced each other without knowing how to begin, but then Charity realised that they had briefly met each other at the Summer Ball.

Charity could instantly see why Stefan was so attracted to the elegant woman standing before her, and Georgina felt guilty that she had tempted a man away from such an attractive wife.

Georgina spoke first, apologetically shaking her head. "I am so sorry for what I have done."

Charity stopped her in her tracks. "Please. You have nothing to be sorry about. What has happened is as much my fault as anyone's. Stefan only followed his natural instincts and I told him to, providing he left me alone physically." She approached Georgina and took her hands and they gently kissed.

The pair sat down on opposite ends of the red leather sofa, perching on its edge, as businesswomen might, with hands clasped and resting on their laps.

"Thank you for your letter. Thomas slipped it under my pillow. You are so thoughtful but I don't understand why." Georgina's eyes pleaded for Charity to explain.

"Stefan has told me most things about you." She hesitated and looked away towards the window. Mustering up some courage she continued. " Except... except," she stuttered.

"Charity, don't let your mind torment you. He loves you and wants the woman back whom he married; the young girl he has known all his life whilst growing up at the village school. The pretty, intelligent and happy girl who is not full of despondency. Stefan sincerely believes that you will, one day, become that woman again." Georgina spoke to Charity softly but sincerely. "We both cannot carry on our lives like this, Charity. Our sufferings are immense. Fulwar has a terrible problem with his drink, and he cannot control his outrages but he doesn't understand his strength. Sober, he is a good man but a demon invites himself into his mind when he is drunk."

"Georgina, please do not let Stefan hear you say how immense your suffering is. Many, many more people have a much more stressful life with no recourse whatsoever to medical help. Yes, I grant you that we have problems but far from the same degree as many on the streets of our great cities and towns." Charity's sympathies, similar to her husband's, lay with the poor.

"I am sorry, Charity, I didn't mean it in such a manner. You are quite right. What I meant to say was that we both need to resolve our problems and lead healthier lives, and perhaps we can then both go out and help those poor people who have such undeserving living standards." Georgina wasn't at all sure how opinionated Stefan's wife actually was.

"What do you intend to do, Georgina, if one day you divorce your husband?"

Georgina felt the question was more to do with Charity wanting to know where Stefan stood in the affair, and didn't give a direct answer. "It depends on what happens to the children. If they have to return to Stokesay then I will live close by. I sincerely hope that they will remain in my charge but, as you well know, women do not have the upper hand in divorce proceedings."

"Yes, you are quite right. We don't have the upper hand," Charity replied meekly, trying not to imagine the outcome of her own marriage.

"I should not be so rude to ask you, but why is it that you and your two sisters don't want your brother back at Bibury? What has he done to make you all hate him so much? Even Stefan doesn't really know why, and the four of you almost grew up together." Georgina was prying. As much as she knew Faith, and had asked her the same question, Faith had never given her a complete and truthful explanation.

At first Charity was reluctant to say anything and Georgina waited patiently. Having studied her own interlocked fingers for some time she looked at Georgina. "Edgar was considerably older than us, I think eight or nine years older than Faith, and he was thoroughly disliked. A bully, you might say. Just because our father owned the Court at Bibury, Edgar felt that he could rule the roost in the village.

"Because of his awful attitude, it reflected back on all of us. We were his sisters and the people in the village hated us as much as they hated him. It was an unfair judgement but people are fickle and they rightly choose their own preferences and loyalties.

"He scared us a great deal, me more so as I was the youngest. If we said anything about his behaviour he would make our lives a misery. We didn't know any better at the time but as we grew older Faith began to understand how he truly was a bad brother. He wasn't intelligent and it seemed when he finished school he would just loiter around the estate upsetting everyone.

"What really hurt Edgar was when Father and Mother realised how academically gifted Stefan was, and so they decided to send him to Wellington School.

"When you said we grew up together, it wasn't quite so. Stefan spent a considerable time away as a boarder. He wouldn't have known what an awful man Edgar was turning out to be. People even began to find work elsewhere because of him. Suddenly and out of the blue, it was announced that Edgar was to join the army. Someone had arranged a commission for him, and the whole village was relieved.

"When Stefan eventually finished at Wellington, young as he was, Father put him to task as the estate manager. Although Edgar was then in the army it incensed him even further when he found out about Stefan's position. He absolutely detested Stefan for it, and still does.

"Some years later Stefan and I decided to marry, and Edgar made a point of taking leave and coming home to spend the entire time complaining vociferously that I shouldn't marry a commoner. Eventually, there was a monumental family argument in the drawing room one morning, and Faith, Hope and I were completely embarrassed, and after about a half hour Faith suddenly stood up and screamed for everyone to shut up.

"It all went deathly quiet, and Faith demanded that Edgar accompany her out of the room. To this day no one knows what she said to him but Edgar left the house without saying another word to anyone that afternoon, and up until November we've hardly seen him, especially when he was in India.

"Months passed but from around the time Edgar joined the army Mother hadn't been well. She was afflicted by problems similar to my own, and Stefan and I decided to marry sooner rather than later to prevent further conflict.

"Mother died four months after our wedding, and although he was in England, Edgar did not attend her funeral. Neither did he attend our wedding. No one knows why he didn't come to the funeral, and he never gave an explanation, and Father didn't seem to mind that he hadn't turned up."

Charity paused for thought and was about to elaborate but thought better of it. "Edgar is simply a horrible, undeserving man and everyone has to suffer when he can't have his own way. I am sorry but that is the way he is."

Georgina said nothing. She didn't prompt Charity further, despite being far from convinced that Charity had told the whole story. There was more to her hatred than for a bullying and overpowering brother. What Faith had planned for him far outweighed his misdemeanours.

Charity brought Georgina back from her thoughts. "Come along, Georgina. I think we had better go and see the others. There is a lot to talk about."

The journey back to Bibury was a little more congenial, and Charity seemed as though she had a great load taken off her mind. She was much more talkative, even though she had great doubts about the final outcome. Faith reassured her that it was best for everyone who were involved with the two despicable men, especially for Charity herself, who couldn't stand the sight of Edgar.

Maria had seemed much more pliant especially now she knew where Georgina was staying and appearing to be much healthier. Also, Sir Charles and Edward would now be informed of her whereabouts, although the children were still to be a mystery to them. Maria would send a letter to Stokesay, which would start the ball rolling.

Faith was now more confident that everything would go to plan, and she hoped within two months the issues at both estates would be finally resolved.

Chapter 45
Maria's Letter

For Willie Greyffos the surroundings were little different but his client, although rather agitated, appeared to be relatively sober. His agitated state was a sure sign that the whisky bottle had been left alone for the last two or three days, and he was suffering from withdrawal symptoms.

Fulwar took an envelope from the mantelpiece and handed it to Willie. His hand shook uncontrollably as he did so, and Willie wondered whether the cause was his craving for a drink or his temper getting the better of him.

"Read it! Your assumptions could well have been right." Fulwar ran his hands through his hair and turned away and sipped a glass of water.

Willie studied the envelope. It was postmarked from Cheltenham, and the address was written eloquently by someone who had had a good education. He slid out the letter. .

My Dear Fulwar

In the past I have said very little about your situation with Georgina but I know it must upset you greatly. Charles and I do hope that one day there will be reconciliation between yourselves, and a permanent one at that.

This brings me to mention two incidences that have occurred over the last weeks that I know will interest you greatly. First of all, one of the estate employees was drinking in a public house in his home village of Andoversford and overheard a conversation between two gentlemen sitting in the corner. They were discussing the position at the Bibury Court estate, and two names were brought up, one was Edgar Collison and the other, surprisingly, was Georgina. It was difficult for our employee to hear as there were other people chatting around the bar but it sounded as if this Edgar Collison character and Georgina intend to set up home together. He is apparently going to take up residence on one of the numerous farms on his father's estate, a name by which he couldn't quite catch but believed it sounded Irish. We have since done some investigation and believe it is a large farm north east of Bibury that goes under the name of Kilkenny. Where Georgina is at the moment, we still do not know but she must be staying somewhere in the Bibury area. This collates with the other incident, which I will relate to you now.

Edward had to travel to Cirencester the other Friday morning and whilst he was there he was almost positive he saw your children. They were with a well-dressed gentleman who he did not recognise. Edward hasn't seen the children for over a year, and they have undoubtedly changed in that time, but he was more than sure that they were your children. Indeed, the boy stared at Edward for some time, and Edward tried to follow them but lost them amid the crowded market.

As you are probably aware, Fulwar, Charles and I are desperately worried about their welfare and will do all we can to assure their safety. Evidently, Edgar Collison is not to be trusted. If we find out any more then we will let you know.

With Love, Maria

Willie folded the letter up and pushed it back into the envelope. Fulwar stared at him expecting some sort of analysis. "Well! What do you think?"

"From what you have told me in the past your aunt seems to have changed her tune somewhat. Suddenly, from you being a hate figure she is now deeply concerned for you. Why might Maria suddenly change her attitude?" Willie cocked his head to one side. There was perhaps something he didn't know about.

Fulwar looked uncomfortable as he paced back and forth before the fire with his hands clasped firmly behind his back. He suddenly stopped and slapped his forehead with the palms of his hands. He looked at Willie. "I think she knows where Georgina and the children are hiding. She and Uncle Charles are well aware that when my Father dies I inherit the entire estate, and I could quite easily oust them from their position at Brockhampton. They need to be seen to be supporting me but, as you say, it is definitely a sudden change of heart. Georgina is Maria's niece, and both are from the Buchanan family, all of whom usually hate me."

Willie had to be careful with what he had to say. He had to compare what he actually knew with what Maria had written in the letter. "There are things you have to consider. Whether Georgina is definitely moving to the Kilkenny Farm with Mr Collison. If she is then are the children going with her? Once their whereabouts is made known then no court in the land would stop you having custody of them. The courts are always in favour of the father, especially in the privileged world of the aristocrats. Parliament passed the Matrimonial Causes Act only ten years ago, and she would have no chance, especially as it would take little to prove she is an adulteress." Willie paused as Fulwar pondered over what he had told him. He then continued. "I think you might have to tread carefully for a while, and be patient. Once you know where your children are the courts can use their powers to return them to you. First of all, we need to find them and also confirm that your wife is living at the farm with another man."

Fulwar held his jaw in his hand and gently stroked its greying stubble. He was deep in thought. Suddenly he looked up, "I would sooner this never went to court. Settling amicably would be better for all concerned." He knew his own behaviour would be exposed and his family's reputation tarnished.

"I don't think for one minute that she would relinquish those children to you unless it goes to court. It is probably what she wants. If she loses them then she will at least have had her cards placed on the table." Willie's assumption was that Georgina would hang on to her children for as long as she could, and at any price.

"There must surely be another way around this," Fulwar said, deep in thought. "We'll have to take the children back in the same way they took them from me. Kidnap them." Fulwar was adamant.

"Before we become too rash, there is something you don't know. It is something that Edgar Collison tells very few people, and in the current circumstances it would never be exposed." Willie could see the intrigue written on Fulwar's face.

"Tell me! What is it?" Fulwar asked impatiently.

"Edgar Collison is married to a woman of Indian descent who has three children, none of whom are his own. She comes from an extremely wealthy family, and he has been trying to have her moved here for some months but there are problems with immigration. Also, the legality of the marriage is being challenged in India by her parents; she is a Muslim and they do not recognise Christian marriages. He married her shortly before leaving India whilst serving in the British army." Willie smiled. He was almost certain Fulwar would use the information for his own purposes and it would secure his own immediate future in the pay of Georgina's reckless husband.

Fulwar paced up and down, again stroking his stubble in thought. "How can we put this information to good use?"

"Send Edgar Collison a letter threatening to expose him to the press for everything he has done, especially for the abduction of your children. Tell him what you know. He will be just the same as you, reluctant to end up in court. Give him a week to reply or, if he doesn't, the London Weekly will be informed forthwith. He will have to answer because he will not want his old army colleagues to find out about his behaviour towards somebody else's children, especially by reading it in a national newspaper. God knows how many journalists will be down in Bibury searching for them. Meanwhile, I'll return to Bibury and try and find out where they really are in case it does go that far." Willie stopped and wondered if Fulwar would take the bait and agree.

Fulwar, desperate to have his children back nodded his head. "Yes, I will go along with that but there is a problem." He held his hands out and they shook like a windblown bush. It was obvious that handling an ink-pen was impossible.

"I'll fetch the headed paper, and if you write it I'll sign it. We can post it off today. But how do we know that the London Weekly will publish the story?"

"I can guarantee that they will," Willie said, confident about Gerard and his contacts on the London business circuit.

Willie left the post office in Ludlow a contented man. He had mailed the letter he had written for Fulwar, and had sent a telegram to Faith telling her of his day's proceedings and his forthcoming visit to Bibury.

Most importantly, he had Fulwar Cavner's signature and a spare sheet of headed paper.

Chapter 46
The Mill at Withington

Mealtimes for the staff at Bibury Court were always a raucous affair. It was a time when they were allowed to let their hair down. The Brigadier insisted on a pleasant working environment and believed that the better the staff were treated, the healthier were the returns.

During working hours they were tidy and dignified, especially towards the family and guests. Few of them were ever late and would often work longer hours should the need arise but not without some compensation or other.

Lionel entered the refectory and the noise abated. He had the day's mail in his hand, which was mostly for the live-in staff, and as he called out their names a cheer erupted as if the recipient had received a lucky prize. When he left the room he had one letter remaining and the handwriting was distinctively Mary's. He took it away for his own private perusal.

In the quiet of his room Lionel read her letter. Strangely, there was another note folded and sealed inside the envelope that was addressed to Stefan. Lionel was puzzled. Mary wrote that she would be down for a couple of days over the weekend but she was going to Cheltenham before her arrival at Bibury, and she urged Lionel to join her there. She also informed him to pass on the inserted letter to Stefan straight away.

He rose from his seat and scratched his head whilst studying his own letter and the unopened insert. Something was odd, he thought. He put on his coat and went to find Stefan.

At the gatehouse he saw himself in and walked into the kitchen. The stove was roaring but there was no one in sight. He called out and a muffled voice came from along the hallway, "I'm here, come on in."

Stefan was actually working on his book about the Coln River, which surprised Lionel. "I thought you had given up writing that?" he asked.

"No, but I have done hardly anything for months apart from jot a few things down. I really must get started again, although I'll write a shorter version than I intended." Stefan shrugged his shoulders almost wishing he had never begun the project.

"Well, I don't want to spoil your good intentions but this arrived this morning." Lionel placed the sealed letter in front of Stefan. "It was inside a letter addressed to me from Mary. I'll leave you to it." He turned to go, anxiously hoping Stefan would ask him to stay whilst he read its contents.

Stefan said nothing, however, and Lionel left him alone with his odd dispatch. He tore it open and read the first lines. His heart began to race. It was short and simple. Georgina wanted to see him and she would be staying at The Mill Inn at Withington for one day and night the coming weekend. He went to his calendar hanging by the door to verify the date. Friday, 18th of January. Where has she been all this time? He squeezed the note in his fist and shook it up and down. The excitement was already getting the better of him. In three days he could see the second woman in his life and hold her in his arms. Stefan grabbed his coat and went to find Lionel.

"Stefan, I am not lying to Charity for you. You'll have to make your own excuses to stay out Friday night. Tell her you're going fishing for the day. Take your rods and tackle and say the members of the angling club are having a competition and there is a drink or two involved afterwards. I'll meet you up there because Mary will undoubtedly want to see Georgina after all these months. I will be meeting Mary off the train at Cheltenham and we will be returning here on Saturday. As long as we both leave separately and don't arrive back together, Charity will be none the wiser."

"Where do you think Georgina is coming from? Did Mary say anything to you in her letter?" Stefan asked, itching to find out.

"She didn't even mention Georgina coming along. What you have in your hand is as big a surprise to me as it is to you. You'll have to ask her when you see her. There are a lot of questions unanswered but just appreciate that she is alive and supposedly well. The letter is a wonderful revelation, but just be patient and wait and see."

The Brigadier watched unsteadily from the drawing room window as Stefan returned back to the gatehouse. His nurse supported his elbow at his side, should he stumble. She knew that something was troubling the old man as soon as Stefan had told him he wouldn't be at the estate on Friday, and would not be back until Saturday lunchtime. A fishing trip had been his excuse.

The young woman coaxed the old man back to his armchair. "Come on, sir. Please sit back down. I don't want you to fall. It's the last thing we want."

He did as she asked. For a while he sat staring at the bookcase and then at the portrait of his wife. She gave the impression that she knew what was going on behind his back but was leaving it for him to find out.

An Armagnac was placed on the side table next to his chair. He smiled with appreciation at his ever-attendant nurse. "What is on your mind, sir? Since Mr Desailley left, you have been unusually quiet."

The Brigadier felt safe to tell her. Indeed, she was now one of the few people he would divulge anything to. "Lionel came to me this morning and asked for time off and now Stefan has asked the same. Both wish to take the same time off; one is going to meet his fiancé and the other is apparently going fishing. I find that rather hard to believe, especially as they are the best of friends. Something, my dear, is afoot."

He picked up his Armagnac and stared through the glass, distorting the vision of his dear wife's portrait. 'I told you, so my darling,' she seemed to say. 'I told you that they would take their revenge'.

The Brigadier looked over his glass and remembered vividly some of the last words she ever spoke. "They will take their revenge,'" she'd said. He sipped the oaken brandy, rested his head back and closed his eyes.

Charity watched from a bedroom window as her husband struggled up into the saddle of his old grey mare. He was laden with fishing equipment across his back, and the saddlebags bulged with a change of clothes. He had used the exact excuse Lionel had suggested; one that Charity knew was a damned lie. She was well aware with whom he was to reconnoitre. She was also well aware that Stefan would be told the truth about everything, and he would return a changed man forever, but whether for good or bad she could not ascertain.

His excursion would be a true test of the strength of their marriage.

Stefan flitted his nymph across the Coln and into a small pool close to overhanging willow branches. He waited a short while for it to sink and then lightly tugged the line, jogging the artificial bait along the bottom of the river in the hope of tempting a lady of the stream, the beautiful silvery scaled grayling. The river was slightly dark because the previous day's rain had brought mud and debris spilling into its upper reaches. For once, that morning, he had begun to concentrate. One more catch and the landlord at The Mill would have his required quota.

Downstream, hidden behind some leafless sallows, Georgina watched Stefan enacting his favourite sport. Her face was expressionless. She had yearned to see him for so long but now that the time had come, her heart was beating quickly, this time with trepidation and not lust. What she had to tell him would evaluate his character to the full.

She stepped out into the meadow and walked towards him as he cast once again upstream with his back to her. He patiently played the line not realising she now stood immediately behind.

"Stefan," she said softly as if not to disturb him, but he did not hear her, such was his concentration. "Stefan," she said a little louder, and he turned his head towards her.

He quickly passed his eyes over her. Neither smiled, they just stared at each other as if they were two strangers in a chance encounter. Eventually Stefan placed his rod on the bank and took her in his arms. "My God, Georgina. Where have you been? I have so missed you." She was cold towards him and he felt the dispassionate feeling through her body. "What is the matter, Georgina? There is something wrong, isn't there?"

"I don't want to talk here, Stefan. Take your fishing equipment back to The Mill and I'll meet you at the King's Head, the little hostelry up around the corner." She turned and walked away, refusing to look back.

Stefan watched her as she made her way along the river towards Withington until she was out of sight behind the copse on the nearside bank. He slowly shook his head and then bent down to gather his belongings. No longer did he believe that it would develop into a beautiful day. Georgina seemed a changed woman, and his expectations had been destroyed. As he staggered back along the riverside with his head swimming full of anxious thoughts he took no notice of two squabbling moorhens or the buoyant, leisurely flight of a red kite. On another day he would have stopped and admired such birds, but his mind this particular day was far away.

Why did she show no emotion towards him? Where had she been these last months, and where was she going next? He stopped and recalled the times that they'd had together in Maidenhead and Fairford, and their first sexual liaison in Sennington barn, of all places. He wondered whether her problem was that she saw their relationship as an erotic encounter between two adulterers that could only follow a path towards marital disaster.

Perhaps he should differentiate between the love Charity showed towards him and the carnal lust Georgina had given him in the recent past. He suddenly asked himself which woman he would be with in his greater hour of need, but he had no answer.

He carried on and at The Mill he off-loaded his fishing tackle and delivered three fine grayling to the cook, telling her that he would be back later. He nervously walked through the village towards the King's Head to meet Georgina, clueless as to what to expect.

Georgina sat on the edge of the bed trying to form a strategy in her mind of how to explain to Stefan what she was about to do without upsetting him so much that he might affect the overall plan. She considered climbing into bed with him, and then telling him afterwards, but not only would he would feel as if he had been used, her guilt when inevitably encountering Charity again would be unrelenting.

Georgina's mind was in turmoil but she had promised Faith that she would explain everything to Stefan without upsetting the applecart at such a critical time, and it was her duty to do so.

Georgina heard the steel latch of the front door open and then gently close downstairs in the bar below. There was a short, inaudible conversation before silence prevailed. Very shortly the stairs began to creak and there was a knock at her door.

"Come in," she said with a dry throat. Her heart pounded, and she felt as if she had been summoned to the headmaster for bad behaviour.

The landlady showed her head around the door. "The gentleman you are meeting is here. Do you want me to send him up?"

Georgina paused in thought. "No, please tell him that I will come down to see him presently. Thank you."

"You can sit in the smoke room. It's quite warm in there and I will make sure that you are not disturbed," she smiled and returned downstairs, where she relayed Georgina's message to Stefan.

Georgina entered the tiny room where Stefan stood impatiently in front of the fire with his hands behind his back. His pewter mug of cider warmed on the hearth. She perched herself on the end of a short wooden bench beside a table, and at first neither said a word, each unable to break the ice.

Stefan eventually chose to ask some questions. "So, what in hell is happening, Georgina? This has become completely absurd. Why have you dragged me this far and then appear not to want to know me any more? You disappear off the face of the earth, have half of Gloucestershire on the lookout for you and your children, and now you reappear at will. I sincerely hope that you have a good explanation. Now tell me what is going on!"

Georgina glanced through to the other bar to assure herself that there was no one listening. She was completely honest with him and straight to the point. "Next week I will be moving to Kilkenny Farm." She watched the expression on his face change from insistence to incredulity.

His eyes squinted as he tried to make sense in what he had just heard. "You can't be. Edgar Collison is setting up home there in the next couple of days. I want to hear the truth, Georgina, and no more 'beat about the bush' stories that emanate between Bibury, Brockhampton and London. I am absolutely fed up with it all." Stefan was beginning to sound extremely irate, which was the last thing Georgina wished. She knew that she had to keep him calm at any cost.

Georgina told him again. "I am moving to Kilkenny Farm." Her brow was raised, emphasising her intentions.

"Doing what, for Christ's sake? Housekeeper! Maid! What?" It did not yet occur to him that she would become Edgar's mistress.

Again, she looked through to see if anyone could hear. There was only one other patron standing at the bar. "We'll have to go upstairs. What I have to tell you, only you must know. Come," she said quietly, "and when we pass through the other side, please don't look so distressed."

Stefan followed Georgina still dismayed at what she had so far told him.

Georgina discreetly stood beside the bed, sitting on it may have signalled sexual intentions, and Stefan closed the door and turned towards her.

"Are you telling me that you are going to live with Edgar?" he asked, dumbfounded. "Edgar Collison, of all people! You are jumping out of the frying pan and into the fire."

"Stefan, please! It is not what you think. Really, it is not. I don't love him. In fact, he makes me cringe. It's just that for now it is convenient. It will not be for long. One month, maybe two, at the most." She turned away with her hands covering her face and shook her head in despair and then spun back around. "We need you to understand, Stefan. Please don't let us down now."

Stefan frowned. "Who do you mean by *we*? What in hell are you talking about?" He went to her and took her by the shoulders. "Tell me, Georgina! For God's sake tell me before this gets out of hand!"

Georgina looked up into the eyes of the man she knew she had lost forever, and she now had to tell him why. "Please promise me one thing, Stefan. When I tell you, do not stand in our way. For all of our sakes do not prevent us from doing what we have to do. Promise me! Please!"

He stared into her beautiful eyes. It was too easy to say yes. "How can any man make a fair judgement when he is unaware of a crime or the names of its perpetrators? Tell me who else is involved. I need to know." He spoke calmly almost assured that he was about to find out.

"Faith, Hope, Aunt Maria and... and... "

"Go on, who else?" Stefan prompted.

"Charity! She knows everything. I have met her." Georgina looked away.

Stefan turned and went to the tiny window and placed his hands on the oak lintel above. He stared out onto the garden below for some moments before turning back to her. "What did Charity tell you?"

"Nothing you probably don't already know. She loves you, Stefan, and she desperately wants to be a complete wife again, and will be if given time. I honestly believe that an issue with her brother is affecting her, and one day soon it will be resolved." Georgina suspected that Stefan had his own opinions as to the cause of Charity's illness, and she wondered what he might reveal.

Stefan avoided the subject. "Who else is involved with all this? Anyone else I might need to know about? What about Mary and Lionel?"

"Mary has an inkling but is having nothing to do with it. Lionel, as far as I know, is oblivious to it all unless he suspects something. James and Gerard, are both fully aware. There are two others whom I only know by name. One is Fulwar's private detective and the other man works on your estate. Both, we believe, are now on our side."

"This chap who works on the estate. Who is he?"

"All that I have been told is that his name is Portlock."

Stefan shook his head in disbelief. "I think you had better start from the beginning. I hope this is all worth it." He sat down on the stool in front of the dresser, and folded his arms and crossed his legs whilst Georgina sat on the edge of the bed. She began the story from when Faith first spawned the idea in her head. Georgina would explain everything with the intent of telling him what the final outcome would be, although she thought that might be better left for Faith to divulge at a later date.

A coach pulled up outside The Mill and Lionel and Mary disembarked. They were in a jovial mood, happy to be in each other's company. Their wedding was just three months away and for them it couldn't come sooner.

The landlord helped them up the stairs with their baggage and showed them to their room for the night. He explained the whereabouts of Stefan at the King's Head, although he knew nothing of Georgina. They gave each other odd looks and shrugged their shoulders believing she must be with him.

"Shall we go and see if we can find them?" Lionel asked naively.

"No! Let them alone in peace. I have a better idea," she said suggestively, and pushed him down onto the bed and pulled off his boots. With her own shoes kicked across the floor, she danced beside the bed and hummed the tune of a mischievous back street tavern song as she slowly shed her clothes and flaunted her sexuality in front of Lionel who, still in his breeches, awkwardly attained full arousal.

She was soon completely nude and tempting him to come to her. Her pubic hair had been shaved, giving her the appearance of a pre-pubescent schoolgirl, and she ran her fingers over her genitals, and feigned an orgasm as she caressed her breasts and gently pinched her nipples, causing them to stand hard.

Lionel could watch no more. He raised himself off the bed and halted her routine by taking her in his arms. Their lips met and their tongues explored each other's mouths. She threw his jacket to the floor and began unbuttoning his shirt and running her cold hands over his slim body. He drew deep breaths through his nose as he explored the milky white skin of her body.

Mary dropped his breeches and underwear and held his penis whilst tantalising his retracting testicles with her gentle female touch. Suddenly close to ejaculation, he gently pushed her hands away and ran his own hand down her belly and onto her shaven groin. His fingers found her vagina and he rhythmically rubbed her clitoris to extrude the conclusive sexual response – an orgasm. She breathed deeply with her eyes closed and her head held back, on a plateau of pre-orgasmic pleasure. Her heart pumped wildly and she began to utter uncontrollable cries of gratification as her whole body generated an utmost feeling of sensual satisfaction, and she pushed Lionel back onto the edge of the bed.

Kneeling before him she ran her soft tongue over his scrotum and upward along his rigid organ, and took the end of his penis in her mouth, where she softly mimicked her enclosed vagina whilst slowly masturbating him.

Lionel ran his hand through her hair and caressed her breasts and nipples. He came closer to ejaculating and so quickly pulled Mary up and onto the bed in order to prolong the occasion, and she climbed above him, straddling his penis tantalisingly by offering his desperate body part a mere touch of her swollen vagina.

Her breasts swung before him and he rubbed and kissed them but still she teased, testing his sexual resolve. Mary bent down and their lips brushed. Finally, she sat back and with her feminine hands guided the despairing organ into her.

She placed her hands on his chest and slowly rocked her pelvis up and down to bring him to his eventual orgasm, and as Lionel clasped her buttocks tightly she also began to climax. He could hold back no longer, and released the feelings he had for his woman into her, and in unison they thrust through their climactic throes.

They had become one being through their love for each other.

Later, with Mary sleeping beside him, with her arm across his stomach and her breath warming his ribcage, Lionel studied the cracks in the ceiling. He wanted to rise but was afraid of waking his dear one. It had been a long journey for her that day.

He raised the bedcovers and eyed her body up and down. The faint fragrance of her warmth and femininity radiated from beneath the blankets and he began to stir once more. His power to resist was weak, and he brushed the hair from her face. She stirred and ran her hand down to his groin. Side by side they were soon engaging in a sexual act of comfortable convenience, during which they kept reminding each other of their love.

For some time afterwards they lay unspeaking, but then Mary suddenly broke the stillness "What do you think will happen between Stefan and Georgina?"

Lionel arched his neck to focus on her eyes. "What do you mean? Are you asking whether they will they end up together? I don't know. It has become all too complicated. Perhaps they will but I hope not, for Charity's sake and the sake of his children. Why do you ask?"

"Georgina's moving to a place called Kilkenny Farm with Edgar Collison."

Lionel sat up on his elbows and looked down at Mary. He asked her to repeat her startling words and she duly obliged. He shook his head in disbelief. "Does Stefan know?"

"That is why she has arranged to meet him here. She intends to tell him. I'm afraid I wouldn't like to predict the consequences when he finds out." She glanced at the clock on the wall "More to the point, now that he has probably already found out. I'm afraid to say that there is something more sinister to it than just an illicit extra-marital affair. I think it is best we go and find them, and if Georgina has told him everything you can extract the rest of the story from Stefan."

With intrigue motivating him Lionel only had a brief wash down before dressing, and he was out of the door before Mary was ready. Outside, Stefan's horse remained attached to a ring post, oblivious to what was happening, and Lionel made his way up the lane towards the King's Head, but soon encountered Stefan striding towards him appearing in no mood to talk. Lionel blocked his friend's path, preventing him from belligerently pushing past.

"What the hell is going on, Stefan?"

"If I told you, you wouldn't believe it. Now let me past! I'm going home. I've nothing more to say." Deep inside Stefan was angry. He had been kept in the dark and now, having found out, felt worse than a fool.

"Come on, let's go back to The Mill and you can tell me," Lionel urged in a friendly tone, and it worked. Stefan mellowed and agreed. At the same time Mary appeared and asked what had happened.

Stefan glanced at them both. "Georgina is going back to Hope's tonight, and I am going home. Mary, go and talk to her before she leaves whilst I explain to Lionel what I have been told." She hesitated. "Please, Mary!" Stefan demanded, and without another word Mary rushed off to find Georgina.

In The Mill Stefan told the awestruck Lionel of what the women were scheming – the demises of both Edgar Collison and Fulwar Cavner. Neither man agreed with their scheme but, on the other hand, neither said that they would oppose such an audacious plan.

A long time before dark Stefan left for home.

Back at the Court Stefan was stabling his horse when he thought of paying a courteous call to his mother and father. After the formalities their conversation took only one direction. It was Marcel who gave Stefan the news.

"Neil Portlock has gone missing. For two days he hasn't turned up for work. I sent someone up to the Catherine Wheel and, oddly enough, he's paid his rent in advance for six weeks. And all of his belongings are still there. It is as if he intends to return sometime, but whether there is work for him when he does is another matter. It is very strange, Stefan. Very strange indeed."

Stefan stood on the opposite side of the table from his father, knuckles down. "Did he not give any notion that he was leaving? Not to anyone at all?"

"No. I do know that he wanted to take over Kilkenny Farm, but that is now impossible. Maybe that is what has skewed his mind?" Marcel suggested, shrugging his shoulders. He knew little else.

Stefan stayed for a few more minutes but his mother could see that he had a lot on his mind. She suggested he went home to see Charity and his children, and he took her advice.

There was a lot to talk about and some serious questions needed answering, and he sincerely hoped that the children would be out of the way when he arrived home.

At the gatehouse he scraped off his boots and left them just inside the door. He then heard excited voices reverberating from the washhouse beyond the kitchen, and he leaned on the doorframe and watched the bath time procedure until little Frankie noticed his father standing there.

Kneeling over the bath, Charity strained to look over her shoulder. Surprised to see him back, she smiled. "I won't be long. Put the kettle on the stove.

With the children in bed they sat down at the table. There was little food prepared because Stefan's return was unexpected. A ploughman's lunch washed down with dry cider sufficed.

Charity was wary of her husband. She didn't know how much he had found out or what he might say, but she trusted his temperament.

He rose from the table and took his plate to the sink, swilled it and put it on the side to drip dry. Back at the table he replenished his cider pot from the demi-john and sat back down. Charity sat with her hands on her lap, awaiting an inquisition.

"I can't let you carry on, Charity. Murdering them is a ridiculous idea, and you will end up on the gallows." He stared deeply into her eyes in the hope that she would see sense and relent. "There must be a more logical way."

"What do you suggest? Edgar hates you. As soon as Father has died he will have you off the estate in no time, regardless of the fact that I am married to you.

"The estate's workforce are already talking of leaving if he becomes the owner, and there is already a problem at Kilkenny Farm. Within two or three years the whole Bibury estate will be on its knees."

Charity went quiet. She could see that the mention of Kilkenny Farm hurt Stefan's conscience.

Faith had been adamant with her that the moment Stefan found out what was going on he would have to be drawn onto their side. That time had come, and now Charity had to use all of her resolve not to allow her husband to upset a very delicate situation. "Please believe me that it is for everyone's good, Georgina included. If Edgar stayed away and had nothing to do with the business then we could put up with it, but that isn't going to be the case. He is determined to stay, and we have to get rid of him for the sake of us all."

Stefan could easily understand the logic in why they intended to cast Edgar aside, but how they intended to do it was contemptible, and the whole plan could end in disaster. He had, however, noticed, the change in Charity's moods of late. Was it because she could see a conclusion to all the disquiet that had been going through her mind these last months or even years? She seemed so much more upbeat.

It suddenly became clearer to Stefan that Edgar was Charity's underlying problem. When he was in India she appeared to be well, but as soon as there was talk of his return, which really began with a letter Edgar sent to his father about three years ago, she had become an altered woman. Whatever the outcome over the next weeks, he was going to lose his relationship with Georgina.

On his journey back from Withington that afternoon he had become resigned to the fact that it was to be the case. His options were stark. Help his wife kill two men or spend years watching her suffer.

He decided to change tack. "Is Neil Portlock involved somewhere along the line, because he has suddenly gone missing?"

Charity thought for a few seconds before responding, not knowing quite what to tell her husband. "If you see him, or even think you have seen him, ignore him. Since Edgar has been home from India he hasn't realised Mr Portlock's true identity. Mr Portlock will reappear using his real name and personality. Please don't expose him, Stefan. We need him and he needs us."

"How do you intend to use him?" Stefan wasn't sure how much his wife knew about what was actually going on but the more he could find out the better. He had heard Georgina's side of the story.

"It is better I don't tell you in case things do not go to plan but please don't draw attention to him by deliberately going to find him. If you expose him as having worked here for Father it will create all sorts of problems. If he finds the right position, please allow him to settle in."

"But where might I have a chance of meeting with him? Isn't it better that I know so I can avoid him? I will have to tell Lionel, who will surely recognise him. Also, more than half of the estate workers will realise who he is, especially if he is still drifting around Bibury. Above all what will my father say if he comes across him?"

"It will be fine, believe me. Another gentleman you need to know about is Mr Greyffos, the private detective. I do not know him, and I don't suppose you do either, but you will probably find him standing on the side of Georgina's husband." Charity couldn't elaborate any further.

Stefan was surprised that Charity hadn't been told that he and Mr Greyffos had met. It gave him the impression that there were other matters outstanding that Charity was not privy to, although she appeared to know most things about himself and Georgina. He again expressed his wish to Charity for her not to become anymore involved but concluded she was already up to her neck in the sordid scheme. He resigned himself to accepting for now what the women had planned, hoping there would be a more reasonable outcome. He wished dearly he had kept his hands off his sister-in-law because she now had him well and truly cornered.

He retired to his drawing room, deciding to let things lie for a few days and await the outcome. Something would surely happen sooner or later. He wrote down a few things before sidling out the door and headed up to the Catherine Wheel.

Chapter 47
Neil Starbury

The Brigadier watched from his window as the estate workers steadfastly moved Edgar's belongings from the Court onto the back of an open trailer. Two shire horses were employed to transport his possessions from what had transpired to be his temporary home to his new life at Kilkenny Farm just three miles away.

Everything had been packed and labelled according to the destined room at the farmhouse, and nothing could go wrong. The Brigadier smiled to himself, knowing that Edgar was to prove his prowess as a Cotswold farmer, and if he failed at Kilkenny Farm he would have little chance of running the entire Bibury Court estate.

Edgar had gone on ahead, and had found Mr and Mrs Kilkenny in the throes of moving out to one of the retirement cottages further down the lane. It was an emotional time for the old lady, having brought up five children there, culminating into eighteen grandchildren, many of whom worked on the Bibury estate in some capacity.

Edgar's saw that his first postage had been laid upon the worn pine kitchen table. The first, he guessed from the handwriting, was a congratulatory letter from Faith and Gerard, but the other had handwriting that he did not recognise. He was about to open it when he heard his name being called from the yard in front of the house.

Edgar went to the doorway and was greeted by one of the older Kilkenny grandchildren sitting bareback upon a magnificent black hunter.

"I met a chap at the Swan in Lechlade last night. Says he's coming out to see you this morning, looking for a job." The horse spun around but soon resettled.

"Should I know him?" Edgar asked warily.

"Says you were in the army together. I didn't ask his name. A clean-cut chap, he is, about forty-odd. Comes from up north somewhere. Says he wants to speak to you." The lad said no more and turned away to stable his animal.

Edgar pondered over what he had been told and then went back inside. He would have to wait for the mystery man to turn up.

He picked up the letter again and slid his thumb through the top of the envelope. It was from Fulwar Cavner.

Standing to one side to allow the labourers to struggle out of the door with the Kilkennys' furniture, Edgar read the contents of the unwelcome post, and when he had finished reading he screwed it tightly in his fist. He had hoped that there would be no repercussions when Georgina moved in with him, but somehow Fulwar Cavner had already found out her intentions. He thought hard of all the people who knew where she was staying in Chedworth, and wondered whose interest it was for them to tell her husband of her future whereabouts.

In two days' time Georgina will have relocated and her children were to follow at the weekend. But Georgina's husband now knew exactly where she would be, and his letter was threatening. The farmhouse would have to be made more secure.

Edgar flattened the scrunched letter before folding it and placing it in his pocket. Answering it would have to wait, although ignoring it was another option.

An old timer had advised Neil Starbury that The Old Saltway was the shortest route from Lechlade to his intended destination, Kilkenny Farm. Correct as the wizened fellow may have been, the winter weather considerably hindered his progress. Except for an odd copse or gully there was little protection from a stern northeasterly wind.

Head bowed in true serviceman fashion, Starbury marched onwards, determined to reach his objective and at least return to Lechlade that evening, disappointed or not. After nearly two hours he had eventually passed through Coln St Aldwyns, and progressed along what was a designated bridleway but in actuality was little more than a footpath.

On the scrap of paper was the final direction. 'Turn right where the paths cross and it will lead to Kilkenny Farm.' The old man was correct, and as he turned into the wind the buildings of Kilkenny Farm loomed in the distance. Sweating from his exertion he pressed on towards his destination.

With tears coursing down her cheeks and dampening her collar, Mrs Kilkenny finally left her home of nearly forty years. Edgar thanked her for the time she had spent but showed no interest in the poor woman's past and family anecdotes. His own future was of paramount importance.

A young maid, recommended for employment by Mrs. Kilkenny, approached him and curtseyed. "There is a gentleman outside to see you, sir. He says his name is Neil Starbury. He has walked a long way and would like a brief word with you, sir."

Edgar screwed his face up. Neil Starbury? He knew that name. He went to the window and there before him stood the man in question. What was Staff Sergeant Starbury doing in Bibury? And at Kilkenny Farm, of all places. He went to the door.

"Starbury! What are you doing here? Of all the Empire locations in the world and you choose to come to Bibury." Edgar tried not to show his pleasure in seeing him.

"Work, sir," Neil said, coming straight to the point. "I wish to move my family south away from the grime of northern England. I stayed in touch with the regiment, sir, and they said that you had moved down this way. Somebody in a pub in Lechlade last night said I would find you here. I simply took a chance and decided to come and see if there were any opportunities. I won't be disappointed, sir, if there is nothing available. I'll just move on."

Starbury would be an ideal employee to install some form of security around the farm when Georgina and her children arrived. "No. Come in. Let us have a chat. Things are changing here and I need someone who will make a difference. You may well be just the man I need."

Neil Starbury stepped up into the farmhouse. With the absence of the Kilkenny family artefacts the building seemed cold and barren. No pots or pans adorned the kitchen walls, nor pickle and jam jars lined the cupboards. It bore no signs of a dog or cat, and the cast iron cooker shed no light. After four decades someone else would have to rekindle a homely flame. Neil Starbury could not imagine the man who stood before him being that capable figure.

Edgar Collison was immediately to the point. "I need a good yard manager. A man who can keep the workforce under control and at the same time make sure the stock turns over correctly, year in, year out. This farm has been underachieving for too long, and my father has been ignoring its interests. I have a new woman coming to live here and she will better the standards within the house. What I want you to do is manage the farm in our absence and keep a secure outlook over the whole business. It's up to you, Starbury. The offer is on the table."

Neil Starbury wasn't taken aback. He knew Edgar Collison when the man was an incompetent army officer entirely dependent on his subordinates. Decisions were taken off the cuff and any mistakes were blamed down the ranks. As a senior ranking man from the lower echelons Starbury knew only too well when to keep his mouth closed and agree with the army hierarchy above himself.

"Sir, I have had a limited amount of experience in the agriculture industry but perhaps enough for your requirements. I have always been able to learn quickly, and I am sure that I have not lost that knack. I would like to thank you and take up your offer."

The two men sat and discussed the forthcoming months. When the subject of security came up, Edgar allowed Neil to read the letter from Fulwar Cavner. Looking agog he nevertheless promised to defend the farmstead in its entirety.

Chapter 48

Starbury v. Greyffos

In the Seven Tuns at Chedworth James Ronssoy and Willie Greyffos mused over a drink.

"So, has Mr Portlock been able to find gainful employment at Edgar's? Did he fall for the ploy?" Willie Greyffos needed to know certain information before visiting Kilkenny Farm.

"He did but from now on we have to use his proper name; Neil Starbury. Everything is so far going to plan. Georgina is moving into Kilkenny Farm tomorrow, and we will be bringing the children along on Sunday. You will have to confront Edgar before Thomas and Jennifer arrive. They've seen enough in their short lives already. Neil will defend Edgar, so expect a realistic physical altercation. Edgar has to believe what he sees, and if you return to Stokesay looking decidedly worse for wear then Fulwar will hopefully accept as true what you have to tell him." James stared into Willie Greyffos' eyes, expecting him to agree.

Willie deliberated over what he had just heard and what was expected of him. There was another question he wanted to ask. "Your brother-in-law, Stefan. Does he know about any of this? He could put the dampers on the whole operation. There is also his best friend, Lionel. Is he aware of what's going on?"

"Let us assume that they both now know. It is not in either of their interests to interfere. Both could lose their livelihoods under Edgar. Stefan has obviously been involved with Georgina, and Charity, his wife, knows that. Charity wants the issue with her brother resolved. She wants him out of sight once and for all. Georgina will now give Stefan the cold shoulder. It is in all our beliefs that Charity's problems elevate when her brother comes into her mind, and Faith thinks she knows why. Stefan will hopefully stay out of the way, and so will Lionel. Please, Mr Greyffos, do as you are requested and begin the finalisation of this long-running saga. The sooner it is over the sooner we can all relax, and you will be paid handsomely."

Willie considered carefully over what the next few days would bring. He looked up at James. "You have to hope both the antagonists will take the bait. What will you do if one of them doesn't wish to take part, or either of them for that matter? Mr Cavner might just decide to take it through a court of law. I think he will give up his wife if only to have his children back."

"We'll have to wait and see. We are extremely dependent on yourself and Mr Starbury over the next few days. Only time will tell." James pursed his lips, he couldn't imagine what would happen if there was a negative outcome.

Willie Greyffos rose from the table and offered his hand to James. "Rest assured, Mr Ronssoy, we will do our best. It appears to us both that neither of those men deserves anything. If you can ask Mrs Cavner, when she is at Kilkenny Farm, to pass a message to Mr Starbury and forewarn him that I will turn up on Friday morning, and suggest to him that he should not wear his best clothes. He laughed and turned away, quietly disappearing out of the door and leaving an anxious James Ronssoy drinking alone.

Back at his house James warned Georgina of what would happen over the next couple of days, and she assured him she would pass the message to Neil Starbury.

Georgina was about to embark on a journey she dreaded; living with a man who, she felt, was as abhorrent as her own husband. The sooner the whole episode was over for her the better. She left James and Hope alone and went to check up on her children.

Thomas and Jennifer were also being thrown into the fray, and would unknowingly play their part in it. It was a risk but they were major pawns in a very serious game. In their bedroom Georgina sat listening to their soft breathing, and tears rolled gently down her cheeks as she thought of the trials and tribulations of the last few years, hoping it would soon be the end of a long, sad story, and the three could live out their lives in peace, happiness and prosperity.

She gently kissed Thomas and Jennifer and retired to her own bed, where her mind turned to Stefan; a love she had found but had had to reluctantly deter.

The image of his resplendent masculinity developed at the centre of her consciousness, but such recollections of their sexual encounters did little to appease her mental torture. She visualised his good looks and clever intellect, and, almost subconsciously, began stimulating her genitals as she lay with her eyes closed.

Her breathing quickened and her heart rate became faster as she concentrated her mind entirely on her lover. She became flushed and the nipples of her beautifully developed breasts rose and hardened. Secretions began to occur in and around her vagina, which loosened and became more receptive.

She drew her carved apple wood dildo from beneath her pillow and inserted it into herself. Soon she was thrusting it back and forth whilst stimulating her clitoris with her fingers. The rush of blood to her pelvic area provided pleasurable warmth around her animated genitals as an orgasm became imminent.

Strong musculature contractions began and each one became more intense than the last, and each tightening brought about a gratifying tingling sensation through her brain, spine and genital area as the muscles all over her body tightened in unison. She moaned with ecstasy and sprayed fluid over her delicate hands. Beneath the bedclothes the aphrodisiacs of her vaginal secretions permeated the warm air.

"Stefan!" she called during her convulsive orgasm as if he may walk through her bedroom door at any moment.

Slowly, the sexual feelings ebbed away and her body began to relax. She lay motionless with her plaything still partly within her, and it was not long until she again began to fear the days to come. She uncermoniously extricated the dildo from herself, dropped it to the floor and, fantasising that Stefan would come to save her, cried herself to sleep

On the landing, the butler had heard everything. He knew of Stefan but did not know why Georgina and her children had been guests at the house for so long, nor did he know why they were leaving in the next few days. He retired to his room.

Willie's carriage had picked him up promptly from the Fleece Hotel in Cirencester, and as he made his way towards a confrontation, he felt himself becoming nervous. An altercation with a healthy ex-soldier ten years his junior was not what he looked forward to that wet wintry morning.

Gone were the days of his youth when he patrolled on foot the dingy streets around Liverpool's docklands, trying to keep the peace between the Irish immigrants and drunken merchant sailors. Trouble had spilled out regularly from the crowded hostelries, which often ended in bloodshed and, sometimes, death.

He had brought a change of clean and comfortable clothes for the return journey along with some towels, should there be any bloodletting.

His carriage took the course of the old Roman road, Akeman Street, and headed towards Coln St Aldwyns, where it veered northward in the direction of Kilkenny Farm. The driver had estimated that the journey would take approximately an hour. Willie gazed out of the window as the fluttering fieldfares and redwings searched for any winter sustenance in the upland meadows.

Willie was yet to understand how anyone would want to spend a lifetime in such a barren landscape away from the hustle and bustle of city life, where almost any commodity was generally on hand at a price.

True to his driver's estimations the carriage pulled up in the lane at the entrance of the farm in just under an hour, and before stepping out he decided to tell the driver to turn the vehicle around in preparation of a possible hasty retreat.

Willie scrutinised his driver. "Whatever you do, just wait here and don't get involved. I will try not to be long." Willie nervously stepped down from the carriage and proceeded towards the farmhouse.

After being alerted by the noisy arrival of a horse and carriage Edgar Collison stood on the steps of his new home and wondered what was going on.

Willie Greyffos approached diligently.

"How can I help you?" Edgar asked. "I hope you are not trying to sell something. You had better not be a hawker otherwise you'd just as well leave immediately. I'll only tell you once."

"No, sir. I wish to speak with Mrs Cavner. I work on behalf of her husband," Willie informed him.

Edgar couldn't believe that someone else already knew where Georgina was after just two days of her taking up residence at Kilkenny Farm.

"Can I help, sir? Is this gentleman being a nuisance?" Neil Starbury had appeared from the adjoining barn. He stared at Willie Greyffos, who at first refused eye contact.

Willie glanced at him but neither showed any recognition of each other. "I am sorry, but this has nothing to do with you. I only wish to speak briefly with Mrs Cavner and deliver this letter."

From down the farmhouse steps Georgina appeared behind Edgar's shoulder. "Who is it? What does he want?" Edgar told her and she screamed. "No! I don't want to talk to him. Send him away."

Neil took Willie by the elbow and politely spoke to him. "Please, sir. You are obviously not welcome here. I think it would be better that you leave."

Willie brushed him away. "I have travelled a long way and I am not leaving until I talk briefly with Mrs Cavner, and hand her this letter. Madam, I know that your children are staying at Chedworth. Other clients of your husband will be visiting there immediately after this brief visit to take them back to their father."

This finally made Georgina go berserk. She flew at him with flailing fists. "You dare go there, you bastard! Get out of here! You leave my children alone!"

Willie pushed her away and she fell to the ground. Edgar, coward as always, looked at Neil for assistance, and Neil delivered a clean punch on the end of Willie's nose. Blood splattered across his face. A fight broke out and both men traded punches, one quick and sharp, the other hard but cumbersome. Neil finally delivered one to the big man's solar plexus, which dropped him to his knees. He then fired a boot into his kidney, which sent him down onto his side, and another kick went into his groin. He squealed as a beaten man does. Neil stood over him, unaware of what was happening around him. "Starbury, watch out!"

Just as Neil Starbury looked up, stars overcame him and he dropped to the ground like a sack of rotten oranges. There he lay unconscious and with several of his teeth broken.

Willie's carriage driver looked at Edgar. "It should have been a fair fight. The man was finished and he was kicking him on the ground." He helped the ailing Willie Greyffos to his feet.

Willie's broken nose bled profusely, and he stared down at Neil before looking up at Edgar. In his pocket he struggled to pull out another letter addressed to Edgar Collison, which his driver handed over. "Mr Cavner said if you won't hand over his wife and children then I should give you this letter." Willie spoke nasally and appeared like a man in a great deal of pain.

Edgar read the very brief note and then stared at Willie before looking at Georgina. Slowly he shook his head in disbelief. "Is he being serious?"

"I don't know. I don't know what is in the letter," Willie said through his fingers, denying all knowledge of its content. "I am just paid to deliver it."

Neil Starbury was beginning to come around, and he coughed blood and spat out a tooth from his painful mouth. He'd bitten his tongue badly and struggling to speak. The carriage driver pulled him to his feet and stood between the pair as a referee would before announcing the winner.

"What does it say, Edgar? Tell me! What does it say?" Georgina pleaded to know.

Edgar read it again still not convinced that anyone could make such a request, especially as none had been heard of in England for at least fifteen years. He even wasn't sure of the legalities.

Willie looked at him soulfully. "Do you want me to take back a reply?"

"Please, Edgar. Tell me what the letter says. It might end everything and we can at least live in peace."

Edgar read the letter once more and then stared at her hard in the face. "Your husband has challenged me to a pistol duel. It is as simple as that. He wants to fight for his family."

Georgina said nothing at first. The challenge was serious. She thought about Edgar and Fulwar firing shots at each other. Suddenly, she grabbed Edgar's arm. "Come on, Edgar. Take him on. You have been a soldier for years, and you know how to fire a gun. The only shooting Fulwar ever does is for pheasants or woodcocks with shotguns, and he's still hopeless. Besides, he'll be so full of whisky he won't know what he is aiming at. Take him on, my darling. You cannot lose."

The small audience waited for Edgar's answer. The carriage driver couldn't believe that he was witnessing an offer of a duel between two feuding men. Over what he didn't have a clue.

Edgar glanced over to Neil for advice. He stuttered his words, "If Mr Cavner is as incompetent as Mrs Cavner says he is, then I would say you have a very good chance of winning. It is your decision, sir, but if you wish I will act as your second. First you must consider what you might gain or lose." Neil thought like a battle-hardened soldier.

"Let me talk inside with Mrs Cavner. Give us just five minutes." Edgar took Georgina inside the farmhouse.

All three waited outside. Willie and Neil said nothing to each other and still didn't make any eye contact but both realised that there was now someone else inadvertently involved; the carriage driver. He would have to be Willie's problem, at least for the time being.

Edgar soon returned with Georgina and stared at Willie Greyffos.

"Tell Mr Cavner that I accept his challenge, but only on behalf of the children. Mrs Cavner is to stay here at all costs, and the duel will be for custody of the children only. If I win the duel then the children will move here with us. For now, until this situation is resolved, the children will remain where they are in Chedworth and, you call off your kidnappers. Do you understand me?"

"I will return to Stokesay and convey your reply immediately," Willie Greyffos said through a handkerchief, and it was apparent that he was finding it difficult to talk. "I assume that there will have to be future arrangements for the event, as well as the weaponry, the venue and, of course, the arrangement for the disposal of a body, should there be one." He was about to walk away but then turned and pointed to Neil Starbury. "As he is more than happy to be your second, would it be wise to make the arrangements through him?"

Edgar, now a worried man looked at both men, and Neil's eyes told him everything. "Yes, and tell Mr Cavner that the sooner it is over the better," he announced with bravado, and Georgina grabbed his arm, pulled him towards her and kissed him on the cheek. "My brave warrior," she said.

Willie's driver, and former showground boxer, drove him down to Fairford hospital, where they cleaned the private detective up and made him as comfortable as possible before he went back to the Fleece Hotel. His nose had swollen and his eyes were blackening, along with several tender body bruises. The next day he paid his driver a large sum of money and began his train journey north to Stokesay.

Neil Starbury fretted over his swollen face and loss of teeth but added up the rewards in his aching head. If all went well he would be set up for life.

When the rumblings of the fracas filtered back to Bibury, Stefan's curiosity began to get the better of him. Confronting Faith was now becoming imperative, especially as she was due on his doorstep at any time.

Chapter 49
The Brigadier with Faith

As planned, Faith travelled from London to visit Kilkenny Farm, and she listened to the intrigue of the altercation between Neil Starbury and Willie Greyffos, and she seemed shocked when she read the letter from Fulwar. Edgar told her everything.

Contrary to a verbal agreement, Georgina had gone to Chedworth that morning to fetch her children after persuading Edgar not to keep their side of the bargain that the children were to be kept away from the estate until the issue was decided. It suited Georgina that they were with her at the farm, and Edgar had naively agreed because it would infuriate Fulwar even more when he found out where his children were, which was the general intention.

Faith left Kilkenny Farm more than pleased that proceedings were going to plan, and it was only the carriage driver who worried her. Also, some of Edgar's inherited workers may well have seen the incident, but the driver had listened to the conversation about the duel. She wondered what Willie had done to silence him.

Neil Starbury hadn't shown his face but from what she could gather he probably didn't want to. Besides that, it was for the better because Edgar did not know that she knew him intimately. She also wanted to speak with Georgina, her last three or four days must have been hell.

Georgina had to be persuaded to carry on no matter what. They had all gone too far, and there was no turning back. Faith believed that Hope would remain as neutral as possible whilst still being supportive. Although Hope knew about everything that had happened, and what was hopefully going to happen, she had to remain innocent. Charity was a problem but she had so far been holding up well. Indeed, letters Faith had received from her over time suggested that she was much better, especially when Edgar had been known to be moving away from Bibury Court to Kilkenny Farm.

Faith had known for some time that the greatest showdown Faith would have was with Stefan. He believed in judicial fairness and Gerard had a lot of respect for him for that reason. Stefan was guaranteed to be difficult, even if his own livelihood came into jeopardy. Faith had a lot of respect for Stefan's parents but there were some things they underestimated about their beloved son – his French blood.

She again smiled to herself as her carriage drew up towards the front doors of the Court.

The Brigadier watched as his elder daughter stepped down from the carriage and confidently took several deep breaths as she surveyed the surrounding parkland before turning and entering the magnificent building.

The Brigadier shook his head. "She is up to no good," he said to himself.

Faith entered her father's drawing room an hour after arriving at the Bibury Court estate, and her father was far from pleased at the discourtesy.

"Where have you been? Isn't it normal to come and visit your father before you go off gallivanting around the countryside?"

"What do you mean *gallivanting around the countryside*? Father, I arrived at Cirencester during mid-morning, and Edgar's new home is on the way here from there, so I went to see him and now I've come to see you." Faith was frustrated by the Brigadier's cantankerous attitude, and she peered at his brandy glass before casting a scornful eye at his nurse, whose name she still did not know.

The Brigadier's voice was laborious and gravely, and he seemed to be struggling with his health, much to do with his perpetual drinking, although his mind was still sharp.

"Faith, you have not sided with your brother for years, so why now? It has appeared to me during these last eight or nine months that you have spoken of him as if you couldn't wait for him to return from India. You persuaded him to take on Kilkenny Farm, and now you visit him before visiting me." The Brigadier concluded his weak tirade by coughing and spluttering, and his nurse bent down and wiped drool from his chin. He slowly regained his composure before continuing. "You hated him for years, Faith, so why the change of heart?"

Faith stood stock still before her father, and she realised that he knew that she was planning something in the near future, but what she was planning was probably beyond his furthest imaginations.

It was the Brigadier who broke the verbal impasse. "Where is the chap who was working for Marcel? The one interested in Kilkenny Farm. Mr Portlock, I believe. He has disappeared, so I am told, and all his belongings are left at the Catherine Wheel." He paused and took some deep breaths. "You were seen to be having serious conversations with him before he disappeared. Where do you think he went so abruptly?" The Brigadier struggled to raise his ailing eyebrows.

Faith turned away and looked up at the portrait of her mother with her strange expression of irony. It was as if she knew what was happening so many years after her death, and telling them all 'I told you so'. A slight smile faintly creasing her brow said it all.

Faith spun around and glared at her father. "You have been drinking too much and your imagination is getting the better of you, Father?" She looked stonily at his nurse and scolded the poor girl, "It is your job to make sure that he drinks less and eats properly."

Faith turned to leave without another word, but the Brigadier stopped her in her tracks. "Don't do anything stupid, Faith."

She turned to face him and saw that he was pointing to her mother's portrait. "Your mother wouldn't want you to come to any harm." His eyes fixed on his eldest daughter, hoping that she would come to her senses.

"I will see you this evening at dinner, Father." Faith left the room wondering what notions were going through her father's ageing mind. Not about the present but about the past.

Chapter 50
Stefan Confronts Faith

At the gatehouse Faith and Charity embraced as if they hadn't met for years, their hearts beating madly. They settled at the kitchen table.

"I am so scared that this might not work, and then what?" Charity squeezed her sister's hand.

"Everything will be all right, Charity. Be rest assured," Faith replied soothingly, trying to calm her young sister's nerves. "Tell me, what does Stefan know? And where is he? I need to speak to him."

"He knows our intentions but he thinks we are all stupid. Perhaps he is right, Faith. Should we really carry on? We may all end up in prison." Charity shivered at the thought of incarceration amongst some of the most depraved women in England's filthiest, rat-ridden prisons.

"Calm down, Charity. It won't come to that, believe me. I have worked out a plan whereby you will not be implicated in the final outcome. Please, my sweet sister, trust me." Faith stroked Charity's hand reassuringly. "Now tell me where I might find Stefan?"

Charity looked up at the clock. "He is probably at his parents' with the children but I know he intends to go to the Catherine Wheel as soon as it opens. If you wait here, he'll be back."

"No. I haven't time. I need to speak to him soon. I am almost sure that he'll want harsh words with me." Faith smiled at the probable outcome, and set out to find her brother-in-law. Charity, quickly wrapping herself in a shawl, followed hot on her sister's heels.

Faith found Stefan in his parents' home, and he wasn't pleased to see her. He put on a brave face and greeted her with charm as did his three children and his father and mother. Faith refused the offer of a drink but indicated that she needed to speak with Stefan alone, as soon as possible. Charity naturally reassured him that the children would be safe, and the pair left.

It was dark as they passed the gatehouse, and Faith broke the silence. "You're quiet. What's the matter? Is it something I've said?" He couldn't see her smile.

"I'm not saying anything here, anyone could be listening. Where are we going? Will the Swan be good enough?" Stefan asked sarcastically.

They sat in a corner in the alehouse out of earshot from anyone, and Stefan tapped out an imaginary tune on his cider pot. How many times over the past few months had he sat in a corner or outside so no-one could hear his conversations? Even the villagers had noticed the change far from his normal self and wondered what troubled him. His anger and impatience were getting the better of him and Faith felt his pent up wrath. Unusually, he wasn't even facing her. She felt that he was about to explode into a diatribe of rage but hoped that his normally intellectual mind would show great restraint, especially in view of where they were sitting.

The situation was now proceeding towards a precarious period in which Stefan had no part. He had been deliberately misinformed in the past, and Faith had every intention to prevent him from standing in the way, whether he was family not.

"So, what is angering you, Stefan?" Faith asked soothingly knowing full well that her brother-in-law was about to try and shatter everything that had been planned over the last months.

Stefan looked up suddenly and glowered at Faith. "Angering me? What do you bloody well think is angering me? From what I have been told you intend to wipe out two human beings from the face of the earth. That's what's angering me. It's tantamount to bloody murder. Have you sat down and thought about what happens if you get caught? You will be in bloody prison for the rest of your life or, even more likely, swinging from the gallows. It is a ridiculous idea!" He stood up shunting his chair back across the flagstone floor and drew attention from the customers at the bar.

He made to leave but Faith strongly urged him to sit back down and listen. After some thought and pacing around he complied with her wish. "What else has anybody told you other than what Georgina mentioned to you the other day?" Faith asked.

"Nothing. All I've heard is that there was some kind of confrontation at Kilkenny Farm. A fight. From what I've been told the bloke who turned up and sparked it all off fits the description of Fulwar Cavner's detective, but that wouldn't surprise me. Other than that I don't know." Stefan shrugged his shoulders, still angry.

"It was Willie Greyffos," she admitted. "Do you know what the fight was about?" Faith asked him, positive that he was not fully aware of the whole situation.

"Well, Fulwar Cavner obviously wants his family back, and Edgar isn't allowing it. Who was Willie Greyffos fighting with? I am damned sure Edgar wouldn't stand up to anyone in a brawl, coward that he is." Stefan kept looking towards the bar and trying not to shout at his sister in law.

Faith smiled. "Who do you think? Of all people, who do you think may have confronted Willie Greyffos on Friday morning?"

Stefan knew nearly all of the labourers at the farm but he couldn't think of anyone who would have stood up and fought for Edgar Collison. "None to my knowledge at Kilkenny Farm would ever get into a fight on behalf of Edgar Collison. I don't know, and I am not even going to try and guess."

"Does Staff Sergeant Neil Starbury ring a bell?" Faith watched her brother-in-law's face with amusement.

Stefan thought hard. He was about to deny ever hearing the name when the penny seemed to drop. "Not Neil Portlock?" He rested his forehead in his palm with his elbow on the table, and his head shook slowly from side to side in disbelief. When he eventually looked up he asked Faith the ultimate question. "For God's sake, Faith, how far has all this gone? It has to stop. There are people's lives at risk, not only from imprisonment but from death!"

He stood up abruptly and went to the bar and except for the barman no one spoke to him. With another drink he took his seat again. "I can't let you carry on, Faith. I can't. Murdering two men is a ludicrous idea. Someone will find out, the beans will be spilled and most of the Brigadier's family will be incarcerated if not hung; his daughters, including my wife, and his sons-in-law. His son may end up dead, or someone from Shropshire who we hadn't even heard of nine months ago. Perhaps both of them will end up dead and buried. No! I am sorry but this has definitely gone too far. I am not going to allow it to happen!"

"Stefan! For one, you have no time for Edgar. For two, although you have only met him briefly, drunk that he always is, you have no time for Georgina's husband either. Now you want to keep both men alive!" Stefan went to interrupt but Faith was having none of it. "Shut up and listen! Of all people, you should understand the economics. On our estate alone there must be at least a hundred workers, perhaps more, I don't know. On the Cavner estates you can probably double or treble those figures. Then there are all the small businesses that depend on gaining work where they can from both estates. Above all, there are the families whose hard working fathers have to support financially, including their children and, quite often, their grandparents. Stefan, you know better than I do that the number of people who depend on our estates amounts to hundreds if not thousands of people." She drew a breath. "For the sake's of two miserable undeserving lives how many people do you think will end up in an early grave because of unemployment, homelessness and subsequently starvation because of their outright incompetence and arrogance?"

Faith paused. Stefan went to interrupt again but she never gave him a chance. "Times will change progressively and economically, I have no doubt, but now is not that time." Faith was resolute. "God forbid those two men who will inherit what has been built up over many years. All those people I have just mentioned and, I 'll say it again, will be jobless, then homeless and finally destitute. Am I getting through to you Stefan? Some already want to leave Kilkenny Farm but they have nowhere to go yet." Faith leaned back in her chair. She knew Stefan would have his own opinion and gave him his chance.

He spoke very quietly. "I cannot condone murdering people just to have it your own way."

"Now listen to me!" she shouted but then was suddenly aware of receiving inquisitive scowls from the bar. "We are not going to murder them," she continued in a lowered voice. "None of us are. We will not be involved." It was Faith who was now becoming annoyed as she tried to make Stefan see reason.

Stefan screwed up his forehead. "Then who is if you are not?"

Faith stared at the window. All she could see in the reflection was a side view of Stefan, and knew that she had to tell him what the shenanigans the day before at Kilkenny Farm were all about, but she wasn't sure how Stefan would respond when she told him.

"Yesterday, Willie Greyffos delivered a letter from Fulwar to Edgar. Fulwar actually challenged Edgar to a duel so he could have his children back. Georgina is not in his equation, he only wants the return of his children."

Stefan looked both stunned and bemused. "A duel. Why would he challenge Edgar to a duel? Fulwar could go to a court of law and easily win custody of his children. If Edgar had challenged him then I could understand, but why challenge Edgar?" Stefan shook his head because of the absurdity of it all. "Come off it, Faith. This is becoming even more ridiculous."

"No it is not. Edgar has already accepted the challenge. Now it is all up to Fulwar Cavner to say yes." Faith watched her brother-in-law closely, wondering if he understood her last remark.

Stefan frowned. He stood up with his drink and walked to the fireplace. He placed his elbow on the mantelpiece and supported his chin with his fist. Faith could see that he was deep in thought, trying to conclude what she had just told him. After a minute or two he finished his cider and bought another before returning, sitting opposite Faith but saying nothing.

"What are you thinking about?" Faith eventually asked him.

He looked at her questionably. "What kind of duel, for heaven's sake?"

Here was an issue for Faith. Something else she didn't want him to find out just yet. "A pistol duel," she told him quietly.

"And how the hell has Edgar accepted the challenge from Fulwar Cavner but Fulwar Cavner has yet to agree. Surely he has already challenged him!" Stefan's temper was rising again.

"Calm down, Stefan. What you don't understand is that Willie Greyffos delivered that letter to Edgar from Fulwar Cavner. Nobody else. The letter was signed by Fulwar. Edgar accepted it and agreed to the challenge of the duel. Willie Greyffos has gone back to Stokesay Castle and will verbally tell Fulwar that Edgar wants a pistol duel with him. It all depends now on Fulwar's agreement. When Fulwar sees the state of his private detective, having been beaten up pursuing the return of his children, then he will hopefully accept the challenge. We'll have to wait and see. Willie Greyffos has travelled back today and will probably see Fulwar tomorrow. Both men will inadvertently think that they have challenged the other."

Faith remained perfectly calm. If Stefan disagreed she had one trump card up her sleeve that she didn't want to use but to keep Edgar from inheriting her father's estate she would not hesitate to lay it on the table.

Stefan shook his head. "You are just a scheming bitch. It's a conspiracy. Do you really expect those two men to shoot each other and everything will be all right. Is it designed to suit your inheritance? Two dead men, Faith. I cannot believe that you have stooped this low. You are putting the whole of the family name on the line as well. Most of who, including yourself especially, will definitely end up behind bars or hanging from the gallows."

"Stefan! We have little choice. Act now or suffer later!" Faith was adamant.

Stefan went back to the bar. His mind began to swirl with a concoction of bizarre information and the winter cider. Faith was calm and collected when he returned.

"So, what are you going to do?" she asked? "Tell everyone, including the police, and spoil it all? You are the only one against the scheme."

"I cannot let you cause the deaths of two men, it is beyond my principles. I am sorry but that is the way I am. There is enough unnecessary killing going on in the world now but this is completely reprehensible. Call it off, Faith. Call it off!" Stefan was resolute.

"I am going to tell you for the last time, none of our family will be implicated. Willie Greyffos will be acting on Fulwar Cavner's behalf, and Neil Portlock – or Starbury – will be acting on Edgar's behalf. It is as simple as that. No one will believe any different. Edgar and Fulwar are arguing over a marriage and Willie and Neil's motivations are purely financial. If the former pair dies, then so be it. And if the latter are caught for aiding and abetting, so be it." Faith hastily stood up. "I'll buy my own drink, thank you." She went to the bar and chatted briefly with some old acquaintances before returning.

Stefan was about to say something as Faith sat back down but she stopped him dead.

"There is something else I have yet to tell you." She spoke carefully and slyly, and Stefan couldn't believe there might be another twist in the plot but there was. "I'm pregnant," she added.

Stefan was taken aback. At first he didn't know what to say. His head was entirely wrapped up in the murdering of Edgar and Fulwar. "Congratulations," he said and rubbed the top of her hand across the table. "I thought you and Gerard had problems in that respect."

"We do, but you have solved that for us." Her face had a deadpan expression.

Stefan was stunned. "What do you mean by that?"

"Gerard couldn't have children during his last marriage. They divorced because of it, and since then his ex-wife has had children. We tried for a long time and concluded that it was a problem of his. He didn't mind me going out and becoming pregnant as long as the father was respectable and intelligent, and that I would have no sexual requirements from the donor ever again. Gerard also bade me to love him afterwards as well, which I still do." Faith smiled across the table at Stefan.

Stefan was dumfounded once again. "Are you insinuating that I might be the father?"

"Who else could it be? Are you suggesting that I am a slut?" she asked whilst raising her eyebrows. "Don't worry, I haven't told anyone else that I am pregnant... yet."

"Yet?"

"Oh, except for Gerard, of course."

Stefan was well and truly cornered. Faith was a scheming bitch, and a clever one at that, and he suddenly realised that he was no longer in a position to say another word against her murderous plan. It was obvious that if he didn't go along with the order of things Charity would almost certainly find out. What the Brigadier might say or do was inconceivable; let alone the general public's view. "Did you actually time this pregnancy to prevent me from saying anything? Did you assume all those months ago that I would be against your *great* plan?"

"Stefan, what you have been told has to materialise whether you like it or not. On our own estate bankruptcy will loom in no time with Edgar in charge, which is very much the same as on the Cavner estate with Fulwar in charge. Sir Charles, Maria and Edward are very concerned about their future. We need a period of stability, and those two fools are not qualified to provide that, by any stretch of the imagination." She rolled her wine glass around with her fingers, quite confident that Stefan would comply to her wishes.

"There are other underlying reasons why Edgar is surplus to requirements, but I am not going to elaborate on that any further. I will ask this though, what will happen if he is ever allowed to bring his Indian wife and children back here? Are you going to be servile to them? Not only that, where then does Georgina and her two children stand in all of this? I am sorry, Stefan but Edgar simply has to go." Faith was unwavering and there was nothing to convince her not to carry on.

"What will happen to the Cavner estate if Fulwar is dead? Who is next in line?" Stefan was suddenly keen to know. He had never imagined Fulwar being out of the equation.

"Technically on the death of Fulwar, Thomas, his son, becomes the heir to the estate. If his grandfather dies quite soon as well and Thomas is still very young, his great uncle, Sir Charles Cavner, will probably preside over the estate until Georgina's son is experienced enough to take over the entire management. Putting it simply, Thomas will become in charge of the whole estate at Stokesay and at Brockhampton." Faith had been doing her groundwork. "You know, of course, who would become heir to the Bibury estate if Edgar should die?"

Stefan sat in thought. He had considered it before, but he had never let it bother him. "You. The eldest sister. Which gives you an even greater reason to dispose of your brother."

"No. Between ourselves the three of us have already come to a decision that we will miss a generation. When this epic is over we will tell the Brigadier what we want. He'll have to alter his will if Edgar dies. Your Francois will be the main beneficiary and heir to the estate. We can't tell Father to alter his will at this time because he'll realise something serious is going to happen, and I'm already under suspicion from him. I'm having dinner with him alone this evening. I don't really want to but someone has to try and appease him, and who else but me?" Faith didn't enjoy the thought of sitting alone with her father. A companion in tow would be a much more comfortable proposition.

"When you go back, call in and see Charity," Stefan urged. "She'll go to dinner with you. She seems so much better lately, and your father would appreciate it if she was present, and she'll be good company for you as well. Tell her I'll be back at eight-thirty to look after the children. I want to go and have a drink with Lionel first; it's his evening off." Stefan had an underlying motive and Faith knew it.

"Are you going to tell Lionel what I have just told you?"

"Are you in a position to stop me?" he retorted.

"As long as he doesn't say anything. As you are good friends, you can also tell him that I am pregnant with your child if you want. Anyway, Father will find out that I'm pregnant this evening, and by the end of the weekend the whole of Bibury will probably know." She smiled at Stefan who was now obviously becoming drunk.

Outside, they briefly kissed goodbye before going their separate ways, and the kiss felt like finality between them, an ending of a sexual love but now the beginning of a business relationship that both had to endure for perhaps a long period of time. It was a love that could save Bibury Court for years to come.

Faith watched her Gallic brother-in-law stagger up the hill towards the Catherine Wheel. She had one small trap to set and then the guns were ready to fire at the end of the plan.

Stefan struggled his way up the hill to the Catherine Wheel. He didn't have much time because of his promise to be back to look after his children but he anxiously wanted to speak with Lionel. He wasn't disappointed. Lionel thought he recognised the cause of his friend's state of his mind: cider. He took him out to his father's sitting room, sat him down and insisted he drank a large glass of water.

"What the hell is the matter? You haven't been like this for a long time." Lionel was worried about Stefan. "What have you been doing?"

"Please, Lionel, listen to what I have to say. I have to go home soon. Believe me when I tell you that this is not made up." Stefan drank water but it barely helped his addled mind. He told Lionel what was going to happen. He emphasised 'a duel'.

"Don't be ridiculous, Stefan. The last known duel in England was probably about 1852 or '53. They are illegal now. Besides, what are they going to use? Bill hooks?" Lionel laughed. "You've had too much to drink. Your best bet is to go home and get some sleep."

Stefan went quiet in thought for several moments, remembering what it was Faith had said. "Pistols," he suddenly blurted out. "Faith said they were going to use pistols." He thought deeply for a few moments but then suddenly looked up at Lionel. "Believe me, Lionel, I think this is going to happen. Edgar and Fulwar are going to have a duel, and come to think of it I know who is procuring the pistols."

Stefan quickly stood up but Lionel dragged him back down.

"When men were allowed to duel the chance of someone being killed by a pistol shot was remote. Wounded, yes, but dying was extremely rare. One of them would always walk away, and the other might have a serious gunfire wound but they were far more likely to survive. And even if the loser does die, the victor will live. It cannot possibly work. Edgar or Georgina's husband will almost certainly live. Then what? Georgina cannot win with either outcome. From what you have said in the past, I am damn sure that she doesn't want to live with Edgar. I think you had better tell the Brigadier and let him sort it all out."

Stefan kept shaking his head. "No, it's not as simple as that," he said remorsefully. She's pregnant, Lionel. She's bloody pregnant!" He raised his head and faced his friend. "She insinuates that it is my child, and if I tell her to stop this deathly charade the whole family, including, Charity, will find out that I have been screwing her." Stefan then went on to tell his friend about Gerard's physical condition, and how Faith had come to get herself with child.

Lionel said nothing for a while, taking in what he had just been told. "Did you ask her how far along she is into her pregnancy? Did she actually look pregnant?" Lionel also had an interest in Faith's condition.

"No, I didn't ask... and no, I didn't notice. We walked up to the pub in the dark, and when we talked she was sitting down. Why do you ask? Don't you believe her?"

"Because I screwed her at the Summer Ball but that was months ago. It's putting it crudely, but you must have been in there since," Lionel said with a half smile.

"Faith has also got my hands tied behind my back, Stefan. She could so easily mention to Mary what happened between us at the Ball."

"You're right. Our hands *are* tied."

"Try to view it sensibly, Stefan. We haven't created this scenario; it's all to do with the women. They want to dispose of Edgar and Fulwar. The women want us to remain with our hands tied behind our backs but on the other hand they want us to know what is going on. I'm sorry but I find it all very confusing. By the sound of it Gerard and James also seem to be accepting what their wives are up to. I suppose it's because they have an interest in the estate." It was dawning on Lionel that the men wouldn't have a say in the proceedings at all.

"You could involve the police and see what they do. They might operate to some degree in the towns and cities but they will soon prove to be defunct in rural areas such as Bibury. The 'powers that be' here are completely different. Other than that, we will have to wait and see what becomes of this bizarre confrontation. Just remember, Stefan, if you had never had a sexual liaison with Georgina in that barn, all this would probably not be happening." Lionel shrugged his shoulders, resigned to the fact that they could do or say nothing about Faith's great contrivance.

"I am not so sure. Deep in the Collison sisters' minds they want to get rid of their brother. Georgina may just have been a coincidence and then the catalyst to start a macabre ball rolling." Stefan stopped in thought, "it's strange, but how did Georgina ever become involved with Faith? And why would she then go along with such a peculiar plan? Georgina and I met purely by chance. I am sure we did. Someone else must have instigated the connection between Georgina and Faith. How else would those two women begin plotting the demise of a brother and a husband? There is more to it than meets the eye. They were in on it together at least as far back as when I met Georgina in Maidenhead, maybe even before that. Come to think of it, something happened between Georgina and Edgar at the Summer Ball."

"Who knew about you and Georgina? Someone perhaps also linked to Faith?" Lionel asked, trying to be helpful by jogging Stefan's memory.

Stefan thought deeply. "Charity asked had I been with another woman because she could smell perfume on me, but that was the day I met Georgina. I think that was on the Wednesday. The following Friday, after a walking tour around both of the villages with her cousin Edward, I spoke with Georgina in the Cavner Arms and she told me about her marital problems. I went to the barn with her the next day. I didn't need to go back up to Brockhampton but believe me, Lionel, she was irresistible."

"So, no one other then Charity knew what was going on?" Lionel's questioning was becoming intense. He felt that only Stefan's dear wife knew of the liaison.

"I suppose not," Stefan shrugged. "I did tell you, of course, and the Brigadier was then well aware after Sir Charles' visit."

Lionel became serious. "You can count me out for a start. So early on, Faith and Georgina could only have become acquainted through two people. One is your wife and the other is the Brigadier. Perhaps they are all in it together, although I would find it hard to understand why the Brigadier is mixed up with it."

Stefan had a far away look. "Do you remember when my father gave me that pair of French duelling pistols on my thirtieth birthday? They were in a beautiful inlaid wooden box,"

Lionel nodded. "Well, I am going back home to see if they are still in the bottom of my wardrobe. If they are missing then Charity must have something to do with all this. Nobody else knew where they were." Stefan glanced at the clock. "I must go. I said I would be back to look after the children."

Both men shook hands and parted. Back at the gatehouse Stefan saw Charity out of the door and then promptly rushed upstairs in search of his prized gift. Feeling around at the bottom of the wardrobe confirmed to him what he already felt. They were gone.

After a glass of Armagnac, he fell soundly asleep in the armchair, drunk and confused.

Chapter 51
Greyffos' Message

Willie Greyffos was asked to wait in the expansive banqueting hall at Stokesay Castle due to his client not being readily available. It didn't stretch Willie's imagination far to think why. He walked slowly around admiring the great portrait and landscape paintings hanging from the walls between the long Gothic windows. Willie strained his neck to view the timbers supporting the roof. They were made from huge oak trees and he tried to envisage the craftsmen building such a masterpiece of construction hundreds of years earlier. Above the medieval fireplace was an elaborately decorated over mantel on which stood at each end a pair of silver candlesticks and centrally, a Lenoir Ravrio gold plated clock.

"Flanders, that one came from," a voice told him from behind, and Willie spun around startled. Isabella Cavner, Fulwar's mother stood behind him. "It was made by the finest Flemish artisans and brought here and installed by the Baldwyn family," she smiled, proud to be the owner of such a beautiful timepiece.

"I beg your pardon, ma'am. I was merely browsing. I have come to speak with your son. Is he not here?" Willie asked her, hoping he wouldn't have to leave and return another time.

Isabella then realised the state of Willie's face. "My God! What happened to you? You have been in the wars."

"Oh, nothing much. It was just a little altercation with someone. Sometimes it comes with the job." He tried to smile but found it too difficult.

"I'm sorry to hear that. I'm afraid Fulwar is rather inebriated at the moment. He had been quite good of late but suddenly he has decided to start drinking again. In an hour or two we might be able to bring him around but whether he'll be able to understand you, I don't know. I've sent two maids up to stay by his side, and when he stirs they'll keep him awake, and one of them will come and let us know. Would you like a tour around the castle? You are obviously interested and there is a lot of history behind the place. Afterwards, we can perhaps go and have some refreshment in the lounge." Willie agreed and they set off at a leisurely pace whilst Isabella described the past times of her Shropshire home.

After nearly an hour they returned and sat comfortably drinking lemon tea. Willie was discreet and refused her offer of something stronger. It could wait until later, he thought.

"So, have you discovered the whereabouts of poor Georgina?" Isabella asked.

Willie wasn't sure if she was being sympathetic or whether there was a hint of sarcasm in the tone of her voice. He had no intention of beating around the bush; there was no need to. Everyone wanted Fulwar to know where his wife was. "Yes. I have but I don't think getting her back here is going to be quite so simple."

Her next remark surprised him. "He doesn't deserve to have her back. Nor the children. I hope you have found them safe as well?"

"I believe the children are going to live with their mother if they are not already with her. I am afraid that there are other complications but I'll let your son tell you if he so wishes." Willie stared into the bottom of his teacup. He was unsure how much information he could pass to her.

Isabella sat forward on the edge of the armchair with her hands clasped between her knees. "How is Georgina? I do hope she is all right? I've been so worried about her and the children. Has she recovered from that dreadful beating he gave her? I really thought she was going to die. Fulwar is such a terrible man, especially when he has been drinking."

What Isabella said astonished Willie. He always had the impression that Georgina had no friends here at Stokesay. "I saw her on Friday. Yes, she seemed to be quite well but I gather she had sustained some rather nasty internal injuries. Injuries I could not possibly comment on medically. Tell me, Mrs Cavner, why didn't you ever try to put a stop to it all."

Isabella Cavner suddenly stood up and began pacing the room, and her body language suggested to Willie that a feeling of guilt was soaked right through her. "*My* husband also beat me. He wasn't quite as bad as Fulwar but he was bad enough. I couldn't say anything so long ago but when Fulwar began the same antics his father defended him, blaming Georgina for being flirtatious or some other pathetic excuse. I am afraid that it is a classic case of 'like father, like son'." She struggled to hold back the tears. "I am only talking to you now because my husband is away in Wales on a shooting trip, and Fulwar is asleep upstairs. Believe me, Mr Greyffos, I have had a terrible marriage, and have lived in perpetual fear of the next beating. I play such a minor role in the household. Our world is entirely patriarchal, you see, and I am afraid that I am not brave enough to try and change the system. There are valiant women out there who have attempted to persuade the powers that be to make the necessary social reforms, but they are often ridiculed, beaten, and occasionally imprisoned. One day there will be change but I am afraid that I am too much of a coward to try and help." Isabella sat down next to Willie on the settee and placed her hand on the back of his own.

"Please, Mr Greyffos, don't tell Fulwar anything that might jeopardise the lives of Georgina or my grandchildren."

Willie felt awkward. He slowly pulled his hand away. "Ma'am, I want this affair to end amicably but whatever I tell your son, it is he who makes the decisions. He pays my wages. I merely do as he asks."

She leaned back, looked up at the chandelier and sighed. Willie studied the profile of the desperate woman beside him. The brightness seemed to have faded from her blue eyes years before. She was heavily wrinkled and probably in her late sixties or early seventies. Once, he imagined, she was a fine looking woman. But she was now almost certainly wearing a wig, and he could detect a faint whiff of perfume that is generally worn by more mature women, the brand name of which escaped him.

Willie continued to study her face from the corner of his eye. "I would like to ask you a question, if you don't mind."

Continuing to stare upward, she answered. "Go on then. I'll try and answer it."

"What if Fulwar left Stokesay for good and never returned? Would it worry you?" Willie waited as she pondered over his strange question.

She turned. "Do you mean if he went to live elsewhere and never came back?"

"Yes. What if he was more or less out of your life forever?" Willie looked into her aged face.

"I shouldn't say it because he is my son, but no, I wouldn't care at all. I have had enough of him. I haven't long left in this world and all he gives me and everyone else is grief. If he went tomorrow and never returned it wouldn't bother me in the slightest. At least there would be a chance of having my grandchildren back, perhaps. I don't know what Frederick would think though because he would almost certainly have a say in it. I am afraid it is hypothetical because Fulwar would never leave Stokesay."

There was a faint knock at the door, much to the relief of Willie Greyffos, and Isabella quickly moved back onto her armchair before inviting the visitor in. They were told that Fulwar Cavner was ready to speak with Mr Greyffos. Willie rose to his feet.

"Please, Mr Greyffos, keep me in touch about Georgina and the children. I am never told anything. I am so glad that I could talk to you today. You have given me just a little bit of hope. Please send my love to them and tell them that I miss them very much." Isabella gently kissed him on the cheek and he turned and left.

As he went to find Fulwar Cavner he almost felt vindicated working for both sides.

"Are you are telling me that Edgar Collison is saying that if I want my children back then I would have to accept his challenge to a duel, and the winner keeps the children?" Fulwar, not quite his full self, was flabbergasted. With his head down he paced around the room.

"I am afraid that it seems there is no possible chance of your wife returning here to Stokesay and she is going to fight tooth and nail to keep the children in her charge. If it goes to court she says she can produce evidence of your behaviour and compare you unfavourably with Mr Collison, who, she says, is a gentleman and good father figure. He is also prepared to be a witness in court. Just remember that she spent a long time in hospital before Christmas, and she never fell off a horse or was ever run over by a carriage. Edgar has seen the damage you did to her. Go to court and take your chances or accept his challenge on the traditional 'field of honour'." Willie hoped dearly that Fulwar would take up the latter option.

Fulwar took a large swig of whisky. Already he wasn't quite listening properly. He was trying to weigh up in his mind what it would be like to be shot at, and then the pain, the humiliation and, of course, the possibility of death. He could only conjure up a bizarre scenario in his mind.

"Listen to me, Mr Cavner! I have been beaten up because of you and I also want some kind of revenge. Edgar Collison may well have been in the army for years but he is a known coward and spent most of his time as a pen pusher. If you think you can shoot quite reasonably then it might be worth accepting his challenge. Don't forget, it concerns you and your children." Willie was slowly plying his powers of persuasion.

Fulwar gulped some more whisky. "I'm not sure," he hesitated, "isn't it illegal?"

"Mr Cavner, the last man who died in Britain from a pistol shot wound at a duel was about fifteen years ago. The chances of dying are very remote. There is a good chance that he won't go through with it, and that will make you the winner. Then you can have your children back. If you really want to accept the challenge I will be your second. You will need someone reliable who knows something about guns. Other than that I can return to Bibury and decline the offer, whereby you will have to go and face your wife in court. It's up to you but I am prepared to help if you so wish." Willie was finding it hard to persuade Fulwar to accept but it was crucial that he did for the ultimate plan to succeed. He had to keep reassuring Fulwar that he would generally be safe.

"Where might this duel happen? Fulwar asked, beginning to thaw to the idea. "And, of course, when?" Maybe the whisky was making him more daring?

"It would be better if it was held halfway between the Brockhampton and Bibury Court estates. There it will be neutral ground and the local judiciary do not have too much sway as to what goes on. As for when, that is what we will have to decide." Willie suddenly became hopeful.

Fulwar lay back down on his chaise longue and for some time he said nothing until suddenly sitting up, taking another large gulp of whisky and smiling. "Tell that bloody fool and kidnapper, Edgar Collison, that I accept his challenge, and God help him." He then fell swiftly to sleep.

Willie walked along the hallway wondering whether Fulwar would remember the conversation in the morning and the importance of the decision he had made.

As his carriage drew away from Stokesay Castle, Isabella Cavner watched him leave from a bedroom window. He looked up and briefly caught sight of her saddened face. He touched his hat to her and she gave an almost imperceptible nod in return.

At least he seemed to have her blessing.

Chapter 52
The Collusion

Edgar gave Neil Starbury a long weekend off to go and visit his family in order to arrange their move to Gloucestershire. Edgar had promised Neil one of the larger cottages at the farm for Neil and his family, and had given him the title of Farm Manager, despite him having little experience in the agricultural industry.

During his visit home he had one appointment that he could not miss and he was now heading to The Commercial, Willie Greyffos' favourite haunt.

As ever it was busy and the two men sat and recalled the last few days. Neither had fully recovered from their staged fisticuffs and Willie's face was still a yellowy black from the bruising. Both admitted that they had gone too far, but shook hands as gentlemen, brushing the incident under the table.

Willie, detective as ever, asked the first question. "So, how is it going at your end? Has anything happened yet?"

"This coming week the 'Ladies' are having dinner at the Bull Hotel in Fairford. They have booked a discreet little room at the back where their conversation will not be overheard. They will arrange the date for the duel, the whereabouts of the field of honour, who will be allowed to attend, and how they travel there. Obviously, they don't want any strangers involved who they cannot trust." Neil went to carry on but Willie stopped him.

"This is all very well, Neil, but someone has to stand between those two men and quote some rules. They cannot just shoot it out arbitrarily."

Neil raised his hand. "No, you're right. They can't. This is an important point so please listen carefully. When the women make their decision on a date for the duel, both sides have to have an equal opportunity. First of all, the date must be compatible between both men. Then the pistols on offer must be acceptable to both sides. They should be able to try them out prior to combat and, if they agree to use them, then so be it. They must also agree where the duel will take place. Normally, a duel will take place at first light when there are few other people around. We must make sure that the duel is conducted fairly but I think there should be a third party there to make sure we do not break any honourable gentlemen's rules."

"Who? You obviously have someone in mind. Who is he and is he impartial?" Willie asked.

"Far from being neutral, he has every reason to want both combatants dead but he fully understands the rules of duelling. Apparently, he had already called for a halt to the stupidity but has now become involved should the duel go ahead."

"Who are you talking about? And where did you get your information?" Willie was intrigued.

"Stefan Desailley. It is he who owns the duelling pistols. People talk and I then put two and two together. Before I left Bibury I worked for Marcel, Stefan's father, and he often told me stories of his past when he was living in France. The way he spoke he gave me the impression that he was the man who organised duels in his particular area of France. Stefan Desailley, who you know, is his son and is normally a man of high ethical standards. I am sure that he would sooner this duel doesn't take place. Stefan knew a long time ago why I came to Bibury, and he told me to stay away from his brother-in-law. I think someone is intimidating Stefan and has coerced him to take part. My problem with gleaning information is that I no longer have direct contact with the people on the Bibury estate, and I have to rely on second hand hearsay from the Kilkenny Farm labourers." Neil held his hands out in submission.

"Then who told you that Stefan had become involved?"

"His wife. She has become a sort of go-between but only so she doesn't have to meet with Edgar. A couple of days ago she came up to Kilkenny Farm to see Georgina, and I helped her down from the carriage. Edgar was away at the market in Cirencester, and I had a brief but subtle conversation with her. I don't receive letters at the farm yet so I am having to depend on those chance meetings." Neil smiled ironically. He raised himself off his seat and pushed his way to the bar.

Willie sat alone for a while in deep thought. Someone had been very clever, as long as the duel came to a successful conclusion.

Neil sat back down. "Penny for your thoughts?" he asked.

Willie stirred. "It might take a long time to explain and still I don't know all the reasons, but why are these two men so despised and people want them dead? Not just to have them out of their lives, but to actually have them dead.

Let's take Fulwar Cavner. He's a terrible alcoholic and a wicked wife beater. His wife has very good reasons to get rid of him in this respect, but if he does die, then I assume the son, Thomas, will eventually inherit the estate from his grandfather. Georgina will in be a very privileged position and, probably by then, head matriarch. You probably don't know this, Neil, but Isabella, Fulwar's mother, doesn't want her son around either. I found it hard to believe but I am sure that it is true, judging from the conversation I had with her the other day.

Another person who would sooner see him eliminated is, of course, the so-called ethical Stefan Desailley, who we have just spoken about. He could still have ambitions of fornicating with Georgina because she is still a beautiful and sensual woman. Not to be scoffed at, especially if you are denied sex in your own home. However, the people with the greatest reasons to see the man in his grave are probably Sir Charles Corbett-Cavner and his wife and son. If Fulwar survives they might find themselves homeless when he inherits the estate, not just because of his attitude towards them but also because of his incompetence. They don't like him and he knows it. They have to put up with his awful shenanigans and take in poor Georgina for convalescence every time she takes a thrashing. Edward will be left with almost nothing if Fulwar survives, especially when his parents die." Willie took some large gulps of beer and then looked Neil straight in the eyes. "Is there anyone else you might know who would want Fulwar Corbett-Cavner dead?"

"Only Charity Desailley but that is because Georgina Cavner would be free to go and find another love and perhaps leave Stefan alone, but that's purely supposition."

"Well, let's leave Fulwar Cavner out of it for now and talk about Edgar Collison, your current employer. Similar to Fulwar, there is deep suspicion that he will bankrupt the Bibury estate. His three sisters seem adamant that this will happen and appear to use it as the excuse to dispose of him. Neil, believe me, there has to be more to it than that. There are three men involved. Stefan, who we have already spoken about, Hope's husband, James, and then the most well educated of them all, Faith's husband, Gerard. They all married into money, and each one of them must want to see the estate well maintained because of their own inheritance. We both know that they all want Edgar dead. He has been away for many years in the army, but as soon as he was demobilised and returned home all hell was let loose. Charity becomes ill, Faith is seen in Bibury more than ever and Hope takes in a lodger who, putting it mildly, is more than a hot potato."

"Which means?" Neil asked.

"It means that all of them want the two men dead!" Willie leaned back and made the chair creak with his girth.

Neil had listened long enough. He had his own opinions. "Then there is the other parallel. One we are loath to talk about," he took a deep breath, "I gain a substantial amount of money if Edgar Collison dies, especially if I instigate it or even murder him. You know that but you are in the pay of both sides, and when the duel takes place you will gain two pay packets, regardless of the outcome. If Edgar doesn't die I might have to go on the run for the rest of my life from people who want their money back because I failed to kill him. There is something else that you don't know about. When I found out that the tenancy of Kilkenny Farm was becoming available I applied to take it over, not realising that it had been earmarked for Edgar. So, I have more than one reason to see the man dead. In fact, there are other reasons but I cannot divulge them to you. It is about something which happened in the past."

Willie sat pondering. "Those two men have to kill each other and then no one can prove that any of us had anything to do with it. But what are the chances of that?"

Neil was quick to the point." I need them both to die or for Edgar to win the duel outright then I can sort him out afterwards. Now please listen to me, Willie. I need you on my side. If all goes ahead as planned, we'll have first practise with those pistols. I am sure that neither will fire accurately but I will work out where each gun fires, be it high, low, left or right. I will mark them almost indiscernibly according to each gun's accuracy. Only Edgar will know which one is which, and whether he wins or loses the toss he will have the advantage." Neil hoped Willie would agree.

"What if we do the same thing and put on our own marks?" Willie smiled at him.

"Well, there is money in it for you if you don't. All I want is for Edgar to initially survive the duel and be the winner. Leave the rest to me."

Both men agreed and shook hands on the amount of money that would exchange hands should the duel go to plan.

As Willie wandered back to his office above the draper's store he couldn't help admiring how Faith had organised such a bizarre execution over the months, whereby the only people to blame would be the executed, but that was only if everything went by the book. He would have to wait and see.

Chapter 53
The Final Indictment

Charity and Hope stood on the bridge in Fairford and looked upstream towards the oxen pens. Both sisters said very little as the fresh January wind blew their hair and frocks, and they braced themselves against another winter squall whilst their meagre umbrellas struggled to remain intact.

Dusk was falling quickly and silhouetted rooks on the wing appreciated the strong up draughts before finally settling to roost in the trees near Coronation Street for another dismal night.

A grey heron stood stoically with its back to the wind at the edge of the Coln River as the banks threatened to burst and flood the adjacent meadows. Cattle, which had earlier taken to higher ground as if in anticipation of the rising floodwaters, huddled together with their heads down, and the beleaguered animals gave Charity and Hope a clear indication that another storm was imminent.

Both women instinctively turned and began the short walk back to the Bull Hotel. They had come to discuss the contest between Edgar and Fulwar.

A little later at a round table in a separate room Faith arrived with Georgina. Georgina looked classically Victorian in her elegant attire. Edgar had begun to rebuild her lost wardrobe.

Georgina's Aunt Maria rushed to hug her niece, and after a long journey down from Shropshire that day and being so pleased to see her, the elderly woman almost collapsed in Georgina's embrace.

The five women sat down and began their first course. Little was said between them at the beginning but things soon changed after a glass of mellowing wine. As was usually the case with women, their tongues began to loosen.

It was a worried Charity who asked the first serious question. "Do you think it is safe to carry on? I mean, what if it all backfires and we get caught? It will surely be the gallows for someone."

All eyes fell on to Faith, the main instigator. It was a question she had been expecting.

"My sweet sister, we have come this far and there is no retreating now. If you so wish, step backwards, I wouldn't despise you because I know how you must feel," she said as she glanced around the table. "If anyone else thinks the same way then please say so. I will tell you now that I am very determined to carry this through."

Aunt Maria followed up Charity's question. "As Charity asked, what if it all goes wrong and the police do become involved?"

"Well, this is why we are going to have to be very discreet so that nothing does go wrong," Faith said, nodding towards Hope. "James, Hope's husband, will search for an ideal place to hold the duel. We decided that somewhere halfway between the Brockhampton and Bibury estates would be fair. Fulwar has agreed to come down from the West Midlands. To avoid any contact with the local bobbies James will explore the woodland around the villages of Chedworth and Withington for an ideal clearing with the brief that we will need carriage access in the area from more than one direction, if possible. Each of those two villages has their own policeman but we believe that they have to visit county headquarters once a week, and we are trying to find out which day that is. Also, the duel will take place at first light, so there will be few people around. We are trying to organise it so there will only be us and people we know witnessing the duel."

"So, we are just spectators if we decide to attend?" Maria asked.

"Exactly. Except for watching we will not be involved at all. It has been planned that the law cannot lay a finger on us. Gerard has investigated the legality of it all, and no one will possibly know that we organised it. Two adult men have accepted the challenge of a duel between themselves. Only Mr Greyffos and Mr Starbury, acting as their seconds, will have any involvement. Mr Starbury has an ulterior motive but that is his business entirely."

"I am afraid that Stefan is going to insist on being there as some kind of referee or adjudicator, and not only him but Lionel as well. Where would they both stand in all of this?" Charity asked her sister with a concerned look on her face. "On the wrong side of the law?"

"If they don't become involved and just act as morbid spectators then there should not be a problem. I'll speak to them but I am sure that I can persuade them to remain in the background... for their own good."

The other four women were not sure of Faith's undertones. "What do you mean?" Georgina asked with a worried frown, and Charity noted her concern.

Faith realised that she had seemed a little harsh but she would not weaken her resolve. "We have come this far and it is too late to back down now. Two large inheritances will disappear if those two men gain charge over their prospective birthrights.

"As women we do not have a say in the inheritance laws of this country, and now is the time to make a stand, and they have given us every excuse to speak out. If you have any doubts at all about the plan, I implore you not to step away now. Speak your minds and say what you believe. Be honest with yourselves, and see that their actions cannot carry on. We have some wonderful people working for us but if the estates disintegrate because of two degenerate men, are we going to be held to blame? No!" Faith went quiet again and looked around the table. "Tonight, we have to make a choice, however macabre, and it has to be the right choice." Faith stood up, politely wiped her mouth with her napkin and excused herself from the table to use the washroom.

After a period of silence Maria spoke. "Faith is right. We cannot back away now. It is not just us but all the workers and their families on both estates who will suffer. They will be forced out of their homes and jobs into the urbanisation and grime of industrial Britain. Fulwar Cavner and Edgar Collison think that they have something to offer but they are living in cuckoo land. Their managerial aptitude is poor and I don't care if Edgar was an officer in the army. Those estate workers have a way of life that must be preserved or it will be lost forever. We have to support Faith and follow this through."

Georgina stared adoringly at her aunt and godmother, and Hope, as always, remained quiet. Deep in her intelligent mind she had her own view but said nothing amongst her present company. She appeared to look fixedly at an oil painting of Fairford church hanging on the wall.

Faith returned and they all smiled as she retook her seat. The main course was brought out and they chatted about its ingredients and the availability of various vegetables. On finishing they sat back and relaxed, inducing a conversation about the quality of the French wine at the table. The Desailley family came to be mentioned but Faith quickly changed the subject.

"Does Edgar have any inkling that Neil Starbury has been working down at the Bibury estate?" Faith asked Georgina.

"He would have mentioned it by now if he had. Besides, he would have been extremely suspicious as to why, and would have surely asked questions by now. If any of the workforce have realised who he is then they are not saying anything. I'd be very surprised if at least one of them has not realised his true identity. Fortunately, Mr Starbury is very respectful to our staff and they genuinely trust him. Some of them who were going to leave because of Edgar have now decided to stay. Mr Starbury is being very careful." Georgina could only ascertain the situation. She couldn't wait until everything was all over.

"If Edgar does find out then Mr Starbury will have to disappear off the scene. It doesn't necessarily mean that he is one of the instigators of the duel, and it can still go ahead. We'll just have to hope Edgar doesn't put two and two together. We have come this far, and nothing must be allowed to stand in our way now." Faith was completely in control and confident that the duel would take place. "Does anyone have any other questions?" she asked.

"Yes, I do." It was Hope. "What do you think Father will do, or say, when he finds out what has happened? Edgar is his only son and Father is not in the best of health either. This could finish him off. Are we going to take the blame for his death as well?"

Faith was about to reply but, to her surprise, Charity vociferously stepped in. "Please! Leave Father to me. I know what you are saying, Hope, but he is more resilient than you believe. If Edgar does lose his life then so be it. Father will be told and we will have to explain to him what it was all about. Father was deeply saddened when Mother prematurely died, but he soon recuperated, if only to make sure we were all right. He didn't have much time to be a grieving husband, but then there was the estate to oversee."

Faith and Hope stole glances at each other, and almost smiled. For a long time they hadn't seen their youngest sister so opinionated. The possible demise of Edgar seemed to be relighting her tired and tortured mind. She had certainly improved recently, and both sisters wondered if Stefan had noticed a difference with Charity.

Georgina changed the subject and asked her aunt the burning question. "What about Uncle Charles? What does he think of it all? And Edward, of course? Let's not forget Edward." Georgina had a soft spot for Edward. He wasn't a robust fellow but he always remained sensible and helpful.

"Sir Charles will not tell anyone what he thinks but then he doesn't believe that the duel will possibly happen. In his mind we are all scatterbrained. Edward is open-minded, and I think he will just wait and see. For him all things are possible, but he feels that whether we persuade the two men to carry the duel through is another matter. We have to prove them both wrong, don't we?"

Maria was determined that Fulwar Cavner didn't deserve a life on earth, especially after he had so badly beaten her niece. Edgar Collison was a different matter. She didn't actually know him but took it for granted how Georgina described the arrogant and self-extolling coward. He deserved the same fate. Let them both face each other in battle, she thought.

Desserts and more wine were delivered to the table, and the ladies were now much more relaxed. Cheese and biscuits were brought out and they were left entirely alone to end their meal and finalise their crucial meeting.

It was the first time the five women had come together. Previously, Faith had made brief visits to them all over the past months or contacted them by post, whilst others had met discreetly in each their homes or at dinner somewhere. Most of them had had little to do with the likes of Mr Greyffos or Mr Starbury but they had, at some time or other, met them both, except for Maria who was not familiar with Neil Starbury.

Faith also had the male side of the Collison family doing as she asked. Whether it was Gerard, James, Stefan, or even Edgar, each one had a reason to listen to and believe in Faith Havrincourt. It wasn't in their interests not to. She was also beginning to believe that Edgar had an idea that if he won the duel, Georgina's son, Thomas, would eventually inherit the Cavner estate, which might give Edgar himself secondary control over another huge business. It was the subject of inheritance that Faith wanted to discuss next.

Faith looked at both Georgina and Maria and coldly asked. "After your husband's demise, Georgina, what are you going to do, return to Stokesay with your children?"

Georgina took a nervous, indirect glance towards Charity. "I'm not sure. It much depends on what Frederick decides. If Thomas becomes next in line to the inheritance, which he undoubtedly should, then yes, I will have to seriously consider returning to Shropshire. Whether I will be welcome there I do not know. First and foremost my children will be at the bottom of my heart. Their physical and mental welfare comes first. I am afraid they have seen too much anguish already in their young lives."

"I received a letter the other day from Mr Greyffos. Other than the general subject there was an unusual postscript. He suggested that you may have a secret supporter at Stokesay who wants to see you and the children back there." Faith nearly smiled.

"Who?" Georgina asked surprised.

"The children's grandmother."

Georgina could only wonder why Isabella had never stood up for her in the past.

Maria queried Faith's information. "Does she know about the duel between Fulwar and Edgar?"

"Not as far as I know, unless Fulwar has told her. If she does then it appears that she doesn't intend to stand in anyone's way, which might be a sign that she too wants her son out of the picture."

Deep down Charity sighed with relief. If she and Stefan were to resume a normal married relationship then it would be much more convenient that Georgina returned north, although she was sure that everyone would remain friends in the future.

"What about you three women?" Maria asked. "Who will become the overall inheritor of the Bibury estate? If your brother ceases to live, there are only yourselves."

Charity went to say something but Faith was astute and cut in. "Francois, Charity's boy, will become the rightful heir, but being so young he will, of course, be tutored as to how to run the estate. His father is extremely adept, as you probably know," Faith raised an eyebrow towards Georgina, "and we have great confidence that the young man will deliver at least another two generations of success there. We three sisters will take a backstage, with or without the Brigadier, and we are confident that the estate will pull through with Stefan involved until Francois is old enough to gain full control." Faith glanced at Charity and Hope for support. It was something they had all agreed upon weeks previously.

Maria wasn't quite satisfied. "And yourself, Faith? When is your child due?"

Under her plumpness Faith could hide her pregnancy no longer. With all eyes on her she smiled, "Yes, I am with child, but there are a few months to go yet."

Her sisters suddenly became jubilant that Faith was having a baby, and glasses chinked across the table and the mood changed amongst them all from sombre in one moment to delight in the next.

Except for poor Hope each woman poured out her experiences of motherhood. Whilst trying to be cheerful Faith watched her middle sister sadly. Charity however, had changed for the better.

Chapter 54
Starbury's Ultimatum

Gerard Havrincourt walked unsteadily up Leather Lane towards his home. The Castle Tavern had been a welcome respite after work that day, and he had over-indulged. Holding the railings he took the few steps up to the door and allowed himself in. His housekeeper took his coat and advised him that Faith was in the drawing room. He politely asked for a bottle of red wine with two glasses before going to see her.

Faith was sitting at a desk that was strewn with letters, and he kissed her on the top of the head and sat down quietly in the corner without saying a word.

He watched her as she re-read the correspondence and then place them in chronological order. The housekeeper entered the room and left the wine next to Gerard on an intricately carved console table. He poured two glasses, examined one and took a large mouthful. He closed his tired eyes and mulled over the day's events.

Faith soon placed her hand on his shoulder. "I have a date for the duel."

It startled him and he nearly spilled his wine. Gerard sat upright and focused on his wife. "Good, because there is something I need to tell you. When is it? Soon I hope, for Mr Starbury's sake."

"Tuesday, 26th February. Why because of Starbury's sake?" she asked.

"Edgar's wife in India has been granted permission to travel to England, and we are about to send the necessary paperwork. From what you have told me if she leaves India Mr Starbury doesn't get paid but not only that he will have to return any monies that have already changed hands. If I remember rightly you told me there is also a cottage or house involved. He could quite easily be in some trouble if it doesn't work out for him." Gerard shrugged his shoulders. There was little else he could do or say.

"Edgar still wants her over here, I take it, even though he's now living with Georgina?" It amused Faith that her brother thought that they would all live as one happy family.

"Yes. Edgar has sent letters to us on a regular basis enquiring about the progress of his wife's emigration documents. He seems determined she'll come here, and now it is certain that he is going to get his wish." Gerard rolled the stem of his glass around between his finger and thumb and tried to imagine Edgar with two wives and five step children.

Faith was thoughtful. "It won't really matter if Neil Starbury has his way and he is accredited with Edgar's death. His biggest problem is that Edgar's wife leaves India before her father finds out that Edgar is dead. If she manages to leave those shores, there will be no going back, with Edgar dead or alive." Faith went quiet. She sipped some wine and then looked up. "How long does it take the post to get to India?"

"We talked about this in the office this afternoon. Apparently it depends on which way the ship sails, the part of India it is heading for, who owns the ship and what the weather is like. It might be travelling to one of three main ports, Bombay, Madras or Calcutta, whichever one is closest to the postage destination and address. In a couple of years they will have completed the Suez Canal, and that will reduce the journey time by months. Currently, the longest journey time is around the Cape of Good Hope, which can be four to six months, again depending on the weather and at which supply ports they stop at. The quickest route at the moment is to go through the Mediterranean to Alexandria, disembark, travel across land to Port Suez and then embark upon another ship to India."

The forever-intelligent Gerard was a mine of information but he was slowly drifting to sleep. After a long day he had eaten out with friends, and now needed to rest. "I am going to bed because I need to be up early in the morning. Perhaps I should visit Mr Starbury at Bibury. Please, my darling, find out when it would be best to travel there," he said, beginning to slur his words. Gerard lifted himself out of his chair and went across to his wife. He gently stroked her now protrusive stomach, kissed her affectionately and headed towards the bottom of the stairs. "Goodnight, my sweetheart."

Faith sat contemplating the outcome of the death of her brother and Georgina's husband. She had no compunction about the outcome of the duel. She believed neither deserved any credit. Both estates would pass into young, sensible hands, educated by reasonably minded adults who had as fair an opinion towards women as they did about men. She studied her diary. The next day would be exactly four weeks until the duel. The following day, Wednesday, there was the market in Cirencester, which would be a good day for Gerard to visit Kilkenny Farm.

As a city dweller Gerard loathed country dogs. They barked, were untrustworthy and were prone to biting strangers. One particular dog owned by one of Edgar Collison's herdsman was no exception and, on top of that, had two different coloured eyes, which, as Gerard perceived it, a sure sign of madness. He remained seated inside his carriage until the animal was tied to a post and brought under control.

Georgina greeted him at the door and invited him in. In Edgar's absence and with tea at the table they talked generally about the farm but the mood soon changed, and Gerard asked the housekeeper to find Mr Starbury, inform him that Mr Havrincourt wished to speak with him and bring him to the house.

Gerard eyed Georgina seriously. "I will tell you now before Mr Starbury arrives that I have a letter here for Edgar, which outlines the emigration of his wife and her children to England. As far as you are concerned you do not know what is in it but she has been granted permission to be here in England with him."

Neil nervously stepped into the kitchen and they introduced each other, having never met. The letter's content was explained to Neil, and Gerard studied the intense look on his face and raised his eyebrows slightly. "I believe that you know when the duel is to take place?" Gerard asked.

"Yes, I am well aware but I have to think of the timing. In under four weeks this may be all over, but if Mr Collison's wife leaves India I could be in a lot of trouble and not just financially." Neil stroked his chin in deep thought. He had been taken aback and actually believed Gerard had come to confront him over his fornication with his wife.

"Now listen to me, Neil. For you this might be important. Yesterday I visited East India docks and ensured that Edgar's wife's emigration papers will go by the southern route around the Cape of Good Hope. In four weeks' time Edgar should have deceased. If we can get the message of his demise to India before those emigration papers arrive, it will ensure you receive your final payment." Gerard went to carry on but Neil stopped him.

"Excuse me, please. May I ask you why you are so concerned that I receive payment in full? After all, I intend to make sure your brother-in-law dies during this duel." Neil stared at Gerard Havrincourt intensely. For one so intelligent, a city lawyer, he thought Gerard seemed very helpful.

Gerard leaned forward, eyebrows raised and forehead wrinkled. "If everything goes to plan, Mr Starbury, my wife will be the matriarch of the Bibury estate. She is well aware that you wanted tenure of Kilkenny Farm. In Edgar's prolonged or permanent absence she would be more than content that you secure that tenancy. So, now do you understand why we are all concerned?"

Neil Starbury stood up and faced the wall in thought. Soon afterwards he turned around. "My options are few," he said, glancing at Georgina, who looked on sympathetically. "I have to be seen to murder Edgar Collison." He covered his face with his hands before continuing. "That way, neither family will have any responsibility for either death... should those deaths occur."

Gerard realised that Neil Starbury might suddenly relent and have nothing to do with the duel. He wondered if Neil had stronger human principles than to simply earn money.

Georgina spoke. "Neil, please take your seat again and start from the beginning. Tell Gerard what you told me about your family."

Reluctantly he sat back down and looked Gerard straight in the face before beginning. "Being the eldest of eight children meant that I had few options. My father had been invalided from the docks due to an accident, and I suddenly became an unaffordable child. I joined the army when I was fifteen, and my next two younger brothers did the same, although one of them joined the navy. Anyhow, it was in the rifle brigade where I met Neil Portlock and we became great friends. We just happened to have the same forename. It was his name I used at Bibury." He went quiet, reflecting on the past. Georgina stroked the back of his hand and he stopped daydreaming. "I'm sorry, but we were inseparable, great friends you might say. Neil himself eventually married a woman called Joanna who he had met years previously when they were both young. They had two children and she was pregnant when we were sent abroad to fight in the Crimean War. It was there that Neil died." He went quiet again, reminiscing.

The forever-knowledgeable Gerard brought him around once more. "At which battle?" he asked.

Neil stared over towards the window. "He didn't die at a battle. He died of cholera. Believe it or not five times more soldiers died of disease than they did from battle wounds during the Crimean War. It was ridiculous. That is how my best friend died. I spoke to him the day before, as he lay stretchered out and sickly. With his last words he meekly asked if I would make sure his wife and children were all right, should anything happen to him. Naturally I said 'yes, of course'."

Neil Starbury suddenly stood up, and tears were developing. Georgina took his wrist and tried to pull him back down into the chair but he refused. Eventually, he spoke again. "A long time after that war I came home and went to see his wife. I still vividly remember the step up to the terraced house made from a block of slate, and knocking on her door." Neil held his hand over his mouth, and tears began to run down his cheeks. He stammered. "His wife answered and I expressed my sympathies for her husband's death." He went quiet again and the tears became profuse.

Georgina pulled him back into the chair and rubbed his hand again. "Tell him. Go on. Tell him."

"The British Government or army hadn't even bothered to inform her that her husband and my great friend had died. Quite accidentally it was left to me. At first it was difficult to console her but a baby had been born in his absence and fortunately I suppose she was preoccupied with the child, a boy. I promised her, as I had promised him, that she would be kept, and I married her six months later. The boy will be thirteen this year, and he has two older sisters. Each of them is aware that I am not their real father but they have great respect for their own family. I tell them all the time what a good man their father was, and I try to explain how he had wished them to grow up in the world.

The children do want to move here but so far I haven't a clue what might happen in a month's time. I cannot at the moment make any promises. The outcome is far from certain but not only that, I am really not sure that I will be able to look his children in the eye knowing I helped instigate Edgar Collison's death, however evil he is. The rules in the army are different to those as a civilian."

Gerard screwed his eyebrows up. "What do you mean, *however evil he is*?"

"I'm afraid he wasn't a well thought of man in India, whether it was by the local population or the British administration. I think even Neil Portlock would have wanted to kill him had he known him. It is important that Edgar's new family do not arrive here in England, or better still, they do not leave India's shores. I have a contact in London who will verify Edgar's death for me. It is possible the message might reach Arjun Singh, his father-in-law, before your emigration paperwork arrives in Azamgargh."

Gerard thought hard. "Indeed! I am sure we can pass the information on quite quickly. The electric telegraph, across land from Alexandria to Suez, and then by ship to India. Many things are now possible with modern science but we have only four weeks to send that message."

"Why me, Mr Havrincourt? Why are you on my side?" Neil Starbury studied the man across the table wondering why the Collison sisters were so keen to help him.

Gerard took a deep breath. "My wife has respect for you. Except for your devious intentions there are people out there in the world who think themselves above the law and beyond jurisdiction because of their wealth. I am afraid that my wife's brother thinks he is one of those but she intends to deliver his comeuppance. When you appeared on the scene some months back it was a complete coincidence. The same with Georgina here." Gerard stroked his chin and remained quiet for a time. "I work as a lawyer in London and I earn a lot of money, but financial gain is not my prime intention. Fairness is what I strive for. People, whether men or women, should be treated equally, but most are not in the world. Having listened to what you have told me today it sounds like you are one of those people on our side. You're a person with a direction towards some degree of equality."

Neil Starbury stood up from the table. "I will do my job here. I will be at the duel, Mr Havrincourt. I am not here necessarily for the money but it will help me considerably. A good day to you both." Mr Starbury left the farmhouse.

Both Georgina and Gerard sat bemused. Their tea had gone cold. Georgina tapped the saucer with her delicately manicured nails.

It was Gerard who spoke first. "How are you getting along with Edgar?"

Almost in tears she shook her head. "Please, I cannot wait to be out of this situation. He is awful. I allowed him to have sexual intercourse and there was no love whatsoever. He just climbed on top of me and in no time it was all over. I felt used and physically tarnished and unclean." Georgina held back her tears. "Whatever happens at the duel, deaths or no deaths, I will not be staying here. Where I go, I have not a clue but I feel that I would be better off with a prison sentence."

"Please, Georgina. Do not forget your children. They must surely be keeping your hopes up?" Gerard asked her.

Georgina stared at the flagstone floor before replying. "Just under four bloody weeks! That is all it is! Just make sure that both of those undeserving bastards are dead! I don't care how they die; just make sure they both end up in the ground. This is going to be the longest four weeks of my life!" She began to cough and held a handkerchief over her mouth, and Gerard saw that she had brought up blood. The housekeeper rushed in and knelt by her side to help her. She then politely asked Mr Havrincourt if he would leave.

Shocked at what he was witnessing, Gerard left. As he entered his carriage he tipped his hat towards Mr Starbury, who was watching from the corner of the barn. Both fully understood the severity of what was about to take place, somewhere along the River Coln.

Gerard travelled straight back to London and met Faith in The Castle Tavern, where they discussed his countryside sojourn and what seemed perhaps to be Neil's final revelation. After copious amounts of wine, most of which Gerard consumed, and a traditional dinner the contented couple staggered home.

Chapter 55

The Common Ground

The conversation was bleak and James, Stefan and Lionel sat tapping imaginary tunes on their pint pots and staring out of the window at the horses and carriages, steeds and hacks tethered outside, including their own.

The Lord Chedworth Arms at certain times of the day was a busy trading inn halfway between Cirencester and Northleach, and was usually frequented by strangers or businessmen going about their daily assignments. Stefan didn't mention his former visit but the landlord made a satirical comment about his condition when he had left that day, and was surprised that Stefan hadn't had an accident on his way home.

"Lionel, what date is your wedding?" James asked, trying to keep his two bored companions interested.

"Saturday, 6th April in Bibury. Surely you have received your invitation by now?" Lionel asked.

"Maybe. I don't really know. That's for the women to organise, isn't it? Surely our job is just to turn up, especially to the stag night."

James smiled at the carefree attitudes of Lionel and Stefan but his mind was preoccupied with other dubious matters.

Stefan appreciated that James was nervous, and tried to calm him down. "So why have you dragged us here to Fossebridge, of all places? I could have thought of better places to visit."

"Because of Edward Cavner. He had to visit Cirencester and is meeting us here on his return, and then I am going to show you an ideal spot for this duel to take place. Apparently, if Edward believes it is all right, Fulwar will accept his decision and participate. Personally, I want you both to at least have a quick reconnaissance and hopefully either side will be content that the area is comfortable." James hoped that all three men, after visiting the site, would form a reasonable opinion between themselves.

Edward walked into the inn and immediately made it clear that he was not interested in eating or drinking, and wished to retreat to Brockhampton before dark.

The four set off to Withington woods.

James led them along an obscure route on horseback, keeping to footpaths and overgrown bridleways. He took them over Pancake Hill and along the southwestern side of Chedworth, avoiding the village where possible. The track passed between the Beacon and Chedworth Laines. He knew from walking his dog that somewhere nearby was an area called Pinswell, which was his next destination. After cutting across a field and then entering the very southern edge of Withington woods, James asked his small entourage to dismount when they reached two clearings. They tied up their horses.

The piece of ground James had found was a relatively level fallow field. With enough space for an audience and distance to fire, it was ideal for a duel. A double row of trees separated another clearing that edged alongside a bridleway, which led back to Chedworth, and this meant that the carriages could be parked off track.

All of the men decided that the piece of ground James had discovered in the woods near Withington would be a good place to hold the duel, and so it was settled. The date of 26th February 1867 at eight-thirty in the morning was agreed upon, and the field of honour would be a small clearing hidden amongst Withington woods.

Chapter 56
The Duel

At Brockhampton Court Willie Greyffos eyed Fulwar Cavner up and down. "Are you sure you want to go through with this? I can easily send a message to Chedworth stating that you wish to pull out and return to Stokesay. Your children will be quite safe in the hands of your wife but at least you will be alive and uninjured. It is entirely your decision, Mr Cavner." Willie Greyffos' words were sombre to Fulwar Cavner but the last thing Willie actually wanted was for him to back down from the duel.

Fulwar Cavner stood tall. He had stayed away from alcohol for just over three weeks and his demeanour had completely changed. He was an entirely different character, and probably the one Georgina had originally married, Willie thought. The man had been eating well and exercising out with the horses, and even his mother was surprised. His jaundiced complexion had faded and he was decidedly healthier and much more positive in his attitude, and the servants at the castle and on the estate were much more contented with his new demeanour. Many senior employees, however, debated over how long he would stay sober, although none knew of his underlying motive to retrieve his children by duel from his estranged wife and her new companion.

"I will be a challenger at that duel and I am confident. Years in the army or not, from what you and others have told me, Edgar Collison is a pathetic waste of space. I am younger, sharper eyed and definitely more determined. He will not be raising my children! The pistols will decide!"

"Have a drink. Not much, just enough so you can sleep well tonight. Tomorrow we have to leave at six-thirty. Edward will drive the Brougham, which will give you enough time to steady your nerves. You start firing at approximately eight-thirty or when it is light enough."

Willie had depended on Fulwar being to some degree intoxicated but it was definitely not working in that direction. Fulwar's strength of mind was stronger than he had ever seen it, and he seemed determined that his children should rightly return to Stokesay.

"How are you, sir? You appear nervous. Just remember, sir, that before any conflict all soldiers have the jitters. When the battle commences first thing tomorrow morning everything will change. Fulwar Cavner will almost certainly be intoxicated and probably will not even be able to see you properly. Don't forget what I have told you about the guns, one shoots to the left and the other shots high and right. They are marked, so please don't forget which one is which. You cannot lose. Fulwar Cavner is an idiot, and he has never faced an enemy. For him it will be an entirely different experience. The only people Cavner has ever fought against are defenceless women."

Over the last weeks Neil Starbury had given his employer all the information he needed and now the time had almost come for Edgar Collison to enact his determination by killing the drunken slob that is Fulwar Cavner. He had been insulted but in a few hours he would put Fulwar Cavner's challenge to right and win the duel.

It was dark when Edward steered the Brougham out through the gates of Brockhampton Park. Onboard was his mother, Willie Greyffos and the principle challenger to Edgar Collison, Fulwar Cavner. Sir Charles, Edward's father, had decided to stay at home and have nothing to do with the duel, although he was more than interested in its outcome. This particular Tuesday morning Sir Charles' whole livelihood lay in the balance, as did his nephew's life.

The wind was light and the new moon attempted to break through the sporadic cloud cover. It was dry and the coming day was perfect for a pistol fight.

Fulwar still hadn't touched one drop of alcohol, much to the surprise of the many who knew him, and the consternation of those involved with the duel. No matter how much Willie Greyffos tried to persuade him he had rejected his advice. Sobriety could possibly save his life and have his children returned to him. He was naturally nervous but remained very quiet as they headed south to the ancient Withington woods.

Edgar Collison was quite the opposite. He was full of confidence, knowing full well of his challenger's alcohol dependency. He had had plenty of practice with the guns to be used, under the guidance of his trusted farm manager, who had taught him to believe that all the advantages were his.

He talked a great deal as his carriage trundled northward to the duelling ground. With him was a slightly nervous Georgina and, of course, Neil Starbury, who would act as his second and for security reasons drove the carriage.

The fewer people who knew about the duel the better.

The Brigadier was wary. He lay in his bath trying to focus on his rotten toenails and swollen ankles, both of which were diagnosed as ominous signs by his physician, perhaps portending a malignant finale but, concerns for his own health that overcast morning were irrelevant.

"Something is wrong, something sinister," he kept saying to himself. Stefan and Lionel had asked for a day off together to go grayling fishing but Lionel had a life-long aversion to fishing. A letter had been received two days before stating that Faith and Gerard were coming to visit for a short while, but Gerard rarely left London during the week, especially in the winter. Another occurrence he thought strange was that he had been told that Mrs Desailley was looking after her grandchildren that day, which meant that Charity was also off somewhere. Marcel Desailley would not be available because he had made an excuse to see a doctor in Fairford. Then there was the strange case of Marcel's right hand man, who had disappeared some time ago but had left all of his belongings at the Catherine Wheel.

Nothing added up in the Brigadier's mind. He had hardly seen Edgar since his move to Kilkenny Farm, and had heard that he had hired a housekeeper but who she was he didn't know?

He had suspicions but he couldn't ascertain what it was that blew in the wind, and this caused him to think very deeply. He called for his nurse to help him out of the bath, and she eventually pulled him onto his feet and towelled him down. Cleansed and dry she then rubbed his body with scented water before dressing the old man. Contrary to what Faith had implied, he had no inclination to misbehave with his young nurse.

In the drawing room before the sun had fully risen he drank a glass of Armagnac, his morning vice, and then ate a light breakfast. He stared at the painting of his dear wife on the wall, and he noticed that she still had the expression of 'I told you so'. Along with his feet, the old man's memory was fading, but he smiled back at the picture. This day of all days was one to remember.

The Brigadier asked his nurse for a diary he kept in the bureau in the corner, and with a monocle he browsed through the first few pages before suddenly closing the book.

He stared at his nurse. "What is the date today?" he asked.

The young woman thought but not for long. "The 26th of February, sir. Why do you ask?"

The Brigadier again stared up at the painting of his wife, and her expression had not changed.

It was the date of her birth.

James and Gerard left Chedworth on a small buggy at seven in the morning with the intention of quietly driving to the great beech and oak woodlands near Withington in order to secure the tiny area where the duel would take place. Their wives would follow behind a little later when Charity arrived in Chedworth. The wooden box containing the antique pistols given to Stefan by his father lay on Gerard's lap.

Unknown to both men, very close behind them were Stefan and Lionel as well as a French master in the art of duelling; Marcel Desailley.

When James and Gerard arrived at the destination and parked the buggy in a clearing just off the bridleway, the sun was just beginning to lighten the grey sky in the east, and the moon's startled face began to quickly pale into insignificance. As planned, there was enough room to situate several carriages and horses.

Both men nervously made their way along a short pathway overgrown with brambles. A wren suddenly hissed its annoyance at their intrusion, and a rabbit took a cursory glance at them before diving back into the undergrowth.

Lionel, Stefan and Marcel, determined not to allow the duel to happen without genuine approval, had been riding their horses with speed along the same bridleway. Upon reaching the designated spot, they dismounted, tied their steeds and followed James and Gerard along the same short pathway.

They came together in the clearing and all five circumnavigated the area nominated for the final outcome of the duel between the deceived challengers.

Marcel decided to act and stepped forward to face Gerard, who held the box containing the prized pistols.

In his strong French accent he explained implicitly. "You do not own those pistols, Monsieur Havrincourt. They were a present from me to my son on his birthday. Please may I have them back?"

Stunned, Gerard and James squinted at each other in the poor light. The old Frenchman was going to ruin all the planning over the last few months.

"This duel will be played out by my rules," Marcel continued as the two men hesitated. "These pistols were once mine and I never imagined that one day in England they would be used again. If it is the case then I will preside over this particular contest. Is that understood?" Marcel looked at both men but neither had an answer.

Marcel was suddenly in control, and Stefan and Lionel smiled at each other in the half-light. Gerard and James agreed that Marcel's rules would conclude the outcome of the duel between Fulwar Cavner and Edgar Collison, and the box containing the two duelling pistols was handed over.

Marcel nodded to Stefan, who immediately went back to the horses to retrieve some dry, high quality gunpowder and a bag of bullets.

In Stefan's absence Marcel spoke knowingly of duelling. "These two men have agreed to duel. It is very honourable. It is very brave to accept the challenge but equally as brave to make the challenge in the first place. Both Mr Collison and Mr Cavner have chosen to fight for a principle; a principle that we all have to accept. What happens in this woodland goes no further. The spectators are bound to say nothing. The outcome is beyond judicial law. Do you understand me?" Marcel asked in his basic English.

Gerard and James nodded in agreement, glad that they only needed to stand back and watch. Stefan and Lionel had had their way up to a point. There was now a referee but they both wondered what would be said when Faith and her two sisters arrived. The two friends had to be seen to be completely impartial.

Fulwar arrived next from the direction of Brockhampton. His entourage stepped out onto the spongy woodland floor and he was led through to the clearing, where he was introduced to Marcel. Fulwar and Willie agreed to allow Marcel to take overall control of the proceedings. Subject to Edgar's approval of Marcel's position on the field, both duellists would from now on be kept apart. In his pocket Willie carried a flask of whisky in case Fulwar should change his mind and decide a stiff drink would help him relax.

Maria stayed in the Brougham out of sight from Fulwar and waited for the other women. She wasn't kept long and they arrived soon after. Maria could hear the carriage horses pulling the creaking vehicle along the muddied track, and heard the animals' joy as they entered the clearing, where the driver pulled them to a halt. One rose upon its back feet and then settled.

Out stepped Faith, Hope and Charity, and they greeted Maria solemnly. None of the women sounded as if they welcomed the next hour. Talk of children and families were the last thing on their minds. They were nervous. Edward came and warned them all that Marcel was to referee the duel. He then escorted his mother away to avoid her being seen cavorting with the others when Edgar arrived

Faith went to find Stefan, who was standing with his father. They walked away. "Have you told your father who Edgar's second is?"

"Yes," Stefan replied sternly, and said no more.

"And what did he say?"

"He obviously asked a lot of questions but I managed to persuade him to go along with the charade. You have given me little choice, have you not?" he glanced at her stomach and walked away, allowing her no chance to answer.

Edgar chatted excitedly as his carriage approached the rendezvous. Georgina gazed out of the window, glad that she would never again have to sleep with the revolting man who sat next to her. Even if Edgar survived she would not be returning to Kilkenny Farm with him, and the children were already being temporarily moved that morning back to Hope's home.

Neil Starbury tried to calm Edgar down but it was to no avail. When he arrived at the scene he jumped from the carriage without even attempting to help Georgina to the ground; that chore was left to Neil. Lionel was waiting for their arrival, and ushered them through to what he described in his own mind *the killing field*.

Fulwar stood with Willie Greyffos some way away as the entourage entered the clearing, and after a brief explanation Edgar and Neil agreed with Stefan and Lionel that Marcel would be in charge. Neil then walked Edgar the same distance away but in the opposite direction. Everyone else now moved back and lined up on the edge of the wood, waiting with nervous excitement to witness the rare spectacle.

In his French accent Marcel called for Willie and Neil's attention. "Mr Greyffos, Mr Starbury." The three came together and Marcel smiled ruefully at Neil. "I will tell you the rules, which you must then explain to your principles. Firstly, you are both known as *seconds,* and you must, at all times, assist your principle and pass good and proper advice," he paused, "should they want to listen. I will then ask you both to bring them to the centre of the field, where I will be standing, and the challenger will decide heads or tails. A coin will be tossed to the ground and the–"

"Excuse me, Mr Desailley," Willie said, stopping Marcel in his tracks. "May we both go away and have a quiet word." Marcel agreed, and Willie and Neil walked away out of earshot.

"They are both challengers – or so they think," Willie hissed. "What are we going to do now? Marcel is bound to become suspicious and start asking questions."

Neil thought about the scenario. "Don't worry. Marcel already suspects something and has been warned that I would be attending. We'll ask him to change his rules just for today. Leave it with me."

Willie and Neil returned to Marcel. "Mr Desailley, by sheer coincidence and after weeks of negotiations, Mr Collison and Mr Cavner sent correspondences to each other, but both men made the challenge on the same date, and each letter had the same date stamp on them. Please, just for once, Mr Desailley, ask one of them to call. Neither will know the difference." Neil was lying and Marcel knew it but he reluctantly agreed.

Marcel continued. "Whoever wins the toss has the choice of whichever end of the field of honour he wishes to fire from or which gun he prefers. The loser takes the remaining option. We then decide how many shots are to be fired. One, two, three or a fight until one man expires. The amount of paces will also be agreed upon but twenty paces has always been the average. The closer they decide usually epitomises the severity of the argument. I will ensure that both guns are cleaned and loaded correctly. When in position, they will stand back to back with their pistols pointing upward. You two men will then stand out off the way and I will begin to loudly count out their paces. At twenty paces or, however many are decided upon, I will shout 'fire' whereby they can turn and shoot. No man can shoot the other in the back, and if a man does not turn then he has conceded the argument.

I will then take stock of the situation, especially if there are wounds that need to be attended to. If one man is unable to carry on due to the severity of his wounds then I will call a halt to the proceedings and deem him to be the loser. If both men are not severely injured but cannot carry on, I will deem it to be a draw." It was the last result anybody wanted. "I will take responsibility for reloading the pistols and they shall continue again in exactly the same fashion until there is a result. God bless both men. You will now please go to your principles and explain the method." Marcel took a fob watch from his pocket, glanced at it, peered up to the sky and said. "You have fifteen minutes and then we will proceed," he turned away to prepare the pistols.

The two principles were poles apart in attitude. Seemingly calm and collected, Fulwar was quietly confident in his determination that he that should have his children returned to him. Edgar, on the other hand, was overconfident, and was eager to have the contest over and done with so that he and Georgina could resume their blossoming relationship, with her children by her side at all times.

Fulwar listened intently as Willie Greyffos explained Marcel's rules. He refused both Willie's final offer for him to back out or a quick swig from the flask of whisky. He told Willie that his attitude was if he couldn't have his children returned to him he may as well be dead.

Edgar, on the other hand, barely listened to what Neil Starbury had to say; such was his continual pacing up and down. Neil never suggested that he should walk away and quietly return to Kilkenny Farm. Although Edgar had never told Georgina that he loved her, the duel was one way to prove it so.

The audience lined up at the edge of the clearing, standing well away and quietly waiting in anticipation of the outcome. A carriage suddenly pulled up on the other side of the trees, and they all nervously looked behind to see who had arrived; an interloper was the last thing they needed.

When the man appeared along the footpath it was only Georgina who recognised the showground boxer, Jim 'The Bull' Baker. After exchanging glances, she and Faith went to speak to him. On Willie Greyffos' advice Faith had hired him for one last act of the day.

Marcel suddenly called both men together, and they all returned their attention to the duellists.

. There was no eye contact between them. "I take it that you both understand the procedure?" They nodded their heads in agreement. Marcel retrieved a gold twenty-franc coin depicting the head of Napoleon Bonaparte from his pocket. It was a cherished keepsake given to him many years before.

Edgar chose to call.

Marcel flipped the coin and as it spun in the air Edgar called "Heads".

"Heads it is," Marcel announced as he retrieved the coin and placed it safely back into his pocket. He held open the box with the two primed pistols. "It is your choice, Mr Collison. Either choose your gun or the end of the field you would like to shoot from."

"I'll choose which pistol," he said with careful scrutiny before lifting one from the box.

Fulwar chose the same end of the field of honour at which he had been standing for some time. It was relatively flat and there was little wind blowing through the surrounding trees. He also chose the distance to be twenty paces.

"I will give you both one last chance to decline or you both now stand back to back." Marcel waited for an answer but the contestants simply turned and stood with their backs to each other. Marcel and the seconds retreated.

"At the ready," he shouted and then paused for a moment. "One, two, three... " he counted, and the two men, with guns pointing up to the heavens, matched his counting with their paces.

Charity held a hand over her mouth whilst Stefan held her other hand. Many times she had seen deer shot on the estate or a fox torn to pieces by the hounds but to see two men shooting at each another was an entirely different spectacle, especially as one was her brother.

Faith's expression was deadpan because she cared for neither man on the field.

Whilst Hope was merely solemn, Georgina couldn't wait for the end, and hoped that she would have her freedom from a both a tortuous marriage *and* a pretence of an affair.

Stefan glanced over at Faith as the distance between the two men increased. He didn't agree with duelling but he had little choice. His very clever yet coy sister-in-law had him eating out of her hand.

"Seventeen, eighteen, nineteen, twenty. Fire!"

The men quickly spun around and fired their shots almost simultaneously. Two loud bangs echoed through the trees and puffs of gunpowder smoke drifted into the air.

Edgar dropped to the ground like a stone, and there were gasps from the women. Fulwar, who remained standing, was unscathed.

Neil went to Edgar's assistance, and took his gun. "Where have you been hit, sir? Is it bad?"

Edgar held his hand on his hip, and blood seeped through his fingers. His pain was obvious and he screwed up his face. "He has hit me in the pelvis. Quick! Help me to my feet. This isn't over yet."

As Marcel took his pistol away for reloading he asked Neil if Edgar was able to carry on. "It's what he wants to do," Neil replied, shrugging his shoulders.

Confident and smiling Fulwar waited in the middle for his opponent's return, and Edgar limped back to the starting position with blood running down his leg.

They began all over again.

"One, two, three... " Marcel counted more slowly as Edgar struggled. "Eleven, twelve, thirteen, fourteen, fifteen... " Each step for Edgar was more and more agonising, and Neil and Willie were concerned that he might not be able to carry on. "Sixteen, seventeen, eighteen, nineteen, twenty. Fire!"

Again puffs of smoke flew from the pistol barrels. Wood pigeons flapped away deep amongst the trees. The kschaach kschaach of a frightened jay was heard in the distance as the noise from the bullets fired towards their intended targets. Fulwar's back was grazed as he fired fractionally slower and he winced in pain. Being a muscle injury the wound wasn't serious. Edgar however, had again dropped to his knees. He had taken a bullet into his thigh, on the same side that the first salvo had been delivered. It was superficial but he showed unusual resilience.

"Sir! I told you! The pistol you have fires high and to the right," Neil Starbury told the kneeling man. He needed Edgar Collison to remain alive. "Aim down the left side of the barrel of his pistol. Please listen to me unless you want to lose your life."

Fulwar stretched his bloodied upper back and was now ready for the kill. Edgar was ailing and losing blood. Willie Greyffos told him that his adversary was weakening and couldn't last much longer, although neither man had received a wound into a major internal organ.

Marcel had finished reloading the guns when Stefan walked across to him. "Papa, this cannot carry on; Edgar is badly wounded. He is not capable of facing another shoot out. Please stop the proceedings immediately."

Marcel was very quiet whist he pondered over the situation. He then looked up into his son's face before answering. "Son, these two men chose to settle their argument in this way. I am just holding court over the outcome. If one dies, then so be it. There will be only one more bullet each. After that they will have to take their disagreement to a court of law. That is normally the way of the French. More often than not it never reaches this point. If both men choose to fire the final bullet then that is their choice, not ours." He went very quiet and recollected the duels he had presided over in the days gone by when he had been an illegal judge over many disputes. This would hopefully be his last. The pistols had been a part of his life, and he had hoped that they would never be used again. "Please, my son, there is more to this argument than meets the eye." Marcel scanned the audience. "I see the people watching and know what they want to happen here today. I have worked for the Brigadier for many years now, he wouldn't normally allow this to happen but he chooses to remain aloof. Let it be decided here."

Stefan walked away shaking his head, livid, but honouring his father's decision. Faith watched his every step and shook her own head, hoping Stefan hadn't spoiled the occasion. Meanwhile, the two men were again standing back to back, and Marcel could be heard to warn them that this would be the last firing.

Marcel slowly began his final act of judgement. "One, two, three, four..." and the two wounded men paced away from each other, Edgar barely able to walk.

Except for Faith the women watching were shocked. In her mind she willed the outcome. Neither man deserved to live. "Nine, ten, eleven, twelve..." Willie and Neil looked at each other, realising that it was now or never. "Seventeen... eighteen... nineteen... twenty."

Edgar swung around and unleashed his shot a fraction of a second before Marcel could shout 'fire'. Fulwar was levelling his pistol when Edgar's bullet hit the upper part of his cheekbone, glanced off through his eye socket and travelled upwards into his brain.

Never getting the chance to fire his third shot, Fulwar had died instantly whilst still standing, and as his dead body slumped to the ground Willie Greyffos quickly went to him and with a sign of the cross, confirmed that he was dead.

Edgar slumped onto his knees holding his hip, and Marcel could not take his eyes off him. He was stunned that Edgar had cheated.

Charity ran over to Fulwar from the group of spectators, and took the pistol from his lifeless hand. Willie tried to stop her but she raised the loaded weapon at him and told him to leave her alone. She walked to where Edgar was kneeling with murderous intent in her eyes. The onlookers became anxious for her safety.

Stefan approached her. "Charity, don't do anything stupid. Let me have the pistol, please."

She raised the gun, but this time it was towards her husband. "Stay back, Stefan. I'm not afraid to use it. Even on you... or me."

Faith grabbed Stefan's wrist. "Just listen to what she has to say," she implored, "and then try and tell me that this duel should never have gone ahead."

Charity pointed the pistol at her brother. "You think that this duel is over, you filthy bastard? Well, I can assure you that it is not."

Edgar was confused. He couldn't understand what she meant. "The duel is finished, Charity. I won fair and square. Fulwar Cavner is dead."

"My God! You don't even know that you are a cheat and a liar. Can't you understand the difference between right and wrong? My nightmares returned the moment I heard that you were leaving the army and returning to Bibury. I have spent the last ten months reliving the past when I was a little girl of seven. I cannot erase the memories of you coming into my bedroom in the middle of the night and climbing into bed with me," she paused and tears fell onto her dress. "You had no clothes on!" Charity trembled with hatred for her brother.

"Charity, don't be so silly. It must have all been a dream. You were always a bad sleeper, and nightmares are common with young people. Here, let me have the pistol before you hurt someone." Edgar struggled to his feet and hobbled towards his sister with the intent of taking the pistol from her.

"Get back or I will shoot you dead where you stand!" she shouted, thrusting the pistol at him. He moved back, not trusting her mood. "There are people here who have never heard this story before, and it's time they did. You would touch me all over, and I was so scared. You told me about the terrible things that would happen to me if I ever told mother. You put your tongue in my mouth and then in other places. Then there were the horrible things you asked me to do to you just so you could have your own sexual gratification. You used to say you loved me but how could you care for someone and then do that to them?"

"Charity, you must–"

"Quiet! Every time it happened you left me crying myself to sleep when you had had your pleasure, and those nights have tormented me ever since. So, Edgar, you have had your pleasure. I think it's only fair that I now have mine" Charity pointed the pistol at Edgar's head.

"You're being irrational, Charity. It was all a dream. Put the pistol down," Edgar pleaded with her.

"Far from it, Edgar," Faith suddenly said. "It was far from being a dream. By the time I was twelve you were regularly shagging me. You made it sound normal as if it was what all brothers and sisters do."

"You ruined me, Edgar," Hope suddenly shouted. You ruined me physically and emotionally. For years James and I have tried for a baby but every time I have become pregnant I have miscarried. A Harley Street gynaecologist believes that I have somehow been damaged internally, and he is right. You damaged me when I was a very young girl. I will never bear a child for James because of you." Hope turned and buried her head in James' chest, and sobbed uncontrollably.

Georgina and Maria knew the sisters' story but except for Gerard the men didn't. Gerard knew most of what had happened in the past but it was the first time he had heard Hope and Charity's versions of events. However, all of them were astonished. None could believe that the three women had kept their secret for so many years. The only reason why Gerard supported his wife for so long was that he firmly believed that there would be a good case against Edgar's abominable behaviour. He had risked his whole career so Faith and his sisters-in-law could have their proper justice. As much as Edgar would have been found guilty, an English judge would be lenient with a man of such wealth. At the worst he would have been banished into exile on the verbal evidence of three sisters who detested their brother anyway, only for him to carry on with his appalling deeds elsewhere.

Stefan was visibly shaken and Lionel had a hand around his shoulder. His father held him around the waist. The causes of Charity's years of intermittent depression were laid bare before him. He was confused. Had Faith blackmailed him about her own pregnancy so the duel would come to fruition? And was her blasé attitude towards sexual intercourse to do with Edgar's interfering with her when she was so young? His wife, his dear Charity, now stood threatening to murder her own brother.

Willie Greyffos and Neil Starbury had now realised why Faith Havrincourt so desperately wanted the duel to take place. Edgar was wounded but only the alcoholic wife beater was dead. It was now Neil Starbury's turn to finish the gory business.

Neil stepped towards the distraught woman and Charity trained the pistol on him and then back at her brother. "Stay away from me!" she screamed. "He is not leaving here alive. He should have gone to the gallows years ago. Get back!" The pistol went back and forth from Edgar to Neil. Stefan went to move but was restrained. His father whispered for him to wait.

Neil spoke calmly. Years of experience told him of the virtues of patience in the face of adversity. The difference here was that he faced a woman and not a warrior. "Charity!" he said sternly. "Please! Let me have the pistol. Stefan wants you. His father is with him. Please do not pull the trigger. It is not a woman's task. It is a man's."

"You are going to let him get away with it, aren't you?" She trained the pistol back onto Neil.

Neil stared into her eyes. "No Charity. He will not get away with anything. He is guilty, and no one in the world could disbelieve his three sisters. Please give me the pistol and leave him with me." Neil held his hand out, tempting her to hand it over. "Shoot me first, Charity, but please don't shoot your brother."

"Charity. Do as he says. Give him the pistol," Georgina begged, breaking the impasse. "Everything will be all right if you do. Give Neil the pistol and he will make sure that justice is done."

Charity directed the pistol back at Edgar. "Get down on your knees and beg forgiveness, you perverted bastard!" she demanded, and he did as she asked. "Pray! Pray that God might help you in the other world because that is where you are going. Heaven or hell, I don't care as long as I never meet you again on this earth." She lowered the pistol to her side, much to everyone's relief, especially Edgar's, and Neil took the weapon from her.

Stefan stepped across and escorted his sobbing wife away, gracious that she wouldn't be declared a murderess in a court of law.

Faith indicated for people to leave with a slight nod of her head, and most of the people trailed away along the pathway.

Edgar stood motionless beside Neil as Georgina went over to pay her respects to her husband. Maria and Edward stood by her side. She stared at his prostrate body face down on the wet ground and a trickle of tears emerged. "He was such a fine man at one time; intelligent and considerate. I'm afraid that was before he took to the drink. It changed him into a monster, and I couldn't allow the children to see him like it." She took out a handkerchief and blew her nose. "Mr Greyffos says that Fulwar hasn't drank for some weeks and in that time he has been one of the most charming men he has ever met. Dear Fulwar, it didn't need to come to this. Whoever would have thought it that you died completely sober?"

Georgina turned and cried on Maria's shoulder, and then Edward led them both back to their carriages.

Neil Starbury behaved like a caring soldier towards Edgar until he could barely hear a horse or rattling carriage in the distance. "Where is Georgina?" Edgar asked with a painful expression.

"She is at the bridleway waiting for a doctor." There was no truth in what he said. The pistol was still in Neil's hand. "Tell me, sir, when we were in India, in Azamgargh, were the accounts told about you true? It was said that you used to pay the lower caste people very reasonable sums of money to fornicate with their young daughters. Only now do I fully believe that. Their fathers' morals were no better than yours, but their poor mothers could do nothing about it. Your money alleviated their abject poverty and fed their household, but it also fed your insatiable desire to have sex with children, especially little girls.

From what I have heard this morning from your sisters, in addition to the rumours that circulated in India over many years, you do not deserve to be alive." Neil Starbury refrained from smiling contemptuously.

"Don't be ridiculous, Starbury. Let's get to a hospital and then go back to Kilkenny Farm." Edgar still refused to accept the truth about his abhorrent behaviour.

"No, sir! I am afraid that for you it is all over. One day there will be a single word for people like you who prey on children for sex. It might seem coincidental to some that your wife in India, who wants nothing other than to come here to live with you, has three young daughters." Neil Starbury raised his eyebrows expecting some kind of retort. "You *are* nothing but a pervert, Collison." He told him calmly.

"You are being absurd, Starbury. Come on, help me to the carriage so we can go home!" Edgar, in pain and annoyed, tried to persuade Neil to help him.

"Mr Collison," Neil said sardonically, "*we* are going nowhere. I will be going home, not you."

"What the hell do you mean, you fool?" Edgar asked vehemently as if he was still talking to his lowly staff sergeant.

"You spoke to your men in the army as if they were vermin, you treat women as if they are third-class prostitutes, and you are arrogant and disbelieving of your own actions. I am sorry to say it, Collison, but you deserve to die. I have shot better soldiers in defence of the British Empire." Neil Starbury raised the offending pistol and aimed it at Edgar Collison's head.

"Don't! Please! I am a changed man. All those things you charge me with are in the past. I have Georgina now, and she's a beautiful woman. My wife in India can stay there. Those days are over, Starbury, believe me. How much do you want? Money isn't an object. You can be a very rich man." Edgar was beginning to realise that Neil Starbury meant what he said.

"I've heard it all before from people like yourself. Money buys freedom from justice. I am afraid that doesn't work with me. Your sisters have gone through hell, let alone all the other children you have laid your stinking hands on. How proud will your father be of you when he finds out what you have done to his daughters? I cannot imagine the thoughts of your mother, had she been alive today. I was born into a very hard working-class family, but we all had respect for each other. My parents could not afford a bed each for us but boy lay next to girl in the way that brother and sister should; untouched."

Edgar suddenly stood tall and challenged Neil Starbury. "So, what are you going to do about it then, Starbury? How are you going to prove it?" Edgar winced with pain.

"I am afraid that it is all over for you, sir. Never again will you pursue those young girls to satiate your personal pleasure. And you will never have the opportunity to deny it in court of law. This is your courtroom, and you have been found guilty." Neil's hand trembled as he touched the muzzle of the gun to the forehead of his former superior officer and present-day employer.

"Put that pistol down, Starbury, or I swear you'll end up on the gallows," Edgar demanded, which inspired one final thought to pass into Neil Starbury's mind before he squeezed the trigger. Arrogance.

The bullet passed through the head of Edgar Collison, and the puff of gun smoke dissipated into the early morning air above a distraught ex-soldier standing over the body of his dead employer in a clearing in Withington woods.

It was the end for Edgar Collison, but it wasn't over yet. Neil collected his thoughts before placing Edgar's discharged pistol back into his hand. He turned and walked past the beautiful wooden inlaid pistol box, the bullets and unused gunpowder, towards the body of Fulwar Cavner, which was cooling fast in the early February morning. He placed the other pistol back into Fulwar's hand. Before he walked away he gently tapped him on the head. The scene was set. Neil headed back through the trees.

"Are you all right, sir? You are shaking. Come on. Get in. Your luggage is in the back. I have a change of clothes for you. If we hurry you can catch the five past eleven from Cheltenham and probably be back in Liverpool by this evening."

Jimmy 'The Bull' Baker was being paid handsomely for his small part in the proceedings.

"How can we help you, Mr Baker?" The police sergeant eyed his dubious visitor with some trepidation, knowing all too well of his reputation.

"I was passing through Withington woods this morning on my way from Cirencester to Cassey Compton when I heard unusual gunfire. It didn't sound like normal hunting rifles. It also sounded as if there were two shots going off at once. I stopped to listen, and three times it seemed to happen. I went to investigate cautiously, thinking it might be poachers, and I found two dead bodies in a clearing about thirty or forty yards apart. It seemed to me that they had used pistols to kill one another in some sort of duel. The box, the remaining gunpowder and some bullets were lying on the ground between them. I left everything as I found it and came straight away to tell you."

The desk sergeant took down the details of the whereabouts of the two bodies and organised a patrol to go and probe into the strange information.

After earning his wages, Jimmy 'The Bull' Baker walked out of the station a contented man, and was flush in the pocket. He would travel back to Cirencester to look for Willie Greyffos and have a few celebratory drinks.

Chapter 57
The Brigadier Reminisces

There was a quiet knock at the door and the Brigadier's nurse entered the drawing room. The old man was asleep in his chair, and she gently woke him up. "Your gamekeeper is back. Do you feel like speaking to him now?" she asked.

"Yes. Please show him in." Struggling to sit up in his chair, he swigged the remnants of his Armagnac and hid the glass down by his side. The gamekeeper entered and stood obediently with his cap held before him. "Well, what did you find out? Where were they?"

"Nowhere, sir. I know that they headed upriver because they were seen riding out towards Ablington. I followed the river as far as the grayling fishing would allow, up until Andoversford. From there on it was pointless going any further because it is a mere stream. I saw no one, sir. I heard shooting some way off up in the woods when I passed through Monarch's Way and approaching Woodbridge, but it's not your land, sir and it was quite early this morning. The sky had only just lit up. Where the three of them were fishing, I do not know." The gamekeeper shrugged his shoulders.

The Brigadier suddenly looked quizzical and his eyebrows dropped. "What do you mean the three of them? Who else supposedly went fishing?"

"Lionel, Stefan and Stefan's father, Marcel. Although it was still dark the landlord at the Swan saw them ride by as he was cleaning the front of the hotel. He is a very early riser, sir. Besides, two of them were speaking fluent French so it could have been no one else." The gamekeeper wanted to leave. The Brigadier, although a good employer, was making the old fellow feel uncomfortable.

The Brigadier thanked him and dismissed him. The old man muttered to himself. Other information he had received that morning told him that Edgar was not at Kilkenny Farm, nor his housekeeper, whom he knew little about, or his farm manager. He glanced at the clock. It was noon and it was not long until he was expecting Faith and Gerard. His nurse poured another Armagnac. After a small snack of bread and cheese he dozed off again beneath the portrait of his dear wife looking down upon him.

Faith woke her father. He stopped dreaming, spluttered spittle down his front and tried to sit up properly. Gerard helped him as his nurse wiped him clean. For a few moments he tried to recollect himself and then eventually realised where he was and who was in his company. Faith gave him a large kiss. Gerard, deep down, grimaced at the thought of kissing him, and shook his hand instead.

"Where have you two just come from?" the ailing old man asked coyly.

"Hope's. We stayed there last night for dinner. How are you feeling, Father? You haven't been very well, have you?" Faith squeezed his old fattened hand.

"Something isn't right, Faith. Something isn't right at all. Do you know what date it is today? It's a special day." The Brigadier was tired of asking repetitive questions and having no answers.

"It's Mother's birthday, Father. We've come to have dinner with you." She knelt beside him, and her pregnancy showed all the more.

"Who's doing the cooking? Mrs Desailley has the grandchildren." His face was expressionless.

"Charity is with her children. I've just seen her at the gatehouse. Stefan and Lionel are drinking in the Catherine Wheel. They were supposed to go fishing but went on a binge instead. They don't change, Father, do they? I can only assume that Mrs Desailley is in charge of the kitchen tonight."

Gerard felt extremely uncomfortable. "I'll go and find out, otherwise we might have to eat out." He left his theatrical wife talking with her dubious-minded father.

Dinner was subdued. Charity attended as if it were a doctor's appointment, and Stefan still hadn't arrived home. Faith and Gerard tried to make polite conversation but the atmosphere was that of a committee discussing a sewerage problem in London.

Halfway through dinner there was a knock at the door, and a maid entered and whispered into the Brigadier's ear. He wiped his mouth with a napkin and nodded to the young woman. "Show them in, please." He looked across the table at Gerard, and was glad that he was in attendance.

"It is the Cheltenham police. What in hell might they want?"

The two men entered the small dining room apologetically. The one who was dressed casually introduced himself as Detective Inspector Davies. "I am sorry that it is an inconvenient time for you, sir, but may we speak with you alone?"

"It is all right, go ahead. These are my two daughters and Gerard is my son-in-law; he is a lawyer" the Brigadier announced whist trying to imagine what the visit entailed.

Pushing her chair back Charity stood up abruptly. "I must go, Father. I told my childminder that I wouldn't be long." She went around the table and kissed her father on the head before excusing herself and scurrying out of the door without looking back.

When she had left, the Brigadier gestured for the detective to explain his visit.

"Some time this morning we were alerted to a strange occurrence in Withington woods, which is about eight miles from Cheltenham. When arriving we found two bodies about forty yards apart. They had apparently killed each other in a duel. All the evidence at the site, such as pistols, gunpowder, bullets and so on, points to a serious altercation between two feuding men, and I am afraid, Mr Collison, that we have identified one of the bodies as being your son, Edgar. There are some questions I would like to ask but I'll leave it until tomorrow to give you time to come to terms with your own personal grief. I am afraid that we have not yet identified the other body. I am sorry to be the one that has to tell you this tragic news, and you all have our condolences." The two policemen dipped their heads, turned and quietly left.

The Brigadier sat shocked and bemused. Faith had her elbows on the table and her hands covered her face. She seemed visibly taken aback, and Gerard placed his arm around her, which was as much as he could do to console his grieving pregnant wife.

"Who in hell would Edgar have been having a duel with?" the Brigadier eventually asked.

Gerard was sheepish. He studied his father-in-law's wizened face and tried to understand how much the news was affecting him. "I have been in quite a lot of correspondence with Edgar of late, sir, and his wife in India has been much on his mind, but there has been an issue with another woman. A woman that he took on as a housekeeper at Kilkenny Farm."

At that point Faith decided to go and find her younger sister and left the room, leaving Gerard to explain Edgar's situation. "It is a woman you might well know about."

The Brigadier shook his head and shrugged his tired shoulders.

"Georgina Corbett-Cavner. She was here at the Summer Ball."

"Do you mean the woman married to that raging alcoholic?" he asked angrily.

"Yes, sir. Fulwar Corbett-Cavner. The man who slept on your chaise longue." Gerard desperately wanted to get away but knew that there would be many more questions.

"The Brigadier eyed his son-in-law with suspicion. "Did you know anything about this so-called duel? Were you a part of its organisation?"

"No, sir. I am as shocked as you are. Faith has never mentioned anything either." Being a man of public standing Gerard found it difficult to lie and was treading on very dangerous ground.

"It is strange that Lionel, Stefan and his father should disappear off the estate this morning. Charity went off somewhere as well and then you and Faith turn up on the same day, which is your mother-in-law's birthday, as it happens. Marcel's right hand man disappeared some weeks ago, and leaves everything behind at the Catherine Wheel. I have seen more of Faith over the last few months than I ever did over the years she has lived in London, and now my son is found dead in peculiar circumstances." The Brigadier gazed up at another portrait of his dear wife.

"Sir, let's not surmise. We don't yet know who the other person involved is. This is all hypothetical talk. It might be to do with something from the past, uncovered since Edgar has been home. It would be better if the police finished their investigations and they can conclude how and why this tragedy occurred." Gerard thought it odd that the Brigadier didn't seem particularly perturbed that his only son had died. "Are you all right, sir? I'll get you another drink."

"I'll be fine. Come on, let's go to the drawing room; where it's so much more comfortable. I have something to tell you, something you should perhaps know." Gerard helped the Brigadier to his feet and walked him very steadily to his favourite chair in the room next door.

With each holding a large glass of Armagnac the Brigadier began to reminisce about a very sad story. "Many years ago, when I lived in France and owned a little farmstead, I had a very good friend – Hubert, his name was – and at that time he was courting Eleanor, who eventually became the girls' and Edgar's mother and who would have been your mother-in-law, had you ever known her." The Brigadier referred to the portrait on the wall. "Hubert was a Frenchman and had met Eleanor during one of his frequent visits to England. They planned to marry. Hubert's family and myself were all very good friends.

"Tragically, Hubert died in a hunting accident three weeks before their wedding. A lot of money had already been spent on the impending wedding, and the shock of his death was great, especially for Eleanor. Naturally, we all had to console each other as best we could. His funeral was a very, very sad day, and was probably not what he would have wanted, but it was difficult not to be so heavy-hearted. At his wake we ate and drank solemnly and talked about his life and what we would do without him. Many tears were shed.

"Later that day, after having had far too much wine, I was talking to Eleanor alone. She was distraught. I remember stroking the back of her hand to comfort her and, completely out of character, I suddenly asked her if she would marry me instead." The old man went quiet and took a deep breath.

"Straight away my embarrassment overcame me because it was a terrible thing to say on such a day. I held my head in my hands and tried to apologise but Eleanor stood up and walked away to talk with her parents and Hubert's father. We were outside on the lawn at the time, and suddenly everyone went quiet. There I sat alone with my face buried in my hands for what seemed like an age, and all eyes were directed towards me. But then, just as suddenly, people began to talk louder and began to laugh and joke, which made me even more convinced that they were jesting about what I had stupidly said to Eleanor."

The Brigadier stopped. There was almost a tear in his eye and he sipped slowly from his glass. Gerard leaned across and replenished it because he had unexpectantly become interested in hearing the rest of the story.

"I stared into my wine glass with my head bowed, but a loud thud on the wooden table disturbed my reverie, and someone slapped me hard on the back. I turned to see that it was Hubert's father. There in front of me was a bottle of Armagnac, and he told me that what I had done was the most honourable thing he had ever heard. Soon it seemed that everyone in the village was around me, and again celebrating a forthcoming wedding that would be brought about in the most bizarre of circumstances." He mused over that fateful day in France for a while.

"Eleanor had said yes. I had liked her but she was Hubert's woman. Never would have I crossed that path and interfered with my friend's partner if he were alive." The Brigadier never elaborated on whether he would interfere with a stranger's wife. "We soon married. We married at the expense of Hubert's parents on the same day that their son would have married Eleanor. It was a wonderful day, and without a trace of animosity. The whole village turned out. We have all remained great friends, and to this day we send letters to each other's families, although many are now dead and buried, of course. It was a strange state of affairs, Gerard. For years when I lay with your mother-in-law I could never stop thinking about Hubert. He was the one who should have lain there with her, not me." Now a trickle did run down the old man's cheek, and not because of the news of his son. His past was catching him up but he hadn't finished.

Gerard was reminded of the episode told to him by Neil Starbury weeks before about how he came to marry his wife. They were such strangely similar circumstances.

"I think you should go and have a rest, sir. There are going to be some difficult days ahead."

"No! Please! Just listen. I need you to listen. Now is the time." The Brigadier was distraught but determined. He desperately wanted to get something off his chest to alleviate his ailing mind.

"As soon as we married, Eleanor announced that she was pregnant, and Edgar was born in France. Several years later my father died and I was called back to England to take charge of Bibury Court. Sadly, we had to 'up tail and move'. We both enjoyed living in France immensely but the Bibury estate was my inheritance and I was duty driven by my father and mother's belief, and their ideology, that the people who depended on their livelihoods from the estate should be protected. I reluctantly sold the farmstead in France, as it was too far away to maintain, and Mr and Mrs Desailley decided to come with us. Stefan was then very young. Just a baby." The Brigadier smiled.

"When the estate was back up and running, Eleanor and I began to increase our family. Faith was born and then Hope and then Charity. Although they were much younger than Edgar, everything seemed rosy. Edgar was born eight or nine months after we had married. I was probably naïve. I do not know to this day whether he was my son or Hubert's, but by then it didn't matter. Whatever, he was Eleanor's son and we brought him up as our own." The Brigadier was visibly shaking as he sipped his Armagnac. "In those days we used to hire head housekeepers because Eleanor was busy running the estate in much the same way as Stefan does today. One of the housekeepers we had took ill and passed away, and so we employed another, a former hospital matron from a children's ward. She was recommended to us and proved to be very astute." Again he stopped and thought about what to say next.

"Not long after her arrival she felt that our girls were acting oddly, especially Charity, whom the matron thought seemed very nervous and wouldn't talk much. Because of her suspicions she started to keep an eye on them and one night decided to stay up late to read a book. It was then everything began to come clear to her. On hearing footsteps along the landing she went to investigate. She waited whilst hiding in one of the airing cupboards and after half an hour Edgar was seen leaving Faith's bedroom. The matron was puzzled but did nothing at the time. Another night she saw him entering Charity's bedroom and her suspicions became fully aroused. The next morning she took Faith aside and gently coaxed from her why Edgar was visiting her in her bedroom at night and what was actually happening. Faith, who I think was about thirteen at the time, quite naïvely told the matron that Edgar was having intercourse with her and it had happened many times before. Edgar had persuaded Faith that it was normal to do such things as a brother and sister, but not to tell anyone."

The Brigadier stuttered but held his hand up when Gerard went to intervene. "I'm sorry, Gerard because Faith is now your wife but please let me finish what I have to say. Faith suggested to the matron that he had also been interfering with Hope and Charity, who were some years younger than her, but not only during the night. He would often corner them in one of the farm buildings or catch them out in the cornfields. I am afraid that at such a young age he had become a dangerous sexual predator, but as far as we knew he had only preyed on his sisters. The miracle was that he impregnated none of them, but looking back he still hasn't any children of his own. Maybe God was their saviour to some degree."

Gerard stroked his brow in deep thought. Although Faith had told him most of the things that had happened to her years before, and he had heard the sisters' indictment only that very morning, he never imagined that the Brigadier would sit before him verifying their condemnation of their own brother.

"So, how did Edgar get away with it?" he asked, prying into the Brigadier's tormented mind, but he now desperately wanted to hear the end of the story.

The Brigadier was struggling. "Eleanor was devastated. It was as if all three of her daughters had died in an accident at the same time. I had to confront Edgar alone but he obviously denied it, describing it as young girls' fantasies. I told him that I would have all three of them in with him and they could compare their stories. Thankfully, he backed down. That day while the girls were at school I arranged for him to leave the estate immediately and had him sent down to the south coast with an old friend of ours while we decided what to do."

"Why didn't you get the police involved?" Gerard asked.

"Gerard, you know as well as I do the stigma attached to this sort of family behaviour. What would the community think of us? We employ ninety five per cent of them, and our household cannot bring up three girls respectably. We, and especially the girls, would have been ostracised everywhere. All of our friends in the upper circles would have never spoken to us again. Imagine your own son raping his sisters. I can tell you now that if he was Hubert's son and Hubert was alive he would have taken him somewhere quiet for a heart to heart, and extricated the truth from him before shooting him through the head without hesitation." The Brigadier stretched for the Armagnac bottle, but Gerard refused another drink for himself.

"So, then what happened?" Gerard asked wryly, trying not to smile as he thought about how Edgar had probably died.

"A friend of mine, who was oblivious to Edgar's crimes, was heavily involved in armaments manufacture for the British army. He suggested that Edgar should be bought a commission. Edgar wasn't very bright but to keep him away from the estate it was all we could think of at the time. The physical and mental health of the girls was imperative, and so I gave him a choice; join the army or have the police investigate what he had been doing. He chose to join the army."

Strangely, the Brigadier suddenly stood up without assistance, and gazed at the portrait of Eleanor. He turned back to Gerard with immensely sad eyes. "Not only did he sexually assault his sisters, he also killed his mother. Eleanor was so shocked that she became ill, blaming herself that she hadn't been paying attention to her own children's needs. There was nothing she could have done, of course. It wasn't her fault that her son was a rapist, but she could not forgive herself that he had committed the atrocities under our own roof and against his own siblings."

The Brigadier stood and cried, and Gerard asked him to sit down but he refused. His son-in-law then tried to help him back into his chair but the old man feebly threw an elbow at him.

"Eleanor never recovered. She stopped eating and became so gaunt as if her guilt was eating her from within. As if the girls hadn't gone through enough, their dear mother was dying. A year after the discovery of Edgar's appalling deeds Eleanor lay on her deathbed. Over some time different physicians, one after another, packed away their little black cases and concluded that she was willing herself to die, and that there was little they could do for her."

The Brigadier then sat back down as if he said all that he wanted to say, but he hadn't. "In that one year before her mother's death, Faith, your dear, dear wife, grew up emphatically. She had come to realise the callousness of her own brother's foul deeds and what he had done to the three sisters, and she made up her mind to never to let it lie.

"Faith went to her mother's bedside before she died and defiantly told her how she felt about Edgar. Faith's last words to her mother were 'don't worry, Mummy. I will not let Edgar get away with it'."

The Brigadier stared at Gerard. Now that he'd explained his side of the awful story, he hoped that Gerard would enlighten him about the demise of his son.

Neither man said a word for a while, and the clock ticked laboriously. It was Gerard who spoke.

"Are you going to be remorseful over Edgar's death? Or are you going to tell the police your opinions? A feud over a beautiful woman between two aristocratic families that ended up with the tragic deaths of two duellists? If so, sir, would you also mention your diabolical son's incestuous perversions?"

Gerard knew the law so well that he was positive that his wife would never be sentenced for her part in the death of her brother. He leaned towards the Armagnac bottle and poured himself a drop more. He was sure that nobody could now say anything without recriminations falling back onto themselves.

With a strong conviction that the Brigadier would never say anything against his eldest daughter, especially after what he knew she had been through, Gerard told the Brigadier everything. He began at the very beginning, and told the Brigadier about Faith's ambition to have her brother eliminated without any retaliatory charges brought against anyone. Faith's ultimate plan began by pure coincidence when Stefan met the unfortunate but beautiful Georgina Corbett-Cavner, and shortly afterwards Edgar announced that he was leaving the army and returning to Bibury.

Gerard told his father-in-law of the final involvement of the three sisters, Maria and Georgina; five women that Gerard had come to think of as 'The Ladies of the Stream'. The Brigadier listened intently and Gerard finally came to the closing act; how both men had shot themselves duelling over Georgina's children. There was only one thing he didn't explain, and that was who had fired the final shot.

The last thing Gerard told the Brigadier was all the names of the witnesses at the duel; three of whom Gerard thought the old man had never met.

Satisfied that he had put the record straight for the Brigadier and his three daughters Gerard leaned back in his chair. Should the old man wish to tell the police he was welcome to do so, but Gerard was positive that he wouldn't.

Before Gerard left to find Faith he called in the nurse and told her of Edgar's death and asked her to make sure the Brigadier was as comfortable as possible that night.

The Brigadier sat staring at Eleanor's portrait, and more tears began to trickle down his cheeks, but not for his son. He raised his glass to his dear wife. "It's all over now, my dear. You can rest in peace. Your daughters have punished their predator."

The police discovered the identity of the other body as being a Mr Fulwar Corbett-Cavner. No one offered any information as to why the two men fought, and the story read in the local newspaper as a tragic occurrence between two illegal duellists.

Edgar Collison's body was taken to Woolwich Barracks and buried. Apart from the pallbearers, only three people attended the funeral, one of which was Neil Starbury. There were no family members in attendance.

Chapter 58
The Wedding

Jimmy 'The Bull' Baker had two jobs that evening. One was to drive Lionel's stag night entourage to Lechlade, and the other was to act as a guardian should any of them find themselves in trouble with the local louts. Lionel and Stefan couldn't afford any facial damage with the wedding only two days away. The idea was to visit every pub in the pretty village and end up in the disreputable Swan Inn, where a penis was engraved in the stone, high up on the front of the building. It was notorious for its wild music, excessive drinking and loose women, as the strange advert announced.

The evening went well and they became thoroughly drunk. What happened after the inn closed was nobody's business but a good time was had by all. The next morning seven very dejected men climbed aboard Jimmy's carriage and they were back in Bibury by nine o'clock.

The wedding began at eleven o'clock in Bibury church dedicated to St Mary the Virgin, of all people, and Lionel and Mary were soon leading the guests along the riverside heading towards the Catherine Wheel for an informal reception.

Lionel was dressed resplendently in top hat and tails with pin-stripe trousers whilst Mary wore a pretty off-white dress and bonnet and carried a posy of red roses.

The friends and families followed behind the newlyweds. Gerard laboured as he pushed the Brigadier's wheelchair over the rough ground, but he smiled at the thought of the old man having a bottle of his own Armagnac squeezed down by his side.

It seemed as though the whole village had turned out to wave on and wish the very happy couple a long and successful marriage. The local children ran, skipped and hopped alongside the new husband and wife, and some children scattered posies around the happy pair in the beautiful sunshine.

As Lionel and Mary crossed the bridge over the Coln, a pair of swans performed their mating ritual beside them, and with their heads together the royal birds created a perfect white heart, which rekindled an old superstition in the village that within a year twins would be born to the newlyweds.

Walking alongside Gerard was Faith, who was now close to having her own child. Stefan glanced over at her, curious as to how many people knew of the architect of the unborn chid. Like a worried father-to-be he added up on his fingers the number of months he thought Faith had been pregnant.

Charity watched him and marvelled at what might be passing through his intelligent mind. Her own pregnancy was now beginning to show, for which there was only one architect.

The reception was jolly, exactly as the couple had planned, and everyone intermingled and chatted incessantly. At one stage the Ladies of the Stream stood talking to each another about the events of the past year. Georgina, dressed resplendently, had travelled from Stokesay, where she now lived with her children, out of Stefan and Charity's life.

Neil Starbury, now fully ensconced at Kilkenny Farm, tried to explain to his wife who was who but to little avail. Time would lubricate her memory.

Willie Greyffos was in attendance, and had reconciled with 'Aunt Maria' and 'Uncle Charles', as he now refers to them affectionately. Edward escorted a new, rather elegant woman in his life and introduced her as Lara Nieuweboer. Her family connection was, as yet, unknown.

Stefan approached Gerard and asked him about the two pretty young women who were accompanying him that day.

Gerard glanced across to them both and smiled proudly. "I wondered when you would ask that question, Stefan. They are my daughters from my first marriage."

Stefan looked across the room towards Faith, who smiled smugly back at him, patted her stomach and raised her painted eyebrows as she realised that Stefan was now well aware who the two young women were.

Gerard had been absolutely right when he had concluded those weeks before that no one could possibly say anything about anyone without reprisals.

Faith Havrincourt had thoroughly done her homework – with the help of The Ladies of the Stream.